T0195778

Their kiss was a melting consummation for all eternity . . .

In the grotto, moonlight radiated through clouds of mist whirling off the hot spring pool, pearl-pale as starlight. Ferns tumbled from rock walls and emerald moss carpeted the ground.

Naked, Moira stepped to the water's edge, touched toe tip to water, then dove into the hot springs. Her beauty cut Wulfsun like a dagger, as he, too, stepped into the water's enveloping warmth.

He was not sure who moved to whom first, but Moira's arms were around his neck and his hands were on her smooth hips. Her eyes glistened with the pale fire of stars. His awareness of her brushing against him was so acute, it was almost pain. His hands travelled slowly. He would learn her body, what pleased her . . . what excited her . . . His mouth covered hers and tasted all that was sweet. And more. . . .

SWAN BRIDE

BETINA LINDSEY

POCKET BOOKS

New York   London   Toronto   Sydney   Tokyo   Singapore

An *Original* Publication of POCKET BOOKS

POCKET BOOKS, a division of Simon & Schuster Inc.
1230 Avenue of the Americas, New York, NY 10020

ISBN: 978-1-5011-3378-7

First Pocket Books printing November 1990

10 9 8 7 6 5 4 3 2 1

POCKET and colophon are registered trademarks of
Simon & Schuster Inc.

Printed in the U.S.A.

for James . . .

If you care to know
How much it is I love you,
Stand at Tago bay
And count the number of waves
As they roll in toward the shore.
　　　　　—Fujiwara No Okikaze

And thanks to my editor, Caroline Tolley.

Prologue

The forest of Myr was an enchanted place and the ancient haven of the Swan Sisterhood. Myr's secret rested in the condition that no one harboring the heart and weapons of war could travel the ley path into its realm. In these times there were few men of peace afoot in Britain and none with the turn of heart to pass into the realm of Myr. Indeed, Myr's legendary peace and tranquility were sustained by the absence of men.

On the midsummer's eve of Moira's twenty-first year her kinswoman, Epona, made a heart-stopping announcement. She unfastened her smock, folded it neatly, and said, "It is time we walk the ley path into the world of men to attend the celebration of the Mother of all living." Epona spoke flatly as she might say the bread is done or the water is warm.

Moira's hands stopped on the strings of her harp. Before the airy tune rang into stillness, she breathed, "Now? This very night?"

"Yes," said Epona with maddening calm.

"Thank the Goddess! At last I will see a man!" Moira clasped her hands joyously. She set her harp aside and pursed her lips. Her eyes sparked with anticipation. Had she not awaited this adventure nearly all of her life? She had never traveled the ley path, which enabled the swan sisters of Myr to cross into the world of men, and, in truth, she'd never seen a man.

The spring had left her with something akin to discontent. For the first time the peace and beauty of Myr was not enough, nor was the loving companionship of Epona and the other swan sisters of Myr. Intuitively, she understood that now was the time and the season for her to join with man and conceive a child. Others had left Myr for such an adventure, and most were younger than herself.

In seasons past Moira was content to daydream by hearth and home fire like any other maid, but no longer. Now, come full moon, the estrous fever drove her to couple, and to do this she must venture into the world of men. She knew tradition held that the first kiss between man and swan maid would leave the man hopelessly enchanted by the maid's beauty for one moon month. At the next full moon the man would be free of the enchantment.

Moira reasoned her own mother must have traveled the ley path into the world of men and become the fertile garden for a wandering warrior's seed. Unfortunately, she knew little of her mother and father, because Epona refused to speak of them.

She looked over at her grandmother and gnawed her lip with aggravation. *She thinks to protect me, but I am no longer a child. Perhaps now, as I travel the ley path, she will speak to me of men.*

Her request was spoken softly. "Epona, tell me of men."

Old as a Methuselah's wife, Epona was yet straight-backed and slim-hipped, with white hair worn knotted atop a still beautiful face. She looked at Moira as if seeing her for the first time. Her pensive grandchild had lengthened and ripened into womanhood, transforming into an embodiment of beauty that few eyes had ever seen.

Like all the swan sisters of Myr, her granddaughter was of dual nature. She was both woman and swan. A child of the world of faerie, she had grown tall and strong in nature's wildness. She was slender-boned with flowing black hair, and her opalescent eyes, fearless and discerning, held the swirling rainbows of a nether world. Her skin shone soft and pearl white, and her lips and cheeks were blushed with the light rose of hawthorn flower. Her limbs were straight and strong as rowan boughs. Her swan mind, sun bright and full of wisdom, was as age-old as the Mother of all living.

Epona added to this, her granddaughter's inheritance, the legacy the White Goddess of Myr bequeathed to all her daughters: power. This was not the power to control and subjugate, as in the world of men, but the power to heal. Hers was the intuitive intelligence to commune with beasts and nature, to interpret dreams, and to work enchantments for the good. Whether it was in the dimension of Myr or in the world of men, Epona saw with shining clarity that Moira was one in ten thousand.

If only her mother Creirwy could see her, Epona thought. She pushed the notion away and turned her eyes to other tasks, not wanting to resurrect old heartaches. "Daughter of Creirwy, to speak of men is to speak of riddles," she hedged.

"I will hear your riddles," pressed Moira, not foreseeing she might end up more confused by the telling. Epona remained silent while Moira dogged her steps from one task to the next until at last Epona doused the fire in the cave hearth and turned to her granddaughter. "Be patient, my swanling, and I will tell you."

She raised a staying palm and eased herself down on a gnarled stump stool. "Eight millennia ago, the Goddess birthed man and woman." She paused, counting her fingers, then said, "Or it may have been seven millennia ago, or perhaps nine. I get confused in my old age. On any hand, man was puff-breasted, like the grouse, swift as the stag. He was bee to the flower. While the flower slept, he sparked fire, and with fire he forged blade. With blade man ruled woman. She wept for her freedom and her tears formed a lake. Taking pity on woman, the White Goddess transformed her into swan, and she lived summer long upon the lake. In fall, during harvest moon, swan flew and alighted in a forest of Myr, where she transformed back into woman.

"The Goddess wisely veiled man's eyes from the forest of Myr, and man became a wanderer. No sunrise found him where sunset left him. But come spring, being of loving heart, the woman pined for man. Truly, even a goddess understands loneliness, and she made the ley path so the woman might leave Myr and travel into the realm of man, yet return."

Moira shifted, and her swan self reminded, *This is an old story. She has told you this since you first stepped into the pond and we grew feathers.*

Impatient, Moira interrupted Epona. "But, Grandmother, tell me of man. Why did man forge blade to rule woman? Why did the Goddess not take the blade from man? You have not told me enough," she complained.

Epona touched Moira's forearm. "You are the hare jumping over the turtle. Within your womb is the riddle of life. Learn first of womanhood before you undertake the riddle of manhood. It is enough to know that in the world of men the gift of giving life is not so revered as the warrior art of taking it. Perhaps this becomes the greatest riddle."

"But—"

"Enough." Epona cut her short.

Certainly, Moira had no wish to be a man. The gift of womanhood was one gem every daughter of both realms, Men or Myr, could place in her crown. Perhaps she would solve the riddle in time, when she coupled with man. Her womb would swell with life, continuing the circle of the Mother of all living. Anticipation suffused through her as her hand lowered and rested on the soft hollow of her midriff. Even now she felt yearnings within her body, and her senses hummed expectantly.

Epona fastened her handspun cloak and stepped to the cave entrance to sight the setting sun. "It will soon be twilight. Come, we must go to the henge in the meadow."

Moira did not hesitate. She followed Epona out of the cave along the well-worn moss-edged path which sided the lake of glass. Soon the trees parted and the stone-henge came within Moira's view. From early childhood

4

she had danced and played within the circle of stones during celebrations of the full moon and midsummer. When she became older, Epona had used the placement of the stones to school her in the ancient knowledge of heavenly bodies, the course of star, sun, and moon.

The setting sun's rays capped the tall stones, giving them the appearance of shimmering beacons to the heavens. Already mist rose in swirls around the stones' shadowed bases. The last light of sunset, the in-between time, became magical. Only this night of Midsummer could those who stood within the perimeters of the stone circle travel the ley path between worlds.

She followed her grandmother's lead into the henge circle. Epona walked into the center and stood beside an arch where two upright dolmens were joined by a flat stone lintel. The rays of the setting sun fanned through this doorway to the ley path.

Epona lifted her hood to cover her head. "I will step through first, then you follow. May the peace of the White Goddess fill your heart, Granddaughter." With that blessing and an embrace, Epona walked beneath the stone lintel and passed into the mist. Moira's heart skipped a beat, and for a moment wonderment mingled with nervousness as Epona disappeared before her eyes. Moira took one last sweeping glance of the forests of Myr surrounding the meadow and drew in a deep breath for courage. Then she, too, walked beneath the stone lintel, following Epona on this uncommon journey into the world of men.

Now, Moira anticipated as she stepped from the mist, *I will see a man.*

But then how are you to tell? her swan half asked.

Because the man will have a sword, she reasoned blithely.

Through the blurred vision of mist she saw figures appear. Yet the faces first to greet her eyes were all familiar. Looking past the women, she could see the circling stones and the nearby forest. She blinked her eyes once, then twice, certain she remained in Myr after all!

Epona, knowing her all too well, stepped forward and

5

took her hand. "Daughter of Myr, your disappointment is written on your face. Alas, we are all women here. I see I must explain one more aspect of the riddle."

Epona began, "The realms of Myr and Men are the same, but in spirit different. Do not forget that in a forgotten time ago Myr spanned all the earth. When man forged blade, he choose to worship the blade of death rather than the chalice of life, and Myr retreated. Now greet your swan sisters and join with them in the celebration of the Mother of all living."

"Are there no men to join with us?" asked Moira. A gentle laughter encircled her ears.

"You will meet men soon enough," assured Epona with a tolerant sigh. "Now join in sisterhood for the celebration of life."

In silent, graceful ritual the women slipped off their cloaks and clothing. They interlaced their arms, and in unison their voices rose in a soft chant, pouring out from their hearts a low floating song to touch the stars. Moira moved beside Epona, falling easily into the chant which called the Moon Goddess from deep heaven into the midsummer sky. Three times the women slowly snaked sun-wise beneath the lintel stone. Three times they chanted each sacred song, praising the White Goddess.

When at last the moon rose in the cobalt sky, the women slowed their chanting and turned their voices to a deep healing song to Mother Earth. Around them the earth force began to flow into the great stones. Moira stretched out her arms and spanned the massive dolmens with her two hands touching each side. Immediately she felt a strong tingling sensation radiate through her palms. She felt giddiness as the earth force trembled through her arms and into her body, swirling within her womb like lifeblood, wet and warm.

Suddenly she underwent a powerful transformation. Lightheaded, she drew in air, floating with the energy of the spiral flow. Her spirit mingled with the women's chant and swirled up. Up and around the henge, past the dancing women's skein, above the lintel stone. She felt her chest swell tighter with every breath, unbalancing her, transforming her into sister swan. The wind of song lifted her wings up, aloft into the perpetual twilight of the midsummer's night. No longer earthbound she dared fly beyond the protection of the henges. She soared, a cygnet shadow across the Queen of Heaven's opal face.

Beyond the outlying stones, crouched on the forest edge, huddled Arn the poacher. He patiently waited the passing of a roebuck. An other-worldly sound carried on the night breeze, and he shifted, uneasy. Surely 'twas only the hoot of owl or cree of hawk, but the sound hung in the air. His nervous eyes darted across the meadow, fixing on the rock monoliths, remembering the story of the magical dancing stones. 'Twas only a child's tale, but in truth tonight the stones illuminated a fire's glow. He swallowed hard and then summoned his hunter's nerve, convinced the stones only reflected the light of midsummer twilight. But still he riveted an uneasy eye to the stonehenge, for so near the place he did not like to be. And then his hunter's sight caught the movement of a white swan spiraling in the cobalt sky above.

By God's teeth! Tonight he would bag not roebuck but swan. He left the forest cover, stepped into the clearing, and drew taut his bow. He let fly an arrow into the night. The shriek sounded more human than fowl. Wings flapping in vain, the great white swan toppled from the sky, tumbling down past reach of star and eye of moon.

The sharp-eyed poacher, game bag in hand, slung his bow over his shoulder and ran a direct line to his quarry. The great wings hung askew and the long neck folded limply on the feathered breast. A seasoned hunter, Arn felt no remorse as he removed the arrow, and yet the earlier uneasiness crept through him like a chill. He looked warily over his shoulder toward the stonehenge. Did he see shadows moving toward him? His heart began to pound, and deftly he stuffed the huge bird into his bag and slung it over his broad shoulders. He would make delivery to the convent now and save himself the effort of gutting entrails and plucking feathers.

Covering the half league to Mergate Abbey, he strained under the weighty load. All the while he was heartened by the knowledge that a bird of this size would trade for sweet honey as well as beeswax candles. Stealthily he approached the high walled quadrant of buildings which overlooked the sea. He circumvented to the south and disappeared into an outcropping of stones. He stooped down into a well-concealed passageway tunneled underground to the heart of the convent. Mole-like he moved and eventually halted at the passage's end.

He knocked thrice on the wooden door and waited. Soon he heard movement from within as the iron bolt was slipped aside. The door creaked open, and he lowered the brim of his hat from the exposing candlelight. The face of a dark-robed nun peered through the door's opening.

"I've brought thee fowl," Arn whispered.

The nun leaned through the threshold and eyed the bulging game bag.

"Let me see."

Muttering, he slung the bag from his back to the ground. "'Tis a weighty bugger. I'll have a fair trade from thee." Amid the flurry of white feathers he shook out the game bag.

For a breathless moment Arn the poacher could not believe his eyes. Ice touched his heart.

The nun nearly dropped her candlestick. "'Tis a maid! What deed is this?"

"Nay, 'twas a swan, I swear!"

The nun bent and put hand to pulse.

"She lives. Carry her inside. Quickly."

Mumbling incoherently, Arn did as he was bid. He lifted the bleeding and naked maiden into his arms and followed the nun into the black mouth of the doorway. "'Tis bewitchment. I'm blameless. Do ye 'ear! A night of devil's work. A devil's spawn I've pinioned."

The nun gazed on the pale, ethereal beauty of the maiden. Arn watched her cross herself and heard her whisper, "Have I not prayed all my life for one small sign from heaven? Now God has answered." She spoke assuredly, "Nay, not devil, but angel. Hunter, you've shot an angel from heaven." Arn felt distraught and confused. His eyes rolled fearfully.

Behind the secret entrance was a storage room. The

nun took a moment to ready a pallet on the floor among piles of wool and sacks of grain. Covering the maid with white linen sheeting, she ordered, "Put her here. Gently." Arn did as he was told, still trying to hide his face from the nun's observant eyes. The nun turned to hurry healing preparations, but the maiden moaned and she turned back and knelt beside her. Eyes the color of marsh fires lulled open, and the nun drew closer.

"Where have you come from?" she asked.

"I fell . . . from the sky," she answered breathlessly.

"Above the henge," whispered Arn, peering from the shadows.

"From heaven?" asked the nun hopefully.

The girl licked her dry lips in the effort to answer. "My grandmother is yet there."

"Your grandmother is in heaven. Is she an angel, too?"

"I have come to see a man. I—" Her breath became a gasp as she faded into unconsciousness.

Arn drew farther back into the shadows, his mouth hanging open nearly to his knees. The nun turned on him and said, "You heard for yourself, she is from heaven. Now be off with you! Say nothing! God does not abide men killing his angels. If she dies, you'll forfeit your immortal soul."

"Me tongue's dumb. But 'tis witchery," he muttered, unconvinced. Not needing a second prod to leave, he stooped through the door, scrambling down the black-throated passageway and out into the midsummer's night.

Chapter 1

From her view through the arched bell openings of Mergate Abbey's tower, Moira eyed the scape of sea and land. Somewhere, over the moorland rise, was the stonehenge and forest; beyond, the nuns had spoken of castles and villages. She despaired of finding her grandmother. Where was Epona? Had she returned to Myr? Moira's fingers massaged her still tender shoulder, thinking one hunter's death arrow near her heart was enough to dampen her curiosity about the world of men. Her swan mind was equally cautious.

How can I, a wild thing, live in a world that hunts me from the sky and entraps me behind high walls? her swan self wondered.

Moira's breast fell and with a slow sigh of resignation she thought, *Until I have the strength to fly, we must remain here.*

Her one month stay in the abbey had not been easy. Thanks to the watchful care of Sister Justina, Moira's life was saved. Even so, the nuns now believed she was an angel from heaven and took it upon themselves, with zealous vigilance, to shelter and safeguard her all too well. At first she'd tried to explain to Sister Justina that she was not an angel, but Justina would hear nothing of her explanations.

"I have a pouch full of your feathers to prove it. The pardoner would give me gold coin for these relics, but I believe such things should not be sold. Thanks be to God for sending you to Mergate to renew our faith."

Moira had not ventured beyond the abbey walls, but declared to Justina she hoped soon to see a man. Disapprovingly, Justina said, "I speak truly, you have missed nothing. Men are beyond understanding. They are callous and sadistic, no atrocity is beyond giving them pleasure. Thank the Virgin for Convents where we women might flee for sanctuary and find a little peace."

Daily, Moira observed that no one entered or left the abbey without the consent of Abbess Hildith. This was strictly enforced because the sole key to the great door hung about the Abbess's abundant waist. Feeling her strength returning, Moira now spent her evenings in the bell tower gazing out toward sea and moorland and her afternoons in the abbey library reading the writings of men. The histories spoke of bloody dates and crimson battles, the commandments of God and the rule of kings.

Away from those musty vaults and standing in the light of day she breathed despairingly, *Where are the women? Where is the White Goddess?*

Her swan half reasoned, *Where God is male, the male is God.*

Moira shook her head sadly. *Then there is no balance. Epona said the world of men was a riddle, and now I believe her.*

They have forgotten the Mother of all living and instead believe woman to be a serpent's temptress, mourned her swan self.

Aye, the nuns dare not rejoice in their woman's body, but cover and bind it with shame.

It is not easy for a free soul like myself to be pious, complained her swan self.

'Tis true. How I yearn to cast off this rough homespun robe with the restricting beliefs of men, and again answer the call to revel in the dance of the full moon and in the renewal of life.

Slim shadows flickered inky designs over Moira's face and she looked up. Two ravens hovered in the wind above her, muting the sun's glare. The ravens' cries called her and her eyes followed as they winged out to sea, lessening into the horizon. A shiver crept down her spine as a feeling of menace enveloped her. This was a warning and she knew peril would come from the sea. A storm? There was not a cloud in the late summer sky.

The breeze picked loose the single braid confining the length of her black hair and spider-webbed it across her eyes. With her hand she brushed the strands away, breathing in the tangy sea air. Suddenly above her the bell for vespers rang. With her hands clamped over her ears, she raced down the tower steps. Rays of sunlight streamed through arrow slits, illuminating the circular inside. At the bottom sister Justina pulled the bell rope evenly to and fro. She smiled at Moira. During the next minutes the ringing reverberated from the abbey's heart, floating to castle and croft, along shore and cliff, rolling with the waves out to sea.

Justina retied the bellpull. "Eventide, my angel." Ears still ringing, Moira returned the smile. Justina opened the south door of the tower, and Moira followed her out. "You look well. I am glad to see that you feel strong enough to climb the stairs."

Moira lowered her lashes. Her eyes were a betraying succession of changing colors, ever reflecting her emotions. "I am ready to walk the moor as well."

Justina frowned. "I suppose you still wish to see a man."

"Yes." Moira's eyes brightened.

"I cannot reason why, but in time you will have your wish. Now, Abbess Hildith has requested my help with vespers, and I did not finish stacking the hot loaves of bread on the cooling shelves. Would you go to the kitchen and complete the task?"

"Aye," said Moira, glad for the opportunity to miss vespers. Always her knees became sore on the cold stone floor.

"Peaceful eventide," said Justina as she hurried off. Moira turned down the opposite path.

Through the cloister into the court her footsteps were a sighing echo upon the stone surface. She passed the open chapel doors where the smell of beeswax candles erased the salty sea air, turned down a winding corridor, and disappeared into the scullery.

The large kitchen, sultry from hot baking fires, held the heat of noonday. It was ever tidy, crowded with worktables, washtubs, cooking pots, folded piles of fresh laundered linen and clothing. Herbs, onions, bulging sacks of food, strips of meat, and utensils hung from low ceiling beams. At the far end black kettles hung within a huge stone hearth. The room radiated the heat from the dying fires, and the air held the aroma of baked bread. Moira's eyes wandered to the round russet loaves stacked on the center table by the ovens.

She began the task of carrying the loaves to cooling shelves in the larder closet, thinking that if she worked slow enough, she need not attend vespers at all.

The task all too quickly completed, she looked about for something else to busy herself and set upon straightening cupboards at the back of the storage room. In the process a pouch of salt fell off the cupboard top and became wedged behind. As she reached for it, she discovered the cupboard moved easily forward. When she bent to reach the salt, she discovered something else. A hidden door.

She had suspected the existence of such an entrance. It explained her own mysterious arrival on midsummer's eve. When she asked Justina how she'd found her, Justina merely said, "You fell from heaven." Yet when wild game suddenly appeared in the larder, Justina covered by saying, "God provides for his righteous."

Well, Moira concluded ebulliently, *I have been provided for.*

As the moon waxed full she'd felt the fever of estrous warm her blood, and an unsettling restlessness had seized her. This drove her to explore, and now the opportunity was at hand.

She moved behind the cupboard and slipped the bolt of the hidden door. It opened easily. Cool, musty air from a dark tunnel breezed through the doorway. Reaching back for the beeswax candle flickering on the shelf, she stepped into the secreted passage. Despite the candlelight it was very dark. Worried that bats might fly toward the light, Moira raised the hood of her habit and shadowed her face with her hand. The air was pitchy, the passage extremely claustrophobic. She stepped cautiously, though stumbling once and stubbing her toe. Off balance, she steadied herself and then spied the far-off rays of light at the tunnel's opening. Anxious to be out of the passage, she hastened her steps. At the opening she set the candle in a hollowed earth shelf and snaked upward.

Pausing cautiously for breath and bearings, she furtively peeked out of the opening expertly concealed within a rocky outcropping. Except for a grazing ewe with her lamb on the hillside, she could see no one. Feeling a great sense of freedom, she climbed out of the opening. A glance at the low-riding westerly sun told her she hadn't much time to explore, but perhaps she might go a short distance inland and find the village. Surely there she would see a man.

Belly low, Wulfsun raised his head above the knee-deep heather. His calculating eyes moved across the landscape to settle upon the monastery on the headland's high airy summit. The midsummer's air carried the hum of bees and the heather's peppery fragrance. His mind leaped past the headland's point across the northern sea to the shores of Hordaland, where wiser men than he would be feasting and celebrating this night of midsummer.

But not Wulfsun. While other men reveled, he would be raiding Britain's coast, hoping to carry off gold and silver from Christian coffers and provisions from tradesmen's stores. While other men amused themselves with beautiful women at kingly courts, he would sit belly empty, gaunt as a wolf in hard times, stalking the unwary. While nobles enjoyed the peace and warmth of castle hearth, he and his vikings, teeth clenched to numbing cold, would be rowing through night's long hours. Mayhap to go *a viking* was not a comfor-

14

table occupation, but, Wulfsun reasoned, 'twas lucrative.

His blue eyes studied the monastery's layout with a predator's intensity. He watched the sun sink in the sky and ruminated over the plan of attack. It was sited well, protected by treacherous sea cliffs to the west and high walls to the east. The great wooden doors would require a battering ram, the one weapon impractical to his armory. Two vikings might scale the walls and open the gates from inside, yet if it came to misadventure, the alarm could be too easily sounded.

Suddenly, on a nearby rocky crag, his eye caught movement. A robed figure crawled from the burrow of the rocky outcropping. Wulfsun quickly ducked his head but continued to wonder and watch. The robed monk set out arrow straight toward his hiding lair. As the monk neared, Wulfsun's practiced eyes widened in appreciation. 'Twas no monk, but a woman! Hair the color of night escaped from beneath the hood to frame a face of rare beauty, a face he would not forget.

Reluctantly his eyes left the woman's uncommon features and returned to the outcropping, to the headland, then back to the outcropping. Luck was with him—a secret passage into the very heart of the monastery! With pagan cynicism he knew this woman's errand was easing the pangs of a virile, but celibate brotherhood.

She neared. He lowered his head. Schooling his breath and readying his dagger, he crouched, buck still. She passed so close he was tempted to reach out a hand and catch the white slim ankle. Too long he'd been without a woman. He felt the tightening of arousal in his loins. 'Twas the day for it, the place for it, and clearly the wench for it, but unfortunately not the time for it. After she passed, he raised his head and signaled to Jacob the Freed, who waited in a stand of gorse farther along the slope of the hill. Jacob withdrew an arrow from his bow. Wulfsun's eyes still followed the woman's graceful form. She would never know how close she'd come to death, but then unwittingly she'd done them a good turn. They could not but repay the favor.

* * *

Moira felt excitement when she spied the stone cross at the forest edge. Perhaps it marked the path to the village. Pausing, she caught her breath and saw the setting sun was a fading crown on the horizon. It was time to return to the abbey. Perhaps tomorrow she could set out again. Absently her fingers slowly traced the grooves of the stone cross and tried to make out the inscription. *A furore Normannorum Libera No Domine.* "From the fury of the Northmen, God deliver us."

The nuns had spoken of the Northmen raiders, of how they burned the abodes of their victims and jested as they murdered babes. She turned and looked over the moor in the direction of the abbey and a wave of apprehension swept her.

I sense death on the prowl, prompted her swan self. *The ravens forewarned as much.*

The sea . . . the danger was to come from the sea. The Northmen raiders! Quickly she turned and raced back across the moor, over bank and stream, through gorse and heather, desperate to reach the abbey.

Her heart sank as she neared, for something was clearly amiss. Smoke curled up from the abbey's center and screaming rang from within. Panic-stricken, she ran toward the rocky outcropping and climbed down into the passage. At last, through smoke-stung vision, she saw light at the end of the tunnel. The door was open and the shelving had fallen aside. Smoke clouded the air in the now empty storeroom. She passed into the kitchen trying to remain calm though her heart pounded with every step she took. She peered around the corner of the doorway and across the smoke-hazed court. Like ghostly specters, giant shadows stalked the abbey courtyard and ransacked chapel. Northmen raiders! She had wanted to see men, but these were most definitely the wrong sort!

In her despair she remembered the bell and knew if she could sound the alarm, help might come from the distant village or castle. Taking the opposite route, she fled along the deeper shadows of the cloister and entered the south door of the bell tower.

At the same instant a tall figure, illuminated by the flickering torchlight, appeared in the opposite archway. Moira froze. Fascination overrode fear. She should scream, she should run, but she couldn't, for she was face to face, eye to eye, with a man!

In his hand he held a sword.

He looked nothing like the flat drawings in the abbey library. His eyes caught the light like shimmering sun on a blue sea, his nostrils flared thrice as if he breathed her woman's scent. The cold, hard Nordic face held depth, shadow, and plane. His hair, textured streaks of gold, hung waist length over mighty thewed shoulders. Flowing muscle knit to a slender frame rippled beneath sun-bronzed skin.

She was tall but he was taller, and in all else they were opposites. Hair, fair against dark, eyes blue against aurora, skin furred against smooth. Moira found the sight of his male anatomy arresting, his stone-hearted savagery awesome, and his innate arrogance, which played about his lips and touched his eyes, intimidating.

What was the Goddess thinking when she created man?

How could the opposites of man and woman ever be compatible? amazed her swan self.

Outside, women's shrieks punctuated the bedlam as if bands of frenzied demons stalked the abbey, but in the room between them the air held death's silence. Like a serpent ready to strike, his hand held the hilt of his sword and his fierce eyes held hers in threatening sway. He took her measure with a gaze that could turn bones to dust, muscle to clabber, and a mind to prayer.

Moira was fascinated, but not afraid. So this was man, she contemplated irreverently. The riddlemaster stood before her in all his virility, arrogance, bloodlust, and mayhem. She would not break past him nor cower against the cold unyielding wall. Fear was the greater weapon, and without fear she knew his sword was useless.

As if to show who was master he pressed the icy tip of his sword to the hollow of her throat and traced a deliberate path to her belly. In one swift motion the tip of his sword severed the cord binding her robe.

She did not flinch.

The robe gaped open enough for Wulfsun's burning gaze to follow the beginning curve of soft breast and white hip. Flawless as alabaster, she was the most beautiful woman he'd ever seen. Her eyes sparked with myriad colors of light and dark. He recognized her as the woman he'd seen on the moor and smiled inwardly, thinking she was even more comely at close quarters. Speculating, he studied her. She was not trembling, nothing close to fear lit her wide shimmering eyes. He'd never seen such calm in the face of his aggression before.

He felt his body tighten with desire as he envisioned her lying beneath him on soft furs, her lips swollen from his kisses, her slender legs opening to his passion. Without taking his eyes from her, he lowered his sword and stepped forward.

Though her eyes widened fractionally, she held his own hot gaze and her lips seemed to beckon him. Something about this strange, beautiful woman fevered his loins with anticipation. Possessively, he cupped her delicate jaw in his hard, lean fingers. His thumb slowly brushed across the soft, pliancy of her coral lips. He wanted to taste those lips.

Moira felt a sudden rushing warmth. She had the feeling that he could have lifted her in one hand. His touch made her feel shaky inside, not with fear, but with the same wild restlessness that always possessed her during full moon. Suddenly, she knew without a doubt, that he could give her pleasure, that he could fill the aching emptiness that left her yearning in the night.

Suddenly his arms were around her, holding her tightly to his lean, hard frame. The heat in his eyes intensified. Briefly, as was sometimes given to her, she sensed his inner mind. He was thinking of her in a way that scorched her, and yet she wanted him, too, in just the way he was imagining.

Don't kiss him! warned her swan self.

But the warning came too late.

Fiercely he covered her mouth with his own. Her body reacted instinctively. She raised her hands to his shoulders as her lips surrendered. He kissed her as if she belonged to him, as if he had every right to her, every right to demand anything and everything from her. Under the pressure of his lips the heat and smell of him surrounded her. Every bone of her body, every fiber of her flesh, every instinct of her femininity responded to his overwhelming maleness.

The jolt of pure desire that shook Wulfsun when he kissed her took him by surprise. Suddenly his blood was fire in his veins, his breath caught in his throat. No woman should ignite such a fire. No woman should surrender to him so guilelessly. No woman should taste so sweet. Yet in his arms he held such a woman. He felt the faint quiver of her body as his tongue thrust between her parting lips and invaded the moist hollow of her mouth. He felt the honey gloss of her tongue swirl and mesh with his own. His heartbeat bolted into a wild rhythm, and he wanted her in a way that he'd never wanted anything before. The instant he kissed her, a searing dark heat had gripped him more powerful than iron bonds, more sure than an arrow straight to his heart.

A hundred years might have passed between them.

Someone shouted into the doorway, and the spell was broken. Though Wulfsun's loins were throbbing heavily, his mind reconnected with duty. This was a raid, not a tryst in a spring meadow. He pulled back and cursed between set teeth.

The same moment, remembering her errand, Moira reached for the bellpull. In a deft maneuver the Northman's sword slashed the belfry rope, the blade sharply grazing her knuckles. Her fingers flew to her lips, and the surprise of pain awakened her creature instincts. A daughter of the wild, she realized suddenly that she was the prey and this man, the hunter.

Run! Up into the tower! cried her swan self. *We must fly. I'm not sure I can.*

You must take the risk. It means freedom. After that kiss of sorcery, the man will stalk you to earth's end.

Moira darted up the spiral stone stair of the bell tower.

He followed her, but she was nimble-footed and had a head start. She hurled herself upward, near flying already. She heard his breathing and the quick slap of his step close behind. At the top the exertion caused her to stop. The wound in her shoulder had reopened and the sharp pain unsteadied her. She paused for a breath to shift shape and to spread wing for her escape through the tower's arched opening.

His shout thundered in her ears as he caught her. His arms clamped around her, and she felt the first suffocating, muscled strength of man. Despite her struggles, he was unshaken. He was an unflagging wellspring of bonecrushing force. Swirling with indignation, her eyes clashed with those of the fair-haired raider. His sea-blue eyes went flat and wicked; he smiled, the coldest smile she'd ever seen. With the last might left to her she gathered and flung herself free. A starry flash! Then all went black . . .

The woman lay limp in Wulfsun's arms. Concern etched his face. In her wild flailing she'd knocked herself out against the stone wall. He wondered how she could seduce him with so sweet a kiss one moment and then for fear of capture be willing to fling herself off the tower the next. He and his vikings had no intention of capturing anyone. Some would have their way with the women, but he would take no captives. Treasure was all he sought; altar gold and silver did not whine and thirst long days at sea.

He eased the woman onto the stone floor and sheathed his sword, Wolf's Claw, in his baldric. He bent down beside her on one knee and touched the swelling welt on her temple. The light of the rising full moon radiated through the tower opening and pooled around her.

As if she were some unknown creature to explore, his fingers caught a swatch of her long black hair. He turned it over and over in his hand, examining its texture and moonlit shimmer. He let loose her hair and caressed the smooth curve of her neck and throat, up to her moisture-glistened lips. His thumb lightly brushed the softness of her mouth. A tingling from the faint breeze of her warm breath flowed into his thumb tip, lingering. The honey taste of her still clung to his tongue. A part of him wanted to take her upon the cold stone floor by light of the moon. Mayhap he should stay beside her until she awakened; such beauty needed savoring.

Long lashes draped her eyes, eyes whose color he could

not recall. Violet? Or had they flashed like dappled sunlight in a forest green? His hand slid downward, opening her robe. Her beauty lay uncovered before his hungry eyes, and he savored every inch from the soft swell of her breast to the shadowed mound of her womanhood. He realized the monastery was an abbey and knew her to be a maiden. Untouched innocence radiated from her. Why else had she shown no fear until he raised his sword to sever the bell rope? Without doubt she was a virgin, and now he yearned to be the first to sheathe himself in her sweet depths. His mind clouded with the desire to possess her, brand her as his own, so no other man would ever think of trespassing.

His forefinger traced the swell of her full, white breast. He felt a sticky moistness and peered at the dark stain on his fingers. Blood! His brows knit in puzzlement as he slipped the robe off her shoulder. Anger seized him. Which of his vikings had wounded her? But on closer inspection he saw the wound near healed and just reopened. Disappointment washed through him. Taking pride in his reputation for barbarity, even he was not so ruthless as to take a wounded woman in lusty pleasure.

Shouts, calling his name from below, drew his attention. His companions were tiring of their aged virgins.

He must go.

Yet he remained very still, his desire burning, all thoughts of raiding wiped out of his mind. Never had he been so aroused by a woman and so acutely aware of it.

He closed her robe, covering her bewitching beauty, and forced himself to stand. He strode to the stairs, but on impulse turned and looked back. Like a sleeping goddess, she appeared even more comely in moonlight. The slow fire still trembled in his loins. He wanted her like no other. A rose amid withered blossoms, he did not relish leaving her behind in this unprotected stone fortress. He returned then, and lifted her into his arms. This night he claimed a single captive.

Chapter 2

Sounds of lapping water amid rhythmic splashes echoed within the throbbing caverns of Moira's head. Slowly she opened her eyes to the gray light of dawn. Swaying as though in a cradle, she lay awkwardly on her side, her cheek chafed by splintered wood. A shooting pain over her right ear prompted her to raise her hand, only to find both wrists bound tightly with a twisted leather thong. She raised her bound hands together and gingerly probed the lump.

Not dead. Then where am I? She rolled onto her back and sat up. The movement set her head pounding. Regaining her composure, she looked around only to find the backs of over two dozen oarsmen absorbed in rowing.

Struggling to stand, she stumbled. A swift hand caught and held her.

"If you do not sit, I will also bind your feet," said a hoarse voice. She faced a chestnut-bearded, stout, muscular man, his dark eyes looking sternly over the broken bridge of his nose.

Another voice, hoarse as well, merged into her awareness. "If you jump, you will drown."

She turned to face the tall flaxen-haired Northman. The sound of his voice was like wind on dry rushes. She stared at him, knowing him, yet feeling uncertain. She tried to shake off the haze and confusion. Then her eyes riveted past his face, landward to a dark pillar of smoke. Mergate Abbey! Memory flooded back and intensified the pulsing pain in her head.

Her wrists twisted against the restraints, and her eyes lashed back to his face with outrage.

In the morning light he appeared just as forbidding. Ruthless cunning and savage strength marked his every feature. Leggings knit to muscular thighs, and against his bare, muscled chest a strapping of leather held a sword. The rising wind splayed his long, sun-streaked hair over his broad shoulders. The chiseled contours of his fiercely etched face glowered at her. Shocking blue eyes penetrated her own with a hard-edged threat.

Look long, look well, swanling. This one is bound to you by enchantment's kiss.

Still staring at his hard, arresting face, she caught her lower lip with her teeth, feeling as if both her natures would suddenly drown in wretchedness. She had wanted to do her own choosing, but now she was acutely sensitive to him, and she wondered if she had been in some part enchanted as well. He stood before her, looking at her with narrow intent eyes, and she remembered the heat of his kiss, and a frantic sense of no return washed over her.

"Sit!" he commanded.

She set her teeth, refusing to cower. Challenge filled her like the smoke billowing from the burning abbey. "I will sit but not because I am afraid. I do not fear a man who raises his sword against women."

Wulfsun glared, his sea-watching eyes wintry. Her insult was a blow to his pride. It astounded him, and he felt like seeing if she might fear a man who could strip her of her maidenhead and dignity within a single score. The mere sight of her aroused him. Hours had passed since that first kiss, yet the desire still lingered in his loins.

Still, he knew she spoke the truth, for he saw no fear in her eyes. Her eyes . . . he couldn't stop looking at them. Before they'd been light and now they were dark. In truth he couldn't tell what color they were. Up close, they were a smoldering rose verging on scarlet. He saw innocence in them, but mostly affront. The rest of her was woman enough and more.

"You would be wise to fear the fearless," he warned.

m"And where are the fearless?" She looked about. "I see only those who, from fear, strap swords at their sides. The truly fearless walk the earth weaponless."

He threw back his head and laughed a scoffing, deep sound. "Kind Freya! You are a dove!"

Her eyes smoldered a deeper scarlet, and he realized her mood was reflected in her eyes. He knew a captive with no fear was not obedient. Even so, she might not fear him, but she could be angered.

"Mayhap I will have to put the fear in you," he hissed.

Her coral full bow lips flashed open and showed pearl-white teeth straight and shimmering. "Do what you like. I will not scream or beg for mercy. Death comes to all."

"I was not thinking of something as drastic as death, holy woman. I can and will exact a sweeter price," he threatened and then, in rough undertone said, "One you may be loath to give."

He stepped nearer.

The little spokes in her pupils whirled with challenge. "I would loathe giving only that which is stolen."

He hadn't intended to touch her, but suddenly his hands gripped her waist, roughly pulling her toward him as he bent to claim her mouth. Shifting, his hands clasped the rounds of her soft hips and lifted her closer to the throbbing juncture of his own. His tongue thrust deep, where his manhood could not, spearing fiercely inside the moist folds of her mouth. In front of all, a sensual ferocity overtook him, and his kiss claimed, invaded, and demanded her to respond. Slitting his eyes he sought her own. They were closed. Her thick, black lashes sooted her cheeks, and then, amazingly, he felt the play of her tongue stroking his. Mayhap he'd been wrong thinking her a virgin. She yielded as no virgin would. His body was on fire, throbbing, aching, and wanting her in a way that was beyond reason. His hands tightened on her hips, and a low, rough sound rumbled in his throat.

In morning twilight the full moon slipped below the horizon, but its wanton magic still stirred Moira's blood. A startling heat seared her as the Northman's tongue dived and tasted the moist velvet of her mouth. The connecting pleasure was so satisfying, so intense, that her mouth molded to his, welcoming his invasion with gentle parries of her own. At last the incredible thirst and wanting that burned inside her began to explode with the heat of his kiss. She wanted to lock her arms around his neck, and her hands strained against the thongs binding them.

Suddenly he lifted his mouth from hers, the sharp disappointment causing her eyes to fly open.

His blue eyes burned her. "You say you would loathe that which is stolen. Mayhap you have nothing to steal!" Deep throated laughter sounded from those surrounding. She glanced at the craggy faces with confusion, not understanding the jest. Already she'd witnessed more than she cared about the violent nature of this man.

"Why steal what is willingly given?" she asked with disarming frankness. Their laughter again circled her ears. Her eyes darted to the others. She did not fathom their amusement. Her gaze returned to her captor, still uncertain. "The night past, you pressed upon my lips a kiss which I willingly received. Then you chased me to the tower and struck me down."

Inner mirth touched his eyes but not his lips. "Knocking you silent was not among my black deeds of the night past, holy woman. Your own thrashing did that."

"In truth, you did not strike me with your sword?"

"I do not lie."

"But you steal," she accused steadily. A flush tinged her pearl pale cheeks, but her changeling eyes never wavered.

"I steal. I pillage. I kill," he said flatly.

She sucked in her breath, but her face held hard-won composure and she muttered, "You are very savage."

"I am a warrior. Have you never met a warrior before?"

"No, you were the first man I had ever seen."

His golden brows knit together over his high-bridged nose. "I . . . the first . . ." Amazement filled his voice. In truth, she was a virgin and the thought caused his pulse to quicken, his cods to stir, and his eyes to flame. His lips pursed and he expelled a low breath. By Odin's bow! What was wrong with him? He felt like a stag in rutting.

"Aye."

He gave a harsh laugh, rife of amusement. "No wonder you are a fearless lamb, for you have only known women in that Christian Abbey. You have been done no favor. Now you are the sole woman among men." He snorted lightly. "You will suffer for your ignorance."

He now clearly understood why she tried to fling herself off the tower rather than be captured. Mayhap death might be better for one so fearless—one so beautiful. She *was* beautiful. His eyes dropped to the gap in her rough homespun robe, which revealed a hint of white curved breast. He kept remembering the pale translucent skin in the moonlight, her breasts, her stomach, her thighs. He kept imagining what a woman with no fear would be like in his arms. His face remained impassive, but his loins ached with need.

"Sit!" he commanded once again. His arousal made him irritable. She sat. He shot her a dismissing glance, turned heel, and strode to the stern of the ship to force his mind to other matters.

Following the retreat of his broad back, Moira surveyed the length of the ship. What of the other women? Did Justina escape? In a quandary, she again gazed at the strangeness of the men shipboard. All too soon she found herself staring intently at the tall Northman, pondering the grim circumstance of her misfortune, which at best was dreary.

The sail unfurled, winging to flight a black raven on crimson setting. The rowing ceased, that labor left to the freshening wind. Seated on low chests filled with supplies and loot from past raids, the Northmen busied themselves with weaponry. Shields, yellow and black, lay along the planking, mingled with cooking pots, skins of drink, and pouches of dried foodstuffs.

Whistling, the dark-haired man with the broken nose sat near Moira and sharpened his halberd on a whetstone. Occasionally he gave her a watchful eye. The sun had climbed mid-sky when he took pity on her, tossing her a skin of drink, which she took gladly. She drank, grimacing from the lingering foul aftertaste.

"Thank you," she ventured when she returned the skin bag.

"I am called Jacob the Freed by my comrades," he answered curtly, taking off his bronze conical helmet. Long curly brown hair sprinkled with gray fell to his shoulders.

"Why do you prey upon the innocent?"

He gave a sharp laugh as if the naïveté of her question was justification in itself. "I make no apologies for myself or my companions." Under black brows his eyes held steady on his task. "It could be worse for you. I say this because you are a holy woman and I but half-heathen."

"What happened to the others? Did you kill them?"

"I did not. Most escaped to the forest. We have no liking for captives."

"You have taken me."

He snorted in a half laugh and nodded down the ship to her captor. "Not I. The young chieftain, Wulfsun, he has taken you."

Moira's tongue had no more questions for Jacob the Freed. She looked at the Northman called Wulfsun and gnawed her lower lip anxiously as her spirit plummeted.

Oh, heart of the Goddess! No wonder he took me captive, he could not help himself!

Do not despair, swanling. Within the strong-boned frame and ripple of muscle the Goddess has made him vulnerable, only if by way of enchantment. There is swansdown under the tempered armor of stamina and muscle, as in woman there is a wellspring of strength beneath her fleece of fragility. Until the next full moon you must seek this place and quell the ferocity of this man if you are ever to survive his choosing.

Nay, we will fly, countered Moira.

Bound in any way, we can fly nowhere.

Moira looked down at the leather thong binding her

hands and frayed her wrists against its bondage. *Enchanted, he will be love's fool. He will release me.*

Look at him. Enchanted or not, that one is no one's fool. She looked to the hard chiseled line of Wulfsun's profile and knew her other half spoke the truth.

Time passed and Wulfsun leaned into the steering rudder, trying not to look at or think of the woman. Something about her told him she was not like any woman he had ever known. During this night's raid he would leave one man to guard her, but then he wondered which one could be trusted. Though he was confident none of his vikings would dare touch what belonged to him, he knew each man had ravished her in his thoughts a hundred times since daybreak. He had himself. With some effort he pushed the woman from his mind.

The chastening wind hastened his finely crafted ship in plunging leaps across the swelling waves. The carved dragons fore and aft gave the vessel the look of a great beast slithering through the water, and he knew the Britons were awed by such a sight. During this night's raid his strategy would be the same as when he laid seige to Mergate Abbey. He would sail into a river inlet and wait until after sunset to strike. Then on the morning tide he would swiftly make for open sea.

His eyes narrowed and his jaw clenched as he looked down the length of the ship and saw Jacob speaking with the holy woman. He trusted Jacob better than he trusted himself, yet a sudden primitive urge to confront his longtime companion seized him. He muttered a curse to himself. What was wrong with him?

He turned his gaze out to sea, but his thoughts remained on his captive. Her long, obsidian hair brushed below her hips like a silken cloak, and when she moved, her full breasts quivered as if born for sensuality. At night he knew his desire would flare as he slept beside her as protector. Even so, irritation pummeled him, for he knew he could not touch her with all his vikings about. Times past he had shared women with his men, but he would not share this one. Nor would he give them the satisfaction of watching his own pleasure. He wished himself apart from his vikings and wondered how long before he might have such a night alone with her.

The ship paralleled the coast northward until late afternoon. About a mile off shore he ordered the sail lowered, and the oars again hit the sea. Coming to a juncture of sea and river, he steered the ship up the river channel. Disciplined and powerful, his vikings rowed unhaltingly for an hour more. At dusk he gave a short command and the rowing ceased. The ship drifted, then scraped and grated against the shallow river bottom. They lowered anchor as mists began to rise over the gray water. Dense fog quickly settled on land and river; nearby faces became phantomlike, then nonexistent.

Moira listened to the Northmen whisper softly among themselves, their voices carrying easily on the untouchable veil. She could see nothing, but her ears were tuned to anything that gave an idea as to what was happening. She sensed men were climbing over the side into the river water. Had they taken advantage of the mists to fall upon another defenseless abbey? Why else would they sit covertly, if not for a raid? She reasoned that if she could not see them, they could not see her. Her mind began churning, realizing the ship's crew had dwindled to a handful. There might be a chance . . .

In a whisper her swan self prompted, *Now! Slip over the side. They will not miss you for a while.*

Quickly she eased over the side and nearly shrieked as the icy water bit through her clothing.

Minutes passed. She floated downriver into the cloaking mists and finally climbed out of the water up an abrupt banking. Trusting to luck, she set her direction inland.

For a long time she scrambled blindly through the darkness. Hampered by wet robes and bound hands, she stumbled through the thick undergrowth of thorny gorse, into trees and rocks, over gullies and into holes.

You must find someone to cut your bonds, advised her swan self. *Then we can fly.*

The lump on her head had begun to throb and her

shoulder ached. She stopped to catch her breath and sank to the ground in the damp bracken. After a time she smelled fire. She knew the warriors had attacked some hapless victims.

Men must have no souls, her swan self reasoned.

Her mind more than weary, Moira returned, *'Tis truth.*

At the cracking of a twig her eyes leaped open and caught a shadow in the darkness. She held her breath and scanned the night, catching another shift of shadow. Did her eyes fool her? Did she see a gray shape and flash of canine eye?

The mist had lifted and the sky cleared to reveal the waning moon. She came to her feet, and the shrubbery rustled with her passing as she broke from the overgrowth into a clearing. Her eyes blinked against the flame of torchlight, and she heard muffled voices.

"Aye, 'tis a woman," said one low voice.

Five or six grisly-looking men encircled her. Unlike the Northmen who wore helmets and carried swords, these men wore coarse clothing and held wooden clubs and pitchforks.

One leaned forward and spoke in a rough voice. "Who be you?"

"I was captured by the Northmen," she answered. "I escaped from their ship on the river."

Much interested in her revelation, his wrinkled, hairy face leered within inches of hers. The others circled her and spoke among themselves. She turned her face from the man's rotting breath and asked, "Cut my bonds with your dagger so that I might be free."

His guttural laughter hit her ears. Suddenly his hand caught her jaw and painfully twisted her face back to his own. He took her face in his calloused hands and tried to kiss her mouth.

Oh, Sister Moon! You do not need another man panting at your heels with enchantment, cried her swan self.

Moira tucked her chin and butted him in the mouth with her forehead. His comrades laughed. He swore at them while his mauling hands caught and knocked her to the ground. The man came down heavily on her and nipped her neck painfully. She let loose a shrill cry and kicked at him. Again and again she screamed, until the man grasped her neck and choked away all sound.

Down on one knee, in the cover of gorse, Wulfsun's eyes glittered blue ice in the moonlight. He watched the men surround the holy woman. He had heard her pleas but waited until every man's full attention was centered on her. A possessive rage, cold and deadly, seared through him. He knew what the Britons had in mind, and he cursed himself for forgetting to tie her feet before he'd left the ship. Luckily, the Britons' torchlight served as a beacon for her as well as for himself or he'd never have found her. Suddenly her scream split the black and silver night, and he was up, springing from his cover.

As if appearing from nowhere, his sword flashed wild. The devil on top of the woman flew sideways—at least his head did. Chest heaving, heart flaring savagery, Wulfsun lunged and lashed out at her attackers. All around the Britons fell with wrathful shrieks, while one ran into the forest.

Moira gathered in a crouch and tried to crawl for cover. Blood sprayed her cheek, the taste, warm and salty, wetted her lips. Then all went still. Men lay strewn on the forest floor, and the air hung heavy with death. Nausea and revulsion swept her as she stared at the wanton butchery. Moonlight glinted off the now motionless death blade. A single specter loomed before her. She touched gazes with the unmistakable viking Wulfsun. His cold, ruthless face was devoid of love's enchantment. Frantic, her heart pounded against her ribs and her nostrils flared for breath.

You are dead! her swan self cried. *For this man it is easy to kill!*

Ice crept through Moira's veins. For the first time fear clutched her heart. Her swan's instinct clamored to escape to the river as the warrior turned his intent upon her. Fleeing from the wolf, she was caught by the vultures only to be snared again by the wolf. A woman could not win in the world of men.

There would be no outrunning him, but she would try. Sucking in her breath, she bolted into the trees. Between her still-bound hands she clutched her tangling robes leg high for a freer stride. Tree limbs and brambles whipped stinging blows across her face and legs. How she ran! Her sides began to ache, her lungs burned, and she thought she might collapse. A clammy sweat broke out over her whole body, trickling down her back and ribs.

Glancing back, it was as if a wolf stalked her, and any moment she expected to feel its hot panting breath on her neck and its fangs at her throat. She broke through a copse of trees, pitched forward, and fell down the steep embankment to the river. Over and over she sprawled to the water's edge. Strength was gone in her arms and legs and the long night's escapade had left her with no reserve. Her hunter loomed over her, not wolf but man. Her run had merely saved him the work of dragging her back to the ship, which floated within a whistle's sigh.

Unable to forget the bloody scene in the forest, nausea gripped Moira and she retched. Wulfsun knelt down and in an unwarranted gesture, swept the curtain of her hair away from her face. She sensed his movements, felt the warmth of his body as he came closer. With a strong hand he gave her trembling body support and allowed her to gain some semblance of control. He leaned to the river's edge, cupped a hand into the water and pressed the coolness against her lips. He murmured softly, consoling sounds in rich, mellow tones.

Her wary eyes met his own.

His held concern, not the coldness or cruelty she had witnessed before. "Why did you run from me?" he asked, his voice low.

She could not answer. His savagery flashed in her mind and her senses were overwhelmed.

He can be kind as well as cruel, one part of her consoled.

Aye, but this duality makes him the most dangerous creature in existence. He is quick, he can swing a sword, and he plots destruction. He takes pride not in his goodness, but in his strength. He has mistaken brutality for strength. You cannot forgive him this.

"You need not fear me." His voice stayed deceptively soft.

A shiver trembled through her. The ferocious power of his hard-muscled body stunned her. Even as his hands touched her face, she felt the lean strength that only moments before viciously cut down the others. She swallowed back her shock and hissed. "You lie! I *should* fear you. I run because I fear you. As you vowed, you have put the fear into me."

His deep-sea eyes narrowed sharply in a cold controlled gaze. "I do not lie!" he said steadily. "Of all men I am the first you saw and the last you should fear."

Moira's eyes widened. "Then of all men I will fear you first and last!"

He cupped her upthrust chin, a touch that shocked her by its possessiveness. "Then fear me! Of all men you will be mine, first, last, and only!"

Moira pulled away. Not ready to admit complete defeat and submit to him, she struggled to stand on her own. At the attempt her knees buckled and she collapsed. Wulfsun was quick to catch her in the hard circle of his arms. He heaved her easily over his shoulder, clasping her knees to his waist. Her long hair swept the ground as he waded into the river toward the ship.

Tears of frustration trailed down her cheeks, and in a final act of despair, she raised her still-bound hands to the sky and softly chanted, "Lady of night, Lady of light, shield me from harm, this is my rite."

Two nights without rest, Wulfsun was ready for sleep by the time the ship met the sea. Magnus One Eye took over the tiller, and Wulfsun strode to where the holy woman crouched with her head resting on the hill of her knees. He sat down beside her, pulled the bulk of a grain sack to shoulder his body, and stretched his full length. He used his body to corner her in a protective barricade.

She lifted her forehead from her knees and looked at him through the curtain of her hair. "At least you are comfortable," she said, her voice cold. She shook back her hair, shifted this way and that, making a great show of her bound hands.

"I am comfortable because I did not try to escape and betray my captors," he observed heartlessly.

33

"I may have escaped," she conceded, "but I did not betray you."

"I heard you with my own ears," he said, his voice harsh. Her proximity provoked him, and weariness from the past days of raiding racked through him. Sighing with aggravation, he patted the grain sack. "Lay your head here." He turned on his side with his back to her.

He sensed her hesitation, but then felt the weight of her head behind his. To his annoyance she burrowed up against him, and his senses were off and running. She curved her body around his, and her hips pressed to his. Her nearness inflamed him, and his imagination leaped.

"You are warm," she whispered in a logical explanation.

She was not. In truth he felt her shivering against him, and she smelled like gorse and river water. He cleared his throat and tried to breathe his irritation away.

Sitting up, he said, "Take off your wet robe."

"I cannot, my hands are bound," she announced.

He felt his control slip and wondered again what had possessed him to take her captive, but the rigidity of his loins proved that puzzle easily answered. "Hah!" he scoffed. "Free-handed you would take my sword and slay me while I slept."

"Free-handed I would touch you," she said cautiously. "I could ease those places of weariness in your back and arms."

Her words left him off balance. How could she know of his weariness? He was tempted to accept her offer, but he was no fool. He straightened to his full height, towering over her, and reached to ferret a length of rope. "I will unbind your hands, but first I will bind your feet."

Lines of displeasure dusted her black-winged brows. Surely she did not expect him to allow free movement on his ship. Going down on one knee, he lifted her feet to bind her ankles. "Your feet are like ice!" he exclaimed.

Her dark gaze was on him with unreadable emotion. "I am very cold," she admitted.

He had no choice then but to kneel at her feet. "I will rub some warmth back into your bones." His heart started pounding the moment he touched her, but he steeled himself to calm. Feet were not the best part of a woman, but they were a beginning. Mayhap the fire that burned in him would spark and warm her as well.

Though the full moon was waning, Moira knew its magic was strong upon them both. At first she could not forget that just hours before she'd run from him, nor could she forget the horrors of his bloody handiwork. Now when he lightly touched her feet as if they were delicate flowers, a warm tingling trembled through her. The duality of her own nature troubled her.

His violence appalls me, and yet I am welcoming his touch.

Aye, 'tis the moon and your own instinctive need for union. The enchantment may expand his heart. If not, you must gentle him. You will find it a wearying task to bring balance to his nature, but for a time it means your life and freedom.

His warming touch became firmer as his fingertips glided along the outer and inner contour of one foot, then the other. Expertly he stroked the arch, sliding his fingers between her toes. His fingers paused. Her heart missed a beat, for she felt him discover the thin webbing that connected her toes. Hopefully, he would think it a deformity.

He said nothing, and then she felt his fingers move again. Her toe webbing was wildly sensitive and her teeth caught her lower lip to keep from moaning aloud from the sweet sensation. Cupping her heel in his large, strong hand, he gently rolled each toe between his thumb and forefinger, reviving, stimulating. She felt the warmth return to her feet and experienced an awakening connective flow between herself and Wulfsun.

She felt ripples of pleasure as he began stroking the upper part of her foot, moving up gradually to her ankle. She breathed deeply, letting go a long sigh. It felt so good, but then he suddenly stopped.

"Oh, do not stop," she said, a little selfishly.

"You must take off that wet robe, or you will never be warm," he answered, a hint of tiredness in his voice. She watched him bind each ankle and hobble her feet securely. Frustration seized her and she kept her eyes lowered, refusing to look at him when he moved to unbind her hands. Feeling his watchful eyes upon her, she dragged off her sodden robe.

Moonlight etched the soft contours of her naked body, her breasts, her thighs, her stomach. But for the healing wound on her shoulder, Wulfsun had never seen such flawless alabaster skin, skin as white as pearls in a Byzantium bazaar. His breath halted for a whisper as he devoured her startling beauty. Desire swelled inside him like an incoming tide, and he wanted her more fiercely than ever before. He wanted to press his lips to those coral-budded breasts, his mouth to the silk of her thighs.

Nearby two of his vikings spoke between themselves. He heard a snicker, and he turned on them, growling a ripping reprimand. The glittering lust withered in their quickly lowered eyes. Mayhap he could use the moment to school all his vikings in a lesson of self-control. But first he must learn to control himself.

He unfastened his fur-lined cloak. "Wrap yourself in this and I will spread your robe to dry." She readily took his cloak. Almost with relief he turned away and hung her robe to billow in the night breeze. He lay back down beside her. "Are you comfortable now?" he asked with sarcasm, his voice strained.

"I would be more comfortable if my feet were free."

"Say no more, woman," he commanded. "I am weary and you are much trouble."

In the moonlight Moira saw the dark shadows and glaze of his tired eyes and knew he begged for sleep. He moved to pillow his head beside hers, but pointedly turned his back to her. She heard the mumbled voices of two men nearby. She turned her gaze to them, and suddenly she was glad Wulfsun rested beside her. Closing her eyes, she curled up in the cloak and turned toward Wulfsun's comforting warmth.

"Why bring you a woman shipboard?" Thorfinn shouted. Though at Wulfsun's side, Thorfinn's words were near swallowed in the wind. The ship ran with the storm while he and Thorfinn manned the steering oar with unflagging tenacity. "It is bad enough we battle a storm from Hel and are afloat on open sea."

Wulfsun, gripping the tiller, clenched his lips tightly. For three days he'd listened to Thorfinn's complaints. The storm was a nightmare, and mayhap if it continued in strength the sea would take them all.

Feeling doomed, he held an inward conversation of hindsight. His first error was to mistake a convent for a monastery. What fools these Christians were with their god of peace and love, refusing to arm themselves, all the while leaving their women defenseless. In Hordaland it was different. A man protected his possessions.

His eyes rested on the woman. Through the pelting rain he stared at her intensely, noting her fair face waxed pale. His second mistake had been a whim. From his first sight of the woman on the moor he'd wanted her. Then to come upon her again in the convent . . . She remained too much in his thoughts. A chieftain should demand better control of himself. Thorfinn was right, a ship was no place to pursue a woman. Even now the others believed she had brought the storm.

He licked the sea spray from his lips and cursed the wind ripping at his sails. His vikings had lashed down everything including themselves. Unable to take bearings or plot a course, he had sailed on the open sea two storm-lashed nights and three storm-battered days. He knew they were off course. He wondered if they would ever reach the coast of Jutland.

Suddenly the longship pitched into a heavy sea swell, and dark swirling water washed over the crew and deck. The ship rolled like sea sand in riptide, and Wulfsun felt the tremor and shift of ballast. By Odin's blood, they were doomed!

He heard the woman's screams cut through the howl of the storm. His gaze leaped to her. Agnar and Magnus One Eye had seized her, cut her lifeline, and were preparing to throw her overboard. His heart slammed into his chest as he yelled a curse and lunged forward . . . but he was too late! The men had pitched her over the side. Hesitating not a moment he dived in, groping for her, knowing he could drown himself.

It was her unbound hair, swirling like seaweed, that saved her. He caught a clump in his hand and pulled her toward him. He clung to her, fearing he'd lose her in the depths of the cold sea. Suddenly, he felt her arms coiling around his own. The lifeline around his waist became taut, and he knew his vikings were set on rescue.

Struggling against the sea and the shifting of the ship, the vikings at last hauled them onto the sea-drenched planking. The woman lay in the protection of his strong arms, his long golden hair tangled with the wet black strands of her own.

He laid his hand upon her breast and with relief felt the rise and fall of her breath. Her eyes opened to his. The clamor of the storm seemed to recede and her lips parted with a weak whisper. He turned his ear to her lips.

"Give me your dagger," she begged.

His mouth broke wide in disbelief. "By my word, I am your protector. You need no dagger."

Beseeching, she held out a hand. "Give me your dagger or we all shall die."

The ship pitched wildly. Wulfsun looked to Jacob the Freed and then to the craggy faces of his vikings. They might be fearless, but they were also superstitious. Suddenly her hand caught the hilt, surprising him. Dagger in hand, she struggled to her knees. With the sharp edge of the blade facing the coming storm she thrust it into the ship's floor. He heard her voice calling in the strangely lilting chant of sorcery.

"Hear my chant, Ancient One, O spirit of the Air. Split wind, halt gale, harm none."

Soon the rain ceased, the wind slowed, and the sea no longer boiled like a bottomless cauldron. All stood wordless.

Though she had just saved their lives, Wulfsun realized his vikings would again throw this woman overboard, but for different reasons. His own eyes narrowed speculatively, though he was not one to fear sorcery. Mayhap the woman's charms and chants might prove useful to him. He stepped between the vikings and the woman, a glint of bedevilment in his eyes.

"I have seen her in a dream," he declared, his eyes flinty. "She is our talis-woman. And you fools would throw her into the sea. It is a waste of a fair face." There was no laughter. He did not expect it, but he knew they would be content to leave her alone.

Jacob the Freed stepped forward, distracting everyone by calling out orders to tend to the ship before it sank from neglect. Aside to him he scoffed. "You saw her in a dream. Humph!"

His mouth quirked. "It was a waking dream. The best sort."

For the moment it seemed as if Moira had been forgotten. Her eyes riveted to the dagger within inches of her grasp and then to the sky.

Now is the time. Seize the dagger, cut your foot bindings, and fly, urged her swan self.

Her heart leaping, she reached for the hilt. "I would have my dagger back." Wulfsun's voice was cool and alert as his large hand closed over hers. She raised her eyes to him with uncertainty. His gaze locked on her face, and his eyes sliced through her. She quivered from the chilling discernment in his face.

"If I am to be thrown in the sea each time you meet foul weather, I would have my feet and hands unbound," she declared bravely.

"Do not ask it." His voice was tight. "I am no fool. Mayhap you would escape by walking on water like the Christian hero."

Not understanding, Moira eyed him with confusion.

His big hands clutched her shoulders, and he leaned very close, so close his nose almost touched hers. "Do not make me regret saving you," he warned softly.

She narrowed her eyes indignantly. "I will not thank you for that one good deed, nor my capture!" she sputtered, her teeth clacking with cold.

His grasp loosened on her shoulders and he laughed, but his laugh held contempt. "It is bad enough we are blown off course. Now I must contend with a thankless woman as well!" Abruptly he turned away.

Shaking with chill, Moira shuffled to sit. She glared at his broad back as he searched inside an oilcloth bag and retrieved his dry, fur-lined, scarlet cloak.

Wulfsun turned back. "Take off your wet robe."

Quickly she rose and slipped off the robe. Once again, she stood shivering before him in her naked beauty. He muttered. The sight of her warmed his cold bones faster than a noonday summer sun. When he draped the cloak around her shoulders, the back of his hand brushed against the swell of a bare breast. His heartbeat increased as his eyes dropped. She was so soft, so delicate, he wanted to bury his face against her. Loki's beard! He should have let the sea have her rather than be distracted by his need. He set his teeth and turned away from her to take bearings.

But from behind, her quiet voice sounded. "What course do you plot?" He glanced over his shoulder at her. His curiosity overruled his arrogance and he spoke, "Northeasterly."

Forming graceful slender fingers in a circle she raised her hands to the sky and peered through them. She rotated her hands slowly, then made a half arc turn to the right and pointed her hand out to the gray horizon. "This is your course."

Wulfsun was wary, but he knew this woman possessed uncommon power. Her changeling eyes and her rare ebony hair marked her apart. Even so, she could be setting their course back to Britain, but it was a risk he would take. Besides, the skies would clear and he could turn the ship around. He called abrupt instructions to the rudderman, and the ship turned a few degrees.

For two more nights and a day they sailed the gray sea, sky and water blended into one vast endlessness. Moira continued to plot their Northeasterly course. In the afternoon of the third day the sun broke from behind the cloud covering. The casual pace of the ship quickened, and Wulfsun and Jacob the Freed assessed their course.

Moira pretended indifference to the outcome. She tore a hunk off a loaf of soggy brown bread and chewed slowly. After a moment Wulfsun looked to her, then nodded circumspectly aft to the rudderman. Murmured comments rippled the crew, and many curious eyes turned to her. She knew the ship was exactly on course and tried to school her face. A smug smile played the corners of her lips.

More than once after this Moira found Wulfsun studying her with a hard-eyed gaze and she wondered what he was thinking. In truth she was becoming used to his casual scrutiny and found herself returning the attention. What else was there to do during the long hours at sea but to study this mystery called man? Even with her eyes shut the imprint of his face hovered in her mind. Unruly, flaxen hair, astonishing blue eyes, and the hard line of his determined mouth seemed impossible to erase. His deep voice she knew, whether he thundered orders to his vikings or spoke in a soft flow to a single companion. She became accustomed to sleeping against his broad back at night. In daylight her eyes sought his wide-legged stance and often followed the gait of his long stride from bow to stern. She watched the other men, but no one drew her eyes like Wulfsun.

Eventually, the skies cleared, leaving only a feathery layer of cirrus clouds. Subtle whiffs of land mingled with the sea air, something tangible to stabilize her wandering mind. Off the bow a cloud of gulls swirled over dark shapes in the water.

Moira watched the bow wake. Her eyes grew wide and her mouth dropped open. Small sea serpents leaped above the water. "What are they?" she asked Jacob the Freed wonderingly.

She leaned over the ship's side. Ladened with loot, the ribbed ship rode low in the water. The sea spray sprinkled her face.

"Sea hogs," said Jacob the Freed, who had moved to her side.

"Sea hogs?" At that moment the sea hogs leaped nose first from the water, falling back into the sea on their slick bellies. Others came to the side for a better view, among them Wulfsun. His powerful forearm bumped against Moira's as he held the ship's side. Her pulse quickened. The sight of his large muscled arm so near her own smaller one turned her mind to the paradox of the man beside her. How could a hand now so benign, become the ruthless slayer of those men in the forest? A skittishness rose from the pit of her stomach to the hollow of her throat, and she moved her hand away. She was torn by her instinctive need to twine herself around him, and yet was repelled by the violence of his nature.

Turning his strong-boned looks to her, he said, "They

often follow the bow wake." His features softened and Moira smiled at him.

"Perhaps they are as curious of us as we are of them," she replied. "Look, they are laughing at us. They frolic, loving the sea and their freedom." She particularly lingered on the word *freedom*. Watching the graceful creatures as they surfaced and darted rapidly through the waves took her out of herself and helped her forget her own loss of freedom.

"It is a life as good as any," Wulfsun said, with the bold gaze of an adventurer.

Jacob the Freed took his bow in hand. He drew an arrow and targeted it toward the leaping animals.

Dismay seized Moira. She felt a twinge of pain from her own arrow wound. She clutched her shoulder. "You cannot!" Both men looked at her oddly.

"'Tis fine sport," said Jacob, drawing back the bow string.

"Nay! To break the chain of life is never sport!" Moira cried. Had these men no sense of connection to other creatures? Did they not know all that walked the earth were bound together like tide to moon and sun to season?

She opened her mouth and began to sing, a high-pitched warning which carried over the water to the sea hogs. Even before Jacob's arrow left the bow, the animals plunged deep beneath the water's mirrored surface. All eyes watched the surrounding sea for some moments, but the sea hogs did not reappear. Then Wulfsun turned his look to Moira.

Her lashes lowered demurely, and she blanked her face with innocence. "They have gone."

"Mayhap you can sing them back!" he said irritably, clearly not fooled.

She didn't bend to his imperative, and with an uppity tilt of her chin she returned, "Mayhap . . . and mayhap not!" His eyes narrowed and she knew he didn't relish back talk from a woman.

Someone shouted and all heads turned to the caller, who pointed easterly. A great clamor among the men burst forth as they sighted a ship with red checkered sails off the bow.

Jacob the Freed laughed, "The bloody berserker!" Moira saw a humored calculation in Wulfsun's eyes as he surveyed the distant ship.

"Do you know it?" she asked.

"It is Bjorn's *Elk Wader,* a sister ship." He turned from her and began showering the length of the ship with commands. She craned her head for a better view.

Wulfsun took the tiller, and soon, with sails straining, he deftly turned the ship and bore down on the *Elk Wader.* The ship clipped swiftly through the water, the salt spray sprinkling faces and clothing. By the joviality on board, it seemed to her they were involved in a competition of sorts.

They are such daredevils that they will drown us all in sport, worried her swan mind.

Aye, there is no boundary to their daring.

'Tis so! I believe men make the world as dangerous as possible to justify their existence.

Despite her anxiousness, Moira smiled at the notion.

Reeling like a gull in flight, the ship held its collision course until the last possible instant. Amazed, Moira watched Wulfsun, now in his element, his lean-muscled body animated, heel the craft to the right with a powerful stroke of the tiller, and in a banking roll, the two ships passed within a hand's breadth of each other.

Raucous gestures and name-calling volleyed between the two ships. The race was on. The *Elk Wader* nosed a lead. The *Sea Steed,* sleek and quick, soon made up the difference amid taunts and oaths from both crews. The ships raced toward a long sandy beach, and the moment became anxious. Wulfsun's ship knifed through the surf to win the race. As the craft slugged to a halt on the sand, Moira let loose a slow breath of relief.

Chapter | 3

Shipboard, Moira watched lean dogs nose their way to the water's edge ahead of a handful of women and children. A poor settlement, the eggshell beaches disappeared into low hills of long grasses where no animals grazed. Boats lay turtlelike on the sands, a sign of a sparse livelihood from the sea. Ignored, Moira adjusted the bindings chaffing her ankles and watched the vikings unload the two ships. They put their booty around a dragon-carved totem at the foot of the huts, and the fair-haired residents inspected the sea chests with hopeful curiosity.

The afternoon heat bore hotly through her woolen robe. She picked up a discarded rag and fanned away the insects. Across the water the saffron sun fused a nimbus of light in a lengthening golden column. With mind adrift, she sat watching the mime of conversation, the movements of those on land. Her eyes followed the shore and lingered on the crimson-caped Wulfsun hefting sea chests through the surf.

Among the vikings she'd seen nothing of gentle emotion. The pillars of manhood were strength, stamina, and invincibility. It was as if Wulfsun woke each morning only to prove himself a man each day.

He trods upon the Earth Mother as if she must be subjugated rather than embraced, observed her swan self.

Does he feel pain, shed tears, need love, and suffer loneliness? Has he a love mate and children? Has he no mother?

I think he spawned himself, decided her swan self.

That is impossible. Besides, I have seen on his stomach his birth nub. He is no hatchling.

He may as well be. In the world of men all is created by God, and he alone.

'Tis foolishness to forget the Goddess.

Aye, but it makes for a more heroic story and keeps the Goddess in her place.

Moira smiled to herself and gazed thoughtfully at Wulfsun. *'Tis a pity one with so much potential is so ego-bound.*

He looked toward her then, as if hearing her thoughts across the distance. He waded through the sea and came to the ship's side. "Climb over."

"Cut the bindings on my feet and I will," she said, making no move.

He cast her a baleful look and a low, rough sound rumbled in his throat. Suddenly he was beside her, his large hands circled her small waist, and his snapping blue eyes boldly met her surprised gaze. His earlier fine-edged friendliness was gone, and temper lines bracketed his lips. She averted her eyes as he hoisted her into his powerful arms and eased back over the ship's side. Tight-lipped, he carried her above the thigh-deep surf toward shore.

His dour mood irritated her. "What is this place?" she asked, trying to coax him into conversation.

"Jutland," he said with no more elaboration.

"Will you sack and burn it as you have the others?" she asked curiously, wishing to provoke if she could not please.

She saw his jaw tense and felt him prickle. He took himself so seriously. Unanswering, he muttered under his breath and shifted her weight in his arms. Afraid he'd drop her, the start of imbalance caused her to grip her hands around his neck. His face was close to hers, his breath stirred the hair at her temple. She stared at his firm lips, remembering their heat and fire against her own.

Abruptly he put her down on the shore. After sitting cramped-legged on the ship, she swayed as the land still held the roll of the sea. She fell into him and caught his arm to steady herself. He allowed her a second to catch her balance and then stepped away.

Wulfsun frowned. Her nearness seemed to manacle his wits. He was not prepared for the jolt that her closeness ignited in him. When he'd clasped his hands on her narrow waist to carry her from the ship, his heartbeat increased and his body responded to her womanliness. In past days he'd paced the ship with a wild restlessness. Every time he'd passed her or looked in her direction, his need intensified. He'd taken to bathing shipboard in cold seawater to cool the desire that heated his loins.

"Chieftain," called Thorfinn as he strode toward him, his face grim. "The booty from both ships is laid out. Some may not wait through the night before snatching their share."

Wulfsun's hard, impassive face flickered, betraying his irritation. He fingered his sword, knowing he was the only one to hold them at bay. "If need be, I will guard it."

Moira looked over to the totem and watched the vikings settling themselves around driftwood fires. A huge man standing by the fires drew her gaze. Matted red hair hung from beneath a conical, bronzed helmet, and below red bushy brows protruded vulgar gray eyes, unclean eyes, eyes that could strip the dignity of even the Goddess herself. He unclasped a wide leather girdle that tightened against a bearskin tunic and roughly pulled one of the settlement women toward him. She struggled, but not for long. A few vikings voiced encouragement as he went down upon her.

Growing up in the forest of Myr, Moira had seen the mating of hart and hind, drake and hen, boar and sow, but never had she seen man and woman. In the lore of Myr the union of man and woman was something wondrous, though she saw nothing wondrous happening now. The woman was reluctant and sullen. Tears streamed from the corners of her eyes as he moved back and forth on top of her. He was quickly finished and as soon as he released her, she ran for the shelter of a stone hut.

Moira turned wide questioning eyes back to Wulfsun. The corners of Wulfsun's mouth quirked in a frown. "You must stay the night in a hut," he announced. He did an odd thing then. He lifted the long, thick swatch of her hair aside and raised her hood to cover her head. With his hand possessively pressed against her back, he guided her toward the stone huts.

He parted a sealskin serving as a door and motioned her inside. Moira stooped through the entrance. Inside, a mulling fire glowed, and by the smell, a soapstone pot full of broth simmered. A fair-haired woman tended the pot, and beside her sat a girl on the brink of womanhood. Dressed in rough woolen kirtles, they crouched together, speaking in Norse. The place must have been a conquered settlement and a common layover for the Northmen after raiding Britain, reasoned Moira.

The woman put aside a naked blue-eyed child who rested on her lap, and both women kneeled to Wulfsun. He spoke, softly, but their eyes remained lowered in deference, and also, Moira concluded, in fear. The older woman fetched leather thongs hanging from the roof beam and gave them to Wulfsun.

"Sit," he directed Moira, and then he knelt on one knee and began to bind her wrists. She complied, but when he looked up, their eyes met in a smoldering clash of wills.

"When a man owns a treasure, he must know how to keep it. A treasure with two beautiful legs can run away." In a flourish of crimson cape he left.

He wishes to humble you. 'Tis the way of men, observed her swan self.

"I am not humbled, but enraged. Not a moment passes, but I plot escape!" she anguished aloud.

She realized the two women were staring at her oddly. She smiled self-consciously and ceased talking. The older woman smiled back and offered her coarse bread. Hampered by bound hands, she accepted. The woman eyed her curiously, looking long at the tiny silver cross dangling from the linen tie about her waist. On impulse, Moira offered the cross to her. The woman immediately unfastened it and took a length of spun wool, threaded the cross on it, and tied it around her neck.

After Moira had eaten, she scooted into the shadows and leaned against the stone wall. She couldn't get the red-bearded viking's treatment of the woman out of her mind. The detachment of the coupling shocked her. She had heard no love-lilt sung from the woman, nor had she seen any ritual of self-disclosure by the man. Perhaps loving was different in the world of men, but once a swan sister's love-lilt passed her lips, she was bonded to the man life long. It had been so with Epona. Even after Moira's grandfather, Dylan of Llochin, died, Epona returned to Myr never espousing another. Though the story of her own mother, Creirwy, was shrouded in mystery, Moira knew that to her death, Creirwy had remained bonded to her father.

Moira wondered if her father was such a one as these Northmen. Was he fair or dark? Did he love battle above home hearth? The questions were not new to her, but tonight they seemed more urgent. If she'd only known her father, she might better understand her captor, but then, her mother would have never loved a man so barbaric and ruthless as he. No, she thought as she drifted into sleep, my father would have been life's guardian and wisdom's wizard.

Late in the night Moira woke to the crackle of low embers. The hut rested in stillness except for an occasional cough. Smoke from the driftwood fire clouded the hut and stung her eyes. She yearned for fresh air. Since no one was on guard she plodded a slow and noiseless path over the discarded remains of the meal, around the reclining bodies, to the door. She cautiously parted the sealskin and struggled to her feet, hobbling out into the tangy, refreshing sea air. The warm sea breeze carried the musty smell of salt and sand.

A hasty glance assured her that most of the vikings lay immersed in sleep beside the glowing beach fires. The sea beckoned her, and she hobbled to its edge. The black waters swirled around her feet in stingy retreat, and she looked to the brightness of the moon. How she wished she were back in the peace of Myr with her swan sisters, dancing and rejoicing at the height of midsummer.

She began singing, softly. The waves in their monotonous embrace of land bore her song of solace below into enchanted depths and above into timeless expanse of sky and heaven.

Suddenly two strong arms encircled her back and knees and hoisted her with great ease into the air. Panic gripped her. She lurched, off-balancing her captor, and together they toppled into the water for a thorough drenching.

"By Loki's beard, you are troublesome!" Wulfsun cursed as he bumped against her. Their gazes held a moment. Moira squarely faced his ice-blue stare. The lean lines of his face became an arrestingly youthful profile. Yet his eyes seemed older, ancient as storm-battered sea cliffs and as impenetrable as stone.

She tried to stand, but her bound feet caused her to stumble and fall into the water again.

"You must be half duck the way you take to water," he declared.

She said nothing, so close to the truth were his words. Then his eyes riveted toward her feet, but they were under the water. Even by the light of the moon she saw the hint of suspicion in his eyes.

Frantic to distract him, she fanned her hands across the water and splashed him playfully. "'Tis you, not I, who bathes thrice daily in cold seawater."

"I've enough of your taunting!" He caught her hands in a tight grip and drew her up out of the water with him. "Mayhap I have reason!" His large hands clasped the rounds of her hips, and he pressed her softness against the hard bulge of his own.

The waves lapped against their legs, but he held her tight. She tried to twist away, seeing by the twin flames of his cheekbones, the husk of his voice, the glowing of his eyes, that he was a smoldering vessel of enchantment. Yet when his mouth covered hers, the fire in her own flesh leaped to meet his. Her bound hands looped over his head, and she twined her fingers in his hair. For that moon-shimmering moment his lips tasting hers seemed to be the only thing of importance on earth. His mouth was fierce and demanding, and even as she responded to him she writhed inside with reproach because she knew his passion was driven not by love, but enchantment.

Suddenly a groan rumbled from Wulfsun's throat, and he jerked back. His eyes flew past her face to the totem, where like the vultures they were, he saw the belly low movement of two vikings, closing in on the booty. Quickly he swept the woman up into his arms. She blinked like an owl waking to dusk, and he inwardly cursed the duty that was his and the heat that still simmered his blood. In hurried strides he carried her to the totem and set her beside the fire. In a deft move he drew Wolf's Claw from his baldric and sliced the air in a threatening display. Just as suddenly the sneaking, crawling vultures anchored in mock sleep.

He turned back to the woman. Eyes wide, she was staring into the shadows, the breeze ruffling her hair. The firelight threw a warm, rosy light over her, and her hair fell around her. She was still woefully tempting, but the moment was beyond salvaging. He sat in the sand across from her, though his eyes still sifted the darkness for movement.

"You should have stayed in the hut." His voice was soft and detached as if the uncontrolled desire of the past moments had never been. "Had you hoped to drown yourself in the sea?" he asked, putting more wood on the fire so they both might dry. "It seems you prefer death to captivity in the hands of we Northmen."

"I cannot reason why," she replied quietly. "You are such gentlefolk. You appear when least expected to share the goods of others. And on cold nights you ignite the frigid with your fires. To any who desire a ship's voyage, you offer free passage, though in stormy weather a soul might be thrown overboard." She pursed her lips consideringly, then added, "But I suppose 'tis only your benevolent way of feeding monsters of the deep." She burrowed her toes into the warm sand, which still held the heat of day.

Wulfsun smiled, genuinely amused. He leaned back with his arm resting on a bent knee. He watched her, waiting for her to say more, but she kept silent. His eyes lingered on the gap in her robe. The temptation to leave his duty as guard and sweep her up into his arms and make for a hut became overpowering. His brilliant eyes devouring her, he swallowed back and cleared his throat. Oblivious to his thoughts, she turned her palms to the fire, which licked the belly of a sea-washed log. Her graceful fingers curled to the fire's heat, and a warmth of another sort relentlessly burned through him.

He had planned to have her this night. But he had not calculated crossing sea roads with the *Elk Wader*. Now he was duty-bound to guard the booty, for he was the only one all trusted—or all feared. He was not sure which. He shifted. Sleep haunted him as well as a headache. Two nights before the dragon dream had come, as vivid as ever, and in its aftermath the dull hammering throb.

The woman. His thoughts and eyes ever came back to her. Thorfinn claimed she'd bewitched him, but bewitched or not, he would fall into no woman's arms unless it was by his own choosing. Had he not struck a wager with Thorfinn and Jacob on that account? "The woman will come to me, not I to her. Then you will see who is bewitched," he had boasted. He looked over at her, her small hands clasped delicately in the cleft of her lap, her long hair flowing down over her shoulders, and her strange, ever-changing eyes glowing as softly as a candlewick.

He spoke. "I have sailed my long ship to many lands, but never have I seen a people with changeling eyes. Is it common in your homeland?"

At the same moment her delicate nostrils tightened, and her eyes met his own in a bold stare. Ignoring his question she posed another. "Is it common in your homeland to force your women?"

"Force our women? What has this to do with the color of your eyes?" he asked in exasperation.

"Nothing and all," she snapped. "The one with the red beard, he . . ."

Things clarified for Wulfsun. "You speak of Bjorn Bloody Hair. You must see the woman had no protector." He thought to add "as you do," but he would not beg the issue. "When they see our ships, the hut men run and hide until we leave. Unlike Bjorn, most of us like our women willing, but Bjorn doesn't often find willing women. Even so, this is the first I've heard complaints." His eyebrows raised and his mouth opened with a shrug. "It is a man's right."

"And what is the woman's right?"

Her directness made him uneasy, and his nostrils flared at her challenge. "A woman has none. If she is wise she attends to a man's needs, and he will treat her kindly." He paused thoughtfully for a moment, and then, as though to put credence to this inequity, he added, "It is the way of things."

"In your homeland, it may be, but in mine a woman does her own choosing. She gives herself from love, not force or fear."

Not liking the conversation, he replied. "If you were a man, you would better understand."

"I understand you disregard me because I am a woman."

Wulfsun's lips turned to a frown. "Mayhap you understand enough." His face masked in cocksureness, he looked away to the mesmeric embers of the fire.

He is very arrogant, mused Moira's swan self. *Mayhap this one needs humbling.*

Shall it be air magic or earth magic?

Please yourself.

Moira raised her eyes upward to the night sky and began to hum.

Suddenly Wulfsun sneezed. And then he felt himself in a fit of sneezing as bits of feathery swansdown floated with the breeze around his head. She did not laugh, but he did not fail to see the impish delight in her eyes as he swatted at bits of feathers tickling his nose. By Odin's eyes, he cursed inwardly, the woman could sing sorcery!

He stood and tossed more driftwood on the fire, more aware than ever of how his temples were throbbing. "If we are to sit here at odds all night, why not make your mischief useful," he glowered. "Mayhap you could make good your offer to rub the weariness from my shoulders."

"Unbind my hands and I will." She smiled softly.

He mumbled darkly, but moved to unfasten her hands, thinking at least she was willing.

"You must remove your tunic . . . and your sword," she prompted.

He unfastened his baldric and sword, taking the precaution of thrusting Wolf's Claw point downward into the sand within easy reach. Then his long arms winged to lift his tunic off. She sat down on a log, and he sat crossed-legged before her.

With her first touch he tingled. When her nails lightly raked across his shoulders to move aside his long hair, gooseflesh beaded his broad chest and back. Gently she began working her fingers at his temples.

"You have a headache," she said.

"How did you know?"

"Your life pulse lacks harmony. I feel it in my fingertips. Breath deeply," she advised.

Momentarily he felt defensive. If the woman could know this, what else did she sense? Despite his wariness, her very touch soothed him, and he felt the tiredness and the dull ache dwindle with each slow breath. The softness of her fingers circled behind his ears and then lower to the nape of his neck. He swallowed back with relief.

His voice loosened, "You have magic in your hands."

"I am a healer."

He took comfort in knowing some of her sorcery was practical. "A man grows tired wielding a sword all day. You are one woman I would take into battle."

"I am one woman who would not go."

His chest rose and fell with a half-laugh. "And you said you had no fear."

"'Tis not fear that would keep me away, but good sense."

Her hands worked the muscles of his shoulders, and he

felt his nipples stiffen. "Hummm . . ." He sighed and shifted. A lusty wanting had replaced his head pain, and he knew if he had good sense he'd stop her ministerings.

Her hands moved down the taper of his back. His skin fairly vibrated, and he cursed the need to stand guard. Scanning the beach fires, he knew still not all the vikings slept. Some waited for any opportunity to help themselves to booty . . . or even to the woman. She may disdain my sword and think me coward, he thought, but all that is between her maidenhead and these vikings is my sword point.

"Have you a comb? I will plait your hair," she offered, her fingers leaving his back to gather up his long hair.

The unexpectedness of her suggestion surprised him, though he realized nothing she did or asked was common. He took a moment to rummage for a fish-bone comb, then passed it over his shoulder.

He was not used to the pampering touch of a woman. He felt her carefully smooth his hair and then divide it into three strands.

"Your hair is thick as a unicorn's tail," she observed as she plaited.

"And how know you that? Unicorns are beasts of legends."

"In your land it may be, but not in mine."

"I must visit this land of yours."

"So you may hunt them to the last as men have done in your land?"

He smiled to himself, thinking she was a dove with a sharp tongue. "Nay, such a beast would be worth a king's ransom. I could capture one and make a fine profit." He felt her fingers binding the end of his braid in a slim leather thong.

"To profit at another's expense is no profit." She snapped the length of his braided hair against his back in chastisement. "Now you can comb my hair."

Fascinated by the reciprocity of her request, he asked, "You would ask a warrior to do a woman's task?"

"You have wished to touch me since we first sat beside this fire. Your eyes speak it. I think if you wish to touch me, you should begin by combing my hair."

He near choked with affront. "You think me a clumsy oaf like Bjorn that you must instruct me in the art of woman wooing?"

"I did not say it."

He settled some, seeing the humor in it. "I will comb your hair, lady."

He stood and moved behind her. He went down on one bent knee and picked up the comb. The moment he touched the silk strands of her hair, something shocked through him. Her hair flew up and stayed on his fingers, alive as lightning. The connective current danced over the comb and across his fingers. With supreme difficulty he managed to keep on his task, but one part of him wanted to toss away the comb and take her into his arms. He stifled this desire and concentrated on combing her hair. Loving the feel of the soft, thick masses, he combed gently, smoothing the tangles as neatly and patiently as he would mend a fishnet.

Slowly he coiled the thick loop of hair around his fist and pressured her head back so her face angled to meet his. The spokes in her eyes widened and whirled like a many-faceted ruby. His mouth hovered inches from hers, and he let his gaze roam over her face with uncloaked desire. He caught her woman's scent, a scent musky as spring and as beckoning as mandrake. He wanted her, but he was a waiter and a placer of priorities.

"You are an enchantress," he said, his voice husky with wanting. His eyes lingered on the soft, trembling fullness of her lips as they parted slightly in the hot fire of his possessive regard. Then slowly his gaze settled to fathom the unearthly depths of her eyes. "You make me a stargazer entrapped by the beauty of your eyes. Yet you would escape me if you could. I wish you were an armlet I might clasp to me, and so fastened, I would never lose you," he whispered. His mouth hovered above hers, like a hawk hovers on wind. "Tempt me no further. This night I am duty bound." He drew away and reluctantly let go of her hair. It fell and splayed across her shoulders and down her back. "Go to sleep."

This once her obedience surprised him. After arranging some skins in a soft palette beside his feet, she curled up in sleep. Watching the shadowed contours of her face, he let loose a deep sigh, thinking it was going to be a long night!

In the early morning mist Moira sat on the beach by the carved totem. Before dawn the vikings began sorting all of their goods. Everything, including herself, sat before the gargoyled representative of fairness. The men methodically valued the pieces one by one, put them in their separate hoards, then packed them off to the ships.

She watched Wulfsun stuff a chalice from the abbey altar into a sea chest. Being chieftain, he had first choice of the spoils. She'd been his first pick. She felt apprehension, but at least he was a known entity. He, with the others, continued to pick and sort through the loot like pointed-nosed fishwives. Then he helped another man carry the last of the spoils down to the ships. The villagers scavenged through the castoffs lying about, various items from a cracked earthen cup to an unmatched woolen slipper, none of which the vikings deemed important enough to take.

By early tide black fire pits marked the only evidence of the Northmen's landing. She waited on the beach as the vikings climbed shipboard and manned the oars. At surf's edge Wulfsun easily hoisted her over his shoulder and clasped her thighs tight against his broad chest. Her black hair fell over her shoulders to eddy in the sea froth as she peered at the world from upside down, the blood pulsing to her temples. A throb of another sort erupted when she realized Wulfsun shaped her buttocks with his hands. Her lips parted with an intake of breath as his emboldened fingers caressed and cupped the mounds of her backside, moving along the contours to softly pressure the intimate cleft between her thighs.

Lady of Light! Her eyes widened. She'd never known a touch to trigger such warm expectancy. What was he about? She gripped his lower back with both hands and struggled to force her head up. "You take unfair advantage," she challenged to the folds of his crimson cloak.

In answer, if one could call it so, she heard a low chuckle, and his hand playfully slapped her right buttock just as he lifted her on to the planking. Landing on her hobbled feet, her pride stung more than her backside. She stood before him and glared as he hefted himself shipboard.

His sea-watching eyes glinting in the sunlight, he answered, "Astride my shoulders you are a sweet burden. Now sit that I might bind your hands."

"No!" she flared. "I am done with being bound like a sparrow caught in netting."

He regarded her through narrowing, sleep-starved eyes. "Take care, woman, it is not uncommon for us to cut off a toe each time a captive disobeys."

"I am not so easily threatened. A captive with no toes is of little use."

A dark satisfaction touched his mouth. "With one as fair as you a missing toe would not matter." He snatched up a piece of rope off the planking, caught her wrists in his tight, single-handed grip, and retied her hands with a painful jerk.

"Do you think it is tight enough?" she baited in a soft voice.

"Fool woman, if you find it too tight, sing it loose!" He turned heel and strode off to other matters.

The fool here is plainly not you, consoled her swan self.

Aye, but then again, toes do not grow back. Moira sighed, overweary of the Northman's domination.

Chapter 4

Shadowing the coastline, the viking ships sailed farther north, and though the warmth of day yet spoke of summer, the nights gradually turned cooler. A love of the sea blossomed in Moira. The abundance of life in air, water, and land filled her passing hours with endless entertainment as the two ships meandered around islands, headlands, and shoals. The passing days revealed country in the green of full summer. Occasional fields of sprouting barley and rye began to appear, rolling gently to the sparkling blue sea.

As the ships neared more populated land, she saw domestic animals and peasants, weapons at their sides, working the fields. More than once, calls of alarm passed across the fields as the dark shapes of the dragon ships sailed into view.

She looked to Wulfsun standing at ship's prow, his long wheaten hair blowing wildly over his bare bronzed chest and shoulders. She wondered if the fear of the peasants gratified him. Did he feed on their fear as a wolf fed on a fresh killed carcass? Did he derive his strength from the fear of others?

She thought to ask him, Is it pleasant to have one and all quail and run from your passing? But she knew well enough to hold her woman's tongue. Like summer lightning, already too much of the unspoken was snapping between them. She pushed away the discord that regularly plagued her when she drew close to him each night for warmth. Instead she began to sing a soft song to pass the time. Her voice, sweet and clear, floated like a golden butterfly on the wind.

Across from her Jacob the Freed spoke when the song ended. "Holy woman, do not stop, 'tis a long time since I've heard such singing."

Agreeably Moira opened her mouth to sing, but her eyes met those of her captor. Again the air between them crackled with tension, and by the glaring disapproval in his eyes she knew better than to raise her voice in song.

"The woman can save her songs," said Wulfsun. "We near Kaupang."

Her heart quickened and her curious eyes moved past Wulfsun to see turrets rising in the distance. The town followed the semicircle of the natural sea harbor and was at least a mile in length and breadth. An earthen rampart fortified the town on three sides, north, west, and south. Three stave watchtowers rose from this defense stockade, making it fairly secure against attack. Anticipation filled Moira. She would see a town.

Wulfsun called curtly to his men. The sail furled, oars slapped water. After a time the rowers maneuvered the ship next to a wood and stone breakwater, which arced midway across the harbor. Wulfsun and two others leaped to the pier and tied the ship to massive bollards. The *Elk Wader* moved alongside. Bjorn Bloody Hair threw a length of mooring rope to Wulfsun, who lashed it fast. Bjorn jumped gracelessly ashore, immediately taking off his skin shirt and exposing his red-furred chest to the day's warmth. While he briskly scratched himself, Moira could not help but see his resemblance to a great bear. She marked the contrast between him and Wulfsun as they moved together in counsel. Bjorn was ornamented with bracelets the length of his arms. From his neck hung chains of gold and silver amulets of luck which glimmered in the sun's light. Wulfsun, on the other hand, wore no jewelry or show of wealth. Except for the red of his cloak, his clothing was so spartan as to be a token covering. Outwardly, he looked a civilized man and Bjorn Bloody Hair the bedecked beast. But Moira was not fooled . . . Wulfsun's civility was a thin veneer which could explode in sudden violence. It would take a savage to win a man like Bjorn's fealty as well as to lead such a pack of plunderers.

Trade goods unloaded, Wulfsun carried her ashore and sat her on a wooden sea chest. "You will wait here. Keep your eyes down. Town people believe you holy women have the evil eye."

"What is the evil eye?" she asked.

"You do not know?" His gaze rested wonderingly on her face. "You are a strange one. You have all the powers of a witch, yet you do not know of the evil force."

"The only evidence I have seen of an evil force is the sword at your side," she said flatly.

His eyes narrowed. "Then be warned. Your spells can be no match to the sharp, swift swing of my sword."

His underlying threat caused her to draw up and glare at him. "I have no wish to be your match—not in savagery, not in barbarity, not in brutality! If I am to cast a spell, it is to heal, not maim, to protect, not curse."

"So be it, woman. I hold you to your word." He turned heel and was off to beckon a skinny runt of a man with an empty cart for hire.

Moira looked down then, but felt her cheeks burn with temper. Men were impossible! *He* was impossible! She raised her eyes to glare at Wulfsun's broad back, almost wishing she had the evil eye. If a look could scorch, he would have a smoking hole between his wide shoulders.

After a time the raven-sailed vessel was unloaded. Wulfsun returned to her and in a short word commanded her to follow him as the procession of vikings wove their way down narrow muck-paved streets through the throng of pushing humans, animals, and carts pregnant with tilting loads. At first she tried to keep her eyes lowered, but all was so new to her, she could not help but stare wide-eyed at this town of men.

She marveled as on every side rose buildings large and small, stave wooden houses designed and built with rare craftsmanship for the rich, and in superior numbers, wattle and daub with reed-thatched roofing for the poor. Above one doorway a whole cow, mottled with buzzing flies, hung skewered in sacrifical style. After peering into a hovel as a horse cart squeezed past, she was glad to be out of doors with the noise and dirt rather than inside with the smells and who-knows-what companions.

Wonderingly, her eyes scanned roadways and alleys. Women worked and gossiped, children scurried with hairy pigs and speckled chickens, idlers lounged, and beggars begged. Men talked excitedly in tight groups while others gambled and gamed, setting cock to cock and dog to dog. A mélange of salt, fish, and humanity surrounded her as they made their way to the center of town. Fascinated, she watched peasants and seafarers, traveler and trader whose origins were from the farthest perimeters of the medieval world. In helmet and turban, tunic and cloak, pantaloons and leggings, they chattered in the pidgin tongues of barter, their clothes as varied as their languages. Matrons, fair-headed and whitescarfed, and wearing long, pleated, embroidered dresses, ushered thick-braided girls through piles of fruits and odd vegetables. Craftsmen plied their skills as potters, weavers, and jewelers. She saw wondrous wares of glistening ceramics, scented oils, herbal remedies, and magenta wines. Voices called attention to fish and fabrics, charms and fortunes, weapons and crockery, falcons and furs in a nonstop harangue.

Suddenly her horrified eyes settled on a group of people bound in ropes, rags, and dejection, their faces gaunt with mistreatment. Still staring, she stumbled into Wulfsun, who had stopped in front of her.

He turned. "Don't dog my heels, woman."

But her distraught gaze did not shift to him. "How can this be?"

"How can what be?" Then he saw what drew her attention.

"How can those people be so needy in all this abundance? They look hungry and ill-treated, yet around us I see food. Why do they not eat?"

"They are slaves. It is to be expected."

"What are slaves?"

He looked at her incredulous. "You do not know? They are captives like yourself, taken in raids to trade at market. See, there in the tent is their master, a Greek slave trader."

That sight wounded her anew. The Greek slaver, resplendent in brocades and tassels, feasted in an open tent, with the attendance of dark-skinned slaves, capped and shirted and empty-faced. Oblivious to the hunger of the men, women, and children who sat piteously nearby, the slave merchant stuffed his jowling mouth. All the while his squinting eyes followed the swaying hips of a dancer at the market's hub. It crossed Moira's mind to wish a bellyache upon him, but she would not misuse her powers for ill.

"To trade in flesh is wrong."

"Mayhap, but it is profitable. Do not look if it bothers you." Then he turned to direct the cart man to move to an opening between two trade stalls.

Unlike him, she could not turn away, and she continued to look and fret. She was a captive like them. She lowered her eyes to her own bound hands and feet, thinking death might be better.

She moved to Wulfsun's side and asked him what became foremost in her mind. "Am I to be traded?"

A glimmer of amusement lit his flinty eyes. "Are you in a hurry?"

In the face of his sarcasm she bit out, "No, if I am to be starved and wretched. Yes, if I am to be freed."

"Do not count on it," he said seriously. "Now sit here." He pointed to a shadeless spot by the cart wheel. "And keep out of trouble." He disappeared into the crowd.

She seated herself in the dust of the marketplace and watched the vikings. They took little care for tidiness as they unloaded mounds of luxurious fur pelts, weapons, ivory, and other goods of trade, which included silver cups from the treasure hoard of Mergate Abbey. A few people gathered. Two soldiers paused to heft the weight of a sword and remark on its craftsmanship. One, more interested than the other, began to barter with Jacob the

Freed. He had little success, for after some minutes the man put down the sword and turned to leave. The other viking, Thorfinn, hailed him back. Picking up another sword, Thorfinn pointed out its ornate, twisted silver pommel inlaid with ivory. The soldier, now convinced, produced coins, which the viking weighed upon a small scale. Settlement was swift, and the soldier put his new sword into his Tuscany belt and moved on. Jacob slapped his friend on the back and left the trading to him. He sat down next to Moira and leaned back against a pile of furs.

"Perhaps you should learn trading from your companion," Moira said. She looked to Thorfinn, who was selling a fur pelt to a lady's servant. The lady waited in a litter supported by two red-capped porters.

"Thorfinn is half Rus," he snorted. "It is in his blood to trade." Jacob the Freed closed his eyes and shifted to nap.

She looked at Thorfinn. Though he was doing a brisk trade, he held a quality of reservation. He blandly looked down his toucan-hooked nose at each customer who approached and measured them with luminous eyes, deeply set below a fair ridged brow. Because of the heat he soon stripped off his tunic and exposed rippling muscles to the sun.

Ever fascinated by these men, Moira watched, as she had watched Wulfsun strip and pour seawater over himself during his shipboard bathing ritual. Each afternoon she had watched him, mesmerized by his tall, muscled frame which molded up to a dense rib cage and wide shoulders. He had known she watched him, and with an innate male conceit he had clearly pleasured in her observation. She remembered the night on ship when his own eyes had passed slowly over her unclothed body, and she knew he had found her beautiful.

The chieftain circles, like the peacock ritually struts for the peahen, concluded her swan self.

Mayhap 'tis a good sign. He has not forced me, reasoned Moira.

And would you accept him?

Because I can only conceive at full moon, I am driven to

union. But otherwise I would want a love mate to love me for myself and not because of enchantment. If he proved a gentle lover . . . But I will sing my love-lilt only once and bond lifelong only to a peace-loving man. She was hesitant to admit even to herself that she found herself drawn to the viking.

Then forget that one. He will never be peace-loving. He names his sword Wolf's Claw, as if it were alive. To him a battle cry is his love-lilt, and he has already bonded lifelong to his sword.

'Tis true, conceded Moira, almost wistfully. *Men are nothing like I imagined.*

The smell of freshly baked bread from a neighboring stall set her stomach roaring. She'd never been so hungry. Her eyes lingered on bunches of carrots, berries, and greens as she continued to follow the sights in the market.

She wondered when Wulfsun would return and saw that across the way Bjorn Bloody Hair had entered into a dice game. She had watched the Northmen pass the time playing with dice shipboard and often arguments had broken out. Beside Bjorn sat the Greek slave trader in all his abundance of dress and form. He posed cross-legged on a fine rug clicking the ivory taws in his spatula hands. Beside him sat a smooth-shaven youth in black skull-cap, a soldier with a jeweled dagger glinting in the silk of his sash, and one other—an eastern merchant robed in black from head to foot.

As the afternoon wore on, Bjorn Bloody Hair was clearly losing most heavily in the game of hazard to the slave trader. After a devastating round Bjorn came to his feet and led the trader over to the vikings' cart of goods. Bantering back and forth with Bjorn, the slave trader valued flashing silks and dull wools, fur pelts and weaponry.

Suddenly he turned to regard Moira with astonishment. In stunned awareness his eyes bore hotly on her. "Tut tut! What have we here? A flower hidden amid the market rubble." With the practiced eye of a flesh trader he approached her. At that moment Moira wished herself deaf, dumb, blind, and crippled.

"Feel the weight of this halberd in your fist," spoke Bjorn, turning to display the balance of the weapon hilt in his large hand.

"I will look closer," lisped the trader agreeably, speaking not of weapon, but woman. "Stand up, rise, O blossom," he commanded, his painted and powdered face leering within inches of Moira's own.

With deliberate obstinacy she ignored him.

He reached out and caught her elbows in the fleshy folds of his hands. "Do not be shy, fair one." He lifted her to her feet. "Let me see you. Ah, she stands a head taller than most maids with all the grace and baring of Athena."

She had endured the tittering of children and the catcalls of the fishwives as she was herded through the town, but this puffed-up, honey-mouthed vision of excess infuriated her. His gallant words and exaggerated gestures drew onlookers. The soldier and black-robed merchant came over, and even Thorfinn paused from his bartering.

The slave trader was obviously wealthy. His practiced eye was fine-honed from years of merchandising in flesh. He glanced at Bjorn. "In all my travels, from Iberia to Byzantium, I've not seen eyes like these. Where did you capture this one?"

"Britain," provided Thorfinn shortly.

Moira felt sick. *Please go away,* she anguished, wishing she could crawl under the cart. The trader's fat, clean-nailed fingers pinched her mouth open to probe inside. "Teeth like polished shells!" he exclaimed. She clamped down her teeth before he'd quite withdrawn his fingers. "A she-cat!" The merchant squealed, jerking away his hand. Deep laughter rumbled from Bjorn and Thorfinn.

"She shows spirit. Not so bad a trait," rationalized the slaver in a still pleasant voice. "A sultan might pay well for such spirit to fire his harem."

He pulled down her hood and yanked loose the bound knot of her obsidian hair which glinted in the sun like stars at midnight. "By the gods! Look at these tresses. What other treasures hide you, my beauty?" His quick hand tore open her robe and shrugged it down her shoulders. And with her hands bound and her feet hobbled Moira had no choice but endure. The sickening dread in her stomach was spreading.

A murmur of comment rolled through the gathering crowd. "Ah . . ." he breathed appreciatively. "Breasts of alabaster, budded like plum petals afloat on cream." His hand cupped her breasts, pinched her nipples, and hovered over the rose-hued wound on her shoulder. "A flaw!" He peered closer. "You vikings are a brutal lot. Have you not learned damaged goods bring less coin?"

Thorfinn glowered, but said nothing.

Moira bit the inside of her lip, and with tremulous aloofness she focused beyond the hungry, devouring eyes of the onlookers to a distant point. Expertly the trader's hand slid down over her hips to probe inside her thighs. For Moira the arrow in her shoulder had been less painful than the invading touch of his probing fingers within the softness between her legs.

"Bless the gods! I would not believe it! A virgin yet—and among such captors!" He slipped his fingers from the moist channel and sniffed the tips. "Ah . . . her nectar is sweet." Her chest tightened and angry indignation exploded in her heart.

She began to hum, her eyes following nearby flying insects.

Suddenly his hand flew to cuff his head, and he cried out in pain. Strangely, a wasp had chosen just that moment to sting him by the eye.

You cannot use your magic for ill, cautioned her swan self.

'Twas not for ill, but for self-protection, returned Moira.

While the trader agonized over his swelling eye, she saw, with great relief, a golden head parting the crowd, and the tall-framed Wulfsun shouldered through. Because of the day's heat he'd stripped, and from the hips up he was bare, much like Moira herself. Their eyes met, hers boldly defiant, his wavering as he grasped the situation. She felt his calculating eyes sweep over her nakedness with the same fire as the slave trader but without the devastation.

"What is happening here?" demanded Wulfsun. There

was a look on his face she'd not seen before, like a metal mask, eyes burning, impenetrable, fearsome. In an unexpected movement he lifted her robe back over her shoulders. Where the trader's touch had been defiling, his became restoring. Where the trader's perusal had left her cold, his left her overwhelmingly warmed. "Speak, trader!" he commanded.

Holding a damp cloth to his swelling eye, the trader stepped toward Wulfsun. "I offer to buy this woman."

An unreasonable fear gripped Moira, and her eyes fastened to Wulfsun, searching his features to see if he might be open to this offer.

For enough gold he will trade me, she agonized.

Nay, not as long as he is enchanted, assured her swan self.

I cannot be sure. His ardor runs hot and cold. One moment he burns for me, the next he turns away. Night after night I lay beside him, and he does not touch me. This one is not so easily enchanted.

"Hel's fire!" cursed Wulfsun. He looked to Bjorn, who shrugged ignorantly, then he speared Thorfinn with his golden gaze. "Have you told him she is not for trade?"

"First ask him how much he will pay," said Thorfinn in Norse, ever the bargainer.

Wulfsun rolled his eyes and clenched his teeth. "We have spoken of this before. She is not to be sold," he repeated, still in Norse.

Thorfinn frowned. "You've become the woman's fool. I say she has bewitched you."

"You insult me. I am not so weak-willed. I may want the woman, but you are wrong, I am not bewitched." He looked to the woman, her black-winged brows puckering with apprehension. Suddenly a thought struck him how he might show Thorfinn who bowed to whom. "Look at her, I wager it is my sword she wants in her sheath."

Thorfinn's mouth quirked. "I would see."

"Then, friend, see." His face very closed, Wulfsun turned back to the trader. "For the right price I would sell the woman."

Standing within the close perimeters, he did not miss her sudden intake of breath. His eyes looked a little to one side and rested on her face. Satisfaction niggled within his chest, for clearly she preferred him to the trader. "You are ever eager to be free of my company— now is your chance," he taunted quietly.

Her eyes flared scarlet and her fists started clenching tight against her robe. "I will not go with him," she declared willfully.

"Then he will beat you," he said flatly. "To him your value is more than an eel of linen, but less than a camel."

"And what is my value to you, warrior?" she challenged, her eyes simmering pools of affront.

The corners of his hard mouth curved into twin scimitars, but the humor did not touch his calculating eyes. "I know not." He knew her face haunted his nights and her presence distracted him from his labors. Shipboard, her song had become an enchantment and her beauty a dream. His instinct of self-preservation told him to let the trader have her, but again her mere scent fired his groin with unquenched desire.

"You know not?" she echoed ruefully.

"You are much trouble."

She put out her bound hands and pressed her palms gently against his chest. Beneath his skin he felt his heart expand and his pulse quicken.

"I am a healer," she reminded.

"A sorceress is more the like," he countered. "I am told a wise man closes his door to witchery." He held her eye, enticed by her willingness to bargain.

"A wise man does not close his heart," she said.

Her insistence amused him. "A wise man has no heart!" He clutched her small hands in his own and stepped back. "What you offer I can have from any woman without the sorcery." He made to drop her hands from his, but she twisted hers to clasp his tightly and drew him to her.

"Ask what you will from me, but don't trade me to the slaver."

Her manner and voice were so beseeching, he felt a pang of remorse for allowing her to believe he would discard her to such a fate. His jaw hardened, his icy blue eyes flickered over her. It was time to bargain with this woman, whose beauty kept him at such a disadvantage.

"I will not trade you on the condition you grant me a sole request."

"What is this request?"

"I have not yet decided. But whatever and whenever will be at my choosing."

He saw the hesitancy in her features and knew she would not easily agree. Then the furrow between her winged brows melted and she said, "Yes, I will grant your request, but only one."

"And I will have one kiss to seal this bargain that all watching may see your fealty is to me," he demanded.

Surprising him, her eyes became topaz swirls of consent, and she leaned to him. Her hands clung to his tunic, and she drew him close, seeking his lips. Completely beguiled by her openness he willingly lowered his mouth to capture hers. Her lips were soft, ripe, and moistly welcoming. When had he tasted such sweetness? He fell into the kiss deep and vast, forgetting it was midday and the center of the marketplace. She kissed him endearingly, endlessly, a long wildly exciting kiss, yet a kiss so chaste that deep tremors of anticipation brought a rigid swelling to his groin. His hand involuntarily circled her small waist and slipped to the round of her hips, pressing her to his own.

For Moira, the kiss was a queer sensation, like diving into a deep lake and never surfacing. She had closed her eyes and plunged into his essence, past the warrior, and into the softer shoals of his heart. From the beginning he was the one enchanted, the one whose heart melted with her looks and touch. Despite this, now she was the one swayed by the natural sorcery of his kiss.

Beware, swanling, came the small voice of her swan self. *This one will truss and trick you like a hunting fox.*

For one moon month he is enchanted. And he cannot ask for what I will not give.

What you will not give, he will steal from you. I say beware.

The good-natured jests from Wulfsun's vikings

brought him to his senses, and he drew back. As their gazes met in parting, an unspoken knowing, a knowing of the heart, passed between them.

He turned in a spread-legged stance before the trader and rested his hand on the hilt of his sword. "As you see, the woman does not choose to leave my side," he announced with no little amount of pride, and a sidelong glance at Thorfinn.

Giving a defeated smile, the trader spoke. "Even with one eye swollen shut, I can see her will is enslaved to you, Chieftain. But I will speak truthfully, she is worth a sultan's ransom. Never in all my trades and travels have I seen one such as she. The rose, the lily, the sun, and the dove, she is all of these. But be warned, to hold such a treasure will require more than a warrior's arm."

The warning was not pleasing to Wulfsun. The trader's words goaded the possessiveness within him, and he turned a deadly look on all. He eyed the trader, the soldier, Thorfinn, and Bjorn, and lastly his eyes fastened on the fair and exquisite holy woman. "Even so, she is mine—to gamble, to trade, or to do with whatever I choose."

Chapter | 5

Before dusk the market suddenly disbanded when a fire broke out down at the ship docks. Moira saw the smoke billowing above the rooftops into the evening sky like storm clouds. The vikings rushed to secure the ships, though Wulfsun left a single guard to watch over her and the trade goods. Soon the market became deserted while all ran to the fire. Nearby the slave trader's captives murmured among themselves.

Now is the time to escape, suggested her swan self.

Aye, agreed Moira. *More might escape than I, for the slave trader has gone as well.* Surveying the market and the slaves nearby, she began to formulate a plan.

He has left one guard with two wolfen dogs on chains.

I will use my power to sing them to sleep. Surely it is using my gifts for good. Temptation became her partner, and she began singing a soft song of enchantment to bring sleep to any listener.

Her heart creeping to her throat, she scooted inch by inch near the viking guard, who now slept. She held her eyes on his young face, and though her wrists were bound, with her fingers she eased a dagger from his boot lacing and moved back to her original position. She held the knife between her feet, and began cutting at the thong binding her wrists. After a grueling struggle, she cut free her hands and feet. Before she decided quite how to go about it, she was crawling stealthily toward the slaves. Their guard now slept, as did the two dogs.

She chose a man a little apart from the rest to awaken first. After she brushed his cheek lightly, his eyes opened. She pressed his lips for silence and then cut his bindings. She pointed to the others, meaning for him to help free them, but he jumped up and dashed off into the darkness.

The next man she awakened was less self-serving and helped her in the task of freeing all the others. Somewhere in the night a dog barked, and her attention riveted back to the pair of dogs. Canine eyes flashed open, and one dog's ears perked up. She spoke a soft gentling flow, and the dog calmed. Heart pounding, she continued to hum and approached a remaining slave woman near the guard. When the woman eased away, the guard stirred. Moira continued humming and the guard settled. Leaving her, the man and the woman joined hands and disappeared into the darkness.

Looking skyward, Moira released a slow breath and drew courage from the rising moon. *May the Goddess aid them,* she prayed.

Now fly, urged her swan self. *Be off to freedom!*

Suddenly a strong hand grabbed Moira from behind, twisting her wrist painfully until she dropped the dagger. *Black moon, I am too late!*

"Holy woman, what fox's escape have you planned this night?" Wulfsun's voice stabbed her like a fiery spear. Chest heaving and heart slamming against her ribs with shock, she stood mute.

He loosened his hold for a split second, and she pulled away. His strong hand caught the loop of her long hair so tightly her eyes stung from the pain. He yanked her to the ground and pushed her head between his knees. She felt the pebbles grind into her legs as he tied her arms behind her back. This done, he picked her up, her face chaffing against his leather tunic while she caught a whiff of smoke and perspiration. Why hadn't he remained at the docks?

What ill luck! her swan self rued.

"You are more than a fool, woman!" accused Wulfsun. His lip curled in a sneer, and he pressed her next to the cart, where he hobbled her feet and tied her to the wheel spoke. "Keep still and mayhap your treachery will not be discovered."

"What will they do to me if I am found out?"

"Mayhap torture you in some horrible way and force me to make restitution. Hush now!" his voice was deadly soft.

By now she was smart enough to clamp shut her lips and follow his counsel.

The light from a torch coming from the street drew Wulfsun's attention away to the returning slave trader and another. All too quickly they discovered the missing slaves, and their voices were none too calm. The Greek trader shouted wildly through the marketplace, setting the dogs into frenzied barking. He waved his torch back and forth and ranted with indignation. While the guard rubbed sleepy eyes, Moira began to fear for her life.

The young viking guard now roused was being roughly chastised by Wulfsun. He looked sidelong at Moira, not sure what to think, though uneasy that he had been less than vigilant. Meanwhile, the trader had unchained the dogs, but they whined oddly and ran about in circles. Wulfsun cast one last unspoken warning at her before he and the trader left the market square.

Hours passed. All the while she churned inwardly, and the viking guard dared not take his eyes off her. Once she shifted, for in her cramped position her leg had become numb. The guard started and gripped his dagger. She knew he feared her.

At dawn Wulfsun returned with Thorfinn.

He knelt on one knee beside her. "You did them no favor. When caught they will be punished. A drop of water is of no use to the thirsty man," he moralized with Nordic stoicism.

"A drop is better than nothing," she returned sullenly,

gratified to see his brittle blue eyes were red-rimmed from sleeplessness. "How many were caught?"

His mouth tensed, a muscle along his jaw coursed faintly. "So far, but one."

Her gaze met and held his own, and she knew she was that one.

His eyes narrowed fiercely but were no longer upon her. With calculating intensity, he looked across the market to the ironmonger's forge. Moira did not miss this, and she became even more uneasy. The early-morning ring of hammer against anvil awakened the marketplace like a tolling bell.

He regarded her for a moment, then stood and began rummaging through the chests and baskets in the cart. She watched the immutable lines of his face, hoping for any hint of his intention. Soon he retrieved from a royal jewel chest a gold torque, once a vain throat clutch for a princess.

"Come," he said, releasing her and leading her across the square toward the forge.

The fair-headed ironmonger leaned bare-chested over the high paved hearth and ladled a molten liquid into a mold. A moment passed, and then he turned to Wulfsun, who spoke in friendly conversation concerning the gold torque in his hand. Moira stood patiently by, looking about the forge, until she realized both pairs of eyes were considering her. Then the ironmonger went to the wall where tongs and hammers, wedges and chisels hung. He carefully chose three fine-pointed awls and placed them in the glowing coals. He turned to Wulfsun, and as they spoke, Wulfsun sketched runes into the hearth sand. With a nod and a guttural grunt of comprehension, the ironmonger tested the awls. Head bent, he picked up the gold torque and with a glowing tipped awl chiseled the rune markings on the outside band of the torque. This task finished, he approached her. Taking a step backward, she looked to Wulfsun.

"This goes around your neck. The runes mark you as mine, thrall woman of Wulfsun," he said.

Taken aback she moved away from them both with a defiant glare, though icy fear spread through her breast.

Do not let him bind you in this fashion, swanling! 'Tis the double bind of fire and rune magic. Once his name runes are etched and the gold ring is fastened to your neck, we cannot fly.

"It is not painful," Wulfsun assured her as he took hold of her, bracing her in position with his bull-strong arms.

Terror filled her, but she was helpless against his strength. "Nay, do not do this to me!" she cried, struggling in the hard clamp of his hold.

The ironmonger placed the torque about her graceful throat and cunningly inserted a red hot peg through the small rings, which sealed the cruel necklace in place. She felt the heat of the hot peg sting her skin, and tears spilled down her cheeks.

"Let me free!" she cried desperately. She lowered her chin and let loose a moan so forlorn that Wulfsun released his hold. Amid her wild moaning a gust of wind burst through the doorway, sparking the hearth coals to a blaze.

Suddenly the forge became a whirlwind of smoke, fire, and feathers. While fear and wonder paralyzed the ironmonger's face, Wulfsun watched dumbfounded as the flailing woman transformed into a great white-winged swan.

"By Odin's blood!" he swore. "Don't let her fall into the fire!" He leaped to save woman and swan, capturing in his arms wing and waist. Swan strained against his grip, her bill pecking sharply at his face, her great wings beating against his body.

The thrashing tumbled them both to the dirt. Unrelentingly, Wulfsun held her, his forehead streaming with blood from her gouging beak. He was a novice to sorcery, but he knew enough of legend to know that the torque of gold would keep this swan witch bound to earth.

She thrashed with the strength of a demon, and he trembled with the effort of holding her. In one last wild endeavor she lurched powerfully against Wulfsun's imprisoning hold. He yelled a deep-voiced cry. "Open your gates, daughter of Loki, and I'll follow her into Hel!"

She collapsed.

All resistance gone, she crumpled lifelessly in his arms. She was woman once again. Guilt clutched him like the hand of death. Had he killed her? Stricken with remorse, he searched her inanimate face for signs of life. His head lowered and his lips touched hers. Parting her mouth with his own, he breathed his life force into her. Again and again, softly, until he tasted the wispy breeze of her exhaled breath. He knew she lived.

He came to his feet, lifting her with him. Awe-stricken, the ironmonger cringed backward and raised a hammer self-protectively. With one hand Wulfsun tore the leather-skin money pouch from his belt and tossed it at the ironmonger. "You've seen nothing. Speak of this and I will return to cut out your tongue."

With an explosive thrust of his foot, the door flung open. He left, carrying the still-unconscious swan witch in his arms.

Chapter | 6

Leaning against the ship's railing, Wulfsun stared into the star-dusted twilight of morning, his ear still tuned to the woman's soft sobbing. A day and a night had passed since the ironmonger's forge. He watched the woman he'd once called holy but now knew to be swan witch, huddle shipboard.

If need be he could calm a weeping woman. But what does a man do with a weeping sorceress? Rooted in reality, the practical side of him knew not how to handle her. From the beginning she'd captivated him with that distant look of her changeling eyes and the illusory sway of her womanly beauty. He burned to take her in his arms and press kisses down the curve of her long white neck, suckle the piquant sweetness of her lush breasts, and mount the silken inner flesh of her parting thighs. But now he wondered if in the midst of such delights she might suddenly vanish from his arms. Mayhap Thorfinn was right in thinking she'd enchanted him. But his practical mind did not long dwell on it.

Won over, she would be more than useful. If she could quell a storm, she held the power to brew one. His warrior's mind expanded on the possibilities. If she chose to cooperate, he could be generous, though not so generous as to return to her her freedom. Considering, he turned to study her dark silhouette as though she were a wall to breach or a fortress to storm. He knew about timing, whether it be a woman or a fortress, and he would use every twist and turn of fate to his advantage.

Her black hood was raised over her head like a shield against his gaze. To feast upon her beauty was renewing for him, and he felt angered when she covered herself and turned away from him. Striding over to a sea chest, he searched out a white linen kirtle and gray cloak. He approached her cautiously as he would a wounded animal hiding in a thicket. He held them out to her. "Change into these," he ordered. He might have been more diplomatic, but he would not coddle her.

She shook her head in refusal, her cheeks moist with tears. "I'll not drape myself in clothing stolen from dead people."

Taken aback, he muttered, "You are thankless!" Not used to having his gifts shoved back in his face, his jaw clenched with anger and insult, he vowed silently that by day's end her black robe would be in a ragpicker's bag.

He tied a length of rope to a ring on the baldric that supported his sword, and then to the ring of her gold collar. She did not speak, but he saw tears pool anew in the corners of indigo eyes. Not so calloused, his warrior's heart could yet be moved by a woman's tears. He turned his strong-boned face to hers, his sky-blue eyes filled with reproof. "Lady, you leave me no choice but to bind you."

She said nothing.

Apprehension flitted through him. Memory flashed, and he was a boy again, clutching a fledgling sparrow hawk, running to show the others his prize. He would tame it, hunt with it. Soft, limp in his small boy's hand, it lay dead from fright. His man's hand closed empty upon the past. He wanted her compliant, but he had no wish to break her spirit.

Through the streets of Kaupang, Moira shadowed Wulfsun like a hound on a rope. She lowered her eyes from humiliation as she walked past gossips and idlers, around vegetable carts and mulling animals. She had never experienced hate, but its fire nearly suffocated her each time her drop-dead gaze leveled on Wulfsun.

Do not feed thy enmity, swanling, cautioned her swan self. *'Tis burning that sucks warmth from touch and shrivels the heart into a stony mass.*

Easy for you to say. But 'tis my throat the gold torque grips like an icy hand, not your swan neck.

Do not forget, I, too, flew headlong into the down current of death. By thy warrior's heart was I saved.

He is not my warrior. And only by his life's breath were you saved. He has no heart.

The marketplace wasn't the most pleasant of strolls in bare feet, and Moira briefly regretted not taking the viking's offered garments. On occasion a swan sister might hover a few inches above the ground. Now she was earthbound, this skill lost to her. Once Wulfsun stopped suddenly, and she ran up his heels. More oft someone going the opposite direction would tangle in the loop of the rope. Admittedly, she meandered on purpose to be a nuisance.

When Wulfsun halted at the stall of a knife sharpener, she stopped, too. She felt weak and thirsty. He gave the old man his dagger. The old man pedaled, the grindstone whirled, and the metal sparked. Her patience ebbed as her tongue swelled from thirst.

"I am thirsty," she said softly, somewhat resigned and unable to martyr much longer.

Wulfsun turned. "You are much trouble, woman."

He frowned disbelievingly. "I am thirsty, nothing more."

The man returned his dagger, and he paid him a coin. He led Moira over to a dark-eyed woman sitting beside a large wooden vat. He gave her a coin, and she ladled some honey-colored liquid into a brass cup. He offered the cup to Moira with mock gallantry.

"Thank you," she replied curtly. The drink was very palatable, a sweet ale. She drank three cupsful, and he had to fish another coin from his money pouch to pay the woman.

"You *are* thirsty," he said.

"If it bothers you to pay, why not lop off her head and steal her vat?" Moira remarked icily.

He did not reply. But a look, almost of relief, swept his features, and the corners of his lips quirked. Moira had meant to rankle him, not amuse him. She savored the last swallow of her drink and returned the cup.

He turned his attention to a goldsmith's rich display of jewelry in the stall behind the alewife. "Woman," he said, beckoning her to his side. "I have need of a gift—mayhap you would help in my choice?"

She was surprised he would ask. She became mesmerized by arm bracelets, rings, necklaces, and in particular, one stone, cloudy and crystal-faceted. "Is the gift for a man or a woman?"

He seemed hesitant to say. "A woman," he finally answered.

"Old or young?" she questioned.

"Old," he conceded.

"How old?" Moira pried again.

"Very old, a grandmother." His eyes held an elfish twinkle.

"A grandmother," she echoed as her eyes reluctantly pulled away from the white stone that called her. Her eyes paused on various pieces, a delicate gold chain necklace with a dangling emerald pendant, and a silver ring set with a rare sea pearl. But her eyes and fingers returned to hover over the crystal stone. She felt its essence warm the palm of her hand. Intuitively, she knew this was a magic stone that could promise healing and protection.

"This one," she finally said.

Wulfsun took it from her fingers. "I have seen better."

The goldsmith intent on making a sale said, "'Tis a rare and unusual stone. 'Tis called an ice stone."

Wulfsun shrugged tolerantly. "I will have it then."

The goldsmith smiled approvingly and named his price. A high price.

"Friend, you are more than a thief," returned Wulfsun, a gleam of challenge in his eye. Moira thought this an instance of the raven calling the crow black, though she said nothing as Wulfsun haggled over price. He was a shrewd bargainer, and in the end he came away with not only the ice stone but the emerald pendant necklace as well.

"Your choices were costly," he said.

"Your grandmother will like them," she promised. With one last covetous look at the stone, she watched him put his purchases into his waist pouch.

During the warm afternoon Wulfsun wandered the marketplace. He stood with his broad-shouldered back to Moira, talking to merchant, traveler, and companion alike. At rope's length she sulked behind him as he led her from stall to stall. In one he bought women's things, a red woolen kirtle, more richly embroidered with bluebells than a June meadow, and soft garments to wear beneath to protect against winter's cold. In another he haggled for dainty fur-lined boots and a black-fur-lined cloak, the outside a matching crimson to his own. He did not ask her for her opinion, and she thought most grandmothers would find the bright colors unbefitting.

While he bartered, Moira overheard a fortune-teller read a maiden's future in a bowl of fine sand. She knew he missed the mark and had no gift. He promised the girl wealth and children. Moira sensed she would have neither, but she would be loved, a far better gift.

Wulfsun turned and placed bundles in her arms. "You have seen me pay gold coin for all. You need not shun my gifts a second time, for you will have need of these," he said simply.

"For me? But what of your grandmother?"

"I have no grandmother." He smiled, his clear blue eyes widened with assurance. Then on second thought he said dryly, "If you do not want them, mayhap I can find a grandmother or a corpse bound for burial."

"I want them," she said, forgetting her sulk.

She followed him along, discovering among the bundles a waist pouch containing ivory comb, silk thread, and silver needle . . . and the ice stone. A pleased smile touched her lips, and she looked over at him.

He cocked a golden brow. "It is yours. I have no use for such a stone."

"I thank you." Her cheeks flushed with a hint of embarrassment. She tied the pouch to her waist, wondering why he'd been so extravagant.

This night he wishes to touch more than your hair, niggled her knowing swan self.

Does he hope to buy my favor? She considered the absurdity of it.

It could be that he wishes to make amends, but cannot speak an apology. In truth the ways of men are indeed a puzzle.

Moira shook her head and stole a sidelong glance in Wulfsun's direction. He caught her looking and flashed a smile. Quickly she lowered her eyes.

Early evening Wulfsun left the market, and Moira had no choice but to follow him. He led her down a narrow, meandering street into a more affluent district of richly styled buildings. He stopped beside an iron gateway where a red-capped man stood looking neither right nor left. Wulfsun spoke to him, and with a polite bow of his dark head the man opened wide the gate, and Moira followed Wulfsun into a tiled courtyard.

Water cascaded over the edges of a marble fountain, and she heard the music of flute and drum. The shimmering sounds of tiny bells blended with the other sounds, and two women, dressed in bell-tasseled silks and bead-edged veils, appeared underneath a stone arch doorway. They bowed deeply, took the bundles from Moira, and motioned Wulfsun to follow them.

She trailed behind Wulfsun, and for a moment she wondered if he had forgotten her altogether, so stridently did he follow the women. They passed into large rooms, where men bathed in aqua tiled pools. Some called out to Wulfsun, and Moira recognized many of his vikings relaxing in the water. Her eyes widened with awe, for between the pillars shouldering the roof were nude sculpted alabaster statues of the Goddess. What was this place? She paused, reaching out a hand to touch the curve of stone.

Wulfsun stopped as well. He was grinning, a peculiar, bold appraising grin. "Lower your eyes if such forms offend you, woman. But I warn you, 'tis only the beginning of this night's pleasures."

She started to explain that she found no offense, and to ask what holy shrine this was, but he was off and she had no choice but to lurch after him. He strode along as though he owned the premises, weaving around men exchanging philosophies at pool edge, past dark alcoves, where entwined couples postured and pulsated against silk pillows.

Before an alcove he stopped suddenly, and she stumbled into him. He turned, laughing, and caught her before she fell. He lifted her face, and she found that he was smiling into her eyes. His smile was disarming, and she had to remind herself he was still her captor.

One woman parted the curtains, the other set down the bundles and bowed away. Other women appeared, stripping Wulfsun of his clothing. Moira stared. Her bright eyes swept the flat wine-dark nipples of his bronzed broad chest to the font of manhood between his thighs, and though it was not full moon, part of her burned with the desire to mate with him.

He cleared his throat. "It is proper for a woman to lower her eyes."

Without a blush of embarrassment she asked, "You have told me this before, but I do not like it. I cannot see the world—I cannot see you—with my eyes ever on my toes. I do not understand your customs. If the lowering of eyes is proper for a woman, what is proper for a man?"

He laughed. "I've not met an innocent such as you. A man must turn his back rather than disgrace a lady."

"Is it a disgrace to savor beauty?"

His hand went out to her as though to touch her naïveté. "Nay, 'tis no disgrace." And then he sobered. "We are no longer tied together." A woman stood holding his clothes, the rope dangled loose-ended at her feet. "Do you run, or do you join me in the water?"

Her fingers touched the gold torque at her throat. She was desperately weary of running after him and from him. She breathed and attempted to keep the note of defiance out of her voice when she spoke to him. "I will bargain first."

"And what is this bargain?" His eyes sparked at the challenge. His hands rested on his narrow hips, and his golden hair hung in a loose fall over his muscled shoulders. His masculinity demolished her confidence, and she almost wept from his imposed humiliation. Yet she knew she must speak.

"You have bound me to you with magic. Why do you shame me further with this rope?"

His broad chest rose and fell while considering. "I had no wish to shame you, only to keep you at my side. None know of the magic but myself."

"And what know you of magic?"

"Nothing, but unwittingly enough to bind a swan witch."

"To bind nigh on death!"

"You live." Stoic indifference clouded his face.

She wanted to cry out, *I live, yes! but shackled to your side. I am safe from all else, but am in peril from you.*

Even so, his words were the last spoken, a tradition in the world of men. And Moira held hers inside, learning a tradition of women in the world of men.

He waved the serving women to her then and stepped down into the water. He dived beneath the surface with the sleekness of a merman.

The women attended her, bathed her, prepared her. It was almost sacrificial, the way they washed and brushed her obsidian hair into a shimmering mass, rubbed oil over her clean soft skin until it glistened. Shoulders bared, a silver-threaded silken scarf was tied loosely around her breasts. Around her waist they fastened a crimson silk hip wrap which left to view her long slim legs. A belt ringing with silver and gold fertility symbols was fastened around her hips, leaving her midriff bare.

And Wulfsun watched. She felt his gaze on her, first from the pool, the mist circling his head though not disguising the desire in his eyes. Later he watched from a silken pillow, his narrow hips wrapped in a loincloth. The attendants brought trays of face paints and body scents. The first he waved away, saying he saw no need to blacken lashes already thick as soot, or to redden lips flawlessly coral. The second tray he accepted and uncorked the scent pots. Smelling them, he chose favorites among musks and sweet wild scents and waved them past her nose for her approval.

They had given her wine, and so her resistance melted into sullenness, and in the adventure of Wulfsun's courteous proximity her sullenness mellowed into compliance. Though he was her captor, still she wanted him to think her beautiful. But she was not prepared for the aching intensity that spread through her body when, with two fingers, he touched scent in the parting of her hair and the hollow of her throat.

Aye, because of the enchantment he wanted her. Though she herself was under no enchantment but life's flow, equally she wanted him.

The scent of his virility called her, and she closed her eyes and swallowed back her heartbeat. Upon opening them, the attendants were gone. Wulfsun was not.

He was waiting, waiting for her eyes to come up and meet his.

Interrupting the moment a voice hailed Wulfsun from the far end of the bath, and Jacob the Freed beckoned to him. Wulfsun's chest rose and fell in a sigh of disappointment. "We are called to feast."

Glad for this reprieve, Moira felt his fingers on her wrist, and her own betraying hand curled into his, unbidden, willing. She no longer tagged along behind, but walked beside him beneath an archway and into a room of men who lounged around sumptuously spread tables of food and were deep in cups and joviality.

He chose to sit with his vikings, sitting cross-legged on the floor and pulling her down beside him. His blue-eyed companions appraised her, judged her, and ravished her with bold, undisguised perusals. She lowered her eyes, not because it was proper for a woman, as Wulfsun had instructed, but because she could not abide the devouring lust in their gazes. She was quickly coming to realize that in the world of men, man separated himself apart from woman. Woman became servant, possession, wife, and mistress, but never equal.

"Eat," said Wulfsun, motioning to the platters of roasted fowl, fish, and vegetables. He sliced a half of roast duckling and put it in her hand. She stared at it with distaste.

Grease trickled down her fingers and wrist. "I do not eat roasted flesh."

"Mayhap raw flesh is more to your liking?" Solicitously, he stabbed a blood-red slab of meat with his knife.

"'Tis healthy," spoke Jacob the Freed at her elbow. His dark eyes held a hint of amusement.

"Eat raw flesh?" gasped Moira. "'Tis barbaric."

Around the table the vikings' mocking affront met her words.

"In the company of barbarians it is unwise to condemn the barbaric," Wulfsun said to her on the aside. "Pass the lady a turnip, Sven Blue Coat."

Her trencher was soon piled high with turnips. Wulfsun must have read the chagrin on her face. He beckoned a server, and soon he returned with a selection of fruits, nuts, leeks, and a hot, spicy rye meal. "You see, even barbarians can be hospitable."

The beginning beat of drum and rattle of tambourine drew everyone's attention. A dancing girl, midriff bare, in gauzy skirts swirled into the room, silencing the bawdy conversation. The dancer whirled and pirouetted, twirled and stamped. Moira watched the vikings become mesmerized by the brazen movements. They were thumping time on the table with their open palms and staring that devouring gaze that so debased one.

Suddenly there were shouts. The vikings had swept the table bare of platters. One caught the squealing dancer and set her in the center of the table. Moira's eyes focused on gold-ringed ankles and swirling crimson skirts. The dancer's hips jerked in quick thrusts and her cream-white shoulders shimmied her breasts with wanton abandon, evoking wild oaths and lewd movements from the vikings. Moira wondered at what so incited them and stole a sidelong glance at Wulfsun.

Under intent golden brows Wulfsun's satisfied eyes watched the dancer. His arm draped possessively over her shoulder, and she felt the tremors of his laughter as the dancer stooped provocatively toward him. He received a kiss and an eyeful of her cleavage, before Bjorn

Bloody Hair intruded and carried her across the way to his own table, amid curses and calls from his disappointed companions.

Perhaps it was the wine, or Wulfsun's own desire for perverse pleasure, but Moira felt herself lifted in his arms as he set her table-center as replacement.

She stood frozen, though hands and voices prodded her to dance. It wasn't that she couldn't. For every swan sister the skill of dance was innate. It was just that for one day she'd suffered enough ridicule, enough humiliation. Then she took heart seeing the other dancer's bawdy movements and exaggerated gestures. If she could focus her mind on something . . . or someone. . . .

Her eyes went straight to Wulfsun's. His eyes were very bold in an interested, slightly contemptuous way. His mockery stabbed her to the very heart, but she held his gaze, determined to spark more than contempt in his callous perusal.

The drummer slowed to a sensual beat, perhaps because the other dancer tired. Moira drew up her hands, following the curves of her body skyward, and began swaying to the ripple of flute and pipe. Her movements became fluid, languorous, and melting. Her breasts peaked and quivered beneath the silver-threaded silk, like rolling waves at sea. The tinkling beads and lank tassels on her fertility belt lapped against her round, swaying buttocks. She was suddenly feeling very alive, exhilarated to be able to release emotion from days and months of captivity. She was out under the starry heavens again, her bare feet touching the dark earth and her open lips sucking in the breath and flow of life. Wulfsun might bind her to the earth, but he could not steal her magic. The magic that made her woman.

Wulfsun watched her, his blue eyes lambent and absorbing. Loose silk folds revealed her rounded breasts, and her skirts clung between her legs so he could see the deep cleft between her thighs. He felt his desire rising like never before, and he wanted to hold her as her graceful arms slowly wafted the air like wings on wind. Savoring, his eyes followed the line of her long slim legs, the curve of her hips, and the swell of her breasts. He swallowed back desire which numbed his groin and watered his mouth like magenta wine. A wild, lusting heat began to simmer within him. He wanted this earth witch with her opal eyes and honey voice. He had wanted her through long nights at sea and duty, through the night and mischief of the fire . . . and now a rampant desire ran his blood hot. He was done with wanting!

He pulled his eyes away, circling the craggy faces of his vikings and saw her bewitchment had aroused every man to a slow pant. An angry, hot rush seized him, and he became as territorial as a high mountain wolf. A primitive fire clenched his entire body and glittered in his brooding, hooded eyes. His mouth went dry with desire.

Suddenly he leaped up. His pulse thundering, he pulled her into his arms and clamped his hot mouth down on hers with a fierce desperation. Amid the encouraging shouts of his vikings, his grip shifted, and he cupped the shape of her buttocks in his hands, pinioning her to the hard mount of his loins.

"No!" she struggled against him, not realizing her struggles only inflamed the searing want that burned through him.

"You are mine," his voice rasped.

She broke away, but his hand caught her wrist, his grip unrelenting. She tried to twist free, but he dragged her off the table and strode toward the lamp-lit interior of a curtained alcove. His vikings pounded the table with their fists and raised such a commotion that the musicians stopped playing and ran from the room.

Wulfsun thrust her inside the alcove onto silken cushions, yanked closed the curtains, and turned to her. His gaze sliced through her. Her heart was beating a rabbit's pace, and she could not get her breath.

He took a step.

She drew back, bewildered by his brutish behavior. The guttering lamp danced wicked shadows and contorted his features so he looked wolfen. As he came nearer, his immense straight shoulders, muscled like bas-relief, expanded to block her escape.

"Come, you can be sweeter than this. In dance you call me like a bitch in heat. Now you shrink away." His hand was in her hair, grasping the side of her face, brushing back the long black strands, his mouth brutally capturing the tender flesh of her own. Roughly, he seized her shoulders, and teeth and tongue assaulted her until she twisted her face away. His grip did not loosen, it shifted. He savaged her neck, but ironically the gold torque deflected his teeth. His mouth was at her throat, he nipped and tongued the curve of her silk-smooth neck.

"Stop! Please, stop!" Panic-stricken, she writhed against him and pressed against his bare chest with her fists.

He is a wild man, like Bjorn. What has possessed him?

The darkside of enchantment possesses him. He is frenzied with desire. He will force you, warned her swan self.

She thrashed and turned like hapless quarry within his predator's hold. Struggling against his strength, she anguished, dreading him. The muscular sinewy hardness of his arms crushed her. He was so powerful, she felt the heaving of his chest against her own, and her breath coursed as if she'd been running fast.

You have your wits, use them, her swan side summoned.

Wulfsun dragged her down, where she sprawled onto the cushions. He cast off his loincloth and loomed over her like a bronzed golden god of legend. She had ached for his warm heat and the filling swell of his manhood deep within her being, but not this way. Not this wild predatory mating which offered no love, no tenderness, nothing but possession and release.

He covered her body and pinioned both her hands above her head. Uttering a growl, he lowered his head and clamped his teeth to the careful knot of her silk covering. He tore free the flimsy midriff garment and exposed her breasts to his burning gaze. Looking down at her revealed nipples, his heavy-lidded eyes glittered appreciatively and his nostrils flared.

Her bosom heaving with indignation, she glared at him steadily, her cheeks suffused with a raw blush. His eyes narrowed wickedly, and his mouth, hotly moist, clamped down tightly on her left nipple so intensely, she felt his vitality shock through her body like an indescribable fire, scorching and molten. Still resisting, she writhed; she couldn't bear the pain-pleasure of his assault and inwardly vowed he would not take her this way. Yet her only hope was to divert his unrestrained passion.

And in a desperate plea for tenderness she cried, "Nay! You must be gentler than this," her voice a breathy whimper. "You are driven by enchantment."

He froze.

His lips parted from the tender nub of her breast.

She felt his strong fingers slowly relenquish their hold on her flesh. Then, with a curse that rose like a low, wild growl from his throat, he sank back on his heels and raked a hand across his brow.

She buried her face and tears in the scented cushions that smelled as cloying as overripe fruit at summer's end. Though she did not look, she knew Wulfsun stayed kneeling before her. He stayed, watching her, she feared, like a predator ready to pounce and maul again.

After a long time he spoke in quiet but raging tones, which nonetheless vibrated in the air around her. "Hel's fire, I should have let you drown in the sea! You are more than trouble! But 'tis truth, I had no wish to beat you into submission and wrestle from you your maidenhead."

He moved closer. His hand roughly clutched her chin, and he tilted her face to his. Stormy eyes held hers. "By what came this enchantment?"

Unable to meet his gaze her eyes focused on the fine rain of golden hair on his chest. "That first kiss."

"The night in the tower?"

"Aye." She still could not bear to look into his eyes.

"So I am to be in bondage to your witchery?"

"'Tis not my witchery, but the witchery of the Moon Goddess."

He laughed then. A skeptic's laugh.

"Thorfinn swore you had enchanted me, but I, fool, did not believe him. Instead, I wagered you would come to me wanting, but 'tis myself who is left wanting." Shaking his head woefully, he momentarily searched for answers. Then his eyes brightened. "You must release me. You vowed to grant my request. I make it now. Release me!"

The light seemed to darken, intensify. Overwrought with remorse she said, "I cannot. I am sorry. Truly it was not of my doing. Nor would you be the love mate of my choosing."

For a long moment Wulfsun remained still. He gave a hollow laugh, one that held the echo of wounded pride. "I, too, would welcome a beating rather than bow to the curse of your enchantment."

"Then be done with it. Take from my throat this gold ring of bondage, and at least one of us may be freed," she begged.

Warily, he moved away. "So at first chance you can sing sorcery to freeze my sword arm in heat of battle or wither my manhood at passion's gate?"

"Nay, I would not think it."

"Hah!" he scoffed. "You witches are a heartless, lying lot. Be warned, I am no lackwit."

Taking courage, she looked threateningly at his indomitable face, the jaw, the nose an arrogant profile. "Be warned yourself!" she flared defiantly, scrubbing the tears from her cheeks. "Enchantment of the heart has driven better men than you into madness."

He drew up his leanly muscled frame. "Hag of Hel! To release you would be the greater madness! May you choke on your own magic, swan witch!" He flung aside the curtain and left. The gold torque seemed to tighten on her neck as though he willed it so.

Do not despair, he is still a man, consoled her swan self.

And when the enchantment lifts at moon month, what am I to do with this man who binds me?

What seems sweet can turn sour. In binding you, he binds himself.

Despite their all-night revelry, Wulfsun rallied his vikings and ordered them to prepare to set sail with the morning tide. The swan witch no longer looked a bedraggled captive as she walked beside him through town. Her long black hair waved like sea grass against the background of her crimson cape. He prickled as he saw her eyes meet every admiring gaze, boldly and without deference. Wulfsun was not a jealous man, but he was possessive. He ground his teeth and set his shoulders. The woman was his; no other need look at her.

His mood this day was silent and sullen, and beneath his inky spell he was in even a blacker turbulent quandary. He was not a man to fall in love overnight nor had he ever abandoned himself completely to passion with anyone. Yet now that he was victim to this enchantment, he found himself fired by an earthy, even fierce desire, despite his iron control over his emotions.

He could release her. But because of the bind of enchantment he could not let her go, nor had it ever been his nature to release the reins of power without a long hard struggle. He felt an unswerving devotion to her; the mere sight of her melted his warrior's heart and made him do foolish things. On the one hand he wanted to lay kingdoms at her feet, protect her against harm, and carry her off for passion's conquest, but on the other he raged over his enslavement to her, a woman!

He had walked the streets of Kaupang into early morning hours, fighting a battle like none he'd ever fought on land or sea.

He made his decision.

It would take more than a will of iron, but he would outwardly restrain his passion and resist the woman at every turn. By force of will alone he would break this enchantment.

At the dock Wulfsun's hands closed around her waist, and he lifted her over the ship's side. He handed her over to Jacob the Freed, who stood ready and waiting on the deck of the *Elk Wader*.

He turned on her his wide deliberate blue stare. "You go to the Ravnings on the *Elk Wader*. I will follow on the *Sea Steed*," he announced abruptly.

She did not question, but he saw uneasiness in her eyes. Jacob would guard her better than his own life. Yet a possessive fire ensnared Wulfsun's reason and near caused him to grab her back. He turned heel and hoped that by distancing himself from her for a time, he might regain his common sense.

SWAN BRIDE

He leaped aboard the *Sea Steed* and prepared to take a turn at rowing, thinking physical exhaustion might purge the woman from his thoughts. Thorfinn sounded an order, and the oars hit the sea. Jacob the Freed hailed a farewell. Wulfsun strained to see the woman's face. The irony lay that his last glimpse was not of her, but Bjorn Bloody Hair leering over her. Wulfsun's strong hands gripped the oar and near snapped the stick in two.

Chapter 7

The crystalline waters of the fjord mirrored the looming mountains to each side. Never had Moira seen mountains so high, a land so wild, nor so beckoning. There was not a breath of wind as the two ships glided side by side like waterfowl. The oarsmen's broad shoulders glistened with sweat, and at each turn her eyes found verdant banks and forested hills bespeaking of wilderness. Cormorants called and darted from precipitous nests. Deer grazing at the water's edge leaped back into the forest cover. The passage narrowed, the cliffs to each side closed around her like the stone walls of Mergate Abbey. For a moment she felt a wave of suffocation, and then, gradually, the waterway opened again into a wide expanse of lake and valley.

A horn's summons, sharp and vivid, resounded over green banks and mountains. The Northmen pulled the oars into faster rhythm, shouting heartily as their faces shone of welcome to their homeland. The long arduous journey was over.

"Yonder the Ravnings," spoke Jacob the Freed vibrantly. His expression was no less cheerful than the others.

Moira's eyes followed his pointing hand and saw at the

base of a mountain gorge smoke spiraling upward from the roofs of a group of dwellings. Behind the nested settlement rose a dark mountain, towering above all others. Oddly, the dark heights called her, and she imagined herself flying above the lake and valley, higher to snow-capped peaks. Her fingers clutched the gold torque at her throat, and her vision plummeted from the sky.

Bjorn Bloody Hair ordered oars up as the ship skimmered to a sheltered spot where smaller boats were stranded on the shore. She watched two grazing ponies start at the ship's approach. Tails arched, they romped over the meadow as if making further announcement of the vikings' arrival.

She turned her head to look across to the sister ship, the *Sea Steed*. She easily spied Wulfsun by the fire of his crimson cloak. During days at sea when the *Sea Steed* came into view, she had followed that cloak and wondered why he no longer acknowledged her. Why had he distanced himself from her?

If I am such a pariah, he should let me go.

Because of the enchantment he cannot, reasoned her swan self.

In one week's time the enchantment will end with full moon. Maybe he will be more reasonable.

Do not think it. He will enslave you still or discard you to another.

Her eyes shifted back to Bjorn Bloody Hair, and a shiver trembled through her; sharing close quarters with him during the days at sea had not been pleasant. Though he did not touch her, he watched her, never wavering, even as she attended to her personal affairs. Even now he hovered near her, pretending to pack a sea chest while all the others were leaping from the ship to greet those on shore. She stood and moved away from him, turning her mind to this new land.

Children, fresh-looking, healthy, and strong, ran to welcome the men. All were pure as fairies with Nordic blue eyes and fair hair. Their zestful shrieks of excitement became the official welcome. Down to the water's edge came others: men, women, and handsome youths.

She watched men slap each other on the shoulders and embrace smiling women in greeting. Infinite homesickness for Myr and loneliness crept through her as she witnessed a homecoming that would never be hers.

Jacob the Freed helped her from the boat, and her feet touched the strange land for the first time. Her legs wobbled, and she remembered other times, yearning for Wulfsun's strong hands to steady her. Her eyes sought his red cloak and found him in conversation with Thorfinn.

Behind them a wooden cart came unhurriedly down the track. With each jog, two women swayed easily. Both wore pleated linen kirtles with embroidered overskirts much like Moira's own, but not so fine. One woman was far along in pregnancy, but the other leaped from the cart and ran to embrace Wulfsun. Her unbound hair shown silver white, and her cream silk skin was clear but for the pink blush of her cheeks. Deep-green eyes and chinaberry lips added to her beauty. He lifted her in his arms and spun full circle. She laughed with delight and kissed him. Like a fall wind blowing over the marshes, jealousy whispered through Moira.

Wulfsun set the woman down and searched through his side pouch, pulling from it the emerald necklace. Her joy of the gift became evident as she called liltingly in Norse to the woman in the cart and waved the necklace for her to see. Wulfsun helped her to fasten it around her neck, and then he turned back to Thorfinn. Not leaving his side, the woman turned her head to scan the shore. Her eyes stopped dead on Moira.

Interrupting Wulfsun in mid-conversation, she spoke rapidly. Moira watched her face change from its refined grace to frowning anger as Wulfsun spoke. He shrugged at her show of temper and turned back to Thorfinn. For some seconds, while clutching the emerald necklace at her breast, she coldly studied Moira. Her eyes roamed derisively over Moira's clothes and face. Not shrinking from her glare, Moira held her eyes with dispassionate calm. It was clear from the outset this woman would never call her friend.

Wulfsun motioned for someone to load the cart with goods, and a little while later he and the women wheeled back up the track. Meanwhile, Moira stood alone and forgotten, but for two fair-haired children who stared unblinkingly at her.

"It is time to greet your fate, holy woman." Jacob the Freed walked toward her. He shifted a large bundle easily over one shoulder, his sword and hand ax balanced on the other. Moira followed, prepared for the worst. He whistled lightly as they walked up the grassy track to the dwellings.

"Who were the women in the cart?" she finally asked, breaking the flow of his tune.

"Thorfinn's wife, Brigitta, and Ran the Fair. Both are foster sisters to Wulfsun. Fair Ran is a little fox by better name," he said fondly.

"She seemed angry when she saw me," Moira said, hoping he might enlighten her more.

He chuckled. "She has reason. As a child, Ran's first steps were to Wulfsun. In his youth, before he went *a viking,* he taught her to ride, swim, and hawk. He means much to her."

"Ran will find no rival in me. I did not ask to be captured, nor will I be Wulfsun's thrall woman."

"You have no choice. When the chieftain looks to you, you must please him. He is fair, but do not cross him. He lives hard and is feared, yet respected. None in Hordaland dare quarrel with him, for those who have are dead."

Moira fell momentarily silent. Though she still wished to pry for more information, she was learning men did not readily share their thoughts with women. Turning her queries to another path, she asked, "What am I to do?"

He looked at her then, peering down his broken nose. "You are a captive. Thrall woman to Wulfsun. The runes on your collar mark you as such. You must serve and obey him."

"Has a thrall ever been disobedient?"

"It has happened."

"Often?" she needled, thinking Wulfsun remained chieftain not from adoration, but through superiority of arm.

"A slave does not have a free tongue. You should guard

yours," he warned. "Like you, in my youth, I was captured by the Northmen. For many years I remained a thrall until the Battle of Lade, where Egil Ravn, foster father to Wulfsun, gave me my freedom. Life goes easier if you accept from the beginning what has to be."

"Once free, why did you not return to your homeland?"

"I chose the viking life," was his decisive answer.

"A poor choice to my mind," returned Moira.

"You have much to learn about these people."

"No doubt I will as I step and fetch for them."

"Do not complain or it will go worse for you," he counseled.

She knew he was right, and she steadied her eyes on the wood and stone buildings ahead for fear she would take fright and run.

"At first," began Jacob, "unless Wulfsun calls you, you will be at the service of all."

"Do I obey the children as well?"

"Yes, except for those thrall-born."

"How do I know a thrall?"

"A collar around the neck like your own," he said, then added, "But none are like yours. You alone wear gold."

"'Tis my misfortune," she returned.

"Aye," agreed Jacob. "'Tis easier to lose your head."

Her confidence dissolved, and she saw her throat being brutally cut for the gold torque while she slept. Jacob, seeing the sudden realization of it on her face, merely laughed.

The Ravnings sat like a fortress within the meadow. They made their way to the high-timbered gates and passed under a carved arch which sported the head of a freshly killed goat. Moira swerved to the right and quickly stepped into the confines of the settlement. Her first glimpse took in three long rectangular timbered houses bordering the center of an open yard. The largest of these had doors at each end with ornately carved overhangs. A brightly painted yellow and red dragon's head thrust up from the apex of each roof end, and on the outer perimeters smaller buildings were scattered among stone-piled walls in crisscrossed animal pens. Beyond this, past golden fields of rye and oats, past horned sheep browsing with goats, a clear stream cascaded down the hillside from a gorge above.

Moira felt the stares of people as they gaped and craned their heads to see this strange, finely clothed woman with a gold collar of thralldom. She felt as if she were again being bartered over in the market of Kaupang. A brown-plumed gander, his gaggling harem close behind, nipped at her skirts as though her foreignness might be something edible. She sensed he was giving her a first-hand introduction to the pecking order. She smiled and spoke a soft flow. His long neck swayed side to side suspiciously, and then he honked loudly in a more friendly greeting.

A fair-headed man, of uncommon large arms, hailed Jacob from the forge. "Jacob!" he smiled warmly, saluting him with his hammer. The two men passed a few moments in friendly conversation. Moira stood patiently by and fed dried bread from her pocket to the geese and watched a group of chattering women across the way unload the cart. Wulfsun had disappeared into the longhouse with Ran the Fair and her sister.

After a time Jacob turned his attention. "Ysja, Ysja!" he called. A young girl stepped away from the group. The first thing Moira noticed was the iron collar around Ysja's neck. Knowing that she was not alone in being enslaved did not ease Moira's despair.

As Ysja smiled at Moira, delicate rose tints suffused her cheeks. She looked about sixteen, and her thralldom seemed to have no bearing on her pleasant nature or fresh looks. She listened attentively to Jacob the Freed as he spoke to her. Moira wondered what he was telling everyone about her and vowed to learn this Norse tongue as quickly as possible.

"Ysja will show you your work," he said, and abruptly left them.

She stood awkwardly for a few seconds while Ysja reached out and touched her embroidered dress and cloak admiringly. Moira tried to think of something to say that would communicate her desire to be friends, but she was nervous. Finally she touched her breast and said, "Moira." The sound of her name on her lips startled even herself. It had been so long since she'd been called anything but holy woman or swan witch.

Ysja giggled and repeated "Moira," adding another word which Moira took to mean "come." Taking her hand, Ysja led her across the yard to a longhouse. Outside, Moira saw a bird mew. As they passed, the hawks remained motionless. Taloned feet were tucked beneath feathered breast, ringed and chained to the perch. Moira spoke in soothing tones, causing a stir of wings and answering calls which assured her that though they were not mistreated, they yearned for freedom.

She followed Ysja inside the longhouse. Once her eyes adjusted to the dimness, she saw it to be a great storage house filled with foodstuffs and goods. Ysja climbed a log-pole ladder to a loft and called down to her to follow. Moira easily scrambled up after her. Light filtered through openings between the beams, and she saw that, in various spots, sheepskins were spread, cushioned by the straw. Ysja pointed to a skin and said Moira's name, then pointed to her own beside it. Moira smiled, glad for a place of her own in this new home. Ysja took from her mouth a piece of amber tree sap she'd been chewing and offered it to Moira that she might do likewise. After hesitating, she realized it was a token of friendship, and with a smile she accepted it.

As they labored through the next weeks, Moira rehearsed with Ysja the names of everything in sight. Ysja was not only imaginative and thoughtful, but a patient teacher. Learning Norse became a diverting pastime for Moira as she and Ysja chattered constantly while going about their duties. Ysja pointed out and spoke the name of tools, animals, clothing, and countless other things while Moira repeated.

Ysja told Moira she was a fast learner, and soon she would be more knowledgeable than Ragnorvald the Law Speaker, the scholar of the settlement.

"Ragnorvald presides over the important events of birth, marriage, and the *Althing*," Ysja told her. "All disputes and law settlements are settled at the *Althing*. Twice yearly it is held, and the men will be leaving soon to attend."

"Will Wulfsun go, also?" Moira asked Ysja.

"'Tis certain. Is he not chieftain?"

m"Aye"—Moira sighed unhappily—"that he is."

A new and exhausting phase of life opened to Moira. In long hours of sunlight the crops ripened, and every hand was needed to harvest. Wulfsun had not spoken to her since that day in Kaupang when they set sail for the Ravnings. He remained a silent wall, though he sometimes worked alongside her in the fields. She knew how to work, and fueled by her frustration concerning Wulfsun, she became an able harvester. She could not match his strength or stride, but she did lift arms full of hay and spread them on drying poles which, like thatched fences, lined the hillside. She threshed and winnowed until her black hair was white with chaff. And when the men returned with boats low in the water from the weight of salmon, she gutted them until her hands looked like fish scales, raw and rough.

The air smelled rank with the odor of fish, which hung on drying racks in the sun. Moira watched the thrall children run with clumps of long grasses and shoo off the insects that the stink attracted. While she watched, she longed for sweet air and remembered the exotic scents Wulfsun had touched to her body in Kaupang. She looked across the drying racks at his golden profile, which held a greeting or a word for everyone but herself.

'Tis not easy to be invisible, especially to my enemy.

If you were invisible, he would have no need to ignore you. He sees you first, last, and always, returned her swan mind.

In the afternoon when she served him cheeses, berries, and hazelnuts, she remembered him hospitably offering her roast duck. In the evening, spinning wool by the brilliant light of the rising moon, she watched him idle on the grass beside Ran the Fair. When he leaned close to Ran, Moira remembered his lips on her own, demanding a response she willingly gave. The golden torque of captivity had not erased the fires in her blood that simmered to boiling desire as the rising full moon climbed the night sky. Even now she felt a moistening warmth between her thighs and a dull ache of wanting in her breast at the mere sight of him.

Pulling her eyes away, she agonized inwardly, *I would be better off if I had never come into the world of men! Why did Epona not tell me?*

She could not tell you that which you would not hear. Each soul's path is different. Besides, the chieftain is not the only man to look to on this night of full moon, her swan self counseled.

I suppose you would have me throw myself into the groping hands of Bjorn Bloody Hair. Hah! I am not yet so desperate! With such a father, my child would truly be an ugly duckling.

One ugly duckling is better than none, moralized her swan mind. *But if you intend to be so finicky, I suggest you cool the fire in your blood by sitting in the icy waters of the fjord. If nothing else, it will save you from yourself.*

Abruptly Moira stood up and dropped her spindle onto the pile of carded wool at her feet. She'd had enough of her other mind, she'd had enough of watching Ran fawn over Wulfsun, and she'd had enough of waiting for her destiny!

Her pace quickened as she headed toward the fjord. On the hillside above she stripped naked, tossing off her cloak, tunic, and sheepskin boots. She felt a familiar freedom as the night breeze caressed her bare skin, and she raised her slim arms high as if to touch the moon. Her body tingled with the delight of life.

Then, with a cry of exaltation, she broke into a run. Hair flying, arms spread into wings, she hurled herself down the slope, trying with all the magic left to her and with all her will to transform into swan and fly. In that brief moment at the water's edge, when arm became wing, she caught the up draft of wind, thinking, I will fly.

Her feet left the ground . . .

The icy water bit her face as she skidded across its moonlit mirror, and then she was falling down with her failure . . . deeper and deeper into the chilling, numbing darkness of the fjord. The golden torque banding her throat choked her, and she cursed Wulfsun with a hundred spells . . . all hopelessly impotent.

'Tis flying of a sort, but even a swanling needs air, appealed her swan self after a time. *Up . . . up for breath.*

Feeling a sudden panic, Moira winged upward through the water, spiraling to the surface like a flying fish reborn. She gasped for sweet air, and after a moment returned to woman. Turning on her side, she swam to shore.

Wulfsun pressed his fingers to his temples and tried to will away the sharp throb in his head. The dragon dreams had come again last night and with them the fierce headache. Now he felt as if Thor's hammer pounded in his skull. Looking down the hillside toward the fjord, he tried to see where the woman had gone. Day long he had chewed nearly every root and swallowed every powder in old Halda's bag of cures, and still his head clamored like a summer thunderstorm.

He heard a splash and then with wonderment saw her surface, in the moonlit fjord . . . a white swan . . . then woman. By Freya's crown, he should have guessed even before the ironmonger's forge in Kaupang that she was a changeling. What of the night on the ship when he discovered the webbing between her toes, or later on the Jutland beach? Oh, he'd been enchantment's fool, but no longer! He set his teeth and he walked ahead. This night he would call on her healing powers and nothing more.

His firm avowals were tested the moment she stepped naked from the water. The thunder in his head was soon eclipsed by the pounding of his heart. In shadow he watched her brush the water from her body like glistening pearls. Suddenly he wondered why he had separated himself from her these many days.

He stepped forward. "Mayhap you have need of my cloak again?"

Her back was to him, and the sound of his voice caused her to pause, then she turned and lifted dark lashes to reveal amber eyes. He knew her moods well enough to read a greeting.

"I thank you, but I have mine here."

He watched her bend to pick up the plain thrall tunic and lift it over her head and shoulders. His eyes tasted her nakedness with impatience, impatience spurred by the pulsing in his head. In the silence between them she dressed. Too slowly. He wanted her hands on him, not wringing the dampness from her hair or neatly tying the lacings of her sheepskin boots.

Feeling as though his head would split, he reached for her hand. "Come, I have need of you." He led her up the slope to a moss-grown spot beneath a linden tree. Sitting down, he requested, "Put your hands to my head and take away the pain."

Still not speaking, though her lips did turn up in a soft smile, she came down beside him. She pillowed his head in her lap, and he rested against the soft contours of her thighs. The moment her fingers touched his head, relief swooped through him as comfortingly as a warming wind.

Moira's swim in the fjord had only temporarily cooled the fire in her veins. When his strong hand had cupped hers and he led her up the hill, her blood ignited like blazing longfires. From the depths of her heart she prayed, *Oh, Mother Goddess, I must join with him this night, or I will die!*

Now her hands trembled as her palms hovered over his face. He closed his eyes and she felt the heat from his skin radiating into her cold hands. Delicately she touched her fingertips to his temples. Hot fire like dragon breath scorched her hands! As it burned, she pulled her fingertips away briefly and then pressed them once again. He was suffering, she could not doubt it.

Who would not with dragons roaring fire in their head?

With such visions, no wonder he behaves so wildly, concluded her swan self.

Is it so with all men?

'Tis a certainty! Why else would the world of men be so dangerous if not because they are all touched by madness?

More sympathetic to his plight, every part of Moira reached to sooth and calm the phantoms in his mind. She began to hum softly, and her song became a love potion.

Slowly her fingers moved over his forehead, pleasuring

in the feeling and texture of his skin. Moving down to his golden eyebrows, she skimmed over his eyelids. His lashes felt like tiny spiders' legs against her fingertips. Gently and leisurely she traced the firm and hollow of his cheekbones. She liked the sandy feel of his beard stubble. Her thumb and forefinger outlined his hard jawbone. Perhaps he was not so stubborn as determined, an admirable quality in both man and woman. Her forefinger stroked the length of his nose to the tip. She liked his nose best of all, especially the way his nostrils flared when he felt challenged.

She took her time, paying attention, even comparing the endless details of his face to her own. Caressing above his upper lip, she felt the fuzzy hair growth that shadowed his mouth. Very slowly she traced the edges to the corners. With her touch his lips parted slightly, and she felt the heat of his breath whispering past her knuckles. She wanted to taste his mouth, allowing her lips to explore his face as her hands had done, but he slept.

And then, driven by her own desire, she did something she should not have done. She cupped her hands over his closed eyes and held them there a moment. She sent herself and her desire into his dreaming.

Her swan self did not keep silent. *Do not forget in the world of men all magic has its price.*

I do not forget. But I am desperate. He binds me to him but holds me away. My heart bursts and my thighs weep for his manhood.

He sighed and shifted. A hand resting on his stomach moved and stretched up to caress the curve of her knee. Gently, with both hands, she lifted his head from the pillow of her lap. For the second time this night she slipped off her clothes, and settled herself down beside him. In his half dreaming he wrapped his arms around her and nuzzled against her neck.

"Ummm . . ." His contentment hummed in his throat.

Everything quickened in Moira. She was shaking, heartachingly aware of every brush of skin or cloth against her. The smell of his clothes filled her nose, and the taste of his hair cushioned her seeking lips. She had forgotten his strength and welcomed now the embrace of arms trained to sword and the pull of oar.

His hands roved over her bare skin like the flooding moonlight. His soft stroking crept and swirled through her limbs and into the throbbing emptiness between her thighs. She coiled her long slim legs around him, wanting all of him inside her. He nosed her ear affectionately, gently mouthing and sucking the thickness of her earlobe.

She moaned softly, and then his mouth closed over hers, drinking her juices and swallowing her sighs. Her fingers tangled in his thick hair, holding his face captive to her own. Her hips lifted to him and she wanted his weight on her, in her. . . .

Headache gone, Wulfsun roused into a waking dream. He drank from faerie lips, lips as thirsty as his own. He felt as if the earth had opened and the sky had fallen. His entire body was swamped by his desire, and his manhood throbbed achingly. The ground reeled around him, and her lips seemed to be the one safe haven in the blur.

Suddenly he knew better! Reality came crashing through.

He stiffened and pulled back, his accusing eyes pinned hers. "I asked for pain's relief, and you give me the madness of desire! By the Gods, woman!" Like steel claws his fingers clamped her shoulders. He wanted to shake her and thrust her away, but the flashing confusion in her eyes stayed his hands. "Do you think I'm made of clay, that you can mold and bend me to your whims?"

"Nay, I do not." Remorse rasped her voice. He saw tears well in her eyes, but quickly cooled his sympathy. He could not trust her. Her words sprayed forth. "I could not help myself. The full moon compels me to you and you do not want me."

He looked into her eyes, and amid all those swirling depths of colors saw her otherworld beauty. Golds and coppers and even flecks of silver.

A madman's laugh rose and died deep within his chest. Then he confessed hoarsely, "I am dying for want of you!" The galloping in his heart would not slow, and it no longer mattered if she knew.

"And I for you." Her fingers touched his cheek in honest tenderness. Where she touched, his skin tingled . . . burned! By the Gods! He knew he must leave her now, this instant . . . to break this night's sorcery!

The harshness of Wulfsun's grip on Moira's shoulders paled to the blow of his releasing her. A cry rose in her throat to call him back . . . beg him back as he strode away. A sick abandonment ripped through her breast, and sick shame boiled in her belly. Why had she done it? He was lost to her now!

Remaining beneath the linden tree, she wept. She wept until early dawn, when the commotion of men saddling horses startled her from her misery. With Wulfsun at their lead, the vikings rode up the winding mountain path. With unspeakable regret, Moira watched through tear-washed eyes the crimson flash of his cloak until he disappeared from sight.

While the chieftain and his warriors were away in council at the *Althing,* no one stayed idle at the Ravnings, neither the high-born nor the most aged. Even the toothless old man who Moira discovered groveling around the farmstead waiting for the wastes of the bower house could not chance idleness in this time of winter preparation. Daily he sorted through the refuse as dogs snatched at his hoard. Barely tolerated, he received the scorn of even the very youngest. Once, as she tended the dye pots in the open yard, she chased off some children who mercilessly taunted him.

Ysja walked from the bower house and said coldly, "Have no care for the Man Biter."

"The Man Biter?" she repeated, not sure what Ysja meant.

"The wolf, the dog, the cat, and the bear bite in battle, but a man is greater. For him to bite in battle is cowardly. For that his teeth were broken out at the *Althing* by the law speaker many years ago."

"Your law is too harsh," said Moira.

"No, it is necessary." She looked across the yard, shaking her head sadly. "It is said Olaf the Man Biter was a great warrior once."

"He is old. The old should be honored and respected," returned Moira. She was learning that the Norse people held little reverence for the aged who were unable to fend for themselves. The strongest survived, the weak died. Ysja had told her that men longed for death as heroes so they might enter a place called Asgard, where they could fight battles daily and feast in the hall of Odin at night. It sounded like something the world of men might dream up.

"Respect must be earned. Olaf is a coward." Ysja slowly turned the woolen contents of the yellow dye pot, taking care the dye would bite evenly on the wool.

Moira had learned that the dyes were prized items the men had brought back from Britain. Some dyes, madder root and Tyrian purple, were so valuable that none were used, but locked away in a chest. She had listened to a disagreement between Ran the Fair and her sister Brigitta when Ran the Fair demanded to use the Tyrian purple for herself alone.

Already in Moira's thoughts, Ran the Fair, with her sister Brigitta, walked toward them from the bower house. Comparing likenesses, she saw one tall and graceful, having outward beauty rarely matched, the other awkward from pregnancy, simply dressed, but gently dispositioned. As Jacob the Freed warned, Ran had a devious nature kept only in check by her elder sister's wisdom and understanding. Brigitta took charge of the homestead, being a well-organized overseer, but because of the imminent birth of her child, she now tired easily, leaving much to Ran the Fair, who dominated more than organized.

"Good day," said Brigitta, smiling as she and Ran passed. Both Moira and Ysja said a greeting in return. Ran, however, did not speak. Her eyelids flickered and she shot a look of pure malevolence at Moira.

She averted her eyes to the dye pot, sorry, through no choice of her own, to be the bitter thorn in Ran's side.

"She hates you," whispered Ysja, watching Ran's back. "Since childhood she has always been jealous of Wulfsun's women."

"Are they lovers?"

"No, she was but a maid when last he went *a viking*. But now that he has returned, she is very possessive of him. All expect him to wed her this midsummer hand-fast."

Moira frowned and gnawed her lower lip anxiously. She had not thought of this. What was already complicated might become a hopeless entanglement. On the one hand this news caused her to hope that he might set her free before his marriage, but on the other, she felt a desperate need to join with him all the sooner.

"Is something wrong, Moira?" Ysja asked.

"No. I—" She stopped before she began, not able to share her predicament with Ysja. In an effort to regain her composure, she turned the conversation. "Will Thorfinn return from the *Althing* in time for the birth of his child?"

"Yes." Ysja gave her a speculative glance. "Will you welcome the chieftain's return?"

"No more than any other," she said defensively.

Do not your eyes turn morning, noon, and night to the mountain path in hopes of seeing the returning wave of his crimson cloak? niggled her swan self.

She lowered her eyes with vexation. In an attempt to redirect Ysja's curiosity and silence her other mind, she said, "How came Wulfsun to be chieftain?"

Ysja laughed. "It is an often told saga." Moira realized she was as natural a storyteller as the skald. The past, present, and projected events of the Ravnings were all in Ysja's domain, no matter how closely her stories resembled gossip. "Shall I tell you, Moira?"

"I will listen, but do not make more of your chieftain than he is." Ysja gave her a puzzled look. "Try to understand, Ysja, but for him, I would be free."

"I do understand."

"Go on then, speak your tale," Moira urged, her curiosity undeniable.

"It is truth, not tale!" she declared before beginning. "Wulfsun was found naked and abandoned when he was four or five winters old by Egil Ravn, father of Brigitta and Ran the Fair. Many nights after, a she-wolf howled in the nearby hills and many thought he was a wolf child.

Having no sons, Egil took him to his hall and raised him as his own. Njal the Gray, Egil's brother, became jealous of Wulfsun, for even as a boy, Wulfsun showed courage and great skill with weaponry. He can outswim and outwrestle any man in Hordaland still, and in battle when he takes sword in hand, there is no warrior more dangerous."

Moira thought this was exaggerated but continued to listen to Ysja's story.

"Wulfsun was fourteen winters old when Egil, his wife, Asgard, and Njal the Gray traveled to the summer *Althing*, where Egil proclaimed Wulfsun heir to the Ravnings. They did not go by sea but rode horses and crossed over Ravnjell. On the return journey the weather turned bad and the mists came. It was unlucky for them, for the mists bring unspeakable terror. Njal the Gray returned alone to the Ravnings bearing the unhappy news of everyone's death.

"I was a child but still I remember his white face and quaking hands as he entered the bower house. He boasted of fighting the dragon of the mist, saying that Egil, Asgard, and Wulfsun were dead." Ysja took a deep breath and looked over her shoulder.

"Two nights later, as Njal feasted at the high seat, having proclaimed himself the chieftain of the Ravnings, a stranger came to the gates asking shelter. Njal bid him enter, only to welcome the ghastly visage of Wulfsun. He was barely alive, his clothing torn and bloody. Njal whitened and reached for his sword, which hung on the wall behind the high seat. Wulfsun named him coward for leaving them all to the furies of the black mist, and then he, too, took down a sword from the wall. Though a youth, he matched his uncle in strength, wielding his sword so swiftly none saw the slicing movement that left Njal's legs walking with no head."

"Ragnorvald the Law Speaker pronounced Wulfsun chieftain, though we all thought he would die, so foul were his wounds from battling the dragon of the mist. Even yet, men speak of the youth's courage."

Moira shot Ysja a curious glance. "Have you seen these mist dragons?"

"No."

"Then how do you—" she began, but Ysja cut her off. "I know because the chieftain has black dreams of them yet. Always afterward he is seized by fierce headaches, and he calls for old Halda's remedies, though they rarely work."

Moira pursed her lips thoughtfully, knowing all too well of those black headaches. It would be impossible for her to forget the night Wulfsun came to her seeking relief. "Maybe it was not mist dragons, but Njal who killed Egil and his wife," she suggested, trying to resurrect the fire beneath the dye vat.

"Moira, there are trolls and dragons that haunt the forest and mountains. You should not doubt my words, you who cannot even keep a fire burning." She took the stick from Moira's hand and successfully stirred up the fire.

"I do not doubt. But then I see no bravery in the slaying of Wulfsun's uncle for cowardice. We are all cowards at heart, Ysja. If a dragon were chasing you, would you not run?"

"Of course, but I am a woman."

"Men and women are not so different. Both feel fear."

"But a coward cannot be chieftain."

"A coward may be the best chieftain of all."

"Now you speak foolishness," Ysja scoffed.

Moira shook her head seriously "Sometimes, Ysja, it takes greater courage to lay down a sword than pick one up."

Chapter 8

Surrounding the blue fjord, the golden filigree of change etched the hills. Annatto, ocher, and russet fired forth to warm the eye and heart. Moira's vision was filled with the cornflower sky and forested mountains serving as pedestals for napping clouds. The clarity of the autumn day exhilarated her. She took a deep invigorating breath and turned her face upward to follow the chattering, swirling birds fleeing to warm winter lands. Her swan spirit yearned to fly with them.

It's been four moon passings since we left Myr, whispered her swan mind, despairingly.

Aye, so much has happened, yet so little. The fever simmers within my blood once more, yet another full moon will pass and I will still sleep alone.

She meandered down the hillside and followed the stream from Ravnjell as it formed a chain of pools down the gorge. She stopped to fill her basket with strings of moss, which she would twist into wicks for the fish-oil lamps. Amid the busy hours of harvest and winter preparation, expectancy filled the air as all awaited the birth of Brigitta's child and the return of the men from the *Althing.*

Moira entered the gargoyle archway of the feast hall,

and the clean scent of pine pricked her nostrils. She saw Ysja busily spreading fresh pine boughs on the hard-packed clay floor. Nearby on a long bench sat Brigitta. She poured oil into disk bowls that would be wicked and hung from the rafter beams.

Seeing Moira enter the hall, she called, "I wish to hang the raven emblem of my father. Go to the loft and fetch it from the chest."

Setting down her basket, Moira began to climb the ladder.

"Wait, the key." Brigitta called her back, and her graceful fingers sorted through a tiny container of needles, a small pair of scissors, a knife, and a set of odd keys which hung on the fine chains of her kirtle broach.

"How do you feel?" Moira asked. Fatigue etched at the corners of Brigitta's blue-green eyes.

"Well enough. The child is slow to come." She pressed her hands to the small of her back, stretching her shoulders to relieve some of the pressure.

Moira smiled. "Perhaps he is waiting for his father to return."

"He?" A pleased smile touched Brigitta's lips. "Ysja tells me you have the sight. Do you truly believe it will be a man child?" Her pink lips curled with a hint of expectancy at the prospect.

"Do you wish it?" Moira hedged, though she knew it to be so.

"It is Thorfinn's hope. I wish to please my husband."

"A healthy mother and child, whether girl or boy, should please him," Moira said, taking the key from her and climbing to the loft.

Sheepskins and furs spread the floor of the loft, making it a comfortable sleeping area, though it had not been used since the men had gone to the *Althing*. Rays of light from the wind eyes in the roof sketched sunlit patterns on the floor and walls. The large chest sat in the far corner. Talons clutching the mouth of the lock, a bird of prey carved in fierce viking mode sat spread-winged on its face. It took Moira a few seconds to fit the key squarely into the lock to open it.

The raven banner lay on top. After taking it from the

chest, she shook out the dried herbs tucked within its folds. The delicate smell of sweet woodruff wisped through the air, and she was seized by a wave of homesickness for Epona and Myr.

Sighing, she turned to close the chest, but glimpsed something familiar inside. Her natural curiosity got the better of her. Almond brown and silver banded, she drew out a harp. She should have shut it back into the chest, but it had been so long since she had played her own. Lightly her fingers plucked the strings to pitch. Its tone rang brightly. She paced a few scales and picked out a well-remembered song. It seemed like greeting a long-absent companion. She looked up and saw Ysja standing on the ladder watching her. Her music stopped short.

"It sounds beautiful, Moira. Where did you learn the harper's craft?"

"In my homeland. It seems a long time since I've played."

Ysja looked at her sadly. "Here women are not skalds, it is forbidden."

"I suppose the chieftain decided this. 'Tis a foolish notion a man might think of."

"I do not know who thought it. I think it foolish as well."

She shook her head and placed the harp back inside the trunk, locking it into silence.

"Listen, a horn sounds!" Ysja cried. She turned back down the ladder.

Outside the horn incited the dogs to barking. Moira hurried down from the loft and saw Brigitta, anxious for Thorfinn's return, walking out the door.

"The men have returned!" she sang out excitedly.

Moira's own heart suddenly pounded with anxiety. Nervousness coiled and jumped in her belly at the thought of seeing Wulfsun again. One part of her wanted to climb the loft ladder and hide within the depths of the great chest, but the other half yearned to dash out and welcome him with open arms.

"Hurry, Moira, light the longfires and the lamps," prompted Ysja, nudging Moira aside as she rushed out the door. Moira sighed inwardly. She knew Ysja had a vested interest in this homecoming. Haki Gunnarson, the swordmonger, had left to the *Althing* weeks before with the others. Ysja had hinted to Moira of her affection for him. "Haki is the bravest and finest swordmonger in all of Hordaland," she declared.

It seemed Hordaland entailed only the Ravnings or Ysja knew few men outside, for in her estimation the bravest and the best of Hordaland resided wholly at the Ravnings.

And will not you run out to greet the chieftain of the bravest and the best? asked her swan self.

You know I long to. But I would find no greeting in his face—the enchantment is broken.

Her heart as heavy as ironstone, she filled the lamps and lit the fires. Soon the woodsy smells of pine and crackling fire would be overrun with the staleness of smoke and cloying smell of mead. The intricately carved high seats and long benches, now empty, would fill with sporting and feasting men.

She hung the banner. Then she lit a brass incense burner, which, by its exotic design, had found its way to the Ravnings on a Norse pirate ship, much like herself. Tasks finished, she left the tranquility of the hall.

It was poor timing on her part to leave just as a flaxen stallion with two riders on its back galloped past the hall. She could not mistake Wulfsun astride the horse, the fair Ran behind holding him tight with encircling arms. They looked like golden twins upon a golden steed.

The lessening of the afternoon sun no longer radiated across the fading landscape, and the chilly wind sent leaves twirling and grasses bending. Moira trembled as if the earth were shaking. Wulfsun's face was bronzed from days of sun, and his startling blue eyes were full of mirth.

Seeing him shattered Moira.

Rather than meet his indifference, she would have chosen to to be a rock or a tree. His rejection of her the night of the full moon leaped back stronger than before. Yet it was too late to retreat inside the feast hall. The prancing horse carried its riders up to her. Recognition jumped into his eyes, which met and held the flashing prisms of her own. His gaze leveled her worse than a blow. No matter how it appeared to the outward eye, he and she were alone in the whole of space.

Then Ran spoke and kicked her heels into the horse's flanks. The horse reared, taking his attention from her. Like an apparition, she stole back inside the feast hall.

Warriors, faces radiant in firelight, sat along trestle tables laden to overflowing with cheeses, dark crusty flatbrod, raw and smoked fish, oysters, pike, and salmon. Bending over the long fires, Moira basted reindeer and lamb, with thyme and berry of juniper. It took every inch of her will not to turn thirsty eyes upon Wulfsun, who occupied the high seat. She hated being slave to such longing.

Thorfinn and Ragnorvald the Law Speaker flanked his sides. Behind him his sword, Wolf's Claw, hung on the wall along with the other men's weapons. This traditional display gave the hall the aspect of a vast armory. Ran the Fair sat down from Wulfsun on the women's benches. Her silver hair fell braided in twin plaits intertwined with colorful silk threads and gold rings. At her white throat flashed the gold and emerald necklace Moira had chosen. She reluctantly admitted the necklace suited Ran's beauty. Moira fingered the waist pouch containing her own gifts that Wulfsun had given her in the market. Not a day passed that she did not take out the ice stone and admire its crystalline tranquility. She cherished the stone for its beauty, but more because it was a gift from Wulfsun.

Around Ran the highborn ladies, dressed in their finest linens, chattered pleasantly among themselves. Children ran merrily, playing tag and stealing tidbits from the tables. From behind, Moira felt a sharp yank on her hair. She turned to discover a child hiding beneath the table.

Ysja laughed. "He has never touched black hair before." Ysja's own hair was caught attractively in two ivory combs, gifts from Haki Gunnerson.

"Nor I such a white one," she replied, reaching over to tousle the child's snowy head. He let out a squeal of fright and ran to his mother's skirt. "I'm sorry," she apologized, but his mother turned her face away.

"She thinks you a Christian witch," said Ysja as she basted a joint of mutton. "Ran has put it about that you will bring ill luck to the Ravnings."

"Do you think this, Ysja?" she asked, hoping for one ally.

"You are my friend. If ill luck comes, I think another brings it." She said this looking hard at Bjorn Bloody Hair, who sat opposite. "Wulfsun has welcomed Bjorn to winter with us. He is outlawed from his own land."

"Why?" asked Moira, thinking he must have deserved the banishment.

"Many fear him, for he deals crookedly and has a fierce temper. He is a berserker, one who goes mad in battle." She leaned nearer, whispering in Moira's ear. "It is said he killed his wife. For this he was outlawed." Her words left Moira uneasy, and she inquired no further about Bjorn and his comrades, who guzzled endless amounts of mead.

Ysja nudged her. "Look, there is Haki! Does he look unhappy?" She saw no difference in his expression, but then these Northmen were not ones to carry their emotions on their sleeves. Quick to laugh but quicker to seriousness, they possessed stony faces that one would swear never formed a smile.

"Tonight I will not speak to him." Ysja's eyes sparkled with mischief.

"I thought you liked him best," Moira said, puzzled at Ysja's change of heart.

"I do!" She stood up and sallied past him without a nod. Still sullen-faced, Haki watched her speak to another youth.

She does not speak to him, but loves him? I do not understand this.

Mayhap 'tis a Norse custom to infuriate the one you love, volunteered her swan self. *Look to the high seat, the chieftain is heavy into his cups and with every mouthful his eyes stray to you. Like Ysja, he speaks not to the one he most wishes to speak with.*

I say the enchantment is broken, reiterated Moira.

I say, you can charm him anew.

In the world of men, charms and enchantments are costly. I have learned my lesson well.

Freedom is a dear price to pay for magic, but you need not use magic to charm him. You are a woman, he is a man. That is all the enchantment needed now.

Wulfsun pushed aside his barely touched platter of food and lifted his drinking horn for a passing serving girl to refill. While away he hoped he would overcome the swan witch's enchantment. He had not. Distance was not the remedy. In the past weeks at the *Althing,* even the king's courtly beauties could not distract his insatiable desire for her. Other women no longer aroused him, and he resented this. He resented her hold over him. As his icy blue eyes leveled on her, his temper simmered.

Mayhap he could torment her as she tormented him, he brooded. The night beneath the full moon had she not used sorcery to bring him to her arms? She wanted him, to be sure. He might toy and tease her passions as easily as she did his. He was not without sorcery of his own. If he was doomed by the enchantment, at least he would seek retribution.

Seeing her now, the fire still smoldered, yet he seemed more able to reason with his passion. After weeks of distancing himself, he now saw her as if anew. Moving through the hall, she readily lifted her hand to any task. He could not fault her for being lazy or ill-tempered. Her beauty had not diminished, though she wore the humble white tunic of a slave. He wished she wore the fine clothes he'd given her in Kaupang.

"Skald. Skald," came a roust. Wulfsun, welcoming the distraction, joined in.

"Let us hear your tales, Skald," he commanded from his high seat in a voice deep and true.

He watched the slightly built, gray-haired skald step forward with his harp. Hand fisted, he pounded the table and all around him followed his lead, honoring the skald with a round of table thumping. His poetic gifts were held in high esteem. With great aplomb the skald accepted their favor as was his due. He seated himself on the dais in the center of the hall and strummed a preamble of chords.

"Hear me, O ring bearers, and I shall sing of the three maidens. Urth is one named, she is the keeper of men's past. Verthandi the next, the maker of men's present. And Skuld the third, who knows men's future." Plucking the strings dramatically, in a voice melodic, tuneful, and pure, he seduced the hall into rapt attention.

"There were three warriors named Egil, Slagfith, and Volund. While hunting one day, they came upon three swan maidens on the shore of the sea."

At the mention of swan maidens, Wulfsun's bold eyes riveted again to the black-haired woman standing in the shadows of his hall. Merely looking at her sparked physical and mental shock waves to the depths of his earthly roots. This woman was not of his kith or kin, she was of another race, another kingdom, yet he wanted her without reservation. Would she be his downfall? Legends told tales of hapless men doomed by the enchantments of such women. Who had not heard of youths who passed between the dividing veil of the two worlds never to return, or strong men who wasted away with lovesickness? Wulfsun looked away from her, back to his untouched platter of food and obstinately forced himself to eat as he listened to the skald's tale.

"The fair young maids took the weather-wise bowmen to their arms. For seven winters they did sit, and in the eighth came the swan maids' longings. Volund, Slagfith, and Egil came home from their hunting to find the hall empty. Out and in they went, everywhere seeking. East fared Egil, and Slagfith south, but Volund alone in Ulgalir stayed awaiting, longing for his fair one to come home."

Wulfsun listened closely, wanting the courageous Volund again to find his swan maid, or at least to outwit her. Unfortunately, the skald left that portion of the tale untold. Instead, he sung of Volund's greatest battle and his heroic deeds. It was the first time in Wulfsun's life he was not mesmerized by a tale of battle. At the story's end, when the skald received hearty applause, he tossed him only one gold ring in tribute.

The thrall women returned to dipping flasks into the huge vat and moved up and down the tables filling horn after horn to brimming. They spoke the customary salutation of good health and long life to each man. The skald, disappointed by Wulfsun's tribute, took the dais once more and began telling a short saga designed to compliment his host for his prowess in battle and, naturally, his generosity.

"Upon his high seat sits the most dangerous warrior in Hordaland. To look at him one would not think it. He is young, but born old. When he takes a sword in hand, he greets death with a smile."

Wulfsun felt a shy pleasure as around him voices and horns raised in acclaim, "Wulfsun, wise overlord of the Ravnings!"

He watched the swan witch approach his high seat on her round of horn filling. His eyes raked over her features as she filled Thorfinn's horn and then his own. He willed her to look at him, but she did not.

"Say you no greeting to your chieftain, woman?" he reproved as he raised a silver-gilded horn to his lips.

Her eyes lifted boldly to pin his own. "I greet not he who speaks not."

His voice was level perfect and his piercing blue eyes looked straight at her as he lifted his drinking horn. He drank, but his eyes never left hers as the rim of his horn tipped up. "I need not speak to my thralls. But you must pay tribute to me."

"You are arrogant to expect it. Even so, I will speak tribute to you . . . on the day you set me free!" Her lips tightened in severity, and she looked past him as though he were a formless spirit and walked on.

Wulfsun near clamped his hand to the soft swell of her buttocks to halt her leaving, but beside him, Thorfinn choked on his mead, and he turned his hand to Thorfinn's shoulders. Once he had caught his breath Thorfinn gasped, "Mayhap were she a man, you could challenge her for disrespect."

He laughed aloud, ruing his ill luck, his eyes still following her. "Do not the legends speak of docile, sweet, and loving swan maids who give all to love? Why is it my great misfortune to become entangled with the one maid neither sweet nor docile but iron-willed and talon-tongued?"

"Don't say I didn't warn you," Thorfinn panted with laughter.

Wulfsun continued to watch her as she moved silently on her rounds about the hall. His eyes followed her graceful form as she dodged flying joints of meat and grasping hands. Her flask filled, she neared the bench of Bjorn. She skirted around in an attempt to avoid him, but he lurched and caught a swatch of her long hair.

Outwardly Wulfsun remained passive, but his teeth gritted as possessiveness overpowered his pretense of indifference. His fingernails gouged the table, and he slowly rose to his feet. He could not kill his friend Bjorn over a woman, but he could take the moment to exorcise his pent-up virility. "Bjorn, you use my thrall woman roughly." His voice cut through the roar. "There are other maids willing enough."

Bjorn's glazed eyes bulged drunkenly. "One slap and they are all willing!" He yanked her closer.

The sight of Bjorn touching her gripped him with a cold rage. The woman was his, and his alone. He jumped from his high seat and tossed off his scarlet cloak. "If it is sport you want, Bjorn. I am stiff from the sitting." Bjorn let loose of the woman's hair and rubbed his hands together, the blackness of his nature dispelled at the prospect of a wrestling bout. Men called bets and the matching of odds across the hall.

"You are too drunk to stand, Bjorn. I have won before I begin," he boasted with a dark laugh of pleasure.

"May your hawk foul your shoulder!" Bjorn returned, and hurled himself toward him. Within seconds Wulfsun captured Bjorn in a headlock and held him immobile.

Moira saw that some highborn women began to leave; the more sporting stayed.

"Thrall woman, I would have more drink."

Moira blinked at the command and turned to Ran the Fair. Ran sat chin high, looking very regal, an icy smile on her lips. "I would have more drink," she repeated, nodding to the horn at her elbow.

Moira stepped over and began to pour, but lifted her eyes to see Bjorn suddenly break away from Wulfsun's hold.

"Fool thrall!" cried Ran, jumping to her feet.

She looked down and saw the mead flowing over the horn's brim down onto Ran's lap. "I am sorry," she gasped. But Ran picked up the horn and tossed its contents into her face.

Backing off, Moira sputtered. Ran's hand seemed hardly to have moved, but suddenly she felt the sharp sting of Ran's palm across her cheek. "Leave here! Get out!" Ran spat with outrage.

Before she could attack again, Moira turned heel and left the hall. Feathered flakes of the first snow cooled the sting of her cheek as she burst out into the stillness of night. She closed her eyes, the welling tears slipped beneath her lids and down her cheeks. The wound of Ran's animosity ripped invisibly beneath her breast. She'd been manhandled, but never before in her life had she been struck. Boisterous shouts filtered from the hall as the brawl progressed, and she wondered how a gentle soul like herself would survive in such a world.

It is not fair.

I agree, it is going to be a long winter, returned her swan mind. *We should go into hibernation.*

Swans do not hibernate, though it would be a blessed relief . . .

The snow fell soundlessly, erasing all direction. She stepped into the chaste veil and disappeared across the center yard to the adjacent longhouse. As she moved, feeling her way along the wall to the doorway, she tripped over a mound of snow. It moved, then groaned. She bent down and brushed away the snow and touched a bearded face.

"Olaf? Is it you?" She felt the huddled body tremble with chill. "'Tis a cold night to lay out of doors." He did not answer. A gurgling sound rumbled deep within his chest and came forth in coughing spasms. She dragged his limp body along with her and finally reached the longhouse door. She pulled him inside and climbed to the loft for sheepskins to wrap him in. This done she tried to spark warmth into his skeletal hands and feet.

"Grandfather Frost has touched me," he rasped. "Do not trouble yourself. Why should the man live whom no one loves?" His pitiful frame rattled with each gasp.

"You are the Moon Mother's child. Her love gift to you was your soul's awakening and birth. Feel life's flow from my hands." Filled with compassion, she willed healing warmth into her hands and held them over his heart.

"Nay, I wish to die!" He fell into a spasm of coughing.

"Do not speak so."

"I am glad to die. The fates have deserted me. I am of the blood of Sigurd the Dragon Slayer . . ." He clasped Moira's hand so tightly she winced. "In my youth I was a great warrior. One even prophesied a Norn would bide with me at death." How soft his voice became. "About my waist . . . the Dragon Slayer . . ." He guided her hand within the ragged folds of his tunic, where she felt a dagger. "Some enemies no sword can kill, no fire can burn. . . . Take it." He coughed, retching with convulsions. Finally spent, he was silent. Feeling death's presence, she sat beside him in the darkness, listening to his breathing. She began to sing a separation song to ease his passing.

Before dawn he died, his hand clutching her own. She saw his spirit fly, spiraling out the wind eyes of the longhouse. She covered his body and left.

The snow had stopped, leaving the world covered in slumping mounds of white. Everything slumbered, innocent of the change across the valley. Even the whisperings of her own mind's harpies quieted, as if suddenly aware no one listened. She walked into the sublime silence of first snow, following upward the trickling stream which still meandered down from the heights of Ravnjell. Birches bent in mourning reached thirstily to the water's edge. In the shortening days the sun was a late riser, though the shroud of white washed the hills in its own eerie light.

She climbed the hillside to the largest of the stream-fed pools. She brushed snow aside and sat down on a boulder overlooking a pool so clear she could count the pebbles strewn across its depths. The tranquility freed her mind and healed her soul. This first snow, a virgin's blanket, warmed her, wrapping her in the security and solitude of the Earth Mother. In early forage a quail family scurried from beneath a snowy clump, and with them dawn awoke. The sun rose an opalescent pearl in the cloud-swirled sky.

Moira took Olaf's dagger from her cloak. She fingered its silver hilt inlaid with precious stones and felt sorry to receive this last bequest. For her it held no value and embodied all that was wrong in the world of men. She sensed something heavy and dull lying within it . . . a darkness. She dropped the dagger into a rock crevice.

Suddenly, amid a rush of wings, two magnificent swans sailed down from overhead. Back pedaling, they hung in suspension as their great wings flapped a tide of waves, which rippled the pool mirror. Settling down, they glided serenely, preening silk-soft necks arched hill high. Her heart swelled with welcome, and her swan self sang out to the mated pair.

"My kindred, I greet thee. From whence come ye?"

The pair glided to the pool's edge. "The great Northland. We are the last to fly before the Earth Mother turns her northern face to winter sleep. Rest ye here, sister swan?"

"Not by choice, by capture. A chieftain binds me by fire magic."

"There is no worse fate, sister," mourned one.

"Would we could give you our wings," consoled the other.

"I ask not for your wings, but carry one message to my grandmother. Know ye of Myr?"

"Myr of the dawning?"

"Myr of the everlasting peace?"

"Aye, my birth home. My grandmother, Epona, dwells there still, beside the lake of glass. Seek her and tell her of my misfortune."

Startled by a horse's neigh, with the swift reflexes of all things wild, they took flight. Before Moira could say more, like traveling spirits their powerful wings lifted them upward in a dance of flight.

Moira's eyes filled with tears. *Would that I could soar with them,* lamented her swan self.

Turning, she discovered the reason for the swans' sudden departure. Her eyes met the querulous gaze of Wulfsun. He sat on horseback not ten feet away, stroking his stallion's shaggy flaxen mane. Her nerves vibrated.

Silence held between them.

She could not speculate on his intent. It was time for milking, but the chieftain of the Ravnings would not come to fetch the truant milkmaid. Confused by his appearance, she moved down the hill past him.

Her eyes focused on the spirals of smoke above the longhouses below. *'Tis a chance meeting.* From behind she heard the heavy whinny and snort of the stallion. Glancing back, she was completely astonished to see him racing down the hillside. Snow sprayed in fountain plumes on either side of his stallion. Paralyzed, she stood aghast. He aimed to run her down! He did not slow his speed but leaned to the side of his horse. With a jerk that almost displaced her shoulder, he swooped her up with one arm. As he slung her sidelong in front of him, she shrieked her indignation and struggled wildly to leap away.

"By Hel's gates, woman, you are wild-limbed!" He swore as her thrashing nearly unseated them both. His arms tightened, squeezing her breath from her lungs. He reined the horse in and implacable blue eyes focused full force on her. She did not flinch but gave measure for measure, her most defiant glare.

He spoke with sharp clarity. "I'll not abide sorcery and scheming with your faerie kin. I am your master now! The life you had before is over. You are my thrall woman, my property by right of capture . . . and bond of magic." He continued, though she barely heard, so loud was her pulse pounding in her ears. "For your labors you'll receive food, shelter, and a fair life at the Ravnings."

She felt a crimson heat rise to her face. Rebellion filled her. She stiffened. Drawing herself up straight, she breathed deeply, "Fasten a hundred rings about my throat. Bind me with a thousand spells. I will bow to no man as master!"

To these brave words he said nothing.

She smoldered, wanting to break from his unrelenting hold.

He uses his strength to unfair advantage, she raged inwardly.

Swanling, it will always be so in the world of men, returned her swan mind. *Now, calm yourself. Your strength is not of arm, but mind. Reason with him. This one is not such a brute.*

Hah! 'Tis not your wings he crushes in his steel grip. 'Tis my spirit, something worse.

They passed between the gates of the Ravnings, and he pulled up his horse before the bower house. She moved to slide off, but he did not release her. Her fine jaw clenched, despite her swan self's counsel.

The long tapered fingers of one hand suddenly tilted her face toward his own.

"You waited death with the Man Biter?" he asked, looking at her with a relaxed face as if the previous exchange had never occurred. Refusing to answer, she tightened her lips and averted her eyes.

"Few will miss him, though it is said no man is so bad as to be worth nothing." He said this mainly to himself with his usual Nordic stoicism. "Brigitta is birthing, your healing powers may be needed."

Moira realized now why he had come to find her. Still refusing to look at him, she did not speak but waited resignedly for his grip to loosen.

Suddenly his warm mouth captured her own. At the touch of his lips, she inhaled with surprise, then held her breath in the sweet reunion of his kiss. She felt a surge of desire explode within her like a thousand bursting stars, but she refused to fully succumb to his demand. He nudged open her mouth as his tongue in a swift wet stroke invaded the seam of her lips, licking the ivory texture of her clenched teeth. Her eyes flashed open only to meet the glinting amusement in his own. He drew back slightly, his lids lowered sardonically.

"Thrall woman," he chided, his breath like fire on her skin. "A close-mouthed woman is worth having." His hands released her then, and not urgently he lowered her down off the horse.

Once in the bower house Moira paused, waiting for her eyes to adjust to the dimness. The flicker of the fire's shadows danced from one end of the longhouse to the other. She wondered at the unusual stillness, for the bower was the center of most household activities. At the far end Ran the Fair sat at the upright loom weaving webs and keeping hands busy while Ysja and two others hovered around Brigitta's wooden staved bed. Ran looked up when she entered, and for a brief moment their eyes clashed before Moira turned her gaze to Ysja.

"It started last night, but she told no one," whispered Ysja.

"Is she all right?" Moira asked.

"The first is always the hardest," assured Ysja, though Moira sensed she worried. "You stay in my place, I will do the milking." Ysja bit her lower lip and with one last anxious look, she left.

Moira stood watching old Halda. In a soapstone pestle she crushed valerian and golden seal with other herbs into a powder. She sprinkled the powder into a brew pot which simmered over the fire.

"Turn her on to her back," Halda instructed her. Carefully Moira tried to urge Brigitta on to her back, but she moaned and resisted.

"Why do you wish her to move in a way that pains her?" asked Moira.

"I must feel for the child's head," answered Halda.

"This I can tell you," announced Moira. Quickly she put her hands on Brigitta's swollen belly and closed her eyes, imaging the child inside Brigitta's womb. "The child is turned wrongly. His feet come before his head."

Halda's eyes narrowed. "How know you this?"

"In my homeland I am a healer."

Halda clicked her tongue. "I suspected it so . . . and more." Halda reached for some ropes and began tying Brigitta's arms to the bed staves.

"What will you do?"

"We must bind her so we can pull the child from her."

"Nay, I think not. I can turn the child."

"You?" Ran came near the bed, her lips tight. "How?" she asked, disbelief on her face.

"Painlessly, for both mother and child. See." And again Moira lay her hands upon Brigitta's belly and her spirit called to and then joined with the child within. Slowly she guided it into the birthing path.

Halda's hand probed the birth opening. Her eyes flashed wide. "The child comes!"

"At last!" gasped Brigitta thankfully.

"Quickly!" muttered Halda. "Someone fetch Thorfinn."

"I will go," offered Ran the Fair. She shot Moira an uncharitable look and left.

"It will be soon now," comforted Halda.

Oblivious to everything but her own travail, Brigitta panted rapidly, her chest heaving from the tremendous pressure to push forth the unborn child. Moira moved to support her back as Brigitta clasped her knees in a final thrust. After an outcry of relief, she collapsed backward.

Just as Halda accepted the head, the door opened. Ran entered, followed not only by Thorfinn, but Wulfsun, Ragnorvald, and others. Wulfsun's eyes traveled to Moira for a brief glittering second before looking to Brigitta.

No cry of life broke the air of anticipation. The small form lay limp. All looked on as Halda stood shaking her head sadly. "It was not soon enough."

Moira abruptly moved forward, taking the baby from her. She turned the purple lips to hers and whispered the breath of life into its tiny mouth. Then she called to its spirit by song. "I call thee to awaken to the circle of life. Life is flowing in thee. Thou art the dew of all the Gods, the eye of the Sun, the light of the Moon, the beauty and glory of the Sky, the mystery of the Earth. Awaken to the breath of life." Soon the small chest rose up and down. With a strangled cough he began to cry.

"Thank the Goddess, a male child, perfect in every way." Moira put the child on Brigitta's stomach and

128

smiled. The bower was uncommonly still. All eyes were on Moira. Many showed puzzlement, others suspicion. Her eyes met Wulfsun's, and in his penetrating gaze she witnessed a softening. Something passed between them that she could not explain and then it disappeared. Yet a loving and a knowing settled deep within her breast, and she knew that of all the men that walked the earth, she wanted him and him alone to sire her children.

Halda took a small dagger in hand and cut the bonding cord. She took the child from Brigitta and placed it on the raised hearthstone in the center of the bower. The child howled lustily, the poor wee thing having been wrenched from a perfect environment to this snowy winter's day.

Turning his back, Wulfsun placed a hand on Thorfinn's shoulder and spoke in low tones none could hear. After some thought Thorfinn walked over to the wailing child, bent down, and examined the small body closely. Using a forefinger, he tested the grip of the tiny fist. Finally he lifted the child into his arms and raised it high in the air.

"I see you to be my son." Approval showed in everyone's faces at his words. Ragnorvald the Law Speaker stepped forward with a silver vial in his hand. He poured the oil over the wiggling child.

"You shall be Eyulf, son of Thorfinn, brave in battle and strong of body and spirit. The Nornir have granted you life this day. Grow swiftly to meet your destiny." From his side Thorfinn took his sword and balanced the hilt upon the small pink chest.

"You own nothing but what you can win for yourself with this sword. I give you this, my greatest wealth." The small mouth attempted to suckle the sword hilt much to the approving humor of those surrounding.

"He will become a great warrior," foretold Wulfsun. All echoed in agreement, except Moira.

There is more to life than swordplay, she thought.

"This is a good omen, a death and a birth on the same night," reasoned Ragnorvald as he stroked his gray beard knowingly.

"If death is a feast, birth is an even greater feast," said someone else.

Then Thorfinn carried the child back to Brigitta, somewhat neglected after the show of ceremony. He put the child beside her, and she shone with the radiance of the Goddess.

Chapter | 9

Wulfsun crossed the open yard past sheaves of rye and barley bound and tied to tall posts as offerings to Odin's eight-legged horse who rode across the winter sky. His spirits were high as he anticipated the Yule festivities to come.

He strode up to the sweathouse at the rear of the Ravnings near the stream. He unfastened his baldric and hung his sword on a wooden peg. Easily he slipped out of his tunic and leggings. He winged his arms and rubbed his chest, feeling the nip of the cold winter air on his nakedness.

Jacob the Freed came up behind him. "Mayhap the sweathouse will purge my joints of winter gout. Each season my sword becomes heavier."

Wulfsun chuckled. "Enlist Haki to forge you a lighter one."

He opened the door and walked inside. Muttering a common greeting to Ysja, his eyes riveted to the swan witch at her side. His breath caught in his throat and desire swelled up inside of him. Even in the dim candle light of the sweathouse, this faerie woman's unclad beauty was a rare bloom among the loveliest flowers.

Since the birthing, her normal path was to avoid him.

But he did not mind, for he'd taken the time, through calm rational thinking, to form his strategy. He would drive her as mad as he was himself. He smiled at her in a lazy fashion. He knew he could magnetize her. At first it had been on her terms, now it would be on his. He would use every twist and turn of cunning to his advantage. Her eyes flashed surprise, but her lashes concealed the expression almost immediately.

Clouds of moisture hazed the air, and candlelight lit the dark walls. Jacob pushed in and sat next to her, forcing Wulfsun to seat himself opposite. In the cramped quarters he trapped her thighs between the V of his own. Her slim legs nudged this way and that in an awkward attempt to disentangle herself from his. The touch of her moist, hot skin against his cool thighs was like a brand. He tried to distract himself by speaking.

"Ysja will agree," he continued as the swan witch shifted with ill ease, not realizing she was making matters worse. "No swordmonger in Norway has Haki's skills."

"You speak truth, Chieftain," giggled Ysja, making no secret of her affection for Haki.

"Aye, Bjorn's sword is proof. I would be proud to unsheathe such a blade," replied Jacob.

Eyes downcast, the swan witch settled some. Bedevilment played at the corners of Wulfsun's mouth, for she had no option but to sit still.

He could not help but savor her beauty. Her hair was streaming down her back, falling around her shoulders like a black cloud of some ominous storm. He inhaled deeply and settled his thighs against hers. "A warrior could not do better," he said.

Ysja splashed water on the stones, and clouds of steam plumed as the temperature rose. Wulfsun's senses, disturbed by the subtle scent and nearness of the swan witch, ignited as well. His body was responding to her, growing tense and roused. He willed himself to relax. Reason and control were on his side, yet a hunger gripped his loins each time he felt her move or his eyes found her.

Jacob chuckled. "Aye, the sword will win Bjorn Bloody

Hair honor in battle and the warmth of a fair-faced maid."

"With an obedient sword, what warrior would not find battle joyous play? Even the holy woman might find bloodletting sweet with a feather-edged blade." The taunt in his voice was frank and undisguised.

He noticed the two points of Moira's cheeks flush red with fury. Her eyes locked with his own in challenge.

Ysja suddenly stood, moving to leave. "I must be about my work."

"I, too," announced the swan witch. He felt her legs gather to stand, and he clamped his thighs tightly against her own.

"Your work is here, thrall woman." In a sidelong glance, he gave Jacob an invitation to leave.

Jacob grinned and rose to follow Ysja out the door.

The swan witch refused to look at him, so Wulfsun looked at her as stillness and moisture hung in the air between them. Wisps of her hair plastered in tiny curls about her oval face and her lips glistened wet and ripe. His gaze slid lower down the curve of her swan-white neck to full breasts, nubbed with pearls of coral. So beautiful. His hands near reached out to slide down her smooth waist to the rounds of her hips. With mammoth effort he held himself back.

Instead he picked up a tied bundle of sapling twigs and tossed it to her. "I know you holy women prefer to flog yourselves, but I would have you swat my back. It quickens the blood." He lifted one foot to rest on the narrow bench, and he exposed his muscled back to her.

After a moment she said, "Before I begin I would like to ask you something."

He turned to her with interest, for she'd never deemed it necessary to ask permission to speak until now. "Speak."

"You know I am no Christian. Nor am I a holy woman. You call me thrall woman and think me swan witch. Why have you never . . ." Her words seemed to bind with emotion in her throat. ". . . in all this time, asked me my name?"

Suddenly he wondered so himself. "And have you

one?" He meant to be conciliatory, but even in his own ears his voice sounded condescending.

"Aye, I have. It is Moira . . . Moira of Myr. And I am tired of you speaking past me, around me, above me, and in particular . . . down to me. If you do not speak to me by name, I will ignore you."

"Have I your word that if I call you by name, you will not ignore me?"

Her eyes narrowed. "You would use my simple request to bind me to your bidding?"

"I would."

"Then forget my name. I will come only when I choose!" Her spine straightened defiantly, and she raised the sapling bundle to swat his back. Her hand flew forward with a vengeance.

"Ouch! By Loki's beard! Stop it!" He realized that he'd infuriated her. He caught her wrist and tightened his grip to pressure her to drop the bundle. "It seems I am not the only one capable of barbarity!"

"You asked for it." She stared at him, red fire shining in her eyes.

"Then I will ask for something more," he said huskily.

Raising up, he pulled her toward him and pinned her arms against his chest as she struggled to her feet. With one arm he held her, and grasped her hair with the other hand so she could not twist her face away. Her lips parted in protest, and like the warrior he was, he attacked full thrust, his tongue immediately slipping inside her mouth, subduing her protests. He intended to make the most of the moment, savoring her sweetness with gentle circling forays of his spearing tongue. He took his time, as aware of his manhood hardening against the soft hollow of her belly as he was of his tongue melting in the moist folds of her mouth. Her own tongue began to tentatively slide, tasting, then pausing almost hesitantly.

His nostrils flared with calculating satisfaction as he drew in breath. His tongue parried beneath, thrusting up in a licking motion challenging her in a sensual confrontation. He felt her palms relax against his chest, and then her hands slid beneath his arms to curl around his back.

He held her closer, reveling in the pressure of her soft breasts against his chest.

The kiss raced through Moira like fire. Between full moons she should be able to control herself, but not now. She smelled the smell of his sweat, male and musk, and she smelled the scent of her own nervousness. Pressed against his muscled chest her nipples began to tingle, and his rigid rod burned like a spear's point against her belly. His lips sealed hers, and the juices of his mouth were more life-giving than breath. His one hand let loose her hair and slid down across the slickness of her hips. Her own arms circled around his broad chest, and timidly her fingers explored the smooth muscles of his shoulders, and then more boldly she let her hands track down the warm heat of his muscled torso to shape his hard buttocks.

A low hum of pleasure trembled in his throat, and he shifted his hips to better mold himself to the juncture of her own. A giant of yearning flamed within Moira, more powerful than she could fight. Adeptly his large hands wandered freely, over her back and lower, to enclose her small waist. Then she felt the pads of his thumbs lightly stroke the hollow of her belly, moving lower down the angles of her hip bones. A slow liquid fire simmered in her loins, and a wave of expectant pleasure tingled through the dusky inner lips between her thighs. Lower, lower, explored his thumbs, tracing the outer edge of the dark silk fan of her woman's mound. He seemed in no hurry to ravish her, his movements slow and gentle. The dark memory of the night in Kaupang faded as she melted to his touch.

Suddenly his lips pulled back and left her gasping for breath. She raised startled eyes to his.

He studied her appraisingly. "With your wings folded, you are a tame dove," he whispered throatily. "But it is not so healthy to remain in here any longer. I would not have you faint in my arms." His hands on her waist, he turned her to face the door.

Moira knew not what to say, and she allowed him to send her out the door. All the while her body was near to collapsing from disappointment. Outside she snatched her clothes from the wooden peg.

He stopped her hands with his own. "Moira," he said deliberately, rolling the *r* with teasing mockery, "it is not good to put on your clothes so soon. You must cool off first."

"I will do as I choose," she said. She tired of him telling her what to do.

Then, with a lithe carelessness, he scooped her up in his strong arms. "Put me down!" she shrieked.

"If you wish it!" he shrugged his wide shoulders and tossed her into a deep snowbank.

"No!" she gasped and sputtered. "You have no heart!" she cried, scrambling to her feet.

With hands on hips in an insolent stance, he chuckled. "And you have no clothes!" he challenged tauntingly.

She was on her knees, glaring at him. He stood naked before her, a virile male animal with awesome confidence. Her eyes held his and then riveted down to the bold nest of his manhood. She lifted a dark winged brow wickedly and a slow smile curved her red lips.

"Nor do you." At her side her fingers imperceptibly moved to compress a small ball of snow in the cup of her palm which she suddenly threw at him.

"Hah!" He dodged expertly. "A man with no eyes could do better," he taunted.

"I do not believe it!" she challenged, closing both her eyes and taking blind aim. This second launch hit him in the groin.

He met this with bold laughter. "You are dangerous, woman!" Chest heaving, he came down beside her and leaned on one elbow. His long hair tangled with hers over the snow, and she felt his eyes make a slow appreciative tour of her feminine form. Her senses flared once again under his perusal. He scooped up a handful of snow and piled it on her warm belly. As it melted, it pooled in her stomach's concave. She gasped from the cold. Wulfsun bent his golden head to her belly and slowly licked away the moisture. He tongued the circle of her navel and sucked away the last droplet in a kiss.

When he lifted his head, his ice blue eyes burned.

Moira's nostrils dilated. She could feel the warmth of his body crossing the distance between them. She wanted him to take her in his arms and carry her off . . . anywhere where they could be alone. But he didn't touch her, he merely pursed his lips, lowered his head within inches of her right breast, and blew a white plume of warm breath across the taut pink nub. She inhaled sharply, and a light shudder rippled her shoulders and breasts.

Complacency touched his lips and he drew back. It was a display of his male potency as surely as the peacock struts or the rooster crows. He wanted her on fire and undeniably she was because she was sinking into the melting snowbank. Suddenly, a slow realization settled upon her. He was purposely fanning her desire, pushing her to the edge, and then stepping back. Why would he do this?

She scrambled to her feet and stepped to retrieve her clothes, saying, "I do not understand your ways."

To her back his low voice rumbled confidently, "You will learn."

By the light of the half-moon, Wulfsun looked down the hillside to his ships, lying sidelong, waiting for winter's end. From the feast hall he heard the blustering voices of his vikings as they drank, diced and gamed the winter's night away. Most nights he was content to sit around the longfires with them, but tonight his feet took him to the bower house.

Once inside, his eyes quickly found her, the one he now called Moira. Darkly mysterious—the name fit this faerie woman. With distaff in hand, she spun wool. Fitful firelight danced on her face. He chose a seat beside Ran, but maintained a clear view of Moira's face.

The skald enthralled everyone. He told his tale of Odin's ravens, Thought and Memory, who flew the earth by day and reported to Odin in Valhalla at sundown all they had seen. Wulfsun picked up a web of string. Two golden-haired children giggled in unison as he adroitly manipulated the threads around his fingers in cat's cradle, a ladder, and finally crow's feet. Patiently he retraced each movement so they could follow with their own string. When the tale ended, he caught Moira watching him. She quickly lowered her eyes.

"Thrall woman, your work is done," announced Ran the Fair suddenly.

Wulfsun's thoughts turned to Ran and wondered how far her protective jealousy might take her. He watched Moira dutifully wrap her spindle and place it on the basket of carded wool. From a peg, she took her crimson cloak, a match to his own. She went out the door like a shadow, but long after his eyes lingered on the door.

Ran touched his arm and spoke softly, "Chieftain, it is clear to me the thrall woman clutches your heart in her hand. In truth, is it by enchantment?"

He'd be a fool if he denied what all at the Ravnings knew already. Thorfinn would tell Brigitta and Brigitta would tell Ran. There was no end to gossip. His fingers raked the stray hairs off his forehead, and he shook his head somberly. "Mayhap."

Tears pooled in Ran's eyes, and he moved to wrap his arms around her in consolation. "Do not weep. It could be worse."

"I see not how."

He gave a false laugh. "She could be as ugly as the forest witch, Brunhild. At least this one is gentle-hearted and fair-faced."

"My Norse eyes can see no beauty in her darkness," mourned Ran. "She is a black swan who carries night upon her wing." Her hands grasped his. "Send her away."

"I cannot!" Resignation filled his voice.

He stood, leaving her with tears tracking down her cheeks. It wounded him to see her pain. He knew she loved him, had always loved him, but looking at her was like looking at all women since he'd fallen under the swan witch's enchantment. He felt no quickening of pulse, no rush of desire. Mayhap his affections for Ran had always been of a protective nature, no more than a brother for a sister. He paused a moment to admire the tiny Eyulf as he slept in the hanging cradle and remembered standing as a young boy by Ran's cradle, coaxing forth her tiny smiles. Then, giving the cradle a gentle push to set it rocking to and fro, he went out the door.

The cold air nudged him awake. His wolf, Gray Deer, stirred. The black-lined eyes followed him shrewdly. She was all wolf, thick-pelted, lean-flanked, and broad-shouldered. During winter she always came out of the mountains and abided the Ravnings only when he stayed in residence. The other roaming hounds gave the wolf a wide circle; even the children knew of her wildness and left her alone.

Wulfsun's eyes searched the yard and discovered Moira. She stood with her back to him, her face turned upward to the night sky. His long stride quickly brought him behind her. The northern lights sent quivering curtains of red, yellow, and green flowing like harp's music across the winter sky.

"The Valkyries ride this night, the flash of their armor tells of battle somewhere." Wulfsun's voice was husky with cold. She didn't turn to him but continued to look at the sky. "Do you know the star roads?" he asked.

"Aye, my grandmother taught me of them."

"Can you mark a path to your homeland?"

"My homeland I will never see again, unless you set one thrall woman free."

"And were I to do this, which path would you follow? North, south, east, or west?" he prompted with interest.

"East of the sun, west of the moon," she answered cryptically.

Laughing, he put his large hands on her shoulders and turned her northward.

"You see," he said, "look above Ravnjell, follow up from the highest peak. When too long at sea and lonely for our fjords and women, we turn our longships to the twelve stars that form the wings of the swan, and she leads us home. Mayhap someday she will do the same for you."

"Only if you free me."

"You ever circle back." He laughed. He felt her tremble beneath his hands from the cold. "It is cold. Come inside with me," he said. He encircled her in his arms and turned her toward the gargoyled entry of the feast hall. Firelight flickered between the timbers, speckling the snow with diamond dust. The voices from within filtered into the crisp night air.

He felt her resistance. "You hesitate." His words frosted white in the icy stillness.

"In my place you would do the same."

"In your place I would be eager!" He laughed, putting a firm hand on her and propelling her through the threshold.

So immersed in their nightly drinking bout, few heads turned to Wulfsun as he entered the hall. He left Moira at the foot of the ladder to the loft and climbed to roust out two sleeping men. One stumbled down the pole ladder, the other he prodded with his foot. The Viking rolled over the side and landed on the earthen floor below, still unconscious. Wulfsun leaned down and with a strong hand lifted Moira upward.

"Do you think he is all right?" she asked, still staring at the man on the floor.

"Have no fear. Einar will awake to drink again," he said, not letting loose his hold of her. "There is little to do in winter but warm the bones with mead."

"I can think of better things." Her voice held disapproval.

"Then our minds are the same," he answered with a hint of humor. She drew back, one foot falling out from under her in open air. He caught her. "Be careful or you'll find yourself beside the resting Einar." Not one to miss an advantage, he pulled her closer and felt the pulsing of her heart against his breast.

"I did not come here by free choice. Might I leave?"

He remained pleasant. "You think I am a barbarian. I will not prove you right." He took his hands away. "Go freely." With a careless shrug he turned and tossed off his red cloak. Then he bent over the open chest and brought out the harp. Absently he strummed his fingers across it like a rich man flaunts food before the starving. As he expected, given the chance she did not bolt. She eyed the harp covetously.

"Do you play?" she asked.

"No. 'Tis good company if one has the skill."

"I play," she admitted.

"In truth?" He pretended surprise, though Ysja had proved the tattle early on. He offered the harp to her. "Play then."

She still hesitated.

"I came by it fairly. Not all of my possessions are pried from cold fingers." His eyes lost their mockery and his face sobered.

An unwilling smile touched her lips.

She sat down on a cushion, and soon gentle melodies floated through the air. Sipping mead, he listened and watched.

"By allowing me to go freely, you have not changed my opinion," she retorted curtly, but her eyes were on the harp.

To this he raised a golden brow. "You are honest, but should you not forgive your enemies?"

"I can forgive you without changing my opinion. You remain a barbarian. No amount of forgiveness can change that."

He laughed outright.

She straightened indignantly. "As long as you kill, loot, and plunder you are a barbarian."

"For us plundering is an honorable profession, so long as it is done outside home waters. It may not be so east of the moon and west of the sun, but it is the way of life here. You know little of the world, being fey . . . and a woman. There is so much fighting among the Britons that a viking raid is cause for rejoicing, for one's neighbor is weakened and becomes easier prey. Have you forgotten your adventure with the Britons?" he asked, pressing home his point.

"No, I have not forgotten."

"I have done you a favor, one you may never concede." His face was no longer humored.

"Is it a favor to enslave someone lifelong?"

"No more than it is to enchant someone with love sickness lifelong!"

She opened her lips to speak, "'Tis—" and she then seemed to think better of it.

"Speak freely," he prodded.

"I . . . I do not understand you. Once you learned of the enchantment, I became invisible to you. The night of the full moon you despised and cursed me . . . and then today you—"

"Near took you in the sweathouse," he finished for her. "Mayhap I've chosen to give in to the sorcery."

"But why now and not before?"

Her innocence astounded him. "Like you, I value free choice."

Worry tinged Moira. She knew whatever vices this Northman had, he did not lie. He thought he was still enchanted, and if he gave in to its imagined sorcery, he would cling to her till doomsday. She never would be free. Suddenly, in the muddy mire of it all, she realized, full moon or no, she could not encourage him.

"Thirsty?" he asked.

Her mouth felt dry with uneasiness, yet she said, "No," suspicious that he would try to weaken her will with strong drink. She'd seen the other vikings do so to serving maids before. Instead, she turned her interest back to the harp. Sipping mead, Wulfsun watched her hands with a critic's eyes.

"Know you a tune more cheerful?" he asked when she paused.

Slightly offended that he did not give the praise she expected, she said, " 'Tis a sea beast's song. Your life is at sea; I thought you would like it."

He put down his horn to stretch out on the sleeping furs. "And what do sea beasts have to sing about?"

"Very little, as long as men think it necessary to hunt them down. Mayhap that is why they are so mournful."

He grinned. "Play what you wish. Who am I to stop you?"

Moira plucked two strings back on pitch, in truth wondering who he really was. She finally asked, "Is it true you are a wolf child?"

He gave no immediate reply. She may have broached too far. She was careful to keep her eyes on the harp, but presently she looked up, meeting his considering appraisal.

"As true as your home is east of the sun and west of the

142

moon," he countered, making it clear two could play the game.

"Were you suckled by woman?" Still looking at him, she saw genuine amusement glint in his blue eyes.

He chuckled. "What has Ysja been telling you?"

"She has told me how you became chieftain of the Ravnings and that you are a wolf child."

"So Ysja thinks I am a wolf child." He smiled, lifted the horn to his mouth, and took a long swallow. Then the amusement left his eyes and his face sobered.

Moira had never known him to be so talkative and could not refrain from asking, "Are you?"

His face reflected deep thought, and it was a long moment before he spoke. "I remember very little of my childhood before I came to the Ravnings. I remember darkness, a woman's screams—and crawling through snow . . . I was cold and crying. Then I remember wolves sniffing and licking my face and circling me with their warmth. That is all."

"Nothing more?"

"Only that my neck hurt—and with good reason." He turned and lifted aside his hair for her to see. "Small scars circle my neck. My foster mother believed the marks were left by the sharp fangs of the wolf who brought me to the Ravnings."

Moira leaned forward and peered wonderingly at his neck. "It must be so."

No wonder he is such a barbarian, concluded her swan self. *Abandoned and dragged about by a pack of wolves.*

Aye, it explains much. I am sorry for him.

Despite herself, Moira reached over and her fingertips gently traced the ragged scars across his skin. He turned back to face her, and her hand remained looped around his neck. Their noses were within inches, his scent sweet in her nostrils, and his breath a warm wind on her lips. His eyes penetrated hers and his lips dropped open. Her heart cartwheeled in her chest as her own lips parted expectantly.

"You are lucky to be alive." She tried to keep her voice steady, but a telltale tremor made it waver.

His lips brushed the tip of her chin. "I am a survivor,"

he said softly, lightly pressing another feathery kiss on the tip of her nose.

Her fingers tightened on his neck, and she swallowed back the heat creeping up from her chest. "You must have many tales to tell."

"Many." His mouth hovered for one vexing moment, and then gently touched the point of one rosy cheek, then the other.

Moira dropped black-lashed lids and slowly released a pent-up breath. "I would hear them."

Though her sight was veiled, she was vividly aware of his hand circling her waist as he pulled her close. The harp fell aside from her lap with a muffled thwang. She felt his sanded cheek press against hers as he nuzzled her ear. "It is said among us that only a dullard tells all, nor does a wise man tell a woman his past."

He caught the lobe of her ear between moist lips, and the banked fire of Moira's desire exploded in a shiver that streaked to the tip of her toes. Could she find her voice she might agree. She cared only that his lips at last smothered hers. A moan trembled in her throat, but before she could sound a second, Wulfsun's mouth, hard and warm, deserted her.

Her eyes flew open and collided with the straightforward study of his own. The spokes of his pupils shifted imperceptively. His thumb stroked the hollow beneath her lower lip, and then his fingers fell away. "I would have you play and sing to me now." His hand slipped from her waist, and he leaned back comfortably, watching her from half-lidded eyes.

Stunned, she forced herself to stop staring. Her desire flailed like a wounded gull, and she understood he'd purposely kindled a fire he had no intention of burning. Running her tongue across her lower lip, she averted her eyes. Without a word she took refuge in picking up the discarded harp and valiantly fought back the tears that stung her eyes.

No longer enchanted, he seeks a cruel revenge, counseled her swan side.

Aye, he preens me to soar, then tethers me to earth. Yet never once while he bore the enchantment did I withhold

144

myself from him. Too well I know the longing of full moon's passion to deny another fallen to enchantment's heat.

Her fingers slowly plucked out her misery, and she played her faerie melodies late into the night. The voices below had long since fallen silent. The chill in the air slowed her hands to one last chord, which hovered in the stillness like a gliding gull before swooping down to land. The fish-oil lamp cast a faint light, illuminating a small sphere around Wulfsun, and left all else in shadow. As he slept, she wondered what images, if any, her songs conjured for him. Looking at the sleeping stranger beside her, she saw the ruthless lines relaxed, the mocking blue eyes closed. His face, unguarded, left his soul open to her scrutiny.

And what see you, swanling? asked her swan mind.

I see only what I wish to see.

And what is that?

An innocent. I sorrow for the foundling child, for the youth whose only sense of worth was proof of manhood. And lastly, for the man a law unto himself.

Be careful, daughter, in seeing only what you wish. For when you press him to your breast, you take not child, but man—a man who seeks revenge upon your heart.

Chapter | 10

"Wake up, Moira!" Below, Ysja tapped loudly on the rafters with a stick. "I have already done the milking while you sleep."

Just another minute, thought Moira. It was so warm inside her sheepskin cocoon.

"Moira!" Ysja stood there, shaking her awake. "You cannot sleep—there is work to do." She climbed into the loft and ruthlessly yanked off the covering.

"Ysja, that is cruel," she whimpered as the cold air shocked her awake.

"Do you think a beating is kinder? That is what happens to the lazy thrall." Ysja knelt down beside her and in a furtive voice asked, "Moira, you must tell me what happened!"

"What do you mean?" she asked innocently, all the while knowing what Ysja wanted to hear.

"You were with Wulfsun last night. We saw him follow you from the bower house." She leaned closer expectantly. "Moira, there is not a woman in Hordaland that would not crawl into Wulfsun's bed."

Moira grimaced with exasperation. "More likely you mean there is not a woman in Hordaland who's bed he hasn't crawled into! There is nothing to tell, Ysja."

"Speak truly. I am your friend," pleaded Ysja. "They say . . ." Her voice lowered, and then she clasped Moira's hand in apology. "Do not hold what I have to tell you against me. I am only repeating what I heard this early morning in the bower house."

"What is it they have said, Ysja?" Moira no longer fretted over the cold and sat upright.

Ysja took a deep breath and rattled off hastily, "They say you have cast a spell of enchantment over him."

Her face fell. *I should have confessed to him the enchantment had ended.*

And lose your power to bargain? countered her swan self.

As long as he thinks himself enchanted he will despise me. Any tender feelings blossoming in his heart his spite will crush. I was wrong. . . . "We were wrong," she muttered aloud.

Ysja's eyes looked around in confusion. "We were wrong? Moira whom are you talking to?"

She threw off the sleeping skins. "Myself!"

"Moira, you did not answer me," said Ysja to her back.

She turned. Her brows knit as she weighted the wisdom of telling Ysja everything. She knew it would be unfair not to. She could not let her friend be the last at the Ravnings to know. Sighing, she began, "Ysja, I am not like you. In my homeland we are both woman and swan."

"Moira, you are a swan maid?" Her eyes blinked in amazement. "I don't believe it!"

"It is true, Ysja. And it happens that the first time a man kisses one of us, he becomes enchanted. It happened to Wulfsun. . . . "

Shock mottled Ysja's fair face. "This sounds like the tales the skald sings!" Her wondering eyes scoured nearly every inch of Moira as if searching for a feather. "Can you become a swan . . . now, for me?"

She frowned and shook her head sadly. "Yes and no. When Wulfsun put this collar around my neck he bound me to the earth. I cannot fly."

Ysja reached out and clutched her hands in sympathy.

Tears welled in her eyes. "Oh, Moira. I cannot bear it. I knew you were different, but . . . this . . . ." Her hand flew up and touched the golden torque on Moira's neck. A serious look came over her face. "I will ask Haki to take off your collar. He is the ironmonger. We can do it late at night, when no one sees."

Weariness touched her voice. "It would not come off. That is the way of magic, the one who binds must also unbind."

"Then what will you do?"

"I will do as I have been doing . . . wait and hope the chieftain has a change of heart."

"Well, it is not all bad. I would not mind enslaving the hearts of men with my kisses." Her bright eyes widened at the thought. "Anything I asked for would be mine—jewels, fine gowns. If I tired of one man, I would kiss another. I would need only to snap my fingers—"

"Ysja, before you spend the day dreaming, look at me. Am I so happy? Does Wulfsun run when I snap my fingers? No, Ysja, do not wish for it. 'Tis a curse to enslave the will of another."

Ysja pouted. "I was only supposing, Moira."

Moira managed to curve her lips in a tolerant smile. She sighed. "Come, we have much work to do for the Yule feast."

"It is too bad," said Ysja climbing back down and picking up a bucket of milk. She motioned to Moira to carry the other one.

"What is?" asked Moira.

"That you cannot use your magic to make the animals milk themselves, then we both could lay abed."

Giggling, they left the thrall house and crossed the snow-piled yard to the bower. When they entered, the domestic murmur of conversation paused, all eyes turned to Moira. The air hung heavy with gossip, and she knew she was the focus. A freeborn girl, Gunna, who sat beside Ran the Fair at the loom, continued speaking.

"She has put other spells on the household," she accused. "One day after the chieftain returned with her, the churning of butter soured."

Ran silenced her with a word, then turned her eyes to Moira and said, "Thrall woman, fetch kindling."

She set down the milk, welcoming the opportunity to leave. Outside, when passing the feast hall, the previous night came to her mind. Her mouth moistened at the thought of Wulfsun, but she swallowed back the wanting and walked toward the mountain of wood behind the hall. Turning the corner, she heard the rhythmic crack of the chopping ax. Freezing in mid-stride like a rabbit spying a fox, her eyes collided with the sweaty expanse of Wulfsun's bare back. With each swing of the ax, his muscles rippled and knotted. The sweat steamed off his body in the frosty air. Strands of his hair, bound back in a long tail, clung to his slick shoulders. Her breath halted, and she backed away step by step.

Suddenly he turned and spied her. "Sweet morning, Moira," he greeted, rolling her name engagingly over his lips. His eyes were as blue as a summer sky. He stepped toward her.

Her eyes riveted to the ax still in his hand. His own eyes followed hers, and then a deep chuckle trembled through him like an earthquake. "Mayhap you are thinking I'm wanting roast swan for Yule feast." He leaned the ax against the stump. "Do not think I am not tempted."

Offended, her eyes flashed vivid from the insult, and she turned heel to leave. Someone else could fetch the kindling and face his taunting. Before she could dodge him, he moved quickly, hooking her arm. He trapped her between himself and the feast hall.

"I have angered you." His face softened in repentance. "I am a warrior, and oft times insensitive," he said gently. "What is your errand?"

"Kindling," she said curtly.

"Kindling," he repeated, his voice sounding disappointed.

"If you thought I searched for you, I did not. I have better things to do than shadow you about all day."

"Better things?" he asked mockingly. "What is better than cutting across the open yard to glimpse my passing, or setting your path to collide with my own?"

Her jaw tightened firmly, and the burn of temper touched her rosy cheeks. Where had he learned such conceit?

He tried again. "Mayhap you might offer to take another's duty to be near me in the feast hall."

"You are arrogant to think it."

"I did not think it" His teeth flashed white in raw honesty. "I hoped it."

Her anger melted. During the weeks he'd ignored her, had not she hoped the same of him? Each day just the sight of him left her as expectant as the violet twilight of winter's perpetual dawn.

A horn echoed across the hills. He stepped back and scanned the distance of the gray fjord and spied a square-sailed boat navigating the water.

"Who comes?" she asked. Her eyes made out at least six people in the boat.

"Kinsmen from Olvirsted for winter feast."

"Is Olvirsted near?"

"Not so far by boat, and in summer when the ice road has melted, an easy ride over the southern mountain. I must welcome them." He strode down toward the fjord.

Moira turned to follow, but then turned back, remembering her errand. She filled her arms with wood and rushed to the bower house. She met Ysja in the doorway chattering excitedly.

"Hurry, Moira, put away the wood. Let us go down to greet them." Her enthusiasm infected Moira, and she dumped the wood beside the longfire. Ysja caught her hand, and together they hastened down the hillside. A brisk walk took them to the water's edge as the boat bumped ashore. It was a beautiful craft, a dragon ship in miniature with forbidding figures carved in gleaming wood sweeping fore and aft.

"I would like to ride in such a vessel," announced Ysja. She pointed to a tall man stepping from the boat. "He is Olvir the Shipbuilder. He made the boat as a gift for his wife, Freya." Still seated within were two women, one blue-eyed and clear-skinned with a constant charitable smile. Moira decided she was Freya, for the other woman was much older, wizened and wrapped in black furs. Her attitude caught Moira's curiosity.

"Who is that?" She tried to draw Ysja's attention away from her open stare of one young man leaping from the boat. Alongside him two little boys and a young girl jumped out.

"Kari, the eldest son of Olvir. He is handsome," she said decidedly. Moira agreed he was eye-catching, a mirror of his white-haired father's youth. His cheeks were red and his nose tilted slightly at the end. Well-built, his body moved with a youthful lankiness.

"Ysja, for just a little time take your mind off men. I meant the old woman. Who is she?"

"You should not scold me, Moira. I cannot freeze my feelings as easily as you."

"I do not," returned Moira, slightly defensive. "I wish I could, Ysja. Now, who is the old woman?"

"She is a spakonna. She is wise and foreknowing. Spakonnas travel through the land prophesying at feast time. You know," Ysja said thoughtfully, "last Yule feast a spakonna prophesied I would gain my freedom."

"That would be wonderful. Did she say how?"

"No," Ysja returned, "but I know it will be my fate to be a freed woman. Then I will marry Haki, and our children will be freeborn."

"You could marry him now. He would take you. If you wait for prophecy, you may be an old woman," Moira advised, thinking Wulfsun would never let free any of his thralls.

"A thrall woman's children are thralls. It makes no difference if the father is freeborn, that is our law. Haki would not want his children to be thralls." A faint shadow passed across Ysja's gentle brow, and inwardly Moira anguished for her.

Her eyes fell with resentment on Wulfsun as he welcomed Olvir the Shipbuilder to the Ravnings.

Olvir met him with a hardy slap on the shoulders, while Freya encircled him in her arms with motherly affection. The old spakonna, her lightless eyes peering from behind a woolen hood, remained ignored. After a time Kari gave her an arm for support. He lifted her and the young girl onto a sled and pulled them up the hill to the Ravnings. Ysja and Moira followed, turning back to the work at hand, for there was much to prepare for the Yule feast.

Soon after, Moira was sent to the feast hall with a bowl of barley porridge and a cup of curdled goat's milk for the spakonna. She paused in the doorway to seek direction and watched the newcomers mingling around the hall. She saw Kari arm wrestling with Jacob the Freed, while his father, Olvir, held the complete attention of Wulfsun, Bjorn Bloody Hair, and Thorfinn. He spoke with animation over a small-scale wooden ship on the table in front of them.

Another thrall pushed her forward as he entered with a tray of dried figs, nuts, and honeycomb. Eyes still searching, Moira discovered the spakonna off in a corner. Her shrouded form was specterlike in the smoky haze. Moira approached her curiously. She welcomed Moira with a half grin, exposing the two or three teeth left her. She sniffed the porridge and daintily removed woolen gloves, then held the bowl close to her lips. With two fingers she quickly scooped the food into her mouth. Moira waited for the empty bowl, eyeing her highly ornamented clothing. Embroidery circled her waistband, which was inlaid with stones of green and amber. Pouches hung from her belt.

Moira reached for the emptied bowl and turned to leave.

"Do not leave, Skuld," she commanded.

Facing her again, assuming her eyesight was bad due to her age, Moira said, "You mistake me for another."

"I do not mistake. It is your own eyes that do not see." Lowering her woolen hood, she exposed white hair wound atop a palsied head. Someone stirred and wooded the longfires. Soon spark and light blazed forth, momentarily chasing away all shadow at the end of the hall.

"Epona!" Her mouth dropped open and she saw for the first time who the woman was. "Grandmother!" She fell into her grandmother's opening arms. "How did you—"

"The swans carried your message," said Epona with pleasure. Relief flooded over her, and she took Epona's spidery fingers into her own. "I feared for you. That night we heard your cry and saw you fall from the sky. We all looked, but found only bloodied feathers and no trace of you. I have agonized these past months." She kissed Moira's cheek.

"But your teeth? Your beauty? What has happened to you?"

Epona chuckled with the glee of an old hag. "I'm in disguise. A spell here, a charm there. Child's magic."

"Did the swans tell you that fire magic binds me?"

"Aye." She shook her head slowly and patted Moira gently.

"I might as well be dead!" said Moira, frowning.

"Nay, you have just stepped upon your life path," she assured softly. "Now, what of this warrior who binds my swanling?"

"He is here. . . ." She turned and raised her finger to point him out.

Epona stayed her hand. "No need. I knew him at first sight. When he came to greet our boat, I saw him to be a golden child adopted by the wolf clan. *Otherwise he could not bind you.*"

"'Tis true. I did not realize until now, but yes, on his neck he bears the fang marks of the wolf clan. This one—"

"This one binds you with more than magic, swanling," cut in Epona cannily. "I think he stalks your heart and closes in." Her eyes narrowed to pinpoints, and her lips sealed with knowing.

"Aye . . . Grandmother," said Moira, her voice deeply troubled.

That instant Wulfsun's voice rumbled across the hall. "Thrall woman, bring drink." There were half a dozen thrall women in the hall, but all knew which thrall woman the chieftain wanted, so none turned to serve him. As Moira turned, she knew when she saw Wulfsun's face, examining and shrewd, that he had watched their reunion. While Thorfinn and Olvir had backs to her,

Wulfsun had full view from his place, enabling him to make of it what he might.

Obediently she served him his drink. He studied her face point by point as she poured full his horn.

"The beam secured in this way would give the belly of the ship greater depth," continued Olvir. He pointed to his ship's design, not aware that Wulfsun's attention was elsewhere.

His cup filled, she turned to go and bumped squarely into the son of Olvir. Beside him, Einar, brother of Bjorn Bloody Hair, gave her an affable leer.

Kari stopped her retreat by taking her chin in his hand and studying her face. His ale breath was warm upon her cheek. She could understand Ysja's interest in him, for he was pleasing to look at, with flint-gray eyes set in a youthful, beardless face. "This thrall I do not know," he announced.

"Nor shall you." Wulfsun's voice cut slick the air.

Kari's hand dropped as if her skin were on fire, and a rakish grin, fit to crack his face wide open, covered the wound of Wulfsun's warning.

Moira pushed past him. She bumped into two boys, one thrall-born, known as a bully, and the other, Olvir's youngest son. The pair locked together in a pummeling fight.

"Kari, your little brother, Sverr, is getting his guts juggled," said Bjorn, laughing as he rose for a better view.

The men stepped quickly to form a circle around the fighting boys and enclosed Moira as well. They shouted random taunts and cheered whoever was on top. Bested, Kari's brother, Sverr, backed away, a red stain streaming from his nose. To her amazement, Olvir, his father, pushed him back into the circle toward his opponent. Even the thrall boy looked hesitant, but the men would not let it end a draw. They set them to each other time and time again.

She had enough. "Are you so bloodthirsty you encourage little children to tear each other apart before your eyes?" she challenged the men around her. Then she took a step to intervene, but Wulfsun's arm shot out and held her back.

"They must learn to finish what is started," he said coldly.

"They are boys in a children's quarrel."

"Boys become men." A certain intentness deepened in Wulfsun's eyes. Was he thinking of his own lost boyhood? "*Wulfsun was just a boy when he killed Njial the Gray . . . men still speak of the boy's courage.*" Ysja's words echoed in Moira's memory.

"Aye, boys do become men. But if they are not taught as boys to settle their differences peaceably, then as men they will fight like boys!"

Wulfsun still held her, though his grip had loosened. The boys rolled over and over and bumped against her legs. She bent to them and gently laid the palm of her hands onto their heads. She willed the peace within herself to flow into them. Suddenly the bully's fists relaxed, and the other child took the moment to flee the circle by crawling between the legs of his brother Kari.

Around her, Moira felt the room grow colder, felt the viking's hostility turn on her. Her eyes level, she managed to weather their dark looks. She read more of their thoughts than she wished. The circle tightened. The air was thick with anticipation and aggression which no amount of calm within her would dispel. Suddenly she felt Wulfsun's hand on her. He broke the circle by stepping aside and yanked her along beside him as he left the hall.

Outside, he thrust her against the timbered wall. "Never interfere in the affairs of my vikings again! Had I not been there, you would have been the one fallen victim to their sport."

"'Tis not sport but brutality! I do not understand you." She placed her hand on his chest. "If you had no heart, I would understand. But I feel its beat."

He brushed away her hand as if to deny his heart's existence. "A man's heart is not the same as a woman's."

"I do not believe it!"

"Believe it!"

"What demons possess you?"

In the echo of her question she heard crying. Wulfsun's head also riveted to the sound. Unnoticed until then, huddled in the threshold of the doorway, was little Sverr, sobbing. Wulfsun moved and knelt to him. "A warrior does not cry," he said, not unkindly.

Moira was beside the child, her arms reaching to assure him. "If it hurts he should cry. Why else have tears?"

"Then you tend to his tears and hurts. I have no stomach for it," he growled, raising up to return to the feast hall.

"You have stomach enough to spill the blood of your enemies," she muttered to his back.

His hand gripped the door latch. She saw the line of his shoulders tense. *He wants to strike you.* She steeled herself for the blow. Instead, she caught a mumbled oath . . . something about "stomach enough to cut out a shrewish tongue." He disappeared inside.

She scooped up Sverr into her arms and carried him toward the bower house. "You are bold-spirited," she encouraged. "It takes more backbone to walk away from a fight than to stay."

He looked at her doubtfully from a swollen eye and sniffled. "They will call me maid Nanna and send me to sew and spin with the old women."

"Have no fear. Laugh in their faces. Remind them of Elli, the old woman whom the skald sings of, the one who outdid Thor in a wrestling match in his own hall."

"Mayhap that is so." His brows knit in tentative contemplation, and he snuggled more comfortably against her breast.

Chapter 11

Moira hummed to the harper's music as she circled the trestle tables laden with meats, cheese, breads, and fish. In her mind's eye the melodic cadences took to partner the dancing flames of the longfires as she served highborn women who ate delicately and sipped moderately. Around her, warriors spoke of luck and battle as they drank horn after horn of mead. It was an uncommon night, one of open fellowship. Even Wulfsun joined the joviality as he moved through the hall greeting and speaking with his guests.

Moira's gaze caught the eye of Epona, who sat on the dais drinking a broth of special preparation. Sitting regally, she awaited the ceremonial ritual of the Yule feast. From across the hall Moira sent her grandmother a warm smile. Epona did not smile in return, but sobered her face in pretentious gravity. Putting down her emptied cup, Epona raised aloft a knarled birchwood staff which rested against her knee, and she tapped the rafter beams for attention. A knowing smile curved Moira's lips, and she shook her head, amazed at her grandmother's artful disguise.

Suddenly Wulfsun's raised voice silenced the harper in

mid-song. "The time for the Yule seid has come," he announced. A stillness crossed the hall. "The spakonna shall loose her tongue for each who wishes to know his fate. I reward her well for this visit. You may do the same according to your liking of her words."

Moira watched as the women rose from their benches, coming together to form a circle around Epona. Clasping hands, they began to sway and hum. Epona's eyes circled the ring, pausing on the fire-flushed face of each singing woman. Then she lifted her hand for silence.

"Where is the dark-haired thrall woman?" An uneasy murmur rippled from the women.

I stand here in plain sight.

I wonder what mischief she brews? her swan self puzzled.

She plays her part too well. Remember the time she changed all the periwinkle flowers from blue to scarlet for a season because some invaded her herb garden? She's never predictable.

"Bring her!" Epona demanded.

"The old hag has taken a liking to you," came Wulfsun's voice beside Moira. "Mayhap she means to make you her apprentice."

Moira felt his hand on her elbow and she jumped. He was too close to the mark. "Can I count you as patron?"

"My needs go beyond a charm or chant," he muttered, and firmly propelled her into the center of the hall.

Her appearance was not well met by Ran the Fair. "She is a foreigner and knows not the songs of fate," imposed Ran with ill-concealed anger.

"She knows enough," replied Epona with an impatient wave of her skeletal hand. "She will stand with you. She has great favor with the spirits who give us help this night."

Breaking hands, Brigitta and the wife of Olvir took Moira into the circle. The humming began again, working itself into a vibrant chant marked by rhythmic thigh slapping by the men as they sat in place. With the soft sweetness of a ruby-throated bird of spring, Moira broke into full-voiced song. One woman after another followed her lead. They sang rounds whose echoes resounded off the time-scored log beams above and vibrated into the dark earthen depths below, summoning the sleeping souls from earth's beginnings.

Moira found herself swirling in the pulsing rhythm. Knowing the primeval utterances that loosed men's spirits from the earth, her voice led the runic strains and harmonies. Before her eyes ghostly specters crowded the hall, men and women of noble visage ornamented in golden crowns and flashing jewels. The ancestors of the high and low born of the Ravnings celebrated life's continuity beside their descendants. They stood within the dancing flames of the longfires and wove in and out as a weaver's weft between trestle tables, linking past to present.

The women's circle became a whirligig, and the hall's faces floated past Moira's, faces known to her mingling with those of phantoms. . . .

So queer did she feel. She floated above and looked down on herself below.

"She is fainting." She heard Brigitta's voice.

From above she watched Wulfsun's arms encircle her. Then his essence enfolded her, grounding her to earth. Her weightless hands clung to his solidity. He moved her from the ring of women, past the battle-clad warriors and golden-crowned phantoms, away from the heat of the flaring longfires into the outskirting shadows of the hall. She leaned into his arms for support.

"You feel light as a feather. I vow you will not shape-shift on me this night." His eyes fleered into hers.

Firelight swirled in her own. "I will not. 'Tis useless, for you bind me well."

"As you do me." He tilted his head, brushing his lips across her brow and down to her ear.

Where his lips touched, sensation returned. Her ear felt as radiant as a rising star, but the rest of her still floated. She buried her face in the crook of his neck and turned her mouth to kiss gently the hollow of his throat. She nuzzled her lips against him to seek the substance of his flesh. His arms tightened around her and soon his hand tilted her face to his. Possessively his mouth settled on hers, anchoring hers to his own.

Like a jolt of lightning, awareness exploded back inside her body. The kiss shocked her to her toes. It awakened, it deepened as his tongue thrust between her surrendering lips. She stood transfixed, her senses soaring. His kiss surged a fountain of reviving fire, which gushed through her and blotted out everything but him. Her fire gave chase, and boldly she thrust her tongue inside the moistness of his mouth. He devoured her, near sucking her whole into himself.

Be warned, swanling, he baits and beguiles you. He spreads the feast but has no intention of letting you sup . . . and you, you are burning wild, a fool for his lure again.

She knew her mind spoke true, and for a breath her tongue retreated, but he taunted her back. "Umm . . ." she moaned softly, forgetting her other voice. Her tongue molded and tasted the warm slickness of his own. An overwhelming wave of desire washed through her, and her heightened awareness turned to fever. She felt his hands around her waist and wished them lower, fondling the curves of her hips as he had done in the sweathouse. She wanted nothing between them, hot skin to hot skin. Her hands crept upward beneath the fabric of his tunic, but were thwarted by the fastening of his belt. No longer shy, her searching fingers slipped under the waistband of his leggings and wantonly caressed the lean flesh of his hipbones. . . .

Laughter, rich and deep, trembled in his chest. Suddenly he withdrew his tongue, severing the fire and warmth. His lips whispered at her ear, "Patience, my enchantress . . . it is only the beginning. One night you will feel my kisses burn every hillock and cavern of your body." His lips traced kisses over the circle of her cheek and sought her mouth in a gentle brush.

With swollen and wet lips, she wanted to beg him to let this be that night. His kisses were a maddening venom which entered her blood and ravaged her spirit with his heat. She would waste away if he continued to deny her his bed. But the singing and chanting had subsided in the hall, and the sudden stillness caused them both to turn from the secluded shadows to see what was happening at the dais.

In prophesy Epona's voice, hoarse as crows, filled the hall. "The spring will come early, the summer shall be fruitful, and your larders will overflow. Some shall die, some shall be born, most will be at peace at the Ravnings, but not all. Come forth those who wish to know their fate."

A low murmur swelled through the clouded air as many pushed forward. Moira felt a wave of dizziness, but Wulfsun's two hands steadied her against him. "Are you all right?" he asked, his voice soft with concern.

"Aye," she murmured, wanting only to curl within his strong arms. From the shadows a hand offered a horn of mead. Thirsty, she reached for it, but her fingers clutched air. It had been an apparition, a specter spawned to life by sorcery of the Yule seid.

Nothing around her held substance except Wulfsun's arms encircling her from behind. In confusion and need of assurance, she turned inward again and rested her cheek against the regular rise and fall of his broad chest. He relaxed compliantly and embraced her with protective warmth. She closed her eyes, finding momentary refuge from the phantoms still hovering around her.

"Where is the chieftain?" roused the spakonna's rasping voice.

"I am here," replied Wulfsun. Faces turned to his voice, peering into the hall's shadows.

"Why do you, who is most noteworthy, not ask your fate?" The arms around Moira tensed. She made to draw away, but his arms tightened, keeping her near.

"Until it comes I care not," he tossed back sharply.

The spakonna uttered a delighted cackle. "You do not believe I can tell what is to come, fearless chieftain? Nevertheless, I will tell you unbidden."

More curious than he, Moira turned her head and raised her eyes, in anticipation of whatever Epona might speak. Epona's withered mouth moved once, then twice with no sound. The absence of expression on her aged face held the blankness of a lotus eater.

"Out of the hall there came one maiden knowing many things," she finally hissed out. "The swan sister knew not the power she had. From the wolf lair came the dog of the Nornir, his mind turned to the maiden, Skuld. Here shall we part, spoke Skuld. Then did the dog of the Nornir follow the swan sister to the desert of the dread. He must lose her to win her. He will drown in blood. A loathsome sight I see, a loathsome sight I cannot tell. Much I have told, now I will cease."

Moira's eyes stole back to Wulfsun's face, the muscles in his jaw coursed faintly. His eyes shone brightly like the night-stalking eyes of a lynx.

"You speak a riddlesome tale, Spakonna. Mayhap you have had a knock on the head," he jested, though Moira saw no jest in his eyes. Epona gave another twisted laugh. Moira feared she overdid her part, daring to taunt such a one as Wulfsun.

"Her prophecies are as formless as the spirit shadows that crowd your hall this night," Moira whispered, somehow needing to distract him from Epona.

"Spirit shadows? Your eyes see more than mine, or are you daughter to the one who sits upon the dais?" Mockery filled his voice. She stiffened, and worse, uneasiness clutched her when he suddenly called out. "Mayhap, old woman, you know the riddle of breaking love's enchantment as well?"

Moira's throat tightened. She had neglected to tell Epona she'd led him to believe he was still under enchantment. Even so, her inner knowing assured her she need not fear her grandmother would give her ploy away.

Epona asked circumspectly, "Know you a maid who spurns you for another, Chieftain? 'Tis easily remedied. Gather henbane in the morning while standing naked on one foot." The hall rang with laughter.

Moira swallowed back her anxiety, thinking, *Sweet Epona, this is not the time to make jests.*

As if Epona read her thoughts, she sobered and said,

"If you seek my counsel in breaking love's enchantment, Chieftain, I say but this, to love is to free." And with this she turned her attention to young and old still surrounding her who wished to know their fortunes.

Wulfsun's mouth quirked skeptically and he snorted. "To love is to free. This answer is no answer. She tells the hound to chase his tail."

"Nay, Chieftain, she tells the hound to let go of his tail," said Moira. "She meant to break the enchantment you must *set* me free!"

Now he laughed heartily. "It is you who are unhearing. She said nothing of setting you free. I suspect the young witch and the old are scheming to the same end." Hadn't he earlier, with a speculative watchfulness, seen how quickly the pair had taken to each other? "I am the chieftain, the burden is for me to interpret her words."

She pulled away from him abruptly, but he deliberately pressed her back. She was not so easily held, and with a twist of her shoulders she shrugged him off. Her eyes swirled scarlet and he could not doubt he'd angered her.

"Hah!" she scoffed, a black winged brow arching. Temper of a sudden clutched him as well, for his own scheming was rising against him. More and more he whipped himself. How much longer could he touch her—take her in his arms and not do more? "Being chieftain no better qualifies you to decipher the spakonna's words than the ewe in the stable! By your own avowal, I am the witch here," she continued vehemently. "It is *I* who knows her meaning."

Her insult tested his patience; he wanted none of his vikings or thralls to hear her disrespect. "Then know this—if your sorcery withers me into dust or bespells me into a toad, I will not set you free. To bind you is *my* choice. Mayhap, a fool's choice, but what have I to lose? I am a man already drowning in enchantment." He stepped back and with all the presence of a warrior deeply bowed, then strode off.

Achingly, Moira watched him move back to sit upon his high seat. Soon Ran the Fair was beside him attempting to humor his glowering look with conversation.

Plying tasty sweet meats to his lips, she teased him into eating. It was not long before his arm draped over her narrow shoulders, and he leaned into her laughter.

I did not now love could rise against me, agonized Moira.

Aye, swanling, to love 'tis fire and snow. You give your love and this is your pay. Now you must suffer for being a fool.

And like a fool I am wingless and grounded while he sizzles my heart in boiling honey.

Chapter | 12

The long snows' full moon reigned over the second night of the Yule celebration. The high pitch of Moira's emotions made her wildly restless. The moon affected all, for the feasting far surpassed the first night in gluttony and ribaldry. Eating and drinking were continuous, broken only by brief snatches of sleep, just enough to recover the undaunted celebrants. The vikings' ability to consume food became a marvel to Moira. As a table emptied she hurried to the bower, where women bent over fires, tending pots of boiling meats, spitted fowl, roasting fish, and reindeer. She heaped her arms for the return trip. She carried bread and goat cheeses of such ancient age that a single whiff could knock a sober man off his feet. She followed behind two thralls who shouldered a roasted salmon skewered from head to tail. Inside the feast hall she watched the vikings devour pike and raw oysters as delicacies, washing them down with foamy mead brewed in wooden vats three Yules before.

Despite herself, she enjoyed the gaiety, though her blood simmered with the expectancy brought on by the full moon. Her eyes ever strayed to Wulfsun while she dodged grasping hands and filled horns to brimming. One staggering youth followed her about the hall paying tribute to her beauty by piping clumsy verse. Tonight there were many skalds and poets as drink loosened tongues.

"Do not pass so quickly, my horn needs filling," bade Wulfsun as she neared the high seat. Feeling his hot gaze upon her, her hand shook as she paused to fill his horn. Jacob the Freed rambled on his left.

"Aye, being in my youth I had seen few like her," she overheard Jacob spout as she filled his horn. "Her name, I know it yet, was Katreen. She had sunset hair and skin, silk soft, and thighs . . . like a young forest nymph. When I rode her—"

"Friend, do you speak of maid or horse?" said Wulfsun, chuckling, as he reached for roast goose. Moira made to move on, but his other large hand caught her wrist, halting her steps. "Sit beside me, I have need of your company this night. The young pup can sniff out another bitch to woo."

The young man traipsing at her heels was not so drunk he did not realize it was in his best interest to do just that. He fell in beside another serving girl going the opposite way.

"Eat," ordered Wulfsun, offering her roasted goose.

She shook her head in refusal.

Mock penance furrowed his brow. "Oh, I forget you do not eat such things, for fear it is your kin."

The points of her cheeks reddened with temper. She did not appreciate his humor. She made to rise, saying, "Tonight there are better companions than myself." His grip upon her wrist tightened. For many reasons, she acquiesced but mostly because every inch of her wanted to be next to him. She set her flask on the table and seated herself on a stool beside Wulfsun's high seat.

"I agree, but tonight a more pleasant companion deserts me for another."

She followed his gaze across the hall to Ran the Fair. She sat beside an admiring Kari Olvirson. A gold circlet banded her forehead, and gold trimmed the edges of her azure dress. Deep in the darker recesses of her heart, Moira felt the sting of jealousy.

When Wulfsun's gaze turned back to her, she felt as if her very soul would melt under the hooded fires of his unfathomable eyes. "You have a habit of disappearing."

"Dare I admit it is a habit we thralls perfect so as not to be overworked?"

He laughed a mirth unmistakably his, the same laugh that had echoed out to sea in the beginning when she declared she did not fear him. It floated above the din of the hall, disarming and encircling her. She smiled at her own audacity.

"Mayhap smiling is another habit you would take to mind to nurture." He moved closer. "Let us make peace." There was a smell of drink about him, though not unpleasant. His lips nuzzled her ear. Excitement rippled through her, but she turned her gaze away from him, pretending to watch the entertainments of the hall. "Do your changeling eyes see more ghostly visitors within my hall this night?" He rested his elbow on the table and turned her face back to his own with an uncommonly gentle touch of one long forefinger and lightly kissed her.

Breathing deeply, she pulled back. She knew his game.

His eyes lost their humor. "You are shy tonight." He studied her with the cunning of a predator at a desert water hole.

Resenting his taunt, unspeaking she stared back. She followed his firm mouth to the angular curve of his high cheekbones, to his eyes, which in the firelight took on the fjord's icy depths. It was impossible not to admire such a face, ruthlessly wild yet so perfect. She was no longer aware of the crowded hall as he worked a power over her that she never dreamed possible. He was the enchanter now, and forgetting her wariness, she wanted more of his kisses.

He leaned to her, his lips hovering over hers like a hunting hawk idles on the wind.

Her own lips parted tentatively. Did he know she nearly fell off her stool with anticipation? She feared he did.

With a half-mocking smile, he drew back abruptly and

took his hand from her face. "Do your lips beckon to mine? I would not take even a single kiss against your will and risk further sorcery."

"There is no sorcery in my kisses."

He hissed with disbelief. "Then why does a night not pass that I do not thirst for one?"

"You bind yourself by binding me. That is why."

"So I am to love you enough to set you free. Then you fly off, and I hold empty air, my manhood soft as slush."

After all this time she finally grasped his fear, and his reasoning. He thought if he were to set her free, she would take his potency with her. "It will not be. You are mistaken."

His hand suddenly enclosed hers and lowered it beneath the table to rest upon his groin. Even through the leather of his pants and tunic her palm felt the swell and heat of his desire. His manhood was as firm as the heart of oak.

"Among all women living, only you arouse my dagger thus." He cupped his hand over hers, and the heat and strength of his vitality shocked through her. Her fingers tingled as if pricked by a thousand pins. Steadily she caressed his hero's mound, and the fire of his unsated passion leaped into her like a starving tiger.

Her eyes blinked and widened.

His eyes fixed to hers, intensely burning.

In that long moment she found instinctual pleasure in touching him, and she knew by the breathless halt of his chest he craved her touch as well.

Suddenly he caught her shoulders, and his mouth settled on hers. Like a battering ram against opening gates, his tongue thrust inside her mouth. Her hand retreated from his groin and sought a steadying hold on his tunic. The revelry of the hall receded, and she lost herself to sensation, molding her own soft tongue to the rapacity of his own. His tongue plunged deeper, wildly reaching, calling that primal part of her which she now knew would always respond to him . . . full moon or no.

As quickly as light shifts to dark he broke away. Her hand clung to his tunic, hesitant to release him.

"Enough," he said in a gentle whisper at her ear. "It is I

who must cry halt. Like you, I burn for more. But not this place, or this time."

She realized curious eyes had strayed in their direction, though not so curious was the withering glare of Ran the Fair. She averted her eyes and dropped her hands to her lap, her cheeks blooming from the bite of Ran's venomous look.

Wulfsun stood, albeit unsteadily, and took up his horn.

"Kinsmen, it is time to make tribute to the gods," he announced loudly, lifting his chieftain's horn high. A hearty agreement filled the hall and silenced the harper in midsong. "I raise this horn to Odin that he may give each warrior victory over his enemies!" Moira lifted her eyes as all the warriors rose to their feet with upthrust horns. Their virility radiated through the hall and washed over her like an engulfing floodtide. By the moon! The estrous fever swamped her with a wild wantonness, her nipples became piquant buds, her heart thrummed a staccato pace, and the emptiness between her thighs engorged with the juices of desire. For the first time in her life she rued being of dual nature and wished she was like other women, women like the virginal nuns of Mergate, whose blood moved slow and tame.

"The horn of Odin!" The vikings shouted in deep-voiced unison.

Again Wulfsun raised his refilled horn. "This to Thor, friend of man, that all might trust in his own strength." He drank deeply of the mead with no pause for breath. Again and again toasts were made to various deities. Njord, for bounteous harvest, and Frey, for peace. None slipped under benches as Wulfsun spoke yet another tribute. "Vows will be made in many halls this Yule night. Where better to be spoken than here?" At his side he clapped Thorfinn upon the back. "Thorfinn counsels me to marry. He wishes all to share in his miseries." Thorfinn grinned wickedly. "This vow to Bragi I make: At summer feast I shall pledge my troth." A roar of approval rumbled the hall.

"And who shall the unlucky maiden be?" queried an amused Thorfinn.

Wulfsun scanned the hall randomly, his eyes pausing

on many pleasant faces. Then, with a tremor of uncertainty, Moira saw his gaze hesitate briefly on Ran the Fair. She returned him a flashing smile. Moira's heart fell. Was Ran to be the one?

Her swan mind emerged. *It will not be you. Did not Ysja declare no chieftain has ever married a thrall? And why would you wish it?*

I do not wish it. I fear he will cast me aside when he marries.

Wulfsun laughed. "Our Northern women are so fair, I know not." His hand briefly cupped Moira's shoulder, and this light touch seemed the final taunt. She wanted to flee from the hall, flee from her burning need that held her prisoner like a heel on the neck. But instead, she inwardly vowed that this night she would sleep in his arms, no matter the contrivance.

To Wulfsun someone called encouragment. "Perhaps you should marry two or three!"

"On those odds I am a coward!" replied Wulfsun, lifting his horn. "To Bragi."

Moira looked up and met his twinkling gaze. She hated him for being in such merry humor, when she herself was so impassioned. Many others made vows. One florid-faced reveler even forswore drink, which brought a loud laughter of disbelief.

Kari Olvirson vowed to sail to Denmark and there gain wealth.

"He is sure to succeed," she said to Wulfsun when he sat again beside her. "He is a handsome youth."

"If you like a fool's face," said Wulfsun flatly.

It was an opening. Moira turned her head and raised a dark brow to Wulfsun. A sensuous smile curved her lips. "And what if I might? A fool's lips are warmer than none at all," she dared, ablaze with the agony of her need for union.

He sparked at this. A flush suffused his rugged face, and he leaned to her, his strong hands cupping her face. "Are these fool's lips hot enough for you? Mayhap enchantment is not enough for you. Would it better please you to have me lovesick, chasing through the woods after the backside of sow or—"

She touched her fingertips to silence his lips. "This night I would be pleased if you chased me." Boldly, sweetly, she leaned and kissed him.

Her kiss was like snow in summer on a dry tongue. Wulfsun's heart throbbed against his chest, and he knew the fiery blossom of desire she ignited within him would be hard to root out—but pluck it he must. For a moment, as long as the kiss lasted, he struggled with himself.

She drew back. "I want you."

Her frankness disarmed him, and his desire radiated as if anew. Nor did he miss the desperation in her voice, and he realized he was staring at her lips, wishing they would return to his. "I want you as well," he said truthfully, but felt as of yet he was not well enough revenged. "Even so, it is not fitting for me, the chieftain, to leave the feast so soon."

Her full lips, moist from his kisses, fell downward at the corners, and tears glittered in her eyes. A pang of conscience smote him, but he had to remind himself that this woman was not like other women. She was a sorceress, a sorceress who held him by the cods . . . a sorceress whom he must bring to heel.

"I can be patient," she disclosed, her face resilient. "I will wait for you in the loft of the thrall house."

She stood and he watched her leave, her long black hair flowing down her back. His pulse raced like a hundred galloping stallions, and he ached to follow . . . his resolve to gain the upper hand was melting like wax over fire.

Inside the thrall house, with hot tears tracking down her cheeks, Moira climbed the ladder to the loft. In the darkness she felt her way to a far corner and, heart-stricken, tossed herself upon the sleeping skins. Her senses throbbed with his rejection, and her swan self attempted to console.

Be glad he does not wish to bed you. It would only increase the tangle you are in.

Nay, in love's embrace we might put our differences aside.

And would you put aside Epona's dark prophecies? And

what of the golden torque at your throat? When he strips your clothes, would he cast off that binding as well?

The ladder creaked with protest. She cocked an ear to the sound and pushed away the tears. *He has come!*

"Wulfsun," she called softly to guide him to her. Her heart expanded, and she felt as shaky as a leaf in a windstorm. A strong smell of drink permeated the air. "I am here," she breathed.

He did not answer. Suddenly a rough hand caught her, and a weight fell upon her. She cried out, at once realizing that whoever was upon her was not Wulfsun. She tried to thrust the weight from her. A husky voice grated her ear. "This night my stallion waters at your well, holy slut!"

She knew the voice and that knowledge filled her with terror. Bjorn Bloody Hair! The long matted beard, the barrel of a body, and the stench of his flesh she did not mistake, even in the blackness. Frantically she tried to break loose, but she was no match against his brutal strength. On her face his heaving breath was a wind from hell.

In the struggle she screamed. Bjorn clamped his enormous hand over her nose and mouth. She couldn't breathe and near passed out.

Straddling her, he caught her hands in a merciless grip, then he took his hand from her face and tore her linen tunic. He blasted a lusty laugh, which rumbled through his great chest. Instinctively the wild part of her resisted and tried to break free. This was no time to sing sweet songs or reach out a soothing hand.

Suddenly she let herself go limp. She thought to deceive him into thinking she would be compliant. Bjorn relaxed, murmuring vulgar words.

"I know you want it! I watch you use your witch wiles."

No matter if a hundred full moons graced the heavens, she would never want this! How could he think it? He raised up on his knees and fumbled with his pant lacings.

Quickly, with as much force as she could muster, she kneed where he was most vulnerable. He wheezed a cursing gasp. Weakened, he loosed his hold. Breaking away, she dived over the loft's edge and landed on the floor below. Stunned from the fall, she lost advantage as Bjorn jumped down beside her. He caught her arm, wrenching it painfully.

"By Thor's hammer, I will have you!"

Weeping from pain, she broke free and pushed out the door into the open yard. Bjorn caught her. He slapped her over and over, setting her head reeling. Pain seared through her in cataclysmic flashes, and a stealthy haze darkened her vision.

"Bjorn, let loose of her," came a sharp, swift command.

The grip on her neck relented. He flung her full force across the ice-edged snow. Gasping for sweet air, she rolled onto her back and looked up to see Wulfsun. His eyes gleamed with the clarity of a coiled viper. He didn't look to her, but to Bjorn, who loomed before him.

"I want the woman," Bjorn's roughened voice rasped the biting air.

"She is mine." Wulfsun's answer spoke all. His stance and tone said full. This time there would be no trade or barter, no haggling or good-natured sport.

Bjorn took a step forward, his chest rose and fell as his eyes, blood red, glittered with challenge. "I challenge you, Chieftain, for the woman and all that is yours. After this night your sword will lie on the dung heap, bitch's whelp. I challenge you to Holmaganga!"

Wulfsun stood very still, his composure deadlier than Bjorn's threats. "You know what you speak, friend Bjorn, and I do not walk away."

Someone neared and wrapped her cloak about Moira's shoulders, and comforting arms helped her to her feet. "Come away, swanling," whispered Epona.

Within the yard a bonfire was laid and sparked. Wulfsun stripped off his leathers and prepared for battle.

Ysja was also at her side. "Oh, Moira. I knew there would be trouble with Bjorn wintering here," she mourned.

"What is this Holmaganga?"

"A fight to the death!"

Moira's stomach twisted. "No!" She broke forward

and crossed the distance to Wulfsun. She grasped his arm. "You cannot fight over me. I will not be the excuse for this madness."

"You have no say," he said with steady patience.

"I am the one Bjorn has wronged. Let me ask my boon."

He frowned. "I am your protector, and I will settle it on your behalf."

"I do not wish it settled in this way," she insisted stubbornly.

"You are my thrall."

"I belong to no one."

Unmoved by her defiance he said, "The challenge is made. After this night no one will question who you belong to. In truth, Bjorn wants more than you, he wants the Ravnings as well. Outlawed from his own homestead, he seeks another."

"So you fight not for me, but to remain chieftain."

"I fight for you and the Ravnings."

"And what if you lose?"

"I will not." He brushed her hand from his arm and turned away.

In desperation she caught him again. Her voice imploring, "Remove this torque of thralldom from my neck before you fight."

He smiled, ruefully. "Have you so little faith in my sword arm?"

"Would you leave me at the mercy of Bjorn lifelong?"

"No." His blue eyes held the intensity of midnight. He cupped her face into his hands and kissed her briefly with assurance, but in the cold his lips held no more comfort than frost. "Cease your worry, my swan witch. I will command the law speaker to set you free if I fall this night. If I die, you can fly." He moved to leave.

Once more she caught him. Her arms slipped around his bare chest, and she felt tightness in every muscle of his back. She sought his lips. Grateful tears glistened in her eyes. She kissed him a deep farewell.

He pulled away protesting, "I am not dead yet." An arrogant confidence settled on his angular features and curved the corners of his lips. "Now, which want you more, my death or my loving?"

Shaken by the shrewdness of his insight, she watched his back as he strode off.

From behind her came Epona's quiet voice. "And what is your answer, my swanling?"

She slowly turned and faced her grandmother. Shaking her head, she said, "I know not. But had I magic enough, I would use it on his behalf."

"Then better you do not, for the Fates, not magic, should decide this battle."

"Am I ever to be free?" she despaired.

Epona sighed. "As your hero might say, 'Mayhap.' I tell you only this, when the sun never sleeps, follow Thought and Memory to the dragon's lair. On the ley path you came, on the ley path you go."

Weariness filled her. "Grandmother, I tire of riddles and enchantments. Cannot anything be straightforward?"

"Nothing in life is straightforward, not the stream winding down the mountainside or the oak growing in the forest. The twists and turns make life what it is. Come, move back. Your nearness to the battle will only prove a distraction."

She followed Epona and they went to stand beside Ysja and the other women. From here she numbly watched Ragnorvald the Law Speaker pace the snow and set thralls to pounding hard wood poles to mark boundaries. At the center of these posts Ragnorvald squared his own sky-blue cloak.

Thorfinn, speaking quiet counsel at Wulfsun's side, stood shield bearer. Einar stood for Bjorn. Bjorn didn't strip but donned a bearskin tunic, all the while chewing intently on small handfuls of something given him by Einar.

"What does he eat?" she questioned Ysja, after Bjorn vomited and spat into the snow.

"He chews the herb of madness. He is a Berserker. It is so with them before battle."

Suddenly at Ragnorvald's word, the two warriors

moved like wolf and bear inside the boundaries. Shields raised, swords in hand, they began a slow circling of the cloak. The vikings formed a ring around them, waiting, expecting.

In one stride Bjorn's great shape shadowed Wulfsun. Bjorn lifted his sword and brought it singing down. The edge struck and slid off Wulfsun's shield. Bjorn heaved a belching growl. He took one more step and thundered blows upon Wulfsun's parrying sword, driving him to his knees. Agile, Wulfsun rolled away and found his feet again. Bjorn stalked him with a mighty shout and brought down his sword. The power of the blow sliced Wulfsun's shield in splintered halves.

Moira swallowed back dread. Her eyes rose to the full moon and she invoked, *Lady of the Moon, beneath thy light, protect him well.*

Wulfsun, his eyes alight with an animal keenness, kicked aside the broken halves and thrust Wolf's Claw cannily, using it equally well in either hand. As the fight progressed, he countered Bjorn's every swing and worried his every lunge. Wulfsun's powerful thighs and bare chest smoldered with perspiration. Bjorn blinked aside streams of sweat which poured down his rubric face. Their breath of dragon plumes became a constant exchange.

Moira realized that something predatory drove them to each other. She could not understand it. Wooing death, they reached out, then pulled back again. Blow after blow, swords rang bitterly into the black-iced sky. She looked at the surrounding faces and saw the same savagery creep forth as the day the two small boys had fought. Many, exposed by fire's flame, uncloaked an eager hunger for blood. Ran, her eyes green fire, stood beside Brigitta and devoured each strike. Even the shipbuilder's aged face came alive with youth. Beside him, Kari's eyes filled with the yearning to be part.

Bjorn strained with each lunge, and Wulfsun's muscled legs braced for every ringing blow. Harsh in Moira's ears was that ring, and her own limbs winced.

She cried out when Bjorn's swordtip bit and blood gushed from Wulfsun's shoulder. Blood ran bright red over his chest to spatter in a dark staccato on the snow. Scathed, Wulfsun retreated. Bjorn, his eyes full of terrible madness, charged him. In defense, Wulfsun's glinting sword lashed out. She heard a sickening whack and watched Wolf's Claw slice deep into Bjorn's chest. Bjorn swayed, and with the last and greatest of his might, he bellowed a clarion cry of defeat and let fly his sword. It hurdled into night's heart as Bjorn fell.

She pushed forward and broke past the vikings. When her eyes met Wulfsun's she saw no look of conquest on his drawn features. Leaning against his sword, he nodded her to Bjorn's aid.

She knelt down and lay her hands to his wound. Wulfsun, too, knelt at Bjorn's side. "You have made me an old man, Bjorn."

Bjorn's battle-frenzy gone, he coughed blood. "And you have made me a dead one!" He struggled to speak. "Brother Einar, bring me a horn that I may quench this fire in my stomach. I have killed many men, fought many battles. This is the last." Breath tore his gullet, and she knew he was beyond healing.

A servant came quickly with a horn. Einar held the horn to Bjorn's lips. He drank and retched red spittle.

"In death some choose to walk the realm of the mountains. I will find my haven in the sea." He stared into the night sky. His dark pupils flared.

"The Valkyrie riding steeds of white come for me. It is said no man lives forever whom the Fates doom at dawn." It was his last breath; his last words. Glazed with death's light, his eyes stared heavenward.

"His hour of life is past," spoke Einar. "He feasts in Valhalla!" Agreement echoed among the surrounding vikings. In unison they took up a deep-voiced chant of mourning.

Wulfsun stood and walked around Bjorn. From behind he reached to close the staring eyes, the gaping mouth, and pinched together the nostrils.

She heard a banging sound near the gate and came to her feet. "What is that noise?" she asked Wulfsun in a low whisper.

"Bjorn Bloody Hair was a bad-tempered man. Some

fear his ghost spirit will cause trouble for us. We will carry him from the Ravnings backward so he will not enter again."

She stepped back when Wulfsun, Thorfinn, and Einar lifted Bjorn's limp body to their shoulders. They strode through the gates, followed by Bjorn's seamates in a torchlit procession. She felt an overwhelming sadness, knowing she would never understand the violent nature of these men who slept out the long dark winters of the North.

By the dying fire in the open yard, she stood in the moonlit darkness and watched the procession snake down to the fjord. Torches were tossed to feed the leaping flames of Bjorn's funeral pyre. Death's beacon ship would sail him over dark waters to another sphere. In the fire and ice scape of night, it seemed to her that those who remained at the Ravnings dwelt in death's underworld, and Bjorn Bloody Hair alone traveled to a new life. Despairing, she might have stood there through the night had not a hand touched her shoulder.

"Come, I am in need of you." Wulfsun took full possession of what he'd always claimed his own. She opened her mouth to speak, but a brief look at his face suffocated her words. He was gaunt-faced and hollow-eyed with shadows dark as the sea beneath his brows. Blood smeared over his chest and leggings. She glanced to the moon in gratitude that he was not the dead man.

Unspeaking, she followed him into the feast hall, where he climbed into the loft. She paused to find a flask of water, then climbed after him. He had collapsed on the sleeping furs. She searched a chest for clean linen and sat beside him. Gently she washed the dried blood caked on his chest and shoulders. Carefully she inspected his wound. "The bleeding has stopped and the cut is not deep. You are lucky," she said.

He roused at her words, not quite able to bring up a grin. "And you still have a master. You are not so lucky."

She shook her head. "I have been more unlucky."

"When?" he asked.

"When a hunter's arrow shot me from the sky."

His eyes widened. "So that is how a swan maid found

her way to a Christian abbey. I have seen this small wound on your shoulder and wondered as much."

"Small wound, you say. 'Tis a scar that rivals any of your own."

"Calm yourself." His weary face managed a tolerant grin. "We will take the time to compare . . . and then decide."

Thinking to make a poultice for his wound, she had come to her feet and stepped to leave. "And is that time ever to come?" By now she was in such a state that her pride had fallen by the wayside, and his inference made her almost sick with anticipation.

His hand lightly gripped her ankle for a second. She looked down. His touch was like bellows to hearth coals. His eyes lifted to her own, and for a rare unguarded moment she saw in them more depth of emotion than she'd ever seen before. "I killed Bjorn because he dared take from you what I had not. The time will come, swan witch."

He released her ankle then, and with the echo of his promise and the full moon's magic still simmering in her blood, she climbed from the loft in search of old Halda.

Chapter 13

When Moira woke, Wulfsun was still asleep. Hungry, she stepped over other sleepers and climbed down from the loft to the hall below. Jacob the Freed greeted her as he sat leisurely picking his teeth with a bone splint.

"Does he still sleep?" he asked of Wulfsun.

"Like a dead man," she answered, not thinking to the allusion before she spoke.

"Be patient. Once he takes you to his bed, you will find it sweet."

"Not so sweet as freedom," she said, perturbed that he and most others speculated about the chieftain and his thrall woman's sleeping arrangements.

"To bind is easy, not so easy to set free." He winked a knowing eye.

"You say it well," she replied, taking bread and cheese. "The hall is quiet."

"A storm comes. Those from Olvirsted have gone, the others sleep. The spakonna bid me to give you her farewell."

She stopped chewing. "The spakonna has gone to Olvirsted?" She could not believe her grandmother would abandon her.

180

She always has good reason for her unpredictable behavior, her swan self justified.

This is one time I do not see it! How am I ever to escape without her help?

Jacob continued speaking. "She bid me tell you she will see you again at midsummer's feast."

Moira did not want to wait until midsummer to see her grandmother again. "Is Olvirsted far from here?"

"For the thrall woman of Wulfsun, far enough." He gave her a look of sidelong speculation. "The Norse law is hard on the runaway thrall. If you succeeded in reaching Olvirsted, they would return you to the Ravnings."

She frowned. "What makes you think I thought to run away?"

"I was once a thrall myself," he reminded her. "What slave loves his master but on the day he is set free?"

"Aye." She smiled. "On this we agree." Thoughtfully she sliced more cheese and looked down the table for other delectables. With her trencher filled with food she climbed back to the loft. Others had awakened and were making their way down to the feast hall.

Wulfsun was awake and examining his wound when she returned. He winged the stiffness from his arms and shoulders and flashed her a smile, which tingled through her like the harper's song.

"You have worked your magic well. At last I benefit from your sorcery." His eyes went to the trencher of food in her hands. "What's this? You bring me food—everything I like. I must have died and awakened in Valhalla."

" 'Tis a slothful servant who must be commanded in all things," she said, happy she had pleased him. But it was that extra sixth sense of hers that told her, without asking, what he found palatable.

"We Northmen have a similar saying."

Earlier, she'd taken off her ripped tunic and put on one from the chest. It hitched up mid-thigh as she sat down to mend the rips in her own.

"You Norse have a saying for everything." She took

out her needle and started mending. An uneasy silence settled between them. Covertly she watched him eat. Blatantly he watched her sew. It was hard for her to imagine the fingers that so routinely filled his mouth had deliberately killed Bjorn a night past.

Finally, refreshed from sleep and revitalized with food, he rinsed and wiped his hands. He came over and crouched down beside her. She kept her eyes lowered, intent on her stitching. His long fingers touched the purple bruises on her arms left from Bjorn's mauling. Her pulse quickened, for Wulfsun's every touch tingled like a sweet healing balm. Then he raised his fingers to rest upon her chin. She had no choice but to meet his gaze. "You have received hard treatment at our hands." His lips lowered to hers, and he kissed her lightly . . . too briefly.

Oh, do not begin such sweet torture again, begged Moira inwardly. *I can no longer bear it.*

Drawing back, he turned her head to one side as his clear blue eyes studied the faint splotch on her temple inflicted long months before at Mergate Abbey. He half-laughed. "Yet all the while you remain a virgin."

"It has not always been my choice."

He grinned. "We have another saying, only a woman with no heart denies a man in his need. Yet I have done this to you . . ."

For a breath Moira's needle halted. If he was about to ask forgiveness, she would gladly forgive. She waited.

He said no more, but stood and walked across the loft to the ornate chest. After rummaging through its contents, he tossed her a black cloth bundle. With a wary look, she shook it out and found a black pleated linen dress with an over-apron of red-stitched embroidery along the border.

"I would not want it spoken that I am tight-fisted," he said.

"I have the clothes you gave me in Kaupang," she answered.

"Then why do you not wear them?"

"I am a thrall woman. I wear the tunic of a thrall."

"You martyr to the extreme."

Paying no attention that her voice disturbed others, she said vehemently, "You mark me as a thrall." She flicked the golden torque at her neck to add drama. "I dress as a thrall!" Nearby a man mumbled and turned in his sleep.

"I am your master and you will dress as I say."

"You think yourself my master, but I do not recognize it!" She was angry now. She tossed her sewing aside.

Challenging, he raised a brow. "Does that end it?"

His mocking attitude rankled her. She added for good measure, "No, that does not end it! Though it is more than enough for your barbarian's mind to grasp!" Her temper snapped.

"For a peace lover, your tongue is a mighty sword, but I have battled enough this night." He sighed. "In the North we discuss our disagreements, never argue them. A man who loses his temper is the loser of the argument," he said, smugly collected.

"You forget, I am not a man," she said proudly.

"You seem not to be a woman, either." Sarcasm marked his voice.

She glared at him. "Apparently, I am more woman than you can handle!" With that insult, she came to her feet, swung her cape around her, and left in a flash of scarlet.

The storm descended and marooned everyone within their perspective longhouses. Still another night Moira and the chieftain slept apart. She, in the sanctuary of the thrall house which connected with the stable, and he, in the feast hall.

She thought if he had truly wanted her, he would have braved the blizzard and sought her out. He did not. After midnight she woke, and because of the cold she layered the fine clothes he'd given her in Kaupang over her thrall's tunic. Though warmer, through the snowy night she slept alone and ached from his absence.

The storm ended by early morning, and everyone worked clearing snow from the open yard and breaking paths from one longhouse to the other. Though many of the does were dry, Moira busied herself helping Ysja tend to early milking.

"Wulfsun asks for you, Moira," informed Ysja as she returned from a foray outside. Her cheeks were rosy with cold. "I will finish the milking."

"Let him ask. I have other things to do besides shadow him around all day. As long as you think as a slave, Ysja, you will always be a slave." She began to warm to her subject. "If all the thralls stopped working, the highborn would realize how valuable we were. They could give us freedom for our work. What else could they do . . . ?"

"They could tie the ring leader to a post for whipping," came Wulfsun's deep voice at the stable entrance. She looked around the shaggy flanks of Unna, cursing that Wulfsun should overhear her sedition. Ysja colored and quickly set herself to milking. Wulfsun walked over and affectionately petted the dowager goat.

Moira's temper rose like the milky froth in her pail. At this point she had little to lose, so she spoke smartly. "Is this another of your heroic deeds? To whip innocents until they beg for mercy?" Ysja's milking rhythm faltered as the hiss of Moira's voice became more impassioned.

Wulfsun's tone was measured. "Our laws are fair. It is unusual for the innocent to be punished."

"Humph!" she sniffed skeptically and rose, milk bucket in hand, to leave. Wulfsun insolently leaned with folded arms against the stable beam, thereby blocking her exit. She could have pardoned herself past, but such politeness constricted in her prideful throat. Aggravated, she looked haughtily beyond him, wondering all the while if they were to stand there at odds until the milk froze solid in her bucket.

With a long forefinger Wulfsun turned her chin to his vision line. Their eyes met, hers defiant, his amused.

"I am leaving for the saeter. You are going with me." Moira did not doubt it. Did a linnet fly against the gale?

"Before or after you whip me?" she dared, angry that he commanded her.

"You choose martyrdom?" he returned half teasing, half annoyed. "Do you prefer my company or the whip?"

"Sometimes there is no difference."

A glint of calculation lit his eyes. "Yes, woman, there is a difference, though at first both sting."

She stood, silenced.

"Come to the hall."

She watched him bend out the doorway, and she set down her bucket. "Ysja, what is the saeter?"

"It is the hunting lodge in the high pasture. The chieftain always spends the darkest winter days there. But always he goes alone."

"Well"—she sighed resignedly—"not this time." And upon further thought, a smile curved her lips.

Wulfsun awaited Moira outside the hall. The first sight of her at early morning milking had pleased him. He did not miss that she wore the clothes he'd given her in Kaupang. Mayhap he should have gone after her yesterday, before the storm. Yet what needed to be settled between them would take more than one night's bedding.

He spied her flash of red cloak, and his pulse quickened with anticipation. Soon, he told himself. "Let us be off," he greeted as she approached. Aloof, she adjusted the bundle of her few possessions fastened in a sling over her shoulder. Her eyes did not meet his nor did she return his greeting. This irritated him. He'd enough of temperamental women, beginning with Ran the Fair when she discovered he was to leave for the saeter with the thrall woman. He held up the long wooden snowshoes with simple thong bindings. "During the heavy snows we use snowshoes to hawk and hunt. Lift your cloak aside," he said as he knelt and secured her feet beneath the thongs, first one, then the other.

She took an awkward step and finally spoke. "I feel as clumsy as a great bear."

"I grant you would do better to fly." He laughed, and quickly caught her eye for fear he'd offended her. He thought not, for she continued to smile, but lost her balance and toppled in the snow.

"Take care. Go slowly." He helped her up. He took another pair from the low overhang of the hall and put them on his own feet. He secured his scarlet, fur-lined cape and hefted a large leatherskin backpack onto his shoulders. It took him a moment to adjust its weight to a position that did not rankle his shoulder wound. His sword he carried in his baldric, and his bow he secured to his pack.

From the stables a thrall brought his gyrfalcon, a beautiful bird of blue-black plumage. Wulfsun crooned to it in a low burr as its hooded head crooked and tilted to the sound.

"Remove the hood," he bade the thrall. The falcon's gold-lit eyes flared, then narrowed as she surveyed her surroundings.

"She is keen and sharp-eyed," he said proudly.

"Are we to take her with us?"

"She is a fine huntress. We will need the meat."

"Not I."

He held his tongue, thinking he would try not to tease her. He lifted the falcon to his backpack, and she was content to perch there.

He turned to Moira and placed a tapered wooden pole in her hands. "Use this to keep yourself upright." He demonstrated in a brief turn around the open yard. After this short lesson he set off. She followed, but at the first slope she fell into a headlong tumble. He bit back his amusement and backtracked. "You try too hard. Follow my track." He helped her to her feet. He started again but was careful to set his pace to hers. "The pace will be easier on the uphill slope," he assured her.

He spied Gray Deer shadowing them in the forest cover, and after a time she joined to trot behind. Every so often the wolf darted off into thickets, scaring out ptarmigan and quail. The stir brought unrest to the falcon as her hunter's instinct followed the movement. Her taloned feet flexed and tightened, straining the jesses which bound her.

Wulfsun's eyes followed the rising moon as it appeared and disappeared behind the green-tailed heights of fir forest. The pines thickened, and the way became dark and gloomy. The snow turned patchy, for it could not penetrate the density of the forest. In these places he bid Moira to take off her snowshoes.

As they walked, Gray Deer rooted among rotting logs, disturbing small, winter-colored animals that scurried from cover to cover. In her exuberance she barked excitedly, which caused a small avalanche to cascade down from pine tree skirts, nearly burying her. Wulfsun muttered a scolding curse to Gray Deer, but chuckled and went to her rescue.

Gently he helped her up and brushed her off. "You look like a snow queen."

"I feel like a fool," she said, shaking the snow off her cloak.

In the perpetual twilight, her lash and brow were dusted with fine snow. With a mixture of amusement and desire, his gaze fixed on her snow-frosted lips. His palm cupped her head, and he lowered his face to hers. His frosty breath mingled in a soft cloud with her own. His tongue emerged and slowly traced and licked the snow crystals dusting her lips. She tasted fresh as springwater and sweet as honey nectar. Too long he had waited. Now they were alone, and this moment, this instant, he would begin a careful wooing, a continuous threading of passion through the long dark winter nights to come.

She leaned to him and he felt her lips press against his, seeking—not the warrior, but lover, potent, passionate, and patient. For a time and for her alone he would leash the violence and become a tender and gentle lover.

Slowly he drew his lips away. Tentatively, returning, to show her he regretted the necessity of this momentary parting as much as she.

Suddenly she began to giggle. "Someone is looking over your shoulder." He turned but saw nothing. "Lady Falcon is puzzled."

Realizing, he laughed as well and reached to stroke the falcon's breast. "I had forgotten about her."

"She does not mind. I have told her we are preening and that you are very good at it. She finds your touch pleasing as well."

He walked alongside her. "I am glad you are both in agreement." Intrigued, he asked, "How do you speak with her?"

"I do not know. I just do." She halted a step and tilted her head thoughtfully. "We exchange pictures. That is how."

"So, what if I do the same without speaking? Will she understand me?" he asked.

"Try it."

He thought a moment, and then in his mind's eye he saw the falcon spread-winged. Suddenly the falcon's wings splayed and flapped in the crisp air. "It works!"

"There is no reason it should not. We are all children of the Earth Mother."

"Would unspoken seeing work with you?"

"Yes. Sometimes, I know your thoughts, but not often."

He could not quite believe it, and he was not so sure if he liked her prying into his mind. "What have you seen?"

She paused overlong before answering. "Well"—she stole a cautious sidelong glance—"when you kissed me back there, I saw . . ."

"You saw what?" His tone was not so affable.

She flushed, and then with disarming frankness she said quickly, "I saw myself naked in your arms and you loving me."

He relaxed and grinned. "I cannot deny it. Mayhap I must beware!"

The pine thinned into stark birch. He again knelt and helped her to put on her snowshoes. They traversed over massive snowdrifts carved by the winds into weird figures and etched with moonbeam scribble. But for Gray Deer's panting, all was silent.

The way became steep as they wove up the mountain base. He looked to her and saw she needed a rest. When he halted, she gratefully leaned on her staff to catch her breath.

"We must go on."

"I would like to lay down into the feathery snow and sleep," she confessed.

He smiled with empathy. "You would wake up in Valhalla."

"Not I. I am no warrior." She scooped up a handful of snow, formed it in a moist ball, and began to suck it.

"Eating snow quickens thirst," he said, brushing the snow from her hand. He reached beneath his cloak and brought out a narrow-necked leather drinking skin. "Here, drink. It is warm."

She took it, covering its spout with her mouth.

In his mind's eye he saw her soft lips drinking warmth of another sort.

Suddenly her eyes snapped to his. Quickly he lowered his eyes and pushed away the image. He felt himself at the disadvantage. He breathed an inner sigh and vowed to be more circumspect.

Soon after, they reached the mouth of the high valley. He left her and went a short way up a winding gap that ended abruptly. Here he took off his snowshoes. Using his dagger, he began to pick out footholds along the ice-faced streambed. She patiently watched. At the top he tossed down a rope to her.

"Take off your snowshoes and tie them to the rope."

He drew them up.

"Now it is your turn!"

Her agility to scale up the cliff face surprised him. He took her hands and helped her up beside him. He slipped his arms around her waist and turned her to view the panorama of the fjord and valley below. The mountains rose as black silhouettes, and the land lounged a white wilderness. In the silken stillness he heard only her breathing and felt only her warmth.

Nuzzling her ear he asked softly, "Does your ho eland of Myr hold such peace as this?"

"This and more." A sly smile tugged at her lips. "In Myr there are no Vikings."

He gently nipped her ear in mock retaliation. "Come, it is cold. The saeter is near." He knelt to put on her snowshoes. When he took her small booted foot into his hands, he could not resist and let his hand slide up to caress the curve of her muscled calf.

She spoke. "If you wish to know, your gyrfalcon thinks you have an odd way of preening."

He laughed. "Between the pair of you, I have no chance."

Wulfsun could barely distinguish the saeter from the mounds of snow. Built on a high log platform, the stairway to the door was designed to keep the inhabitants from being trapped inside during heavy winter storms. His eyes surveyed the saeter's southern face, satisfied the mound of chopped wood was enough to last out their stay.

Gray Deer sat by the stairs waiting patiently. She'd chosen her own route to the high pasture. Wulfsun shrugged off his backpack and unfastened the falcon. She hopped-flapped to the stair railing. His fingers were numb, and he had difficulty gripping the thong bindings when he unfastened the snowshoes. He leaned them against the saeter.

"I will start a fire. Come." He climbed the stairs and entered. Inside, as he moved through the darkness, she followed holding to his cloak. His foot hit the hearth stone, and he groped for the tinder box. A moment later short sparks flashed in the pitch black, and then candle-light revealed the room.

His eyes briefly scanned the surroundings. From rafter beams hung bulging sacks of food stores. Cooking pots and tools dangled down as well.

Moira was shivering as she came over to crouch near the struggling fire. He thought to tell her to cover herself in the pile of sleeping furs in the corner, then a better idea occurred to him.

Assured the fire caught hold, Wulfsun turned to her. "Come, I know one way to warm us both." He lifted her into his arms and started back outside.

"Where are we going?" she asked.

"Wait and see," was his mysterious reply.

He carried her behind the saeter to a thicket-clogged ravine. His steps broke a shallow streambed's icy crust, then soon the way was no longer frozen but a slushy trickle. He carried her through the overgrowth into a narrow rock-faced passage to a misty grotto. The moonlight radiated through clouds of mist whirling off the hot spring pool, pearl pale as starlight. Winter had not touched this place, where ferns tumbled from rock walls and emerald moss carpeted the ground.

He felt her relax in his arms. "It is beautiful," she breathed. He set her down. "I feared you would roll me in the snow again, telling me it cured frostbite."

"I would warn you first."

He did not have to tell her to undress. Her hands fumbled at the fastenings of her cape, and her lips pursed with frustration. "My fingers are stiff. I can't . . ."

Used to mastering every situation, he stepped beside her and tried to unfasten the ties with as little success.

He laughed. "Mayhap I must return to the saeter for my dagger." But soon he managed to unloose the ties while she waited as impatient as a child. Hastily she pulled off her clothing. Naked, she stepped to the water's edge and touched her toe tip to water. Her beauty cut him like a scimitar, and he thanked the gods she had learned no shame of her woman's body. While he undressed, she dived into the hot springs. Understanding her natural affinity to water, he soon followed.

Once he stepped into the pool, he stopped thinking and started feeling. He felt the heat of the water glide over his skin and warm his body. The warmth permeated his limbs as he immersed himself into the tranquility. Needle pains shot through his thawing fingers and toes. He could smile and feel it.

He was not sure who moved to who first, but her arms were suddenly around his neck and his hands were on her smooth hips and he was playfully swirling her in slow circles through the water. Her lighthearted laughter rippled the air.

"Are you warm now?" he asked.

"Warm as summer," she breathed.

They stared into each other's eyes for a long time. Her eyes glistened with the pale fire of stars. His awareness of her thighs and breasts brushing against his own was so acute, it was almost pain. Finally he embraced her body, enjoying the contact of his inner arms on her skin. His hands traveled slowly, feeling the curves of her hips and waist. He would learn her body, what pleased her . . . excited her.

Lowering her head, her lips kissing along the red welt of his shoulder wound became a healing balm. His senses exploded as he felt her liquid touch, exploring. Her arms wrapped around him in gentle hugs. He lowered his head and kissed the curve of her white shoulders and the hollow of her throat. With his tongue he traced lower, along the water line that lapped over the swell of her full breasts.

"Humm . . ." She sighed, and her nose tip nuzzled his in an unspoken appeal for his lips. His mouth covered hers, and he tasted all that was sweet . . . and more.

His hand traced her hips and cupped the nest of her womanhood. As he slid his fingers gently across the secret softness, his hard rod throbbed. Insistent, her lips clung to his, and he knew she welcomed the intimacy of his touch. Exploring, his fingers massaged the velvet lips, parted the moist petals, and discovered he could slip but his smallest finger inside her warm, tight virgin well. Wholly chagrined, he was wise enough to realize his manhood might blaze a painful path. From the beginning they had been luckless. But now a careful wooing, and mayhap gentle loving, would be caution enough.

Reluctantly he broke the kiss, for he could not help but chuckle when he felt her small exploring hand lightly tickle the pendants of his manhood.

"You are a mischievous sprite!" he whispered in her ear.

Her eyes and lips flashed with tease. "If you bathe in an enchanted pool, you should expect it."

"Be warned. Mayhap I have tricks of my own." He nipped her ear softly. "But I will save them. Now we must go back to the saeter before the fire burns itself out."

She frowned. "I would happily spend the night here."

He was guiding her to the pool's edge. "No doubt you would, but I am not such a duck as you."

His golden hair floated into the obsidian tangle of her

own. As he stepped out, he gathered his hair and began wringing out the water.

She reluctantly followed him, and still naked, he wrapped her in his cloak and twisted the wet from the loop of her hair as well. "We can dress at the saeter by the fire."

He hastily bundled up their belongings and thrust it in her hands. He swept her in his arms and carried her back into the cold winter's night. Yet he did not feel the cold. His blood ran hot with desire for her, and he felt a primal power shout through his body . . . as wild and vibrant as a wolf king howling at the moon.

Chapter 14

When they entered the saeter, the dying embers of the fire beckoned, and the falcon shifted on her perch. Wulfsun carried Moira to the sleeping furs. She huddled in the warmth and watched him resurrect the fire. She could not take her eyes off of him. The struggling flames danced off timbered walls and shadowed the sculpted contours of his naked body. Full of wonder, she regarded him, running her eyes over his wide shoulders and the tangle of damp thick hair that flowed down his back. When he knelt on one knee, her eyes followed his narrow hips to the prow of his manhood. Expectancy tingled through her.

She pulled her eyes up and looked only at his face. As if she had touched him, he lifted his eyes to hers and watched her with a lover's intentness. In the half light his eyes were as deep blue as heaven's abyss. The flow of desire between them was almost visible. Her pulse sprinted.

She opened her arms and parted the sleeping furs. "Come," she invited, "share my warmth."

In a warning echo, her swan mind surfaced, *Call him to your bed, swanling. Once he has tasted your love, he will never let you go. He will bind your heart as well as your body.*

Nay, for love he will release me. Tonight we share the ritual of disclosure and more. Our loving will nurture his trust.

Do not believe it. He is a warrior first and always. It is not in his nature to trust.

He easily gathered himself and moved to her side. "You need not ask twice," he said, trying to make his voice light, but she could hear the underlying intensity. His hands cupped her face gently, and he looked deep into her eyes. "Moira . . . my sweet swan witch. By the gods! You have given me a chase."

She touched his face, and his mouth lowered to hers. She melted against his warm, bare skin, sliding her hands over his chest and twining her fingers around his neck. She felt his hand slide down, over her shoulder, lower to close gently around her breast.

His hands are assassin's hands skilled at the art of life taking, her swan self warned. She knew it was the power in him that worried her swan half. The power that this moment numbed her with wantonness and commanded every part of her to yield to him—the power of him that could kill as well as cherish. *Oh, swanling be care—*

Be still! 'Tis too late. She silenced her swan mind. She closed her eyes, swimming into the liquid pleasures of Wulfsun's touch and kisses.

His kiss lightened and feathered across her cheeks and eyes. Tenderly he nibbled on her ear, sensuously tasting every curve and crevice until she shivered with bliss.

"You are beautiful . . . my faerie goddess," he whispered, and because he believed it so, she, too, believed it. His lips trailed down the line of her slim neck and white shoulder. His thumb strolled and dallied around the budding spire of her breast. And then she felt sensation jolt through her as the warm wind of his breath . . . then his lips . . . captured her nipple. Goose bumps shimmered over her skin. Her hands caressed his lowered head, and her lips kissed the soft gold of his unbound hair splaying across his muscled back.

Little by little she felt his tongue preen the full circle of her breast. He nuzzled and lapped the furrow between and secreted his tongue's tip along the half-moon fold beneath. She sighed from the pleasure. Near breathless, she felt the slick of his tongue inch across, intruding beneath the velvet tuck of her other breast. Unhurried, as if he intended to sup on every cream-flushed pore, he tasted her plush swell. Slowly, spiraling, he near drove her to beg him to capture her upthrust peak in the softness of his lips. When at last he did fasten firmly on her nipple, the force sent a shock of pure delight to her very fingertips. Her hands caressed his head, and she moaned gratefully.

Soon his head dipped down to rain hot kisses upon the hollow of her belly, and her desire spread like fever to tingle every nerve and pore. His hands slipped around and cupped the pillows of her hips. His golden head lowered, and his mouth gently met the inner velvet of her thighs. She relished the moist stroking creeping up inside each leg in turn. His tongue moved in soft swirls along the outer boundaries of her woman's mound. Indolently her head rolled from side to side, and she knew he schemed to torment her, and meant to hold back. Such sweet torment she could not resist. Lazily, like before, he moved slowly in, debilitating her with desire. She felt a rippling between her thighs and the faint tickle still far from pleasure's heart.

And then he was in her, tracing a fiery spiral within the folds of her moist flesh, tasting the small, sensitive confines. She felt soft contractions and realized her virgin's channel expanded, readying to embrace his shaft. She ached, feeling the soft swell again, and again. Her breath quickened and her hips arched to him. His hero's spear must enter her, now.

Unexplainably, he abandoned her and gently pressed the heel of his hand against her mound. The urgency diminished. She gasped with disappointment and reached for him, clasping his thick hair in her fists and drawing his face up to her own. In the firelight she could see the flash of his teeth as he smiled.

"I am dying for you," she begged hoarsely.

"Not yet, sweet witch." He kissed her full-mouthed. "Through the long months of madness we've endured. Be patient. Soon I will fill the emptiness between your thighs." And his golden head bent, and she felt his lips upon her breasts once more, gently, then sucking more strongly until she near swooned. Her body twisted, seeking his.

"Taunt me no more! I need you, now!" she agonized, pulling his face back to hers and kissing him with the full force of her desire.

She felt his chest rise and fall in a deep sigh against her own. He shifted, saying, "Open your eyes." Reluctantly she did. "Look at me," he commanded.

He was grinning, a peculiar boldly seductive grin. He spoke gently. "I do not taunt you. I have no wish to hurt you by haste. Despite what you have seen, all men do not mate and fly." He reached and stroked her hair and cheek. "Let me prepare you."

Her eyes wandered to his flat wine-dark male nipples, over his broad chest smooth with male muscle, down the full length of his sinuous torso where the spear of his manhood arched rigid. He was strong, so vibrant in his maleness, so sure. But there was more to a swan sister's mating than he knew.

"Might I prepare you as well?" she asked, her voice deceptively dulcet.

Laughter erupted deep in his chest. "Whatever pleases you. I give myself up to your witchery." He leaned back, stretching full length.

She started humming softly. Her song was more than sweet to his ears. Her long slim legs straddled him, and when she settled on him, the hot moist juices between her thighs glossed his belly, and his blood pulsed like white fire. Still humming, she raked the pads of her fingertips lazily down his chest. Where she touched, pure ecstasy chimed through him. He felt as if he had no skin, and she reached to caress his soul. Her lips sought his chest, and she licked him, tongue touching nipple, breasts brushing stomach. The warmth of her body pulsed against his own and he ached to enter her.

As if she read his mind, she drew away her lips.

Shifting to balance on her knees, he felt her small hand encircle his rod, and she lowered herself down on him. His hands gripped the soft rounds of her buttocks and pressured her close.

"Sweet witch!" he groaned full-throated as, easily, he thrust deep his shaft. "Hel's gates!" he cried out deep-voiced. A painful fire seared his rod. A wild agony seized him. This witch was not so sweet! He roughly clutched her shoulders in momentary panic.

Then her lips were at his ear, endearing, assuring, in soft apologies. "Forgive me, I did not mean you hurt, but it is fleeting. I will make it up to you, my heart, a hundred fold. 'Tis the way with my kind. He who first enters must pay such a price. Please, please forgive me."

Amid the fire, he felt the soft silk of her virginity strain, then surrender to embrace him. The pain transformed. It was difficult to tell who penetrated who as their hips began to undulate on a slow-wing. A wild, wild exhilaration swamped him. He felt he rode the shoulders of a thousand warriors, a conqueror of ten thousand battles.

Still at his ear her sweet voice whispered, "Hold back, my stallion. I will promise you a mating like no other you have known."

As he struggled for mastery, the power of motion seemed to fly from his limbs. All awareness drained to the ecstasy she was awakening within his shaft. It was as if a hundred lips enfolded him. His body had become one organ, hungering for her. Her face hovered near his, and the deep fires of her eyes spiraled scarlet. Moisture beaded the shadow of his mouth, and she licked the droplets away. He caught her tongue, sucking her into himself.

Their joining became a molten fire.

No space was between them—a single body, a single breath, a single pulsating. The current moved from his shaft's root upward, setting longfires in his stomach, beneath his ribs. It throbbed in his breast like an exploding sun and lashed to his extremities like a raging sea in storm.

He could hold back no longer. Near wild, he groaned

and twined his legs around her and rolled her on her back and thrust full force. He felt her nails dig into his shoulders, and he plunged his tongue deep into her mouth. Her hips undulated in union with his, and soft moans crossed her lips. His strokes became more powerful with each thrust.

"By the gods!" he shouted as he felt his power explode and his seed spill into her. Turbulent waves of passion throbbed through him.

She cried out—a wild cry, like a raptor winging to prey. The air rustled with the wind of wing, and again he held swan . . . down and feathers wafted the air . . . and then, just as quickly, his arms embraced woman.

He felt her heart pounding next to his own, and he clutched her to him with awe and wonder. How did he, of all men, find such a treasure? He drew a trembling breath and lifted his head to seek her face.

Tears trickled from the corners of her closed eyes. Gently he kissed each eye, and slowly her eye lids slitted, widened into swirling crystalline rainbows of satisfaction. "I bow to you, my swan heart," he said softly. "Your sweetness is beyond my imaginings."

"'Tis only the beginning . . ." Her hands cupped his golden head and drew him down that his lips might touch her own.

During the morning hours, in a haze of sleep, Moira felt his surfeited shaft slip from her, and she sighed from the loss of the sweet connection. She reached for him. "I will return," he assured, kissing her forehead. For a moment she pretended he still held her in his arms. She yearned to snuggle against him and savor his enfolding touch. He was the sorcerer, not she. Through the night he'd pleasured her until she felt as joyous as the sun in high summer. She dozed back into loving dreams.

Sometime later she reawoke. The fire blazed in the hearth, and from its perch the falcon watched her. Where was the man who had loved her through the night?

Where had he gone?

She sat up and rubbed her eyes and looked slowly around the saeter. His bow was gone.

Hunting. Is he so indifferent to my love that he would choose to hunt above holding me in his arms?

He wishes to provide for your needs.

Well, I for one will not eat his kill.

Then what will you eat? asked her swan self. *You cannot live on love.*

She ran her tongue over her lips. They still tasted of him. *Mayhap I will!*

She climbed from the warm sleeping furs. The morning chill raised goose bumps on her naked body, and her eyes searched for her clothes and found them in a neat bundle warming by the fire.

He is thoughtful, you must give him that.

What man would not be when he finds a woman like yourself. A woman whose kiss restores his withered manhood, time after time in an endless night of loving.

He is not alone. You were impassioned enough by his loving to whip up a few feathers . . . I wish you'd make up your mind.

I will when you will.

Moira mumbled to herself with irritation, thinking her two souls would never see eye to eye regarding Wulfsun. After she dressed, she climbed to the loft and inventoried the food stores. She found grains, dried fruits and nuts, lentils, and peas. In the earthen cellar beneath the saeter's floor she discovered root vegetables, apples, and linen-wrapped cheeses. Beside the foodstuffs she came across bundled furs from the fall's hunting. She rubbed their silkiness to her face, feeling sad for the animals that would no longer wear such beautiful coats.

In a soapstone pot she made lentil soup and baked flatbrod on a smooth, flat cooking stone. She turned to every sound, hoping it was Wulfsun returning. She pouted and felt his absence a slight. Idleness being the devil's workshop, she decided to play the snoop and nose through his pack of belongings. On top she found a pouch of arrow points and feathers . . . swan feathers. . . . Momentarily she forgot how pleasing his hands had felt on her body and how thoughtful he'd been to warm her clothes.

Calming herself, she justified, *It is the way of life. One dies that another might live.*

Here you go again, excusing his savagery. Those could be my feathers! Our feathers!

The Norse people believe swans are good luck. He values us.

He values us to pluck our feathers.

She pushed aside the pouch and reached again. Her hands found a familiar shape, the harp. She pulled it out and her heart warmed to Wulfsun.

For a while she lost herself in playing the harp and suddenly realized she'd let the fire burn low. She put on her cloak and went to fetch more wood. Outside, snow had begun to fall, veiling the landscape to the point that she had to use the saeter's wall to guide her to the woodpile. While she made two trips, loading herself up each time, she worried he had lost his way. With the last armful an uneasiness crept over her. It was as if someone watched her behind the veil of falling snow. The smell of skunk or rotten carcass permeated the air, and her senses echoed with foreboding. She couldn't snatch up the wood quick enough.

It is a dark presence I have not known before, said her swan self.

Moira found herself racing for the saeter's stairs, all the while imagining a demon's breath lapping at her neck. She pushed through the door, let fly the wood, and barred the door. She leaned against the door, her heart pounding. The falcon baited at her perch.

"What is it?" she spoke aloud, sure some madness lurked outside.

The falcon screeched a warning, but conjured no answer in Moira's mind. She moved to the falcon and whispered soft words to calm it.

Suddenly a loud thump shook the door, and her heart somersaulted in her chest.

"Let me in, woman!" came a deep-voiced call. Moira unbarred and cracked open the door and peeked out cautiously. A monstrous white form pushed in before she could collect the wit to thrust closed the door.

Wulfsun shook off the snow from his head and cloak. "Would you leave a man out in such a storm?" Gray Deer pushed inside behind him, and Wulfsun slammed shut the door.

"No . . . no," she denied, relieved he had returned.

"I've had the hunting luck." He proudly lowered from his back two rare white-furred foxes tied together by their long tails. Their black muzzles dangled limply, and their staring eyes, even in death, held gentleness.

She knelt and stroked their limp beauty sorrowfully. Tears welled in her eyes, and she began to hum softly.

"Why do you sing?" he asked, his voice defensive.

"I'm apologizing to their life spirit for your violence against them."

"You need not. Did they apologize to the rabbit they killed and shared this early morning? I think not."

"It is different. You hunted them for their beauty, not because you needed food."

His brows knit with offense. "I hunted them for their furs, a gift to you which will keep you from freezing to death in the night."

"I would rather freeze."

Or die in his arms trying, subverted her swan mind.

He snorted lightly, and then his jaw tightened with insult. "What am I to do? Sit in the forest and wait for them to die of old age?" He picked up the carcasses, lifted the cellar door, and disappeared down under the saeter.

Moira brushed the tears from her eyes and thought how insensitive he was.

She prepared what she thought a commendable meal of lentil soup, cheese melted on flatbrod, and stewed wild apples. After a time he came back up from the cellar and sat beside the fire. Wordlessly she offered him a bowl of lentil soup, and wordlessly he accepted it. He tasted it, and she could tell by the lifting of his golden brows that he liked it. He ate three bowls full, but never commented otherwise.

In silence she cleaned up the remains of their meal and returned the saeter to neat order. She could find nothing else to do, so she walked up the stairs and opened the door to see if the storm had slackened. A torrent of snow whirled in like an uninvited guest, and she slammed shut the door. Wulfsun looked up from his work of scraping hides, but said nothing.

She sat on the stair of the loft with chin in hand and surveyed the scene below: Wulfsun, his fair head bent over, Gray Deer chewing on a fresh bone, and the falcon with her head tucked beneath her wing as she napped. In reflection a half smile did curve her lips at the vision of Wulfsun sitting in the forest, a long white beard growing from his face, while he waited for animals to collapse at his feet from old age.

She sighed overloud. He still ignored her. It was the first time she'd sat in a room with someone and felt completely alone. In the next silent hours she suffered sorely from Wulfsun's moodiness.

She worried a snarly knot from her hair and released another dramatic sigh of boredom, which was given no notice by any of her companions. It was not her nature to be mute, but it soon became a point of pride, and the tension began to build.

Her one self argued, *I cannot expect him to cease his way of life because I am of another mind. He is a hunter and warrior. Nor can I insult his prowess at every turn. He thinks to please and win me. I cannot shame his efforts.*

You need not shame him, said her swan self practically. *Merely show him his error.*

He can be gentle . . . . So must I be.

And then her eyes strayed to his busy hands and wished they were busy touching her once again. She felt remorse and knew she must make amends to him. Finally she picked up the harp and situated herself in a comfortable spot by the fire and filled the silence with the music of her apology.

At last he put his work aside.

"Come." He stood up and tossed Moira her cloak. "Let us go to the spring."

"But it storms," she said.

"No longer."

She put on the cape and flung open the door. A clear snowy scape greeted her. "How did you know?"

"A picture just appeared in my mind's eye," he returned smoothly. His eyes held a look of shrewd humor. He was teasing her.

He whistled under his breath as they left the saeter. The moon broke through the clouds with an enormous grin, and its light reflected off the snow like diamond dust. He broke trail for her through the new drifts, and she followed his long strides into the mists of the grotto. Before she'd unlaced her boots, he had stripped and jumped into the water.

The water lapped around her bare shoulders as she slipped into the pool. Her unbound hair floated like tangles of black seaweed.

"This is heaven." She swam a few languid strokes.

"You have an odd vision of heaven."

"No more strange than you Northmen, who think fighting battle after battle and then reveling in Odin's hall by night is happy." She thought it pure debauchery, though she did not say so.

"Each man should choose his heaven," he proposed as he swam nearer to her. His muscular arms glistened wet. "I have my own ideas."

"I will not ask what they are." Still holding a grudge, she moved to sit in the shallows. Did he think he could ignore her for hours on end and then expect her to fall into his arms?

He followed and sat facing her, the water lapping against his broad chest. "It is an unusual woman that is not curious." He playfully caught the ends of her hair and twined them around his fingers.

"Mayhap I do not care."

"Care or not, I will tell you."

He reached beneath the water, and she felt his fingers clasp her ankle. One hand slid along the hard muscle of her calf. As if for the first time, his touch exploded through her. Then he cupped her heel in his palm and raised her foot so her toes surfaced above the water. He lowered his lips to her toes and tauntingly ran his tongue over the webbing between her second and third toes.

"Hummm," she could not help purr. The slow fire crept through her foot, licked up her thigh . . .

"First, I would want a woman faithful to me to life's end," he murmured between her toes.

"Are you willing to repay the favor?" she tossed back, her hands clutching rocks to steady herself.

"Depending on the woman, it would not be difficult." His tongue circled the pad of her fourth toe and then to the silk soft webbing between. His tongue's point probed and flexed against the taunt, transparent skin. "Were she to give me sons, it would be easier."

Like fire to dry kindling, his kisses were igniting her senses. "What is wrong with daughters?" she asked, not daring to tell him a swan sister conceived only daughters.

"Nothing as long as they are fair-faced and quick to marry." He sucked her smallest toe between his lips.

A giggle of pleasure rippled in her throat. "Is that all? You are easy to please, especially for a sea pirate."

Slowly he released her toe and dropped her foot beneath the water. His hand playfully caught floating ends of her hair, and he twined them around his fingers. "You say the last, a ship to sail the sea. Nothing more."

"You love the sea."

"I could not live without it." His fierce independence came across with his words.

"It is a dangerous life," she reminded him.

"Every man must test his limits. Every man must reach out toward death and return."

"Mayhap one day you will not return."

"No man lives forever."

"In memory he can," she added quietly.

"Remember me then." He let loose her hair and rose out of the water. "Come, we will go back."

I will remember, she thought . . . as his statuesque body faded into the veil of mist that widened the chasm between them.

The cold prompted them to dress quickly. Wet-headed, she hurried behind Wulfsun down the ravine. He paused to brush aside the thicket so she might pass more easily. Then, before she realized his intentions, he bent his head to hers and kissed her. As swiftly, the moist warmth of his lips abandoned hers. The kiss, so deftly given, then retrieved, left her wondering if she had been kissed at all. She wanted more. She thought he wanted her to want more.

"The golden bough, you did not see it?" Laughter lit his eyes as he reached to pick a branch covered with bracken. He put a sprig of white-berried mistletoe in her hand. "When enemies meet beneath the bough, they kiss, postponing their battles for a time."

"Are we enemies?"

"I think no longer," he replied as he moved her along with a gentle prod.

Shadows and firelight danced on the timbered walls of the lodge. She sat before the fire's glow, combing her damp and tangled hair. She could not help but contemplate the aspect of the man across the fire. His conciliatory kiss still tingled her lips. Turned away from her, he was intent on shaving his face. The muscles of his back rippled in a wince.

"Is it painful?" She moved to face him and better see his ritual of preening.

"Only when the blade slips. I am told women prefer a man to be smooth of face."

"Have you so many women to please?" Her voice held a slight edge.

"Only whom I choose." Their eyes held, until she averted hers after something contracted, and it was not her heart. It was an area well below that. She continued to comb her hair and watch him.

Soon finished, he sheathed his dagger in his fleece boot and in turn watched her. Suddenly he moved around to her back.

"Let me," he offered, taking the ivory comb from her hand. She released it gladly. In the transfer an odd tingle shocked her fingertips as they touched his. "I have never seen a mane upon a woman such as you wear." His hand gently combed.

She remembered another time he had touched her hair. A time he had been less than tender. The time when he had nearly uprooted every hair on her head, yanking her to her knees in the slave market. Could this be the same man whose voice held sentiment and whose touch quickened her pulse to ardor?

"In Permia I once saw a gemstone the shimmering black of a raven's wing. Your hair is much like it. It pleasures me to look upon you, Moira. Being a captive of your enchantment is not all bad . . ."

His words ran dry, the combing strokes ceased with a static click. A single touch of his finger brushed across her temple. A moment passed, then another.

They hung suspended in the encompassing silence.

She knew before he moved what would happen. She had no will to stop him. This night he was the weaver of enchantments, not her.

Sweeping aside her hair, he kissed her neck, her cheek. She turned to him, and their eyes communed, reaching together as the sunflower joins the blue of sky. He took her into his arms, the feel of his bare muscled skin as warm as gold. She watched his lips lower to hers. She closed her eyes and tasted the sweetness of his lingering kiss. In all her life she would never receive such a kiss. She wanted it to last and last . . . . If he drew away from her now, she would surely weep.

He kissed her gently. He kissed her with passion, which she returned. He kissed her a hundred ways, exploring, teasing, and ploying. How could he, wild and rough of nature, be so skilled in the simple kiss? He wooed every nerve on her lips, until she throbbed with an exquisite ache. His breath, a solar wind, warmed her lips time after time.

"Fill me, or I will die," she finally gasped, her own desire at the point of no return. Wulfsun drew back, cradling her with tenderness. Within the lucid depths of his bright eyes she saw his own desire, his passion.

"My need rides before my patience as well," he murmured. Desire shadowed his leanly fleshed cheeks. She stretched her length beside him as his hands moved to ease her shift up over slim eager hips. Nimbly her fingers unwove the lacings of his leggings as if they had not been.

"I welcome you," she breathed, spreading her thighs. He knelt to her, parting her moist, flushed folds as though he prepared to drink from a holy well. He entered her like a leaping stag. "By the white goddess!" she invoked as his hard rod thrust deep . . . deeper within her very essence. He was sea, quicksilver waters, filling, foaming, and she was earth, loam dark, warm and life-giving.

"Swan witch!" he gasped in the explosion of flesh. He poured his strength into her, her vessel overflowing with his froth. His power surged through her, setting fires, fountaining into starbursts of glowing light.

In the aftermath the room was unusually still to Moira. At one moment it seemed everything in creation had been singing, and now all fell silent. Embers glowed in the hearth circle, and she watched a white feather float from above to land on Wulfsun's muscled shoulderblade. She puffed her lips, and the feather sailed off on the wind of her breath.

She heard his laughter and felt his chest shake against her own. "From where come all these feathers?" His voice was soft in her ear.

"For a swan sister each act of love is a renewal, so we molt, shedding the old for the new."

He chuckled. "Soon we will have enough to stuff a palette."

"Is that why you collect them?"

"I use them to feather my arrows for the hunting luck."

"Humph! You'll find no luck in using mine."

"I thought as much. In truth, your feathers might hex my arrows."

"Only for the good of hapless creatures unfortunate enough to cross your path."

He moved to lift himself, but her hands pressed a protest on his firm buttocks. She wanted to feel him inside her still.

He sighed lightly. "You make me love's slave."

She nuzzled his ear. "Speak you a complaint?"

Affectionately he nuzzled her in return. "Never! I've waited too long. Even on that first night I near took you on the tower floor."

"Why didn't you?"

He contemplated a moment. His thumb massaged the curve of her shoulder and the faint welt of her wound, then he smirked. "Mayhap instinct whispered your virgin's armor could gall my spear. . . ."

Her lips fell sadly and she hugged him to her. "You have not forgiven me. Would I could have taken the burden of pain unto myself."

Now his voice was serious. "Nay, swan heart, I would welcome the fire of your virgin's threshold thrice a moonrise . . . you are one maid whose sweetness is worth the winning. If I am lost to the enchantment, what sweeter doom than to die of love?" His breath tickled her ear. His fingers traced the gold circlet at her throat, as if to reinforce her bondage, which coupled her to his own imagined enslavement.

The gesture compelled her eye to seek the blue fire of his own. In this weak moment she wanted to declare the enchantment over and beg him release her. Yet, as she regarded him she realized with sorrow her swan self had spoken true. He would never willingly remove the collar from her neck and risk losing her.

Aye, he loves me well, too well!

A chilling howl broke her thoughts. The same darkness permeated her senses that she had felt before.

By the fire Gray Deer bared her teeth in a venomous growl. At her perch the falcon creed and pecked at her binding jesses. Moira looked askance to Wulfsun, whose face lost its softness and became a hard mask. His lips tightened with menace. He slipped from her and stood up.

The howl came again.

"Hel's demon!" Wulfsun cursed. "I know that cry!" He reached for his clothes and began dressing.

"This darkness came before, when you were hunting."

He looked to her with concern. "Why did you not speak?"

"I . . . I forgot. I sat within myself, and it's terrors went away."

He gave a half scoffing laugh. "Now it has returned. I fear this time it will not be warded off with a prayer and song."

"How do you know?"

"I know it!" He strode to the wall and took Wolf's Claw from its peg.

"What is it?" she questioned him once more, but the screams outside pushed past her words as if they were never spoken. Again and again they came, tearing her nerves until she covered her ears.

"Tell me what it is?" She restrained his arm as he fastened Wolf's Claw in his baldric.

"It is better you do not know." His answer was abrupt and final. Frustrated with his unwillingness to tell her, her anxiety became anger.

"I must know!"

Droll amusement played at the corners of his bleak eyes.

"Aye, lady, it should be you that goes to chase this mist dragon. After one tune from your harp and some soft-spoken magic, you could ride upon its back."

"Do not tease. You have battled this dragon before, and even more often in your dreams."

"In truth it is an old enemy. It has stalked me since my youth. I first saw it when I traveled over the mountain from the *Althing*. It came from the forest mists challenging Egil Ravn, my foster father, who was then the chieftain, as it now challenges me."

"Why does it challenge you?"

"Because after Egil Ravn fell, I took up the sword in his place. I fought until I could fight no more, and then I escaped. The skald says it is descended from those that haunted the earth before time and was spawned in the violence of chaos. It is a sun eater, a swallower of souls, and no man can slay it with his sword arm."

"Then why do you try?" she asked with bright eyes and burning cheeks, appalled at the futility of such a battle.

The skin stretched taut over his sharp cheekbones. "As a warrior, I know no other course."

He flung on his cloak and opened the door, blocking Gray Deer's exit with his knee. "Bar the door after I go. Do not open it until you hear my voice. If I do not return at the end of this night, at dawn go back down the mountain to the Ravnings."

She reached for him, but her arms caught empty air.

He disappeared out the door before she could cry a protest. She wasted no time in securing the door. Gray Deer took a stance directly in front, appearing none too pleased at being left behind. Another cry pierced the night. It was exultant, as if whatever uttered it knew the challenge had been met.

Chapter 15

Moira waited.

The fire's flame conjured stalking shadows on the timber beams and mud-chinked walls. The shadows leaped and licked in a grotesque mime of her apprehensions. She stood, then sat, paced, then stopped. Gray Deer circled. Time and again she lunged full weight against the door.

Of a sudden, out in the night three cries sounded: swift, short, and piercing. A sharp pain ripped her chest. She clutched her breast and she fell to her knees with a fractured cry.

Enough! agonized her swan self. *You cannot abandon him. He battles a dragon conjured from a darkness within all men. Go to him, or he will surely die.*

In the next seconds she met Gray Deer's wolfen pleas by seizing a torchlight and opening the door. Gray Deer knocked her aside and bounded off into the darkness. She fastened the snowshoes on her feet and rushed in the direction the wolf had bolted. With every step she listened for any sound in the now deathlike quiet of the mist-veiled night.

Movement in the outer limits of her torchlight brought her heart to her throat. Gray Deer appeared. She fretted back and forth, disappearing and reappearing within the bounds of Moira's torchlight. Her lead took Moira some distance from the saeter. Other tracks marred the white mantle. Deep, wide, bestial prints. The snow's fluid texture churned and plaited, dark shadows marbled its white sheen. Her circle of light drew in Wulfsun's humped body, beside him sniffed and whined a vigilant Gray Deer.

Sickening weakness swept her when she saw his shredded leathers. Nausea gripped her as she side-stepped a widening red stain. She rooted the torch in the snow and knelt beside him.

She reached her arms around his limp body and turned him over. Her breath caught as she saw the gaping rips from throat to belly. "Goddess!" she invoked. "Oh, Lady of Light!"

She felt his neck for pulse. Faint, too faint. The night air was freezing, and he felt as cold as a corpse. Using the ancient woman wisdom taught her by Epona, she retrieved from her pouch at her waist the ice stone. Holding the healing stone in her left hand, she began breathing deeply, opening herself to the Goddess and that knowing. The power of earth began to flow into the stone until her hand became hot and tingling. She waved the stone over his body, circling him in a barrier of warmth. "Ice, call forth fire!" she invoked. Then she tucked the warm stone next to his solar plexus.

She laid her hands on his head and began to sing the healsong to stop blood's flow and to sustain him with her own life force.

The healing of New Moon be upon thee,
The healing of Full Moon be upon thee,
May the healing of the Old Moon pass thee;
The healing of starry skies,
The healing of fertile plain,
The healing of ocean's sighs,
The healing of gentle rain;
The healing of warm winds, warm breath, warm sea,
    warm sun be upon thee.
Child of wolf; may they be upon thee now. . . .

Slowly her hands moved down the length of his body, and gradually the blood began to congeal like clabber.

Taking off her own cloak, she wrapped it around him. Wulfsun's glazed eyes opened and closed.

"We must go back to the saeter." Her words misted into the air, and she knew he was beyond hearing. She struggled with his bulk, slipping her arms around his chest, but her strength wasn't enough. After dragging him a few feet, she collapsed from his weight. Gray Deer circled and then moved forward, standing patiently beside her. She looked to Gray Deer's broad shoulders and remembered seeing a pack sled hanging on the saeter outside wall. Time . . . time . . . she had so little time. She must return for the sled—if only she had her wings! Determinedly, she gave an anxious glance at Wulfsun lying still and set off for the sled.

Minutes later she returned, the sled strappings cinched at her waist. He is dead, her fear screamed. But she put her ear close to his lips and felt the whisper of life breath. Breathing deeply herself, she rose and carefully moved him onto the sled.

Refastening the strappings higher up, across her shoulders, her voice broke the deathly stillness of the wintry night. "Come on, then, sister wolf, lead me back to the saeter." Gray Deer moved in front, and Moira gave two false starts before she could shift the sled into motion. The snow held her every step prisoner, and uttering many oaths, Moira summoned all her strength to push ahead. She cursed and wept until her tears frosted her face and vision. Every breath cut her lungs like hot steel. Once Gray Deer halted and growled at the surrounding darkness. Moira sensed the darkness as well and raised her power hand. She drew a circle of protection, and she urged the wolf forward.

Near overcome with exhaustion, she finally came up against the saeter.

"Thank the Goddess, at last!" She breathed, although her words were wasted on Wulfsun. Looping her hands beneath his arms, she lifted him from the sled, then dragged him up the stairs and over the saeter's threshold. A trail of blood marked the path.

Urgency replaced her despair. She lay him on the sleeping furs, built up the fire, and with boiled water, sponged clean his wounds. His skin lay open, and she knew no animal that walked the earth that could rip and tear his body in such a way.

She chanted a healsong, while from her pouch she took her silver needle, the one Wulfsun had given her in Kaupang. With silk thread and shaking hands she began to sew up the wounds. She knew his soul hovered above his body, ready to enter the place of souls his people called Valhalla. With every stitch she muttered an apology and a chant of binding spirit to body.

At last she finished. Along the ragged edges of his wounds his flesh swelled. She bathed the wounds again and washed his whole body. She washed the reddish tinge from his flaxen hair and discovered a raised lump near his right temple. Exploring further, she found no end to his bruises and abrasions. All night she nursed him, refusing to let the waning thread of his own life-force detach his spirit from his body.

Within the early hours of morning, fever seized him. She put the ice stone at his crown and cast a spell to draw away the heat of fever. Fretting that she could do no more, her eyes roamed and found the herbs hanging from the rafter stores. Reaching into the beams, she smelled and tasted the bitter to the sweet, trying to find the ones Epona had instructed were good for drawing poison. Constantly she bathed his wounds in wormwood and steeped hyssop and valerian tea, which she forced between his lips sip by sip.

She found it torment to watch him thrash in fitful sleep. His fingers snatched empty air. His breath would catch, then halt, then begin again. He relived a hundred battles, rehearsed a thousand dramas muddled together in his fevered mind. He begged no aid, called no names, not hers, not anyone's.

This one should be dead, said her swan self. *Let him go.*
Nay, he dies and I am bound lifelong.
He dies and so dies your heart, more like.

In truth, she loved him with a passion that burned a fever, as consuming as the one that racked his ravaged body. Her love had grown like the berry matures to fruit—the shading leaves parting, the treasure found. He was unlike any man she would ever know or meet again.

Three nights passed, then a fourth. Off and on, through the nights, she invoked:

Ancient One of the ancient earth
Older than time can tell
All powerful Mother Earth
You who controls all,
Heal that which cannot be healed in any other way.

She repeatedly changed the dressings and cleansed them in boiling water. She made snow packs and wrapped him in them to cool his fever. She pressed liquid to his lips drop by drop, swallow by swallow.

Suddenly on the fifth day while she sat at his side, the ice stone shattered. She knew it to be an omen of life. At that moment he began to sweat profusely, and the moisture beaded in tiny crystals over his body. Her sigh was near a sob when he opened coherent eyes and offered her a faint smile.

"If you are a Valkyrie, you come too soon," he murmured from moisture-rimmed lips.

Moira began crying. She stroked his forehead and kissed him gently.

"Have I disappointed you by living?" he asked.

"A dead man is good to no one." She smiled through her tears. "It is an unhappiness I must bear."

"Never before has a woman wept on my behalf."

She doubted this, for what woman could love him and not sorrow from his parting? He pressed his lips to her tear-streaked cheek.

"I had forgotten tears have the salt taste of the sea."

"You must shed your own. It is very healthy," she instructed as she sat upright and wiped the wetness from her face. "Drink, you need strength." She put a cup to his lips. He made to raise on his elbow but collapsed, unable to hold his weight.

"What have you done, woman?" he gasped. His groping fingers touched his wounds.

"If your garment is torn, do you not mend it? I have mended your skin."

He knitted his brows. "This was your sorcery that night! I could not fathom the stinging pain you put upon me. You revenge my weakness with stitchery."

"Do not complain," she flared back, "unless you think it braver to walk about showing your entrails. It is easier to mend a man's body than his thinking."

"You are a woman. You will try to do both." He took the cup from her hands, and she held his head while he drank. Finished, his eyes circled the saeter walls and he asked, "Where is Wolf's Claw?"

"I . . . I suppose out in the snow where you fell."

"You left my blade out there to rust?" He made to rise, but far from recovered, he collapsed back, overtaken by weakness.

"What use have I for a sword? Your life was my concern."

"You must find it. Now!" he ordered.

She was not all good works. "What if your dragon is still lurking out there?"

"It is not."

"How do you know?"

"I know! Now be off with you. Or I will go myself."

"You cannot."

"Do not taunt me. I see no fairness in it."

"I see no sense in rushing out to find a sword that will be easier found when the snows melt in spring."

"You are the one who speaks to the beasts. Take the falcon. She is of keen eye and will do the searching. Bid her."

"All right," she relented. He settled back and soon fell into a doze. Her eyes went to the black gyrfalcon on its perch. She slipped on Wulfsun's leather gauntlet and urged the falcon onto her arm. They left the darkness of the saeter for the outdoors. The air smacked with cold, and the sky showed pale gray against the white landscape.

She removed the falcon's hood, unloosed the jesses, and raised her arm high above her head. "Now, my sister, Wulfsun would have his sword, and we are to find it." The bird pushed off, flexing the strength of talon and wing. Her own spirit soared with the falcon's exhilarant *kree . . . kree. . . .* The bird circled high into the winter sky and swooped some distance from the saeter and perched on the dead bough of a fir tree. Moira put on her snowshoes and slowly made her way in that direction. The air cut her lungs, but she felt invigorated.

The stain of battle still darkened the snow, and in the twilight she saw more blood was spilled than Wulfsun's. A stench still lingered, and she raised her cloak to her nose. Quickly she spotted the half-exposed silver glint of Wolf's Claw. A few steps and her small woman's hand reached to grasp the hilt.

"Lady of Light!" she cried out and jerked back her hand. Her palm burned. She thrust her hand in the snow as the tears welled in her eyes.

The weapon glows with the battle fire, and one such as you cannot touch it, realized her swan side.

How am I to take back a sword I cannot touch?

She looked to the gyrfalcon, still perched nearby, and called her. The bird swooped down onto her outstretched arm. "We might as well make good use of your leather bindings." Though her fingers and palm still smarted from touching the sword, she unfastened the leather jesses from the gyrfalcon.

"Wulfsun will have his sword and you, sister, will have your freedom. Now, be you off to freedom!"

The bird stretched and lifted off until she became a pinpoint shadow against the sky. For some time Moira watched, catching sight of her once or twice above the pointed noses of grand dame fir. Then, sighing an envious breath, she turned away and began tying together the jesses into a cord. Carefully she looped it over the hilt of the sword and proceeded to drag Wolf's Claw behind her through the snow. All the while she grumbled to herself about the nature of man. Could they not put their wits to better use than death craft?

Scuffing snow from her boots, she lingered at the saeter door before she entered.

Expectant, Wulfsun's head raised up from the sleeping furs as she came inside. "Have you brought it?"

"I could not touch it, but yes, I brought it." She yanked it through the doorway and thrust it in its sling at his feet. She splayed her hand for him to see the rising blisters. "Look! I, too, am wounded by your death blade."

"Come closer," he commanded.

She went and knelt beside him, putting out her poor hand for him to view. His own gently clasped hers. "I would take away your pain if I could. But that is your gift, not mine." He turned her palm and touched his lips to the backside of her hand. "On my kiss I vow to pleasure you tenfold when I am able." Now both sides of her hand burned. She withdrew it from him and turned away.

"Where is my falcon?"

"Flying free," she said proudly.

Not speaking, Wulfsun's face changed, his features difficult to read, but she sensed that he was not pleased.

As the days passed, Moira learned his moods, and in most things they moved together. Yet at times he became lost in deep silences. Physically Wulfsun had few equals. But though strong and fit, his recovery was not swift. His injuries were slow to heal, and most of the time he was in great pain, which he endured in stoic silence.

On a morning in late January he came to his feet and slowly began dressing. Moira watched approvingly, for until now he'd not made such an effort.

"I wish to go outside," he said in explanation.

"It is too soon and I have much work here," she answered truthfully. She continued to kneed the flatbrod dough.

"You are overly dutiful, but you forget, your duty is to obey me. I say you are to come outside with me."

She ceased her work, wiped her hands, and stood up. She did not look at him and thought he must truly be recovering. His usual arrogance replaced his temporary humility.

"I will go, but only because you should not go without me." She thought he grinned as he put on his cloak.

Outside it was a different sort of day than the never-ending gray blandness. Like the first whiffs of spring, the air held expectancy, though snow was yet deep on the ground. When he bent to put on his snowshoes, his jaw tensed and color drained from his face, but no complaint crossed his lips.

"Let me help you," she offered. He frowned, but stood patiently while she did the fastenings. Cautiously he tested his balance. After putting on her own snowshoes, she turned to him.

"South," he directed, and with staff in hand he set out to the south. After a short distance he crested the top of a sloping hill, and here he drew up on its edge. He panted heavily, and she felt concern that he'd undertaken too much too soon.

"Look to the horizon," he said while catching his breath. She came up next to him, and within a few moments the snow-gray landscape became brilliant as the gray sky turned to red, then gold. Together they witnessed the first appearance of the sun since winter's dark had descended two months before. Almost worshipfully she watched the golden messiah lift regally into the lower sky. Its light thawed frozen fjord, warmed winds to fill sleeping sails, and forced darkness into retreat for a season. She looked to Wulfsun, and a rare splendid smile crossed his lips. A smile a wife preens for, the sort a mistress wins. His dark pupils were pinpoints in circles of blue, and in those eyes she met the sun's flame reflected.

She smiled brilliantly. "I had forgotten there was a sun."

"Through your own stubbornness you might still be sitting in the dark of the saeter."

"You might have told me the sun would return today."

"You did not ask."

He was maddening. Abruptly she turned her face back to the sun, but his hand gently tilted her face back to his.

"I have angered you. I did not intend it."

He reached to her and lowered her cloak's hood. He drew out her hair and shook it free so it caught the sun's warmth and light. His mouth lowered to hers and he gently kissed her.

That sunrise seemed a beginning for them both.

Through the rest of the day Moira felt Wulfsun's eyes on her, not the usual mockery, but a new look, shadowed and considering.

Their relationship fell into an easy compatibility, and in the evening while she played the harp, he sang Norse songs and oiled his bow. He told her of his sea adventures, which she found fascinating.

"I have traveled to most places in the known world," he boasted. "At fourteen I went *a viking*. Our longship sailed down the Dnieper to Kiev, then we crossed the Black Sea to Byzantia. I have seen the Masjid of Jerusalem and the marble temples of Rome. I wandered a land where snow never falls and the heat of summer is an endless longfire. It was a land where no man should live."

"Then why were you there?"

"We were lost," he said, laughing. "In Alexandria and Iberia's sunlit gardens my sword has battled Egyptian and Moor. Seven years I was *a viking,* then I returned to the North."

"Why did you return to this cold Northland when you could live where the sea is warm and food abundant year-round?"

He shifted in a futile effort to be comfortable and set his unstrung bow at his side. He stared reflectively at a slow-burning log. "Among us it is said, unhappy is the man who must live in a foreign land. As for me, I think it is a woman who holds a man to a place."

"In my experience it has been the man who holds the woman to a place," she said honestly.

He chuckled. "You think wholly on one side, enchantress. But we will not ruin an evening's pleasant conversation in the debate of it." He picked up his bow again and peered closely at its arc. "Will you give me a lock of your hair?"

"What for?" she asked, puzzled at his request.

"My bow needs restringing," he answered, taking up a dagger.

"How much shall you cut?"

"The length, your smallest finger thick," he said raising his little finger. She turned her back to him, and he lifted her hair from her neck. His fingers threaded out and cut a long swatch. His touch brought goose bumps to her skin.

"Let me tell you a saga," he began. She watched his long tapered fingers twist and work the hair into a fine strong cord. "It concerns a man, Gunnar Hamundarsun, by name. He was a tall powerful man, outstandingly skillful with arms. He was excellent at archery, and his arrows never missed their mark."

"Much like yourself," she could not help but add teasingly.

"Mayhap," he agreed, giving her a tolerant eye. "Though I hope not to share his fate, for he married a troublemaker named Hallgerd. She stirred in his affairs so, finally many men sought to kill him."

"How do you know? Mayhap he caused his own troubles."

"I do not know," he said with irritation. "But the tale says so. Do you intend to hear it as it is told or not?"

"I will hear it."

"Her plottings so enraged him, he did slap her once, a slap she did not forget," he continued. "One night as he slept, his enemies approached. They were not sure if Gunnar was at home. One went right up to the longhouse to find out. Gunnar caught sight of the attacker's tunic and lunged out, striking the man with his halberd. Upon going back to his companions, the man was asked: 'Is Gunnar at home?' "

" 'That is for you to find out,' he replied, 'but I know that his halberd certainly is!' And with that he fell dead." Wulfsun paused, amusement on his face.

Moira was not equally amused. "Go on," she prompted flatly.

"The men surrounded Gunnar's home, and after some time of fighting, Gunnar had wounded eight men and killed two. He said to Hallgerd, 'Let me have two locks of your hair, and help your mother plait them into a bow string for me.' "

" 'Does anything depend upon it?' asked Hallgerd."

" 'My life depends on it,' replied Gunnar, 'for they will never overcome me as long as I can use my bow.' "

" 'In that case,' said Hallgerd, 'I shall remind you of the slap you once gave me,' and she turned her back. Gunnar defended himself with great courage and wounded ten or more. But in the end they killed him."

Moira looked to Wulfsun expectantly. "So?"

"So! What a stiff-necked woman that Hallgerd must have been."

"So! What a rough-handed man that Gunnar must have been to slap his wife," she said, defending her sister. "You have told only Gunnar's side of the tale. Mayhap he hit her more than once. He seemed a violent man with many enemies and not all of his wife's making."

"You know nothing of women," he said, putting aside her lock of hair.

"I happen to be one," she said, tired of his superior attitude.

"You've said that before. I would welcome the proving."

His challenge was undeniable.

She laughed with surprise. "You are ambitious for one just returned from death." His lips did not curve with equal humor, nor did his deep steady gaze waver from hers.

"Make my return worthwhile," he challenged.

"Mayhap I will," she agreed with a small smile. She settled herself beside him. He'd stripped soon after they'd returned from outside, and as usual she'd bathed his wounds with herbal brew. She'd thought she'd grown accustomed to his nakedness, but now a soft warmth radiated between her thighs, and she desired him. She pursed her lips and scanned the red crisscross welts that scored his bare chest and thighs. "Where am I to begin that my touch won't hurt you?"

He carefully shifted his lean hips and cupped her chin in his hand. His eyes pinned hers. "Are you open to counsel?" His thumb slid slowly back and forth over the moist swell of her lower lip.

"I think not!" Her teeth playfully caught his thumb, and she circled its head with her tongue tip.

Her taunt incited him, and he pulled her to him, but the effort made him wince.

She giggled. "Lie still." She pressured him away. "You cannot make love to me, it might be your undoing."

"It need not be my undoing. I will teach you the way of it."

"I need no teaching," she said haughtily. "I know what will please you. Your desires flash to my vision each time I touch and bath your wounds. Sometimes at night when I lie awake beside you, your dreams come to me. You did more than battle Moor and Egyptian in your travels. I would wager not all your scars are from sword, but more oft from long nails of lusty women panting for more."

Deep-throated laughter shook his chest. "You are jealous!"

She sniffed. "There is no shame in it. Is my love not sweet enough for you?"

He reached a caressing hand to her face. "Enough and more. The countless harems of Byzantia are no match to you."

"I do not find that so reassuring."

"Do not hold my past against me, my swan heart. I am but a mortal man. Is not my love sweet enough for you?"

She relented. "Enough and more."

He leaned and kissed her deeply . . . and drew back. "Never doubt me," he requested softly, "even when our time alone ends. Valhalla can be no sweeter than your arms, Moira."

"And must it end?"

"Soon, when I have strength, we must return to the Ravnings. Today I heard the ripping echo of the ice breaking up in the fjord. Our food stores are low . . . and—"

"And the sea calls you." She looked over to him with a pang of regret, wishing things were different. She wanted time to hold their loving in place, veiling their differences and her fears for the future.

"You are sad-faced. It does not end what passes between us, now the bond is stronger." He cupped her chin in his hand and searched her eyes.

"I have wondered . . ." She hesitated for a long moment.

"What have you wondered?" he asked lazily.

"Had there never been the enchantment—"

"Would I have still desired you?" he finished. His eyes fixed on her, then his firm lips broke into a smile. "Do not fret over something that will never be known. You will be an old woman soon enough."

"That is no answer."

"It is answer enough."

"What if there was no enchantment? Would you unbind me that I might return to my homeland?" The question hung in the air between them.

"This night your silver tongue asks too many questions." He stroked her cheek. "Were good asleep, you would awaken it; were it lost, you would find it. You are a woman in ten thousand, Moira. I could never let you go."

"But you said yourself, unhappy is the man who must live in a foreign land."

"Are you so unhappy in my arms?"

"Nay. But I wish to return to Myr."

"Then I will take you."

She sighed despairingly. "You cannot."

"Tell me the star roads. My ship will find the path."

"'Tis not so easy. Myr is a peaceful kingdom, and no one harboring the heart or weapons of war may enter."

"If it's so peaceful, who's to stop me?"

She frowned. His answer was the problem in itself. He could not see. "Yourself."

"Hah!" he scoffed. "By the gods! Only women would abide such a place where to be a hero a man would be no hero. Nay, you will stay with me. I am not stingy with my love or wealth. All I have is yours." His mouth captured hers, and because her body and heart burned for love of him, she did not refuse.

But in the recesses of her mind her swan self mourned. *All but freedom . . .*

Chapter | 16

Glistening icicles hung like gaping fangs from the saeter's roof. When Wulfsun pulled shut the saeter door, some fell and a pleasant clinking clitter-clatter encircled Moira's ears. Gray Deer danced impatiently within her harness at the head of a small pack sled piled high with furs from the fall and winter hunt. Wearing her snow-shoes, Moira set out over the crusted snow. The day's brightness watered her eyes, and she squinted in the sun's glare. Rivulets of icy water, no longer held prisoner by winter's hand, tunneled beneath snowy banks and gushed over rocky crags down the mountainside. Pines shook off white cloaks, birches yellowed with rising sap. Soon the trees would shake soft buds into leafy chimes. Spring's promise filled the air.

Overhead a bird's kree drew their attention. Moira looked up and spied the black gyrfalcon circling above. It had been two moon passings since she'd set her free. Wulfsun whistled sharply. Appalled, she watched the black gyrfalcon ring lower to land on Wulfsun's out-stretched arm.

"I have missed you, my sharp-beaked huntress," he endeared, stroking the feathered blue-black plumage. The falcon chirred with pleasure.

"She is trained to your whistle," Moira said with flat disappointment.

"And to my handling. She hunts for no one else."

"I thought I had freed her. You should have told me."

"You did not ask." His words irritated her. "Besides, you take so much pious delight in setting free the captive, I did not want to ruin your pleasure." The falcon splayed her wings and side-stepped up his arm to perch comfortably on the backpack.

Moira stared at the bird. Like a slap, the realization hit her that as long as she opened her arms to Wulfsun's loving, he would never, never release her.

I warned you, reminded her swan knowing. *Your compliance to him binds you as truly as the golden torque at your throat.*

While they traveled down the mountain, Moira wrestled with the quandary. The only path open to her lay in denying him what he sought most from her.

'Tis wrong to barter love, nettled her swan mind.

'Tis wrong to enslave another. Do you want your freedom?

Aye. I suppose 'tis worth a try. But I do not think you can find it in your soft woman's heart to deny him, especially at full moon.

I must!

When they crossed down into the valley, Wulfsun did not disguise his eagerness at first sight of the longships tilted sideways on the fjord shore. His pace quickened until Gray Deer strained to keep up. Grassy shoots patched the snow, and Moira stooped to pick a golden crocus from its snow cradle. Below, sheep and goats nosed around rock and thicket in search of tender buds. She inhaled the familiar whiffs of wood smoke and settlement. Scenting their arrival, dogs barked and children came scrambling up the slope.

The snow became too slushy for snowshoes and sled. Wulfsun unharnessed Gray Deer, and the wolf ran off into the forest. Two familiar figures strode up the hillside toward them. Moira recognized Thorfinn, his braided beard swinging to his waist, and Jacob the Freed, shirtless and grinning. They hailed Wulfsun warmly.

"By Odin's eye the spring will be early," said Wulfsun cheerfully.

"The spakonna prophesied it so," said Thorfinn. "I see you have had the hunting luck." He patted the mound of furs on the sled.

"It was a good winter for all," said Jacob.

"In most things," commented Wulfsun, and she felt his blue eyes on her. She turned her head, refusing to meet his gaze. Because of her sudden silence on their journey down, she guessed he thought his woman-luck needed improving.

The three hoisted the sled to their shoulders. Wulfsun walked in front, Thorfinn and Jacob on each side. Moira carried the snowshoes and trailed behind them. A feeling of constriction tightened her chest as she spied Ran the Fair coming up the hill. Sunlight silvered her fine-haired tresses. She could have been the goddess of spring with arms outstretched in welcome. Moira admired her beauty, but her admiration passed as she saw Wulfsun's genuine regard at Ran's approach. He took her in his arms and they kissed—overlong.

Moira's resolve to distance herself from him hardened, along with her heart. She quickly lowered her eyes before Ran could see how this reunion upset her.

"Have you wintered well, thrall woman?" inquired Jacob the Freed.

She looked over to him sullenly. "Yes, and you?"

"My fingers itch for other sport."

"You are not alone," She remarked flatly, noting Ran and Wulfsun laughing together. It became more and more difficult for her to walk behind them. When they entered the Ravnings, she went the opposite direction.

"Moira! Moira!" called Ysja, hurrying from the bower house. Moira greeted her with a warm embrace.

"Ysja, I have missed you." She was glad to see Ysja again. They walked to the hall. Brown-winged sparrows bathed and pecked in puddles by the doorway. She lifted the snowshoes and hung them under the eaves. "Spring has wasted no time in coming."

Ysja began to giggle, "Oh, Moira, have you nothing else to say?"

"What do you mean?" she asked, trying to think of something to tell.

"How did you pass the winter?" she prompted, her face beaming with curiosity.

"Well . . . there is nothing to tell. Wulfsun hunted and . . ." She stalled a little longer, not wanting to tell all.

"And . . ." echoed Ysja, wide-eyed.

"A wild animal attacked him. I nursed him back to health."

"You saved his life!" Her eyes widened in astonishment.

"It was not a big thing. He might have lived anyway," she belatedly added, not wanting Ysja to spread it around the Ravnings. It could ruin his hero's image.

"That is not all." She urged Moira further. "Tell me of the nights."

"I have nothing to tell."

"I do not believe you, Moira. I see it in your eyes."

"Do you see I still wear the collar of thralldom?"

"It is true." Ysja shook her head sadly. "I am so sorry for you."

Moira attempted a small smile. "Do not feel badly for my sake. And what of you?"

"My nights were very interesting," was her happy reply. "I carry a child as proof!"

"Haki Gunnarson's?"

"Yes." She smiled shyly. "Do not scold me, Moira. I love Haki. My only sadness is I am still a thrall and so will be the child."

"I will not scold you, Ysja. A hundred blessings from the Goddess on you and your child! I am glad you are happy. Haki is not such a bad fellow." Moira squeezed Ysja's hand affectionately.

Moira followed her inside the bower house, thinking sadly, It will not be easy for Haki to forge an iron ring of thralldom for his own child's neck.

Wulfsun, Thorfinn, and Ran were inside, inspecting the fur pelts he had brought from the saeter. Seated on a bench, Brigitta was running her hand over the rare white fox. Bent over, the old serving woman, Halda, eyed the fur as well.

"Moira." Brigitta greeted her and beckoned her to her side. "Are these not beautiful? My foster brother is a good hunter."

Before she could answer, across from them Wulfsun spoke. "I fear she does not share your enthusiasm, my sister."

Their eyes met, the first time since returning.

"Where is little Eyulf?" Moira looked away seeking a distraction. "He is not in his cradle."

"He is by the looms." Brigitta said, standing up. Moira followed her to the closed-off area. The women were very careful that the young children not play near the longfires. Brigitta stooped over and picked up a crawling, rosy-cheeked boy.

"He has outgrown the cradle."

Moira put her arms out to him, but he shied and buried his face against his mother's breast.

"I leave a baby and return to a little man. He grows too fast."

"The day will come soon that he will be a fosterling." She petted the taffy head.

"What do you mean?"

"A fosterling is a child raised by those who are not its parents. When a boy child is five winters old, he is sent to another stead to be raised to manhood. It is thought a mother's doting will make him less the warrior."

"I do not agree with that. A child should stay with his mother."

"It is our way," she said with resolve. A spirited debate drew their attention.

"I will take first choice," announced Ran the Fair. Her hands sorted over the hill of fur pelts. "I will take the white fox."

"Your eye is good, but those I set aside for my own use," replied Wulfsun. Ran frowned at his decision.

"In Kiev an Arab king would trade a hundred gold dinars for those. Such pelts are uncommon," interjected Thorfinn.

"You men think of only the price you can get at market. The furs should be worn by your women, not traded." Brigitta stepped forward and gave little Eyulf to Thorfinn. Eyulf cooed happily.

"There would be little peace at the Ravnings. You women would quarrel like cats for best pick," Thorfinn said to her.

Wulfsun had left Ran and moved to Moira's side. "What think you, or are you still not speaking to me?" he said quietly. She knew her moodiness puzzled him.

"They should be worn by those who fit them best, the fox and weasel."

"It is too late for that," he said.

"It may be too late for many things." Pointedly, she walked away from him and pretended to inspect tapestry being woven on the floor loom. She felt his eyes on her a long moment, and then he turned and strode out.

Wulfsun held counsel in the hall the remainder of the day. Moira kept to the bower house. Ysja was in and out as she served food in the hall. Once, in passing, she stopped a moment to gossip with Moira.

"Ran has not left Wulfsun's side. She fills his horn and serves his food. You, Moira, are his thrall woman. It should be you who waits upon him."

"If she chooses to do the duties of a thrall, I do not mind." She tried to suppress the surge of jealousy in her bosom.

"The men will go *a viking* soon. It was decided at counsel. They will go North for the white bear and fish teeth. Einar was in disagreement," Ysja continued. "He called for raids to take captives. But Wulfsun said, 'I have wintered with a captive; I will not spend my spring in pursuit of more.'" Ysja giggled. "Do you not think it funny, Moira?"

"Nay, Ysja, I do not think it funny," she said dryly. "How soon before the men go?"

"When the ships are ready, three, maybe four nights. I have never sailed on a longship." She paused thoughtfully and twirled a hammer of Thor pendant at her breast. "Is it the adventure they say?"

Moira sighed. "I found it so and more!" Again Ysja giggled and her blue eyes sparkled.

Moira looked down to the ships floating in the calm of the fjord. Now the days lengthened and the moon rose midsky before the shade of darkness fell. The men were impatient to go *a viking* and tomorrow the longships would sail.

The rift had widened between her and Wulfsun in the past days. He spent all his time at the ships working on the countless details of preparation and repair. He and the men reworked ropes, scraped hulls free of sea growth, caulked seams, and filled ship stores.

Tonight was the farewell feast. Moira knew her hand was needed to fill horns and carry food, but she had fled the hall's clamor and ribaldry and climbed the hillside to the pool. But even here she found no peace. Yet she couldn't remain in the hall fighting the constant desire to look down the long benches to the one golden head raised above all others. While the moon fever simmered in her veins, she could not stay and watch Ran the Fair as she ate and drank at the chieftain's side.

"Moira."

At her back came the textured softness of a deep Nordic voice, its every timbre and cadence known to her. She did not move; her heart did a cartwheel, and she cursed herself for being so susceptible to him. What sixth sense brought Wulfsun to her now?

"Did you think I would go with this distance between us? Why have you put yourself from me?"

She shook her head, unable to speak. A hundred emotions tore her, jealousy, rage, love, and grief, everything a mind could conjure to put the soul in misery.

He stepped closer. His touch on her arms was fire on ice. He turned her to him. He kissed her forehead, then her lips. Her resolve vanished, and she responded like a starving waif. His kisses became fierce demands as he drew her very breath from within her. A molten sword, his tongue seared and probed its serpent's curve between her parting lips. A giant yearning swept her. His hands moved down with the flow and rise of her body until they encircled her hips and pressured them to his own.

"Let me love you this night, my swan heart. I have missed you at my side." His breath fired her cheek and her blood. His caresses and kisses were laying waste her judgment.

'Tis folly to let him love you! cried her swan self.

I fear folly has come to visit. She felt herself weakening.

"I burn for you. Love me, Moira. This night. Now!" His voice was a harsh whisper. "You make me a beggar."

She placed a resisting palm upon his chest. "Aye, and you make me a prisoner. Sever this gold binding from my throat."

He could not fail to hear the agony in her voice, for it matched his own. He gripped her shoulders and held her eyes with a tortuous dark stare. "I could have you, you know this."

A ripple of despair passed over her face, but she said nothing.

Releasing her, his long fingers raked distractedly through his wheaten hair. "I cannot put my manhood aside like the Christian brothers."

"That is not what I ask of you." Her fingers touched the scarlet stain on his high cheekbones, which betrayed his rising temper. "As long as you enslave me, I cannot . . . nay . . . I will not lay with you." Her eyes stung with moisture, and she blurted out desperately, "Give me my freedom! You enslave my very soul!"

"I will not! Had you freedom, you would fly." His fingers clutched the circle at her throat. "This alone binds you to me."

Tears burned her cheeks. Could he not understand? She searched his face, a swimming profile against the silver of the full moon, a sculpted perfection of strength and savagery.

"Give me freedom. My heart binds me to you stronger than any ring of slavery. Do you chain your vikings to your side? Your wolf? Am I less than them to you?"

"You are more! Because of this I hold you." His eyes were fixed with the blackness of a starless night. "You haunt me. You provoke y manhood, then beg me to use control. I go *a viking* so I might cure the fever you have fired in my blood. But I fear your witchery will follow me. When sea spray wets my lips, I will taste your tears. When night's darkness falls, it will be you, the woman with sorrow-colored hair, who I will want. I bind you, woman, because you bind me!"

He pulled her to him and kissed her, filling and emptying. Her senses shrieked for him, but gathering iron will, she broke away, and ran down the hillside. . . .

He did not follow.

Chapter | 17

The coming of spring softened Moira's parting from Wulfsun. The valley sang with the first bleat of lamb and kid, and peep of chick and gosling. Wildflowers pushed from beneath onion-colored blankets of fall's leaves until the cast of brown became an emerald wash of verdant meadow. The sun hovered above the horizon as darkness and idleness became winter's companions.

The Ravnings took on the aspect of a nunnery, for only a few men remained, the old and the young. No longfire laid in the hall, and for Moira the high seat glared with emptiness. She flung herself into each day's unceasing labors. As she followed behind the plowman sowing barley and rye seed over the brunet turned earth, she thought about Wulfsun and their wintering.

Memories of him wheeled in her mind. Wulfsun carrying her to the warm springs; Wulfsun pushing his way inside the saeter like a snow giant; Wulfsun lying fevered, near to death; their violent farewell the night before he sailed north. She began to regret that night and wondered . . . if she had done the right thing to deny him that which should never be denied.

One afternoon when she passed the bower house, Halda struggled with a wooden stool in the doorway. In one hand she balanced the white fox furs and with the other she tugged on a three-legged stool.

"Let me help you," she offered.

"The light is better outside and my eyes tire," she said, motioning to the exact spot to place the stool.

"What are you sewing?" Moira asked. She was curious as to what the outcome of the prized furs would be.

"The chieftain has me sew his bridal gift."

"Bridal gift?" she questioned.

"It is to be a hooded cloak for Ran the Fair. He said I was to take great care, but have it finished for the handfast."

Stunned, she remained silent.

"It will be a cloak unmatched," continued Halda.

Something fell inside Moira—her heart to the pit of her stomach. She'd been strolling in spring, now she was flung into deep winter. So, she thought, the chieftain has made his choice.

"It speaks well of the chieftain to give Ran such a gift, a gift she has wanted," said Halda.

Slow poison would have been more pleasant for her than to stand there listening to Halda. Yet her legs remained fixed to the spot. A sick desperation clutched her heart and caused her to wish she might enchant Wulfsun anew rather than lose him to Ran.

Oh, swanling, would you truly enchant him again if you could? asked her swan self, aghast. *Has it not been more bitter than sweet?*

Aye, but love's pain encircles my heart like a dark cloud, and what is more bitter than this?

Kari Olvirson with his two younger brothers, Sverr and Rollo, sailed into the Ravnings one drizzling, inclement afternoon. The poor weather had caught them fishing. Welcomed with the usual generous hospitality of the Ravnings, they stayed over the night.

The next morning a thrall child called Moira away from the stream where she was washing and told her she was to go down to the boat of Kari Olvirson. Full of curiosity, she followed the stream down to the fjord and then walked along the shore to his boat. Kari and Ran the Fair stood in conversation while Kari's brothers loaded the boat with bundles of food and gifts that Brigitta wished to send their mother, Freya.

"Thrall woman," said Ran, her face serious, "I have traded you to Kari."

Moira did not mask her shock. Her mouth dropped open, and she looked from Kari to Ran wholly speechless. Kari looked utterly pleased with himself as if he'd been the first to market and gotten the best bargain of the day. Ran was more circumspect.

"Leave us alone," she said to Kari. Hesitant at first, he stepped away and busied himself shouting orders to his younger brothers. Moira and Ran were left facing each other. Though Wulfsun was not there, his presence vibrated in the air between them. Abjectly Moira realized this sun—complexioned woman knew more of Wulfsun than she ever would. She had toddled after him in his youth and rambled with him in manhood. How often had his hands caressed her, or his lips sought the softness of her cheek?

Restraining herself from showing any emotion, Ran's voice was pitched sweet indeed. "It is no secret to me you have enchanted my foster brother. He is unable to send you away, so I must." She opened her hands, revealing silver coins. "Kari has given silver coin for you. If you go with him willingly, I can say as much to Wulfsun when he returns."

A cold wind lapped across the fjord and flowed in to shore. Moira shivered bitterly, realizing that once Ran sent her away, Wulfsun, no longer enchanted, would soon forget her. She would end her days passed from one master to the next, wretched and earthbound. She had nothing to bargain with, so when she finally found her voice, she said, "He will not believe you."

Tension lined the corner of Ran's lovely eyes, and she hastily spat back, "He will believe. For it is common for your kind to be treacherously fickle."

"I will not go," Moira said defiantly.

"You have no choice!" Ran breathed between her teeth and walked off. In a shrill voice which cut across the air she called to Kari. "Take her. Bind her if you must, but take her now!"

Kari frowned and shrugged his cloak off one shoulder. "You said she would go willingly."

"It is no matter what I said. Wulfsun tires of her," declared Ran flatly. "It is I he will wed at summer feast." Her words pummeled Moira like a hundred river stones. "Do not expect your silver back if you do not take her. A bargain is a bargain." Ran tossed back, striding up the hillside.

There was a short silence, while Kari raked his gray eyes over his new acquisition. Moira's fingers knotted the linen of her skirts, and for a brief moment she considered fleeing, where she was not sure.

"Give me no trouble, and I will give you none. Climb into the boat," said Kari, his voice full of false command.

The magnitude of the injustice being done her rooted her to the shore. She thought to threaten Kari with the consequences of taking the chieftain's thrall woman, but she was not sure if there would be consequences.

"All is ready, Kari," announced young Sverr from the boat, his red cheeks blooming with high spirits. He cast a shy smile to Moira. She could not smile back and the bastion of her emotions burst, her lips pursed into a grimace, and she turned her face away as the tears tracked down her cheeks.

"Come," said Kari gently, stepping beside her. His strong arms circled her from behind, and he swept her up and carried her to the boat.

She did not resist, though a wild desolation washed through her, and she yearned for her grandmother's counsel. Then all of a sudden, she remembered her grandmother might yet be at Olvirsted. She need not wait until summer feast to see Epona. Her despair lightened, and as Kari jumped in the boat, she was sniffling away her tears.

As time passed only the gurgle of water and the swish of splashing oars broke the morning's stillness as their boat glided over the fjord. She snuggled in the warmth of her cloak and watched Eider ducks swim in the wake of a wooden fishing cage trolling behind the boat. When the granite cliffs narrowed, Kari lifted his eyes to spy for avalanche or rock slide from above. His brothers were tiring from rowing, but he did not offer to change places. She supposed they were being schooled for the day they would pull the oars of a longship.

The sun was midsky when they turned the boat down an inlet that branched off the mainstream of the fjord. She saw smoke swirling above the trees, and soon two longhouses on the mountain slope came into view. One, opened on all four sides, edged the shore. The overlapping ribs of a longship's hull in the making rested on wooden supports in this open-sided house. The sun broke from behind the clouds, and she recognized Olvir the Shipbuilder working with another man. They saluted and Olvir put down his tool and walked toward their boat. He looked down a hawkish nose and squinted in her direction. In his stance she read disapproval.

"Is she not the fosterling's thrall woman?" he asked Kari.

"She's mine now," Kari said. He helped her from the boat.

"How is this?"

"Wulfsun is *a viking*. I traded Ran two marks of silver."

"That is more than fair, but you may have bought a little trouble," Olvir said, wiping his forehead with a red cloth. "Rollo, take the woman up to your mother."

She felt apprehensive about her new home. The raking glint in Kari's youthful eyes made her wary, and the disapproval in his father's caused her caution.

Following Rollo up the hill, she saw Olvirsted to be on a much smaller scale than the Ravnings. There was no fortress or gates, no feast hall, and only two small outbuildings flanked the single longhouse. She recognized Olvir's wife Freya, but her hopeful eyes searched for Epona. Freya was bent over a rendering pot outside. She looked much the same as she had over three months before at the Yule feast, wide-hipped and heavy breasted. Beside her stood the rosy-cheeked little girl with a snow-white scarf tied over her braided head. Both stared at Moira as she approached.

"Kari?" Freya greeted, and then placed a shading hand over her brow and eyed Moira. "She is Wulfsun's thrall woman. Why is she here?" she asked Rollo.

The boy brushed a shock of reddish gold hair from his eyes and shrugged. "Kari has traded for her."

Freya put her hands on her hips and pursed her lips tightly. Like her husband, she did not approve of what her son had done.

"Come then. There is work." She led Moira into the longhouse.

"Where is the spakonna?" Moira asked, no longer able to contain herself.

Freya stopped and turned, interest marked her features. "It is odd you should ask. We do not know. She is not the same as us. She came at full moon and left at full moon."

"She is gone?" Moira could not believe this. Tears of frustration stung her eyes, and she bit the inside of her mouth attempting to fight back her despair.

"Come now, you can be useful. The fire pit needs cleaning," directed Freya, unaware of her despair. "There is your work." Freya pointed to the fire pit. Moira could see it had been a while since it had been emptied, for the ashes were in high mounds. "Up the hillside is the garden. Sprinkle the ashes there," she said, leaving.

For a moment Moira stood alone in the strangeness of the longhouse, trying to sort everything out. She could not fly, for she was still bound by the golden neck torque. She could not run away because she knew not where to run, and if caught she would be punished. Finally, with a defeated sigh, she did the only thing she could do—she began to clean the fire pit. She wrapped a scarf over her nose and mouth and began the chore.

A little time later she entered the doorway of the longhouse. The smell of baking fish filled her nose. She felt awfully hungry. The men were seated at the trestle table while Freya and the young girl hovered over the cooking. She counted five at the table. Olvir, Kari, the two boys, and the man who worked beside Olvir in ship building.

"Gyda," Freya said to the young girl, whose cheeks

were as red as a summer apple, "give the thrall woman food." Gyda filled a trencher and set it on the table.

"Come, eat," beckoned Freya. Moira sat down beside Rollo. He inched away, nearly falling off the end of the bench. Kari and Sverr chuckled at his shyness while poor Rollo blushed. She sympathized; he was not alone in his ill-ease.

Freya set herring wrapped in leaves and baked in clay on the table. She passed around cheese, flatbrod, and nippy watercress from the spring.

"It goes well at the Ravnings?" inquired Olvir of his son, Kari.

"Yes," replied Kari between mouthfuls. "Wulfsun has gone north."

"On what matter?" wondered his father.

"I did not ask."

Once or twice Moira looked up and met eyes with the silent man. He had not spoken so far. She knew he was freeborn, for he wore no collar of thralldom around his neck. He was neither fair nor dark. Stubble thatched his face, and grime ringed his neck and forearms. He had passive eyes which did not probe like Wulfsun's nor did they leer like Bjorn's. Freya did not sit with them, but the young girl, Gyda, sat beside the silent man. She remained as quiet as he.

"Thorfinn has kinsmen in Halogaland. His father is cousin to Sigvat of Trondeheim," said Freya.

"Sigvat is a lucky man, lucky from fish teeth. I could be as lucky," Kari pointed out to his father.

"There is luck in shipbuilding," returned Olvir curtly. Moira sensed a disagreement between them.

"The thrall woman will sleep with Gyda," announced Freya suddenly as she fastened her coiled hair atop her head more securely. Kari opened his mouth in protest.

"The choice is the thrall woman's," said Olvir, cutting Kari short. The indignant expression on Kari's face caused Moira to bite back a smile. He hadn't reckoned the watchfulness of his parents during his bargain. All eyes turned to her, awaiting her answer.

"I will sleep with Gyda," she affirmed. Kari muttered an oath under his breath and left the longhouse.

As the days passed, Gyda and Moira became close companions. They found enough work to pass the day, but not so much they could not sit and talk, swim in the icy fjord, or ramble over the hills into the forest. Gyda was curious and observant. A little too observant, Moira thought. She told her of many things concerning Olvir and his family. She told Moira what she had suspected, that Kari wanted to go *a viking* but his father desired that he learn the shipbuilder's craft. Thorolf, the other man, was Gyda's father. He was a skilled craftsman, but talked of going south to the Vik now that Gyda's mother was dead.

"Would you like that?" she asked Gyda.

"I could not go. He would not take me."

"Your father is right. Olvirsted is the best place for you."

And you as well, decided her swan self. *If you are to be earthbound, this is a good place.*

At Olvirsted everyone slept outside. Moira preferred it. Winter had confined her too long indoors. The air was sweet and the sounds of night reminded her of Myr. With hands propped behind her head, she gazed into the twilight identifying the hummings and thrummings, the taps and clicks of night.

"You do not sleep," said Freya, who lay nearby.

"The night is too beautiful for sleep," said Moira, turning her face to Freya.

"Gyda's mother and I used to talk into the early hours as we lay here. Since she died, I have been lonely for another woman. I am glad Kari brought you here." Freya's hand reached and touched hers. "At first I was not sure. What is between you and the fosterling?" she probed gently.

Moira thought Freya wouldn't have spoken had she known how close her concern came to cutting the fragile thread that bound her emotions. She had learned that love was a cruel piper. It spared none who heard its song, no matter how innocent, cunning, or wise.

"It is over." She sighed like a tired, old woman. She did not want to think about Wulfsun, but he filled her mind every waking moment.

"I do not think you tell the truth. I see in your face it is not over. The fosterling would not kill Bjorn Bloody Hair on your behalf and then so quickly cast you off. There is more. You had better tell me." Moira knew Freya's concern wasn't for her alone, but for Kari.

She sighed. "Wulfsun vows to marry Ran the Fair. I would not be a mistress."

Freya nodded her head slowly with perfect understanding. "It is a hard thing to share a man, especially one such as the fosterling. Ran is of the same mind. That is why she traded you for nothing to my son Kari." Her voice was soft.

"Aye," she agreed, hardening her own.

"Then it is done, but not over," disclosed Freya. Silence fell between them.

In the sunlit evenings they sat out of doors beside the fire. Moira combed wool while Freya spun it into a thread as fine as spiderweb. Kari and Thorolf carved on a long length of wood that would be the new ship's mast pole. Gyda played round stones with Rollo and Sverr.

"Freya, Rollo has taken my stone. Make him give it back," pleaded Gyda from her knees within the playing circle.

"I won it fairly. If you want it back, you must win it." He tossed and caught the delicately painted stone in front of her nose. Her eyes filled with tears from his taunting.

"I will never play with you again if you keep it," she whined, running to Moira's side.

"Never?" he teased with exaggerated surprise.

"Never! I hope a troll carries you off while you sleep." She twisted up her face at him. "I hate you!" she cried, her crimson cheeks flushed redder still. "I have only three left." She dropped her round painted stones into a small linen pouch. Moira and Freya smiled at each other.

"You are clever at riddles, Gyda. That is the way to win back your stones from Rollo," counseled Freya.

Gyda lit to the suggestion, as did Rollo and Sverr. Soon heads bent together thinking up a riddle.

"I will say it only once," warned Rollo. Gyda grimaced

and closed her eyes in serious concentration. "I am a wondrous creature," began Rollo. "I am long and short. When I bend, the peak of Ravnjell touches my stomach. Odin carries me on his shoulder. What am I?"

Gyda repeated the words slowly . . . "Odin carries me on his shoulder." Her eyes sprang open. A knowing grin spread across her face. "I know it! Give me a stone."

"Not until you say!" cried Rollo.

"Yes, you must say," Sverr echoed.

"Odin's bow! The rainbow!" she squealed triumphantly.

Before giving up the stone, Rollo took a moment to berate Sverr for his poor choice of a riddle. "Anyone could have guessed it."

"You could not, not until I told you," defended Sverr.

"What is this? You cannot guess a riddle, Rollo?" Olvir questioned, looking up from his work.

Rollo glared at Sverr. Sverr grinned. Moira decided they enjoyed getting each other into trouble.

"Guess this one, if you can," challenged Olvir. He rubbed his chin thoughtfully, then spoke. "I have no eyes, foot, or arm, but many ribs. Quickly I pass. I go to return. I am emptied to be filled. What creature is this?"

"That is easy, father. A ship!" answered Rollo, his self–esteem restored.

"Here is another," piped Kari from across the fire. "I am foe and friend. Shaped in fire, I am cold to touch. My master honors me in the hall, yet far and wide I am outlawed. Say what is my name."

Everyone thought silently.

Many things are honored in the halls of the Northmen; most are cold to touch, pondered Moira's swan self.

It would have to be a weapon forged in fire. Just as she opened her mouth to guess, Freya spoke sooner.

"A sword!"

"You are quick-minded, mother," complimented Kari. "Thrall woman, have you a riddle?"

Epona's riddle came quickly to Moira's mind. *When the sun never sleeps, follow Thought and Memory to the Dragon's lair. By the ley path you came, by the ley path you go.* How could she tell a riddle for which she knew no answer? She nibbled her lip and turned ideas over in her mind.

Yes, announced her swan self.

"I have," Moira said aloud. "Though it may be very hard and a slow-minded man like yourself, Kari, will never guess it."

"Then I must pay closer attention." With a laugh, he came around the fire and sat beside her.

"I swim better than walk. The winds carry me above men and mountains. My garment is white," she began.

"Snow," hazarded Sverr. Moira shook her head.

"You are a bird, a white bird," concluded Gyda. "She is a swan!" The children applauded happily.

"A swan maid," Kari teased.

Thorolf spat into the fire. "No good comes from such changelings." His eyes held Moira's darkly. She was scored by his words, his looks, and his unusual break of silence.

"It is said they are so beautiful, no man can resist their enchantments," announced Rollo.

"Do you believe such legends, Kari?" asked Gyda.

"He is young. What do you expect?" Olvir jested. Kari frowned.

"Even you, Father, heard the spakonna at the Yule feast. Did she not tell Wulfsun he would meet a swan sister?"

"He was not pleased to hear such speakings, nor would I be. The old woman is a meddler!"

"Olvir," cautioned Freya. "Be careful what you say."

Olvir frowned. "A month with her under my roof was enough!"

"It is good luck to house a spakonna," said Freya, winding up her spinning. "Our larders were still full at winter's end. None took sick and our sheep have born twins and triplets."

"Well, don't be expecting to be as rich as your sister Thora," warned Olvir.

Freya laughed. "I am content, but you promised me a visit to her. Remember?"

Olvir frowned.

Freya turned to Moira. "I would like to see my sister,

Thora. We are twins. My father named us for the gods Thor and Frey. Life turns out better for those named after the gods, and I believe it so. I have been happy. My sister Thora lives in the hall of the wealthy Sigvat. Her husband Rolf is well-looked upon by Sigvat."

Olvir grunted disapproval. "You know my opinion of your sister's husband and his lord Sigvat, who calls himself the king of the North."

"A man could do no better than to raise his sword for one such as Sigvat," remarked Kari.

"I do not think serving a man that loves wealth before honor, pays men to fight his battles, and lusts after other men's wives is very swordwise." Olvir seemed to have a particular grudge against this Sigvat, decided Moira. Kari muttered.

Olvir's face softened slightly, for he loved his son. "Look to the fosterling, Kari. He is a fair chieftain. I have raised my sword on his behalf before and would do so again."

"He is one mind with you, Father. He thinks I should learn the shipbuilding craft."

"There is time for both," said Freya. "I think it is also time for me to visit my sister in the North. The weather is good and Kari could take us North."

"Do as you please, woman. I will not accompany you nor will Kari. Thorolf will take you." Disagreement showed on Kari's face, but Olvir stood and turned away. Kari left going in the opposite direction. Freya's eyes followed him thoughtfully. Moira could see the rift expanding between Olvir and his son. Maybe Olvir should let him go. He had two other sons to follow his craft.

"You will come as my serving woman, Moira," said Freya, already making plans. "I think you would enjoy a journey North. It is much different from here."

"Yes." Her own agreement echoed in her ears. "I am eager to see the North."

To see your chieftain, more the like, chided her swan mind."

Chapter | 18

It took not two, but three days for Moira and her companions to travel North. A day was lost when fog obscured their sea path. Thorolf put them ashore until it cleared. Moira found him a wordless companion, although Gyda and Freya were happy company.

"Sigvat has more dragon ships than any man in the North," said Freya as their small boat sailed along the ship-lined shore of Halogaland. Moira counted fifteen tipped idly on the beach. The day was sunny, but the gray waters held the feel of ice. The settlement nestled in the curve of a jutting headland. Unlike the Ravnings, it was not hidden in the long arm of a fjord, but faced the sea head on. Behind, glacier-capped mountains rose beyond densely forested hillside.

Thorolf steered them to shore, where the boat halted with a thud. He tossed a guide rope to a youth who had left his work near a dragon ship to aid them. He welcomed them and Thorolf answered in kind. Others came and Gyda hopped with a rabbit's leap to land, heedless of the new dun-colored kirtle Moira had sewn for her. Freya and Moira were helped from the boat to land by a tall, handsome Northman with a red-gold beard. Freya was known to him, though he didn't offer her the courtesy he did Moira—a full-handed squeeze on her buttocks, followed by a flirtatious wink.

"How went winter in Halogaland, Erick?" asked Freya.

"Well enough. We go south soon."

Moira wondered why no one thought of going south during winter. Once when she had asked Wulfsun, he had said, "The sea is unfriendly in winter, and the fish run along the coast in the cold months. The best furs are from the winter hunt. And most important, in winter a man should stay close to his home fires, or he finds another takes his place." His answers made sense to her, but she decided he liked the challenge of being cold and uncomfortable, living in darkness and eating a monotonous diet of dried fish. He was a perennial spartan.

Freya gave Erick a cheering smile. "My sister, Thora, how does she fare?"

"She is well. Her sharp tongue has kept my father's hall in order."

"A man with only sons and no wife needs a forceful woman in his hall," Freya observed.

"She is that!" Erick laughed.

Thorolf remained behind to attend to the boat, but the others followed Erick up to the tall gates of Sigvat's imposing timbered fortress. The staves were carved and painted yellow and red. Dragons rose and twisted from the roof in a fierce grimace to sea, sky, and land. To Moira it seemed a great castle.

At the hall's entrance she peered inside and saw great longfires burning the length. Torch lamps illuminated colorful woven tapestries hanging between carved wooden pillars at all sides of the hall.

In the hall's hub high seats rose like thrones. A gigantic white bearskin, enormous claws and gaping head, hung on the wall behind the seats. Moira could not take her eyes from this ferocious specter and wondered if Sigvat had killed it himself. She could not see any honor in displaying such a trophy.

"Sigvat, spring has brought us fair visitors," announced Erick loudly. He had interrupted his father in mid–conversation. Sigvat turned to them and smiled a welcome. He saluted Freya by raising a ringed hand.

"You are welcome, Freya. And Olvir? Does he yet refuse my hospitality?" he said with amusement.

"Yes, Sigvat."

"He has good reason, I suppose. But it is no good holding a grudge." Sigvat's eyes wandered to Moira. He appraised her. He himself was moon-faced, shaggy-browed, and balding. Not a handsome man, thought Moira, yet age might have improved his looks by sketching lines of shrewdness.

His words told her what he thought of her. "You bring a fair-faced thrall woman, Freya. A gift for me?"

"No, Sigvat." She colored slightly with irritation. "You have enough thralls. She is my serving woman."

A joyful cry rang across the hall. A woman the image of Freya rushed to envelope Freya in her arms. Thora was far from soft-spoken, her voice carried above the noise of the hall.

She questioned Freya about her journey, her family, and her health.

"Little Gyda, come, come." Thora gathered Gyda in her arms. "You are at least two winters taller. Gret and Helga will be happy to see you. Come, we will go to the bower." She went to take Gyda's hand, but Gyda pulled away and clutched Moira's own. Thora was not offended, but noticed Moira for the first time.

"Moira is my serving woman," Freya told her sister.

"A serving woman? She wears a golden collar of thralldom." Thora seemed puzzled.

"Yes, it is a long story, one I will tell you in private," said Freya, her voice lowered. She looked over at Moira and took a fringed linen scarf from her own neck. "Cover your neck. It is best to halt the gossip before it begins."

"It is not usual for Olvir to trade in slaves. I see by her coloring she is foreign." Thora continued to speak as if Moira was not there.

"Kari traded for her, and I have found a good servant and companion." Freya's compliments warmed Moira's heart.

"She is welcome, then," Thora finally acknowledged. She turned and Moira and Freya followed her from the hall.

Moira lost count of the longhouses and outbuildings that housed the men who sailed Sigvat's ships of trade and war. Her eyes were still wide when she entered the woman's hall, the center of housewifery. Here the women and servants prepared the feasts, spun, sewed, gossiped, and tended children away from the politics, counsels, and revelries of the men. She noted happily that crockery and soapstone pots hung in place of swords and shields. Tall, stone-weighted looms, warped with beautiful earthen colors, replaced high seats. The tantalizing smells of baking breads and vegetables simmering with pungent herbs filled her nose while the sounds of playing children filled her ears.

"I am hungry," whispered Gyda.

She squeezed Gyda's hand affectionately. "So am I. Be patient, they will offer us something soon." She knew in the Northland no welcomed traveler went hungry, no matter how scarce the food. Judging by the sights, there was plenty, for Sigvat was a wealthy man.

Thora beckoned them to sit on a long bench beside the fire. She called for food in her loud but amiable voice. Almost immediately a thrall girl, pale-cheeked and blue-eyed, came with mead and bread. At her heels tumbled two white-headed little girls, twins, the echoes of Thora and Freya. Younger than Gyda, they were not shy and quickly made her giggle. The thrall girl returned with trenchers of walnut-colored goat cheese and poached fish in melted butter. While Thora and Freya spoke together, Moira ate and happily prepared herself to settle into this new household.

One week passed. It neared the end of April, a time when the days seemed to last forever and the nights merely winked with darkness. Freya enjoyed her visit, loving the luxury of being waited upon by so many servants. Moira thought Gyda would never want to leave her fast friends, Gret and Helga. As for herself, Moira was ready to return to Olvirsted. Sigvat had taken an interest in her and often called her to his side. She dared not refuse. He found her conversation and company pleasing, so he said. He asked many questions about

Britain after discovering she had been captured from an abbey. He particularly asked about the rumors of treasure and wealth the Christians amassed in their monasteries.

"In comparison to a man of such wealth as yourself, Lord Sigvat," she answered, "they are paupers. You would find no honor in raiding their coffers. A king does not rob the beggar."

"Ah . . . you speak my very mind." He cleared his throat with ill-ease and took another sip of mead from his golden-gilded horn.

Most afternoons Freya and Moira strolled outside the fortress to the headland's northern point. Gyda and the twins laughed out to sea and ran before the waves.

"It is time to leave, Moira," Freya disclosed. "Tomorrow we will depart."

"I am ready." Moira's eyes followed the foraging of a lapwing on the rocks.

"I miss Olvir," Freya admitted. She pushed back a strand of hair loosened by the breeze. "It was here by the sea I first realized how much Olvir loved me . . . and I him. You have heard us speak of the death of my parents on Ravnjell as they returned with Egil Ravn from the *Althing.* At the time Olvir decided to bring me north to Sigvat's hall so I might share my grief with Thora. Sigvat welcomed us and we stayed for a season. Sigvat held Olvir in great estimation because not even Sigvat's master shipbuilder held Olvir's skill.

"A winter before, Sigvat had lost his wife in childbirth, and his eye strayed to me. Sigvat is not as bad as Olvir thinks, but he has many vices. When Sigvat discovered I was a faithful wife, he paid one of his vikings to goad Olvir into a fight. Olvir killed the man and soon after discovered Sigvat's treachery."

"It was a summer day. On this very spot Olvir came to me, saying he was leaving Sigvat's hall. 'I am going. If you choose to stay, I leave you that choice,' he spoke. It is a rare man who loves a woman enough to give her free choice. Olvir is such a man. 'If you leave I have no reason to stay,' I told him. We left Sigvat's hall and never has Olvir returned. But he is fair and trusting and tolerates my visits to my sister." Freya's gaze was distant. She looked out to sea, remembering.

To bind is easy. Not so easy to set free, echoed Moira's swan self.

Aye, agreed Moira, deciding Wulfsun would never love her enough to give her free choice.

"Look, ships!" squealed the girls. Moira looked toward their sharp-eyed gazes and saw the mastheads of one, two, and then three ships. The square sail of the first was taut with the image of a large white bear. The sails of the other ships winged black ravens on the blood-red background.

Her breath halted and her pulse leaped. The *Sea Steed* and the *Elk Wader.*

Freya was quick to discern her shock, because she recognized those sails as well as Moira. "The fosterling. I had not expected . . ." Her words failed, then began, "It would be better if he did not know you are here."

"What am I to do? What if someone speaks of Freya's black-haired thrall woman with the collar of gold? He will know."

"You have covered your collar, most will not think of it," declared Freya.

As the ships neared the headland point, Moira quickly reversed her cloak to show the fur lining outward, and she raised her hood.

"If you keep to the woman's hall, there is no chance you will meet. None but Thora know you are the fosterling's thrall woman. I will speak with her, though it is common talk who a chieftain favors. The tale of Bjorn Bloody Hair's death came north with spring."

Moira sighed. "Then all must know who I am."

"No, they do not. They know only he killed Bjorn over a woman. Such happenings are common in the long winter."

The remainder of the day Moira labored in the bower house, helping with the preparations for the feast that night in the hall. She bent over fires, basting and turning game until she felt as if she were skewered and trussed herself. She finally stepped outside for fresh air. Straightening the crook in her back, her eyes rested on the sky tinged with soft blues and corals of evening. The midnight sun hovered above the horizon, and the air tasted of a spring night. Men and women sprawled across the grassy hillside watching their companions compete in games of wrestling, archery, and spear throwing. She strolled forward, careful to remain unnoticed.

As she peered around heads and over shoulders, she saw the center attraction to be Sigvat's son, Erick. He took a running leap and jumped a remarkable distance. A man paced the area and shouted back the length of Erick's jump. Everyone cheered, whistled, and clapped. Erick raised a fist and summoned another man from the group. The man came forward, a hint of swagger in his gait. The man was Wulfsun.

Is it myth a lover's face is fixed in memory? wondered Moira.

He seems a stranger.

He wore a shaggy beard and his wheaten hair feathered down his shoulders. But the eyes she knew. His eyes flashed with blue clarity as he strode forward with enthusiastic challenge. She wasn't sick, but the sight of him made her feel queasy. She clasped her hands together to keep from shaking.

He prepared for his jump with the easy self-assurance that maddened her.

Look around, swanling, there are other men as handsome, as strong, and as appealing, her swan self prompted.

But she could not look around, for like every other person, her eyes were drawn to Wulfsun.

He ran with the grace of a leopard. He leaped with the stride of a hunter and landed soundly at least a foot beyond Erick's mark. Cheers burst forth. He met the accolade with a reckless grin and proud eye.

He can hazard anything, nettled her swan self. *Hasn't he done so with your heart?*

Moira turned back to the woman's hall and escaped inside. She took up spindle and wool and seated herself on a bench. Pushing the spindle rhythmically to and fro against her thigh, she strangled any thought of Wulfsun in skeins of handspun.

As time passed, she did not need to look outdoors to see if the full moon rose in the indigo sky. She felt it rise, inflaming her blood until her veins pulsed with the wildfire of estrous. How could she not help but think of Wulfsun, so near . . . yet beyond her touch? Should she go to him and reveal herself? Tell him his fair Ran had traded her to young Kari? What good would it do? He still would not free her.

Thralls began carrying food from the bower house to the hall while the highborn women gossiped and chatted as they dressed and combed themselves before joining the feast. Not only the young girls but the married women projected the night's flirtations. She resigned herself to hearing Wulfsun's name as it crossed excited lips.

"His thrall woman is said to rival anyone in the North for beauty," someone prattled.

"She is a witch!" retorted a sagging-faced matron whose great age affixed such a label on her own features.

"A witch?" marveled another. Across from Moira, Freya met her eyes with a cautionary nod.

A squint-eyed woman declared, "One who sails the *Sea Steed* told me himself that the witch has enchanted the chieftain." This was received with gushing exclamations.

"The witch's curse will be on the one the chieftain beds this night. I would not be the one," advised the old matron, eyeing in particular a young girl beside her. The girl's finely arched brows raised in soberness. Moira knew the old matron hoped to discourage the girl's flirtations with a seasoned warrior such as Wulfsun.

"Do not worry, Grandmother. He would not choose you," scoffed a fetching, highborn woman whose yellow hair fell like pale silk over her shoulders. Laughter ran among the women. "Wulfsun's lovemaking would be worth any curse."

Moira lowered her eyes and bit her lip.

"How would you know, Gunrod?" quizzed someone. "He has taken no one to his bed this time North."

Moira felt color rising to her cheeks, and her temper simmered from this gossip. Unable to be still, she spoke up. "It was my hearing that he is a clumsy lover. He puts about the rumors of his prowess himself." Freya gave her a silencing eye. She knew she should not have spoken. More laughter followed her words.

"You lie, thrall woman," challenged the highborn woman, Gunrod. Moira shot her a cool stare. The woman returned a cat-in-the-cream smile.

She knows I lie from the verity of her own experience, thought Moira dejectedly. *Sometime Wulfsun has bedded her. It tells on her face.*

She turned away and choked back her jealousy. The woman rose, tall and willowy, and placed a gold circlet on her head. From beneath beautifully curved golden eyebrows, the green eyes gave her a long appraisal, then she smoothed her saffron kirtle and left.

"Come, sit, let me comb your hair," offered the thrall girl after her mistress departed. Moira felt a headache lurking within her temples, and she knew it would feel good to loosen her tightly plaited hair.

"If you have nothing else to do," she answered gratefully. She sat down and the girl began unfastening her braids. Her combing strokes began to relax Moira and ease her tension.

"My mistress speaks the truth of Wulfsun. He favors her when he comes North." The sure knowledge clutched Moira's heart like a cold hand. "Your hair is beautiful, so thick and long. Wulfsun's witch is said to have black hair like you. It is a rare sight in the North." Moira knew the thrall girl suspected something.

She opened a small wooden chest containing jewelry, combs, and scents in silver vials. "Choose one. Some are very scarce." Moira uncorked two or three and smelled their fragrance. Finally choosing a musky scent, she rubbed it on her wrists and, lifting her skirt, touched a drop behind each knee. This amused the thrall girl.

A hand touched Moira's shoulder, and she turned to

face a young man—Sigvat's personal servant. "Sigvat wants you to attend him in the hall."

Moira looked to Freya. Worry creased her face, but she nodded and said, "You must go. He does not give up easily."

"I will come soon," she assured the servant. She rose to her feet, but the young thrall girl stopped her. As a final touch, she put a silver circlet on her head.

"You are more beautiful than my mistress. You may even catch Wulfsun's eye."

Chapter | 19

The merriment of the hall spurred Moira's nervousness, for she knew as the night wore on the celebration would become unrestrained. She dropped back from Sigvat's servant and attempted to lose herself in the crowded hall. She fell into the company of chatting dowagers, then moved toward the women's benches farthest from the high seats. She skirted into the outer shadows and ducked from one archway to the next until she found a child's stool set back in a secluded corner. Here she planned to stay, seeing, but unseen.

A skald sang, accompanying himself on a harp, and she softly harmonized the lilting refrain with him. She watched dancers, cross-armed, snake around longfires in steady rhythm to a drum's beat. Men shouted for empty horns to be filled on one hand, while with the other they caught flirting women sauntering by. Her eyes rested on Sigvat poised importantly on his high seat. He drank liberally and called out conversation to those within earshot. She knew he would soon send another servant to find her.

Her eyes discovered Thorfinn and Jacob. The sight of their familiar faces was warming. The golden head beside them was less so. The clamor of the hall retreated, and other faces mulled into grayness as her eyes locked on Wulfsun. He frowned, or maybe it appeared so because of his heavy beard. She watched him lift his horn to drink, deliberately but not deeply. For all he drank, she'd never known him drunk . . . brooding, yes. He seemed so this night. His fingers rubbed his temples and a tenseness shadowed the hard lines of his face. A woman blocked her view as she moved to sit beside him. She leaned to him enticingly. To Moira, he seemed to meet her attentions with passive regard. But then with him, she knew it was always so. Solicitousness was not his nature, though somehow he could manage to flame the ardor of even the most high-nosed spinster with nothing more than an inadvertent glance. Even so, the woman beside him was no graying spinster, but Gunrod, the highborn woman from the bower house. Moira, already sick with love's fever, felt her heart plummet like a fledgling from a nest. She shifted her gaze away, but her eyes quickly returned.

Heat flushed Gunrod's face. She took Wulfsun's horn and drank from it, sipping slowly and holding his eyes all the while. Unsuccessfully she swallowed back her jealousy. She ached to gaze into the deep oceans of his eyes herself.

By the full moon! I cannot sit here in torment.

You must!

I burn for him.

'Tis nothing new.

She watched them speak and wondered at their words. He studied Gunrod's face in contemplation. Then his eyes strayed to the mesmeric movement of the dancers. Moira watched as the mute watch those who speak. In an attempt to draw his eyes back to her own, Gunrod laughed prettily and said something that drew even Thorfinn's comment. Wulfsun seemed humored and rose from his seat.

The line of rhythmic dancers passed between and blocked Moira's view. When the space cleared, there was no Wulfsun, and no Gunrod. Moira plaited her fingers and dropped her eyes to the packed-earth floor. She knew what Wulfsun's eyes could promise. To sit by and witness his offer to another made her wish she were as lifeless as the wooden pillars that shouldered the hall. Could she snatch anything from all memory, she would wipe clean what she had just seen.

Tears began to spill from her eyes and gloss her lashes. *My blood runs through my veins like fire, and I sit by and let him take another to his bed. Between my thighs gushes the moisture of desire from the mere sight of him. The moon madness will take me!*

Would you have your child conceived into the same bondage you suffer? A poor swanling never to know flight?

You know I would not choose it.

Something knocked Moira sideways. A man fell against her. The swords of two brawling vikings glittered and clashed above her head. She ducked and, heedless of direction, leaped away. Blood-spattered tables and food, but the skald, with red-specked face, sang on.

"I have found you!" A hand gripped her arm. She turned to face Sigvat, red-faced and watery-eyed. "I honor you, yet you are slow in coming," he said, witlessly drunk.

"I did not want you to think me overly eager," she said, shifting from his hold.

He chuckled. "But I am eager myself." He put both hands firmly about her waist and pushed her beneath an archway into a tapestry-draped corner. Two gargoyled creatures rose at the head of a fur-laden bed. Her eyes circled for an escape route and her pulse quickened as her emotions seemed a cauldron of contradictions. In cheap revenge on Wulfsun, she was almost tempted to throw herself into Sigvat's arms. Sigvat stepped closer, and his tongue licked his lips in anticipation.

No, she thought, I am not so moonstruck as to give myself to Sigvat. Looking over his shoulder and through the archway, she could see the merry-making in the hall. She knew tonight it would be every woman for herself. She forced a tight smile, but had Sigvat been observant he might have seen her lower lip tremble.

She looked about searchingly, circling quickly around him with her back full view to the hall. "We need drink. There is none. Let me fetch it." She made to back out, but he caught her playfully and with the other hand pulled the cord which dropped the tapestry. The light of a single fish-oil lamp lit the alcove.

"I need no more drink."

"I have had nothing. I will be quick," she argued lightly.

"I will be quicker." He picked her up and threw her on the bed. For an old man he was strong. Desire erased the humor from his face, and he came down beside her.

"Let us not go too fast, Lord Sigvat." She pressed her hands against his chest and smiled slowly, enticingly like Gunrod. "I will make you more comfortable." She patted the furs. "Pillow your head and I will undress you."

Compliantly he stretched his length on the bed. She drew up and kneeled beside him. Humming, her fingers busily loosened the laces at his throat. More slowly she unfastened the leather girths at his waist and eased off his tunic.

He relaxed to her attentions, and by the time she had reached the fastenings of his leggings he was sleeping soundly from her song's enchantment, more quickly because he was drunk. Sliding off the bed, she began to step away, keeping her eye on Sigvat while reaching for the curtain.

Suddenly from behind someone grasped her shoulders and jerked her around. She found herself nose to nose with Wulfsun. His beard prickled her chin, and his breath smote her lips. His eyes, flashing like blue flame, stared with wonderment.

"By the gods! From across the hall I saw that fall of black mane—Is it you?"

She looked at him stupidly, her tongue leaden. His eyes left hers, riveting to the sleeping but half-nude form of Sigvat on the bed. In that brief second of his gathering confusion, his hold on her hair relaxed—

She broke free and took flight.

She ran, pushing through the crowd of people and heading for a doorway of escape. Nearly free, she stopped short. Jacob stood at the door! He would stop her, she was sure. After only a split second of hesitation, she slipped behind the tapestry of another curtained alcove. It was blessedly vacant and she thought to quickly extinguish the lamp and hide in the shadows.

Suddenly the curtain was swept aside.

Her heart leaped like a startled doe, and she spun to face Wulfsun again. She saw the bewilderment in his eyes, and for a moment they both held motionless.

"Moira. How came you here?" His voice after all these months was real. Unchanged, deep and resonant, intense, holding her with the same power. Their parting might not have been, though the wish for him had ever been her companion. "Are you a shape changer taking another woman's form to haunt me? Mayhap I am going mad from the dragon's fire raging in my head. Are you a wild vision?"

He lifted both hands and raked his fingers over his temples and through his hair tormentedly. His features were harrowed and his eyes burned like a man possessed.

Flee! cried her swan self.

But Moira suddenly seized on a stepstone to freedom, albeit ruthless and against her nature, but she felt overwhelmed. Her head reared up, meeting his eyes, and she averred, "Aye, I am a wild vision. You *are* going mad—mad with enchantment. I warn you, if you do not free me, you will end your days witless, weeping with the crones."

"Witch! You have conjured this specter of flesh to haunt me!" he growled angrily. He cupped her face in the strong grip of his hands until her opalescent eyes teared from the pressure. "Is it not enough that when I look at you my voice fails, my eyes are dead to all others, my heart pounds, and sweat dampens me like death? Now you will have me spirit-haunted and mad. Oh, my swan witch, your sting of enchantment is a savage wound."

She tried to twist her face away, but he held her relentlessly. Her heart was beating a shattering pace, and she felt a wild arousal mounting within her body.

"'Tis no more savage than the bondage you hold me in. Release me, I beg you."

"Hah!" He laughed coldly. "Desire for you ever runs like a thief through my body. I will never unbind you. If need be, I will hold you into deep heaven."

"No!" she cried, and pushed her hands against his hard chest, trying to break away.

His hands released her face and gripped her shoulders violently. "I've already phantoms to wrestle this night, what is one more! Pull away from me, but do not forget our bargain. You owe me one request, and I would have it now. Whether you be woman or phantom stay this night . . . heal this pounding torment in my head . . . love me . . ." He gripped her like a drowning man, and her senses lashed and thundered like waves upon a treacherous coast. "Honor your word and this night become love's slave. Bring your lips under mine," he commanded, his breath warm on her face. His mouth lowered, rapacious to sate his blazing thirst on the nectar of her lips. "This night I will drink up your soul, swan heart."

"Oh, Lady of Light," she breathed in a sultry husk as his lips silenced hers. She felt the throb of his chest against her bosom. Invading, his hot tongue slid between her lips like a shaft of liquid flame. Forcing her mouth to open more fully, he rediscovered the moist terrain of her mouth, circling the fleshy mound of her tongue, tasting the flowing juices of her desire. Her nostrils filled with the scent of him, and her own hands moved to hug him to her more tightly.

Leave, swanling, before it's too late.

Nay, I can see he suffers, and the healer within me calls to take away his pain, she countered. *Were I not honorbound, I could flee this temptation, but my legs will not carry me away from this man.*

Fall into his arms, and you will hear nothing more from me, but I told you so!

I am near hysterical from want of him. I shake. I am wet with desire, and you bid me break my word and leave the one man who can quench this madness. I cannot. I will not!

She resisted no longer. The full moon fever and long months of separation erupted in a cataclysmic hunger to mate with him. Sensing her surrender, gently, his arms encircled her like the sun's embrace. Not taking his lips from hers, he swept her up in his arms and carried her the few steps to the bed.

Her swan self suddenly invaded, *Sing him to sleep. He will think it all a dream.*

You promised to be silent.

Think of all the people he must have killed, all the women he has surely ravished. At least despise him for those merciless deeds.

You despise him, then. This night I alone will love him.

Their kiss broke when he laid her on her back and came down beside her. He closed his eyes, and she reached over to smooth the tangle of golden hair from his forehead, and she stroked his temples. Through her fingertips she felt the fire of his pain, and in her mind's vision she saw the dark dragon phantom. Moving her fingers from temples to eyelids, she lightly massaged until she sensed the darkness leaving. Where her fingers touched, her lips followed, moving from forehead to eyes, down to his soft lips.

With her kiss Wulfsun felt the thundering ache in his head subside. And with the next, swirling shocks of rainbow flashed before his eyes. As spring renders ice to water, her kisses were a warming wind rushing through his tormented senses.

Her small hands undressed him, slipping off his tunic and leggings. Aroused by her loving care, he felt tingling, warm, and comforted. She removed her own clothing and knelt between the V of his legs and leaned over him, randomly caressing his arms and shoulders. Her hands softly circled the muscled swell of his broad chest, and he felt his nerves awaken to the fire of her touch like birds singing to dawn.

He reached to enclose her in his arms, but she drew away. "Be patient, my love," she whispered and took his hands in her own and brushed her lips over his fingertips. Her lips explored his hand, licking each of his fingers deliciously. The sensations shot right through his body. Her soft lips went to his wrist, and she kissed a hot trail upward to the round of his shoulder. Like a butterfly, her lips alighted to nibble tenderly on his ear, tasting his neck and shoulders. Her breasts and long silken hair brushed across his chest, and he felt his own nipples harden in anticipation of her sweet kiss.

Leisurely she began kissing him all over, moving down his body, tonguing his nipples, his stomach, his legs, his inner thighs. The slow suspense of where she might touch her lips next inflamed him.

His hands closed over her arms. Everywhere her lips claimed him, flesh exploded like stars across a night sky. "Hummm," he mumbled, a low, hoarse groan. He felt warmth rippling through him and blessed her for pleasuring him so.

Mayhap it was all a dream. He cared not—he felt like he was going to burst open. He drew her up to him and captured her moist lips with shattering hunger. He rolled her beneath him. Like a morning glory opens to sun, she opened the lush bloom of her womanliness to him. His swollen shaft blazed into her moist, warm tunnel. His own need rose as keen as a wolf's howl into a star-arrowed heaven. "Swan-necked and swan-breasted, no woman has your beauty," he whispered.

Their next kiss never ended.

All the while she drank from his lips, pouring her own essence into him. Her loving was like a sea dream, and her embrace like the pull of the tide. He felt himself falling into swimming depths, spiraling upward and bursting free in sun-drenched waves.

They swam in a stream of pure love, flowing together and apart. He tempted and lured, yet held back until she begged in a half-heard cry for want of him. The power of creating joined them like the sun's first rays coming over the horizon. He gathered his body, tensed himself, and dived deep into crystalline, primordial waters of creation, coming in a heavy frothing swell like the white horses of the sea pound, then cresting, in a fierce fury on rocky cliffs.

"By the Goddess!" Moira cried out in echoing reverberation, as his silent, sweet violence erupted and pulsed within her. When his seed burst into her womb with searing, liquid pleasure, her flesh rejoiced, and her body felt filled and fulfilled, knowing it was a golden moment of conception.

In the aftermath love's glow cloaked her, and Wulfsun's soft touch gave her assurance as they lay together skin white beside skin golden. Yet her thirst for him was not so easily quenched, and she reached out to him again and he to her until the full moon fell into the morning sea.

In dream mists she left him, to sway and bask in the eddying waves of a union beyond his imaginings. For a long moment she gazed at his sleeping form, torn between the wild yearning to stay and the heart-cutting knowledge that he would wed another woman. She slipped from his side and dressed. She must leave, because she loved selflessly and too well. Even so, now there was a part of him in her, and nothing could take away this hard-won treasure. Swansdown floated in tiny puffs, providing witness to love's reunion and renewal.

In the hall slumbering bodies slouched on benches and across tables; heads nodded over empty horns and snores and coughs interrupted the stillness. Feeling as if she floated, Moira stepped out into the light of early morning. The brilliance of the red and gold of the rising sun watered her eyes. Freya and Thora stood outside the bower house. They ceased talking and together walked to meet her.

"I was soon to come to find you myself," announced Thora.

"Thorolf waits in the boat." Freya searched her face with puzzled scrutiny. Wordless and feeling very fragile, Moira turned away and walked out the tall gates down to the boat. Freya and Thora followed, their heads bent together in low conversation.

She saw Gyda beside the boat gathering pebbles while her father readied the sail.

"Moira, look what Gret and Helga have given me." She raised a small cloth doll wearing a delicately embroidered dress and a halo of golden woolen hair.

"You are a little mother, Gyda," she praised. Still walking in love's dream, Moira gave her a tremulous smile, and her fingers sought the hollow of her own belly.

A bittersweet rush swept through her. She lifted Gyda into the boat and climbed in after her.

Freya gave her sister one last embrace, and Thorolf helped her inside the boat.

The boat moved out to sea, and Moira gazed not forward but backward to the rising dragons of Sigvat's hall, where Wulfsun still slept. She rested her chin upon her hand so she could smell her fingers—they smelled of him.

The sail caught the wind, and Thorolf ceased rowing.

"The wind is cold," said Freya, tightening her cloak.

She had not noticed.

Freya moved to her side and pulled hers more securely around her shoulders. "I see by your face Sigvat has had his way." Shaking her head with concern, she softly patted Moira's reddened cheeks. "Wealth is not enough for him in his old age. Olvir is a better judge of men than I. Sigvat had no need to force you to his bed."

Moira remained silent.

Will you not tell her that it was not Sigvat who bedded you the night past, but Wulfsun? asked her swan self.

I see no need.

Will you see the need when you give birth to Wulfsun's swanling?

When he marries Ran, he will forget me.

You may as well stand in the deep drifts of winter and yearn for summer than to believe he will ever forget you.

Chapter 20

The late afternoon shimmered golden, and the air clung with the sweetness of warm grass, mossy meadow, and pine forest. Moira lounged beside Gyda on the hillside in the warming sun. She'd been picking whortleberries, and Gyda had shown her where to find the sweetest in spots where there was no wind, but bright sun. Since their basket was filled, now they filled their stomachs, making great fun of each other's red-stained lips.

A blue-winged butterfly lit upon a stem's feathered top near her head. Pale, blue-smudged, with black dotted wings, the butterfly fluttered off, leaving an echo of the blue of Wulfsun's eyes. Two months had passed, but the fever of their night of loving in Sigvat's hall still simmered in her veins, and their love child grew within her womb. She, who'd so devoutly lectured Ysja, could now lecture herself.

"I wish it could be this warm in Hordaland the year around," chirped Gyda, bringing her back to the loveliness of the moment.

"I think summer is here," she assured.

"Freya says when you see the first lark, summer is still a month away; when you see the first finch, summer is only two weeks away; but when you see the first swallow, summer has come for good."

"Have you seen a swallow?" she asked.

Gyda sat up. "I have not, but I will look." Sunbeams dusted her lashes as she squinted across the hillside. "Moira!" she suddenly screamed. "A wolf!"

Her eyes flew open. She quickly looked in the direction Gyda pointed. Along the ridge of the opposite hill a gray wolf skirted. Gyda leaped to her feet. The movement captured the wolf's attention, and it started to lope toward them.

"Stay still, do not run. This wolf is only curious," assured Moira. Then she smiled broadly. "I know this wolf."

The wolf bounded toward her, and instead of gaping white fangs at her throat, she felt a wet tongue lapping her face. "She is Gray Deer, Wulfsun's hunter." The wolf nuzzled her, and she kneaded the rolls of furry skin around her neck and ears in greeting.

"I was afraid she would eat us both," chattered Gyda. "In winter the wolves kill the goats and sheep, and Kari must hunt them down."

"Look, Moira." Gyda's eyes were back on the adjacent ridge. Moira pushed Gray Deer's head aside for a better view. On the rise appeared a horseman, then three others. She could not mistake that golden head. Wulfsun was back from the North Sea and had exchanged the roll of his ship for the gait of his stallion. She swallowed back and wished the swirling butterfly migration in the pit of her stomach would cease.

"Come, Gyda. We must hurry back to Olvirsted. Quickly, quickly," she prompted. She clutched Gyda's hand tightly to keep her own from shaking.

"What's wrong?" the child questioned. She twisted her head to see the riders as they came up from behind.

Moira kept her pace deliberate and her eyes downcast as Wulfsun's horse came alongside her. The horse slowed, keeping even with her pace. She marked its lathered withers and the fine gold hairs of Wulfsun's bared muscled calf. Two months ago her lips had pressed fervent kisses the length of that long leg. She did not look up, though she hungered for the sight of him . . . the taste of him.

Not receiving any greeting, nor offering one himself, he goaded the stallion forward and over the crown of the hill down to Olvirsted. Moira sensed his black mood as well as she knew her own. He had not come to speak pleasantries.

Next passed Thorfinn, Ragnorvald the Law Speaker, and lastly, Jacob the Freed.

Jacob pulled back from the others. "Lift the child up and get on yourself." Gyda gave her a look of appeal, for she wanted to ride. Moira handed her up. He put her straddle-legged in front of him. Moira gave her the basket of berries and with the help of Jacob's firm hand hoisted herself up behind him. "So the she-fox traded you off," he commented wryly.

Moira blew aside strands of his hair that brushed her face and asked, "Has he come to take me back?"

"Did you doubt he would?"

She didn't answer.

"We but touched foot to land when he found you gone. Nothing would do but we must mount our horses to come fetch you back. He was as black as the sea in winter storm. Even the fair Ran fled from his temper. It was a rare sight." Jacob chuckled.

Moira saw no humor in it.

At the foot of the hill Wulfsun, Thorfinn, and Ragnorvald remained mounted by the longhouse.

Freya came out to greet them and called to Gyda, "Get down and bring your father." Gyda slipped down off the horse and ran down the path to the ship house. To Moira she said, "Bring drink."

Freya chatted easily with Ragnorvald, asking after Brigitta and the Ravnings household. Wulfsun said nothing. Moira felt his eyes hard on her as she climbed off the horse and slipped inside the longhouse. Hands shaking, she prepared a flask of mead, which she spilled.

Freya soon stuck her head through the doorway and scolded, "You are overlong. They will think we do not welcome them."

Moira gave her a look of dismay. "It is the truth."

Freya stepped inside and touched Moira's arm. "Do not worry. The fosterling wears white peace bands across his sword. Olvir will speak your desire to remain with us."

"He will have me beside him, whether I wish or not." With flask in hand, Moira followed her outside. Kari and Olvir came up the path. "You are welcome to my house," hailed Olvir.

With this greeting they climbed down off their horses.

First Moira served mead to Olvir and Kari, then Thorfinn, Ragnorvald, Jacob, and, lastly, she approached Wulfsun. She knew full well Nordic custom considered it a slight to serve a chieftain last. Eyes downcast, she held the tray before him.

He loomed over her like a sooty, ominous shadow. Gooseflesh sanded her skin. He smelled of horse, sea, masculinity, and a hundred other opiates which called her.

He refused to take the cup.

"Look at me." His voice held the quiet of a death threat.

Her heart shifted to her throat, and no matter how obstinate she might try to be, she could not refuse to look at him. The effort not to look took more than was humanly possible. Slowly she lifted her gaze to meet his.

Time held as she rediscovered his face. He seemed taller and stronger than ever. Sweet Goddess! She loved the sight of him. He stood, hands set on his hips, his strong legs braced apart, and his wheaten hair blazed in the sunlight. What stopped her breath amid the glint of golden features were his eyes. She fell into their depthless blue as they speared her own like sapphire arrows.

"You left me that night. Not finding you, I truly believed it a dream. You wanted me to think myself mad." Perhaps he never really spoke, but either her heart or her ears had heard his accusation of her deception. It was there in the anguished depths of his eyes. Fool she had been to believe a man felt no pain, no agony, no sorrow. Before her, she briefly glimpsed a man fallen from heaven. Then his eyes dilated and masked with a determined coldness.

His words flew above her head. "I think it is known to you, Olvir, on what matter I have come. I want my thrall woman."

The demand chilled her, and she stood before him as if paralyzed.

He speaks not your name, said her swan self. *Again you are a faceless fool.*

This moment I feel it.

"I must speak for my wife, Freya," Olvir finally said. "She tells me there are few serving women with Moira's abilities. She is favored by Freya, a companion to Gyda, and my son Kari thinks well of her."

Still facing Wulfsun, Moira watched his eyes leave Olvir, flit to Kari, and then to her own. She remembered how deeply he could penetrate with a glance. Disgust snarled deep in his throat, and the tightness of his mouth and narrowness of his eyes told her he thought she'd enchanted young Kari as well.

"I speak truth in saying that the thrall woman does not wish to return to the Ravnings with you," finished Olvir.

At that moment the setting sun bowed behind the mountains, and the sky paled. Moira looked at Wulfsun intensely. Her spiraling rainbows held warmth and explanation, but his eyes flashed with midnight lightning.

Ragnorvald raised an arthritic hand in a gesture of compromise. "The law sides with Wulfsun, Olvir. The thrall woman was not Ran the Fair's to trade. The runes on her collar mark her as property of Wulfsun. She was traded without his knowledge, without his consent."

"I paid silver for her!" interjected Kari with a fierce frown.

Wulfsun stepped past Moira, took a weighty pouch from his waist, and tossed it to Kari. "There is your silver."

Kari let it drop at his feet and made no effort to retrieve it.

"You are generous," said Olvir to Wulfsun. He turned to Kari. "It is more than you paid."

Kari only glowered at his father.

Olvir turned back. "I will accept the payment. I have

no wish to take the disagreement further." He stooped and picked up the pouch.

Kari spat in disgust, turned abruptly, and went inside the longhouse. A second later he thrust a clenched fist through the doorway.

"Kari, no!" cried Freya. All eyes riveted on Kari as he stepped out with raised sword.

"It is a waste of one's life to lose it over a woman," warned Wulfsun. He turned his back on Kari's challenge, ending the matter.

Kari boldly lunged at Wulfsun. Moira cried out, "No!"

"Look to your back!" Jacob shouted.

Instantly Thorfinn downed Kari. The point of Thorfinn's sword kissed Kari's throat, and all color drained from Kari's face. Wulfsun slowly turned around. Thorfinn looked to his chieftain. For an endless moment Wulfsun looked straight into Moira's eyes, and she saw with a shock that his held no hint of mercy, only burning rage. If she did not leave with him, he would command Thorfinn to kill Kari.

In the same moment Gyda ran around the corner of the longhouse. She stopped short. Her child's eyes widened at the drama before her. The innocence of her demeanor made the scene even more grotesque.

Moira lowered her eyes. "I will go with you," she breathed in defeat.

Wulfsun gave a curt nod, and Thorfinn released Kari. Her knees near buckled underneath her.

Wulfsun mounted his horse and rode it over to her. He looked down at her from the saddle. She knew he wished her to take the hand up he offered. She hesitated, so great was her agitation. Finally he bent low and in one swift motion lifted her up behind him. She sought hand holds in the furry fleece of his saddle rather than touch him.

"I count this as nothing between us, Olvir," he said.

Olvir's face relaxed. He turned to Kari and said, "Mayhap it is time my son goes *a viking.*" She watched the misery in Kari's face fade.

Wulfsun and Olvir nodded to each other in unspoken agreement.

She wasn't ready for the lurch that nearly snapped off

her head as Wulfsun spurred the horse forward. She failed to brace herself with knees against the horse's flanks, and her hands lost their grip. She slid backward over the horse's silken buttocks. Wulfsun flung back a saving hand and caught her arm and pulled her to rights. It was either hold on to him or fall off.

She was angry. She was angry because she'd almost fallen off, because he had near killed Kari, and because of the power of Wulfsun himself . . . and her own response to him, which now caused her to tremble. She put pride aside and wrapped her arms around the unyielding waist and pressed herself against the bone-hard back. Touching him again was almost pain, as if she clutched smoldering coals. He didn't slow but urged the animal into a gallop. If a horse could fly, that one did!

Wulfsun rode. He rode all shaking thunder, yet he felt not one whit the better for it. His temper churned like rough seas, and the desperate grip of Moira's hands around him served only to flame the fire and spread the blaze of his passion. Suddenly he broke away from the others, leaving them to ride toward the rising moon and Ravnjell without him. He eyed the glowing emerald hillside beneath a moon that poured out light like a shower of pearls, and pulled in his stallion, veering along a flowing stream.

Higher up, the stream formed a small pool. Here Wulfsun drew up the horse and slipped down. Moira refused to look at him and take his offer of a hand down. Full of stubbornness, her eyes rested on some distant point, and she sat firmly on the horse. He was done with bent knee and begging. He stripped off his cloak, the baldric shouldering Wolf's Claw, his tunic . . . everything, until he stood before her naked.

"Get down," he commanded. She turned her face to him. Her eyes widened. His bared chest rose and fell with the steady confidence of a battle-ready warrior. His lips firmed, his eyes dared her to come to him . . . come to him as she had the night at Sigvat's hall. . . .

The stallion shifted and shook its mane with Wulfsun's own impatience. Finally she slipped down, but with her back to him she paused and leaned into the silken flanks as if to gather herself.

He did not move.

She turned. He'd never seen her eyes so shimmering, so vivid. He stood, staring at her. He could hear the stream trickling from the pool. He saw the white linen on her breast ripple with the eruption of her heartbeat. His own pulse thundered in his ears, and he wished her wearing the fine silks he'd given her in Kaupang. Then he wished her wearing nothing.

He stepped forward and bent his golden head to kiss her. A stone might have given him better response. He embraced her, pressed his lips to hers, but she remained passive, and he realized the martyr's game she played.

"I want you!" he declared.

Her eyes flashed crimson, she straightened defiantly, and breathed, "I thought you liked your women willing."

"Tell me you are not," he challenged.

Her lower lip trembled. Beneath his hot gaze her breath halted and her cheeks flamed.

"Say it."

Her lips tightened firmly. She said nothing.

He knew she wanted him. He knew her body yearned for his. Instinctively he knew the heat that fired his loins ignited her as well. He knew this and more . . . he knew she could not lie.

Suddenly the warrior, the part of him he knew she could not abide, ripped her tunic down the front. No longer divided from her by her peasant's garment, he somberly eased it off her shoulders and lifted her, naked, into his arms. If need be, like flaming ray of sun to snow, he would melt her icy mask.

His need raging, he carried her to a moonlit, moss-blanketed spot beside the stream. The power of his desire burned and leaped into his limbs, and he thought he might explode before he united with her once more. Impassioned, with no mind to hold back, he kissed her.

Again she did not respond.

He drew back. The satin of her skin lingered on his lips, and her woman's scent consumed him.

"Swoon not, my lady of the moon?"

Her eyes swirled indifferent opals. He let his gaze flow over her beautiful body . . . over her breasts, full and soft. Her skin appeared more luminous than before, as if one could bite into her and receive a mouthful of cream. A slow dawning touched his thoughts. It had been two months since their lovemaking in Sigvat's hall. He looked back into her eyes, considering.

"By Thor's mother! You carry our child." His hand sought the hollow of her belly and caressed the softness. Laughter rumbled deep in his chest, and he surrounded her in his arms. "Sweet, sweet swan heart." He kissed her, adoringly. "Hel's gates, I am a fool! Can you forgive me for treating you unkindly? Had I known, I would have walked my stallion . . . nay I would have carried you in my arms."

"Had you known, you would have killed Kari Olvirson!" She turned away. Her long black hair covered her face.

He reached out and stroked her head. "Moira, you are mine and I must protect what is mine."

"You protect me by enslaving me, and now you will enslave our child!" She turned her face to his.

"I would not!"

"A child born of thrall is a thrall." Imploring, her eyes burned his. "Now that you are betrothed to Ran, set me free."

"Betrothed to Ran?" He tilted his head as if he'd heard something amiss. "I am not betrothed to Ran. Why think you this?"

Moira's eyes widened. "Halda told me you were to wed Ran the Fair. Why else would Ran trade me to Kari?"

He studied her face with something akin to admiration. He put his hands on her shoulders and drew her into the strength and warmth of his arms. "Thinking this, you still came to me that night in Sigvat's hall?" Moira nodded dismally. "You have given much for me. I will not forget." Cherishing her, he felt a pang of remorse and wanted to explain further. "I gave you my vow that night before I sailed North: It is to you, woman, I have pledged my troth. It is you I wed at the midsummer handfast." Possessiveness tightened in his chest.

"Then I take from Ran what she wants most. You."

"You take nothing from her. She agrees to marry Erick of Trondeheim. She will have what she wants most. She will be the richest woman in the North."

"And I the most enslaved. Bound to you in every way, heart, body, and handfast."

"Can you promise never to leave my side?"

"Can you promise never to leave mine?"

"That is not for me to promise. I am a viking! You must trust I will return to you."

"And I am a swan sister! You must trust I will return to you."

"I cannot!"

He saw the tears brim over her black lashes, and it ripped him more than the bite of cold steel. She began to cry. He lowered his head and kissed her eyes. He kissed her tear-moistened cheeks. "I love you, Moira. . . . Now, more than ever, I need you at my side." He gently caressed her and sought her lips, but she turned away.

Wulfsun's golden steed carried them at the slowest of paces into the Ravnings. Riding behind him, Moira's arms wrapped around his waist in a fragile embrace, and he felt the softness of her cheek resting against his shoulder. His back glossed wet from her tears.

He felt like an ogre and worse. He loved her, cherished her, but he could not let her free for fear she would abandon him. Once he'd discovered she was determined to fly off at the full moon . . . he vowed he would never undo the magic that bound her to him. Tearing out his heart would be easier.

He drew up the horse and let loose the reins. His hands covered hers in caress and with a weighty sigh he unlocked her hold about his waist and slipped off the horse. When he reached to lift her down, she seemed as light as air and as unreal. Her changeable eyes were mist-filled and pathetically red and swollen.

He kissed her lips softly and said, very quietly, "It is not the end of life." But the restless, trapped longing he saw in her eyes stopped his heart. He knew her longing was not for him, but for her freedom.

That afternoon Moira climbed the hillside with Ysja and Gunna and sat down on the grassy turf with her knees drawn up to her chin.

Ysja sighed. "It is a day for idleness. I have no ambition."

"Neither do I," agreed Gunna, who seemed not to have any to begin with.

Throughout the conversation Moira's eyes involuntarily followed Wulfsun's tall golden head as he hawked higher up the slope. After the night past she could think of nothing but the conflict between them. Even so, the day through she sought his face and listened for his voice, a part of her ached for him, nor did he long leave her side.

Her attention was drawn upward to the falcon, wind hovering motionless against the keen atmosphere of the sky. With outstretched wings, it suddenly banked in the wind and stooped for its prey. She saw a flash of movement, then something small broke cover. The fatal mistake! The razor-taloned bird struck it down. With splayed wings Wulfsun's black gyrfalcon clutched the limp carcass.

A thrall ran past, and behind came the voices of the men as they strode down the hillside to inspect the kill.

"She is sharp-set, her hands equal to her sails," said Wulfsun.

Moira turned to his voice and met gazes with him. He flashed her a warming smile and parted from his companions. He stooped beside her and gave a soft whistle. The falcon whipped her wings to flight, and with leather jesses trailing, she carried herself back to her master's arm. With a buffeting of wings she took her reward from his garnished fist.

"When a hawk is starved into obedience, there is more excitement in the kill," said the approaching Einar. He held his own hooded hawk upon his arm.

"I find no pleasure in such a hunt," Wulfsun returned. He ran his fingers affectionately up and down the gyrfalcon's breastbone. The bird's feathers ruffled with enjoyment. Moira's own skin raised with gooseflesh, wanting his touch. "Her spirit is not broken, and her loyalty to me means more than her freedom."

Moira looked darkly away.

You and the black gyrfalcon are chained to the same master, said her swan self.

'Tis so, rued Moira.

"It is the sport and kill. It matters not how the hawk is trained," countered Einar.

"I disagree, friend Einar. Gentleness is known to work on most females." He looked sidelong at Moira, and she lowered her eyes, not in the mood to see the humor. "A hawk of courage and fierceness tames sooner when a soft hand is used. The unwilling vixen covers her teeth when not cornered."

"Chieftain, I think you could woo the scratch from the hag of Hel. For me there is more sport in wenching if the maid has a bite!" Einar laughed deeply and winked at Gunna. Wulfsun gave his friend an indulgent smile.

Moira could stand no more and suddenly stood up. "Come, Ysja, let us go to the pool to bathe." Her message was clear to Wulfsun, and he would not follow. But she saw his pupils sharpen at her brusque leaving.

Up beside the pool Ysja rubbed her lower back before she carefully slipped from her clothes. She was becoming awkward from pregnancy and Moira knew in a few months she would be Ysja's mirror.

"I am sure my child will be a boy. Look how large my stomach is." She patted the roundness of her belly and Moira thought her beautiful. Her small breasts would soon suckle new life, and her girlish laughter would soon please tiny ears.

"A large belly does not mean you will have a boy, but that you may have twins," she pointed out.

"Could it be possible? I would like two boys." Her eyes gleamed at the thought. "Moira, you will attend me as you did Brigitta at my childbed. I am so glad you returned."

"Not by my own choosing."

"Wulfsun was not pleased to find you gone. Ran was

foolish to try and trade you off. He will never give you your freedom. You will be his thrall until you die . . . unless . . ." She hesitated as something occurred to her. "Unless you buy your own freedom."

Ysja caught her full attention. "Can a thrall buy freedom?"

"Few thralls know of it, but Gunnar has told me this."

At that instant Moira remembered the dagger . . . Olaf's dagger. It was hers. No one could accuse her of stealing it. The gemstones on its hilt would put its value beyond the silver Kari paid for her. The wheels spun in her head. The dagger was there, right in the rocks. Her eyes swept the rocks, and she moved to search for the crevice.

"Are you going to get into the pool, Moira?" called Ysja. "Is something wrong?"

Such a shiny object. A wild animal could have packed it off. She fell to her knees and peered into the dark crack. Her fingers probed, frantically, then touched cold metal. It was there! She sighed relief.

"What is it you have found?" Ysja had come to the pool's edge.

"My freedom, Ysja. My freedom!"

Chapter 21

Voices in council from the feast hall filtered to Moira's ears. Overlong she paused on the threshold forming the proper words, the assured demeanor, filling her lungs with the breath of courage. She'd taken care with her appearance. Ysja had combed her hair until it fell into a smooth black silken mantle down her back. She took the short step and entered.

"The bride price is generous," Ragnorvald spoke from his high seat beside Wulfsun. "And Ran the Fair is in agreement?"

"She is," Wulfsun nodded.

As Moira stepped forward, heads turned. Undaunted by the serious specter of these men of judgment, she made her way to the foot of the high seats. Thorfinn sat on Wulfsun's left and Ragnorvald to his right. She did not take individual tally of the others seated down the row of benches, but refused to feel intimidated by their exuding masculinity. The air was smoke-hazed, the hall warm and her hands cold.

Though outwardly confident, it was difficult for her to meet Wulfsun's granitelike countenance. He was now the chieftain among warriors. Where was the gentle lover who had held her in his arms?

"Thrall woman, do you wish to speak before the council?" Ragnorvald asked.

"I would ask the chieftain's ear." The blue of Wulfsun's eyes shifted almost imperceptibly. He gave a half nod of assent. Moira gathered herself to full height and let her voice flow in soft womanly cadence. "It is your law a thrall may buy freedom." An audible pause settled through the hall. No one refuted her statement, so she continued. "I have come to buy mine."

Wulfsun's deep eyes narrowed with slow calculation and watched her with the cool circumspection of any practiced tribune. "What is your payment?" His voice cut the air.

She held the dagger's tip and raised it for all to see. "This." Murmurs of exclamation rumbled the air.

A muttered oath slipped between Wulfsun's teeth. "Blood's fire! There is no bottom to your bag of sorcery!"

"The Dragon Slayer!" shouted the law speaker coming to his feet. "How came it to a woman!"

"She's a sorceress, there is no doubt!" cried another.

Moira, shocked by her own good fortune, held Wulfsun's eyes in a long, tense challenge. He stood then and stepped down from the high seat. Benevolence was lost from his eyes. She shuddered inwardly as if someone touched ice to her spine. He stretched out his hand, a hand with much strength behind it, and took the dagger's hilt. After a brief assessing glance, his eyes flashed back to hers, and he tapped the tip of the dagger to the gold torque on her throat.

"Have I my freedom, Chieftain?" Her eyes were steady. He looked again as she'd seen him that first time. His hard Nordic face held innate arrogance and more. He was so different from her . . . he with his warrior ways. Even so, surely justice was on her side. He could not in fairness refuse her.

"It is not payment enough!" he declared. The room rippled again with disgruntled comment.

Moira's eyes traveled beseechingly to the dour, indomitable Nordic faces.

"A thrall with payment cannot be refused," spoke one warrior who had a covetous eye on the Dragon Slayer.

"It is our law!" summoned another.

By his very stance she could see it was costing Wulfsun, yet he would hear none of it. He tucked the dagger inside the leathers around his waist. The gesture brought silence again to the hall.

Moira's stomach tightened. The distinctive timbre of his voice held a harsh edge. "By my word, only at my death shall this woman be freed!"

Like the ice-cold sea, his eyes held hers. In those depths she found no promise, no pledge of assurance, no yielding.

About the Ravnings word spread quickly that the thrall woman had attempted to buy her freedom from the unwilling chieftain. In the next days time seemed to stagnate for Moira as the thought of her imprisonment became as endless as the streams of water that tumbled down the steep rock cliffs of Ravnjell. She walked. She paced like a wild thing ferreting escape. Futilely her steps followed the stone paths and grass trails throughout the valley of the Ravnings.

She felt Wulfsun watch her. His possessive gaze became an unbidden but connective thread between them. He waited for her. She avoided him and changed her path. As if he could no longer control the fever of possession that drove him, he followed her.

Early afternoon of the midsummer celebration, he caught her arm and thrust her against the fortress timbers. His features were thunderous. He smelled of drink, and despite the pummeling of her heart against her ribs, she said coolly, "You are in happy humor."

He did not sheathe his anger. "Hammer of Thor! Don't taunt me, woman!" His eyes bore into hers like twin stars where neither rest nor peace could be found. He grasped her shoulders like a drowning man clutches flotsam. He bent his head and pressed on her lips a long, vehement kiss. She gave no response, though every nerve and need of her body cried out to him with longing.

He drew back visibly wounded from her lack of response.

"Because I do not weep aloud, you think me heartless!" His voice shook with passion. "Where is your warmth? You are the woman I dream of during long nights at sea. I look upon no woman but I see your face. In dream visions you come to me with your love. By Hel's gates you are a witch to haunt me so!"

"If you think me a witch, then let me go free that you may be rid of my sorcery." She twisted from his hold, but he caught her wrist in his hand.

"If you leave me, Moira, I will find you. I will make war on any who give you shelter and lay low any who give you aid." His nostrils flared. "You are no man's but my own!"

She broke free of him and ran up the hillside until her breath seared her lungs and tears misted her vision. Finally she flung herself down on the mossy turf and sobbed as sorrowfully as a caged nightingale.

After some time a dark jumble of sleep fell upon her and she dreamed. In dream mists she sought to cross the ley path back into Myr. Keeping an eye on the setting midsummer sun, she was running to the stonehenge. Suddenly a great wolf, yellow-eyed and gaping-fanged, blocked her path. It loomed so close she breathed its hot, rank breath and saw the silver guard hairs of its pelt stiffen like quills. The huge beast leaped the circle of dolmens, stone from stone. There were songs a swan sister might sing to still a beast so wild, but in her dream the air was silent, her voice mute and the wolf unhearing.

Time after time the wolf stalked her. Who was this soul? This wild wanderer of dreams who blocked her way into Myr.

"No . . . let me pass . . ." She tossed awake and cried out his name. "Wulfsun!" She sat up, sweating and shaking. In Myr a dream was a dream. The vision path was clear, but here in the realm of men dreams came fragmented, the end before the beginning and the middle after the end.

She rose up from the mossy turf and walked to the stream. There she knelt down on the bank and with cupped hands splashed icy water on her face.

Movement at the opposite bank caught her eye. On a rocky outcrop perched two glossy black ravens. They watched her with a certain knowing gleaming in their onyx eyes. When she stood, they took flight, though not far. They winged to the hall and alighted on the dragon-head apex of the roof. They strutted back and forth, calling to her in garbled cackles.

When the sun never sleeps, follow Thought and Memory to the dragon's lair. On the ley path you came, on the ley path you go. Epona's riddle spun in her mind. This night, on midsummer, the sun would not sleep. Yes, she could follow the ley path back into Myr this night . . . but she was not in Britain.

Do not forget that in the forgotten time ago, Myr spanned all the earth, reminded her swan self.

The birds took flight and circled a tight ring above her. Their black wings and hoarse cries beckoned her.

Follow them, urged her swan self.

Their flight widened as they moved in the unmistakable direction of Ravnjell. She followed and soon found herself far along the mountain slope on the path that led up to the saeter. She scaled the stone trail up the cliff side to the mouth of the high meadow. She remembered that winter's night when she and Wulfsun had stopped and gazed on the valley below. This time she would not look back.

The tinkling bells of sheep and goats carried on the storm-threatened air. A thrall boy shepherded the animals across the mountain pasture. He waved a salute to her, which she returned. She couldn't stop for fear of losing sight of her dark-winged guides. In the distance she spied the mossy roof of the saeter. Heavyhearted, she turned from its sight and those sweet memories which clung like the tendrils of bittersweet to the fringes of her mind.

The path continued over a timbered bridge and beneath a waterfall. The spray misted like steam and the air felt cool. She stopped to quench her thirst and then continued along the muddied trail, careful not to slip on wet rocks. Further on, the path wound its way in switch-back turns up the mountain slopes of Ravnjell. Just above the timberline the path disappeared into open, flower-specked meadow.

The rising wind whipped her hair, and the clouds churned in the gray sky. Around her the silver zigzag of lightning stretched across mountain peaks, and thunder shook the air. A flash, the cutting crash, then a slow rumble sounded over the hills and rolled into the valley below. Full of misgiving, she took cover beneath a ragged rock overhang. Above, the ravens took shelter in the wind-torn stone. She buried her head in her arms against the deafening harangue.

Time passed, and she feared the mountains were crumbling down around her. Then finally, as a wailing child falls into sporadic sobs, the thunder ceased and the rain slowed into a gentle tap. The cleansing was over, the air smelled of earth and sweetness. The ravens took wing with hoarse, expletive cries, and she left the shelter.

Her pulse throbbing, she clutched the gold torque at her throat. But for it, she could take flight and forget the arduous hike of being earthbound. The ravens' calls urged her on.

Suddenly a long eerie howl, piercing and desolate, vibrated from down below. She heard the cry of the wolf! A chill touched her heart. The cry came again, the prey-seeking howl of the hunt. Knowing engulfed her. Wulfsun and Gray Deer were on her wind-born scent in pressing pursuit.

The knowledge impelled her up the mountainside. She found hand holds on rocks and clumps of grass. Using all her strength, she pulled herself upward. The ravens dipped and swooped, biding time as she struggled to match their airy path. Panting and gasping, she threaded her way over the slopes of Ravnjell.

Finally, with heaving chest and aching head, she crested a steep outcropping and met the wild bleak landscape of a glacial iceland. At her back another wolf's cry echoed. Panicked, she looked to the ravens for direction. They frolicked on the wind currents, springing up on the glacier's face, and then disappeared into the low-hanging cloud bank. She sang out to them, but they did not reappear.

She picked up a splintered branch, suitable enough to give her balance, and stepped onto the slippery glacial crust. Two fears encircled her: One was at her back, the other lay ahead.

Once she fell but managed to pull herself back up. She was tiring, winded, and hungry, but the phantom of Wulfsun's pursuit drove her harder.

Soon she disappeared into the fog bank. She could see only a few steps in front and stumbled into a huge rock, which on closer inspection she found to be a great rune stone.

The rune stone is evidence a ley path is near, assured her swan self.

At last the trail lifted her above the cloud bank into a riot of flaming sunlight and on to the crest of the mountain crater.

"By the moon!" she gasped. For below within the hollow hinterland of the crater, rising out of shreds of drifting fog, was a stone circle, an ancient gateway to the ley path. Upon the somber dolmens perched her two raven guides.

Her pulse raced with hope. The ravens had shown her to the ley path so she might return to Myr once more! She scrambled down the talus slope into the crater. Mists swayed over its surface with the beguiling grace of a charmed cobra.

She fell. When she pulled herself up she spied what tripped her, a cairn of bracken-smothered bones. Still on her knees, she suddenly knew she wasn't alone. In the periphery of her sight, enshrouded in the mist, something moved. Slowly she rose to her feet and once more set her path to the stone circle.

A loathsome shadow loomed in the mist before her. The fine hairs on her neck and arms raised. Her breath stopped! Before her loomed Wulfsun's dragon! Around an unhewn dolmen, wings folded, it crouched on clawed feet and coiled like a fearsome guardian. Hooded membranes blinked over red reptilian eyes that burned into her with manlike cogency. A dark tangible evil radiated from the carnelian-scaled head, on down the ridge of sharp spines that stretched from its spiked nose to its barbed tail. Saffron smoke curled from the blackened nostrils, and a glimmer of flame licked from the fanged jaws. Something bitter rose in her throat, and she would have cried out but she could find no voice. Yawning terror gripped her.

Do not fear! counseled her swan knowing. *It is a creature the imagination conjures only in a long sick nightmare. This dragon is a dream of men, the embodiment of their fears. Cloak yourself in a circle of light.*

The knowledge did not make her less afraid. She breathed deeply and began to chant softly, a soothing spell of protection. "Earth, earth, guard my worth. Flame, flame, do not maim."

The heavy lids half closed over the wary eyes, and the creature let her pass into the ring of stones.

Her pace quickened as she neared the two upright dolmens joined by a flat stone lintel. The rays of the setting sun radiated through this doorway to the ley path. Yet her anticipation was eclipsed by the full-throated howl of a wolf! She paused mid-stride and riveted her eyes to the crater's rim.

There, silhouetted against the blood-hued sky, stood Wulfsun. In the sunlight of the in-between time, it seemed to her as if he transformed into wolf. His mighty shoulders rippled beneath a lush gray pelt, his jaw lengthened and narrowed in a jagged-toothed gape, and his azure eyes smoldered canine venery. He flung back his head and loosed a long anguished cry. In answer the mist dragon opened its black mouth and shrieked and spewed a fiery challenge.

Her limbs froze. Her love for Wulfsun was a binding tendon that she could not sever. She loved him better than pride, better than freedom, better than life.

So close, swanling, do not hesitate.

Her eyes went to the sun hanging between night and day and then to Wulfsun. *I cannot leave him to such a fate. Without me, he is a dead man.*

He is ever the dead man. Today or tomorrow he dies how he has lived, a warrior. Leave him!

"Moira . . ." came a soft familiar voice.

Moira turned and saw Epona standing beneath the lintel stone. "Grandmother! You've come! Thank the Goddess! We must help him—"

"Nay, swanling. Would you take his free choice as he takes yours? In the world of men, magic is costly. If you interfere, are you willing to pay the price?"

"Yes! I will pay whatever the cost!" she cried pathetically. "I'll return to him. He need not battle this dragon to the death."

"'Tis too late. The foe he fights is himself. Let the fates decide this day. Come . . ." Epona outstretched her arms.

"No, grandmother I can't—"

"You must!"

Her mind spun in circles and it seemed impossible that her heart did not cease its pace.

He must slay his own dragon, urged her swan self. *If he is to enter Myr, the sacrifice must be his alone.*

Tears brimmed in her eyes. She knew both Epona and her swan mind spoke truth. Sorrowfully she turned away from Wulfsun's visage. In three short steps she undertook the most difficult task of her life; she walked beneath the stone lintel and passed into Myr.

Chest heaving, Wulfsun stood as if on the earth's edge and saw the flash of Moira's crimson cloak disappear between the stones. Too late! Too late to call her back. Too late to tell her, her freedom—anything that was within his grasp to give—was hers. By Odin's blood! He'd lost her!

Deep from his soul rose a full-throated howl . . . a howl that split rocks and shattered cliffs. The cry echoed across the crater's rim in a reverberating torment. His voice raged to sky and earth, "If need be I will follow her to Hel's gates to win her back!"

His wild eyes alighted on the dragon. It swayed with the currents of mist, ready to challenge his right to passage. Battle fire ignited his eyes, and deep-voiced, he chanted his battle song, a low fierce keening.

The dragon roared once, then twice in answer.

Wulfsun brandished Wolf's Claw, and he hurdled down the slope toward his nemesis. Hackles raised, savage and snarling, Gray Deer raced at his side. The air sparked, and he felt power surge through his limbs, and before him, at the same instant the dragon fleered malevolent. He attacked, with the hard driving bite of Wolf's Claw.

The dragon lashed out, equally as vicious, mirroring his every strike. Striving to break past its guard, he savagely retaliated, plying quickness and cunning to blunt the powerful blows of its taloned claws. In answer the dragon spat angry fire, its head tossed side to side, and its wings ripped the air in black madness.

Gray Deer attacked from the rear, aiming at the barbed tail. Her white fangs gripped the coiling tail of the dragon, and she flailed through the air as the maddened beast shook her off.

The serpent demon whirled, attacking Wulfsun's back. Its talons raked him venomously, and he cried out in pain. He lashed out and cut deep into the dragon's side. Blood splattered his brow like rain. That same instant the dragon lunged, and he took a glancing blow across his shoulder and went down. He thought himself a dead man, but the dragon recoiled.

His heart slamming against his chest, he scrambled to his feet. "By Hel's gates!" he cried. Once more he gathered himself. Equally the dragon twisted around and reared. Gleaming-eyed, it rose in the mists before him, harsh and huge. He raised his sword arm, more agile and more driven, and wielded a ringing blow that sliced deep the dragon's foreleg. The dragon sang out foully and with frenzied strength raked his thigh.

Cursing, Wulfsun leaped away. The dragon retreated as well. It had ever been so with this foe, its each biting stroke mirrored his own. In his youth, when he first took up his uncle's sword, wounded, he had fled from it and it had not pursued him. Months before, outside the saeter when he had fallen, the creature had not closed in for the final kill. Why? Even so, the sudden knowledge that the harder he fought, the fiercer loomed his enemy startled him. The stench of blood smote his nostrils, and he felt something within him sour and contract. Around him the air misted bloody, and pooling blood lapped his ankles. His ears rang from the shrill dragon screams, and his skin burned from the heat of it's searing breath. He sprang forward. The dragon swept forth as well and sword and talon clashed. He staggered back, and likewise again the dragon retreated.

Within, he felt the thundering of his own heart, and wondered who this enemy really was? Blood drenched him, soaking his leathers, his hair. Like a raging torrent, the scarlet gushed down the blood channel of his sword. The acridness of it rose bitter in his mouth.

His stomach lurched within him, and he realized he was fighting a battle he could not win. *You will drown in blood* had been the prophecy. He staggered and leaned heavily on his sword as sickening reason edged in on him.

The enemy he fought was himself!

He swayed beneath the crushing revelation of his own savagery. The full force of it was too great for him. The sun would never set . . . and he would fight on . . . endlessly on.

Still mirroring his stance, the dragon quivered, gathered, and waited. As if from a far distance, Wulfsun watched the embodiment of his own war spirit.

The past echoed in his ears, whispering his own condemnation.

Myr is a peaceful kingdom, and no one harboring the heart of war may enter.

If it is so peaceful, who is to stop me?

Yourself!

He looked down at his broad sword clasped tight in his hand and realized it was useless against this dragon. If he was to pass into Myr, he must slay the savagery in his own nature. He must love better than hate, free rather than bind. He sheathed Wolf's Claw in his baldric.

Long moments passed as he determined what he must do. Slowly his hand inched to his waist for the Dragon Slayer, the legendary weapon for the enemy that no sword could kill, no fire could burn. Again, amid its sparkling coils the dragon gathered, baring its shining fangs.

He lunged. The dragon leaped. In collison, he thrust the dagger's point straight and deep into the dragon's heart. Then the world itself suddenly shifted. He felt the dagger's icy bite pierce his own heart. He reeled. Screaming death, the dragon fell, burying him, crushing him.

All he felt was the deadly spread of cold. He lay drowning in the cold-bloodedness of battle, the cold armor of callousness which every warrior donned, and the cold-cruelty of warring might. This moment he entered not Valhalla but Hel. He lay pinned under the stone-dead monster of his own barbarity.

Seven loud heartbeats passed. Then, miraculously, the dragon vanished and the heaviness lifted from his chest. Hands that gripped the hilt of the Dragon Slayer, now clutched empty air. He lay a long moment listening. Only the steady beating of his own heart broke the sudden silence.

Gray Deer came to his side and nosed him gently. He felt her warm tongue and then a strange laughter sounded from his lips. Death's smell clung to his skin and death's taste flooded his mouth, yet he was still alive.

The great cold uncurled inside him.

Time began to have meaning once more. His eyes went to the sun hanging between night and day and then to the stone portal into Myr. Wearily he came to his feet and walked inside the stone circle. Soon he found himself in the center, standing on the green earth before the stone lintel. He stepped forward and hit an invisible barrier.

He could not enter.

Looking down, he spied Wolf's Claw sheathed at his side. The habits of a warrior died hard. He drew out the sword and thrust its point into the earth. At that same moment the mists parted, and he crossed the threshold into Myr.

Chapter 22

On that midsummer eve Wulfsun stepped into a land that was like none other he'd traversed in his life. Tranquility encircled him like a quicksilver cloak. Glittering dragonflies and butterflies sailed through shimmering air, while rare birds swooped into the leafy foliage of tall ancient trees. From the wildwood drifted the scent of honeysuckle and bramble rose. On the turf beneath his feet a carpet of daisies winked white. From behind he heard a rustling and turned to see a moon-pale unicorn nose through a laurel thicket. Amazingly, the unicorn walked toward him, paused a moment to sniff his bloodied hand, and then whickered, shook its head, and trotted off.

He breathed in deeply the peace and contentment as the sound of harp strings, shi mering liquid over the air, called his attention. Ahead sparkled a small lake, and beside it he beheld the one woman in this land he sought. The one woman he had vowed to follow into Hel if need be. Now, instead, he'd found her in paradise.

After seeing the beauty of Myr, how could he ask her to return with him? Deep regret bit his belly.

The weariness was so heavy on him, he feared he would collapse, but he forced himself the few steps onward. "Moira." He meant to call her name boldly, but his voice cracked with the exhaustion and remorse he felt.

She turned to him, her features shifted from night's darkness to the golden of midday. She cast her harp aside and ran to him.

When she went to clasp him in her arms, he drew back. Self-reproach filled his heart and unworthiness etched his soul. Clearly wounded by his distancing, her changeling eyes penetrated his until he wanted to look away from shame.

"I will not long abide in your land of peace. I have come to take from your throat my curse of bondage." He fell to his knees before her and bowed his head, thinking that walking barefoot through a longfire might be easier than begging her pardon. The next words were strangers to his warrior's lips. "Forgive me, lady. Forgive me the unforgivable. I have been a blind man." His voice wavered, then sank.

She fell on her knees next to him and embraced him. "You are a blind man given sight, or you could not have entered Myr." Her eyes met his own. "I forgive only that which needs forgiving."

His chest rose and fell in a solemn sigh. "I will not force you to abide your captivity one moment longer." He reached strong fingers to touch the golden torque. By his own hand he broke the joining pinion. The cruel necklace fell away, leaving a red rash that blemished her swan white neck. Remorse washed through him. Coming to his feet, he tossed the golden torque with all the might left to him. It flew across the lake, transforming into a small golden bird which soared and sang high above the water. He felt tears of relief glaze his eyes.

Moira came to his side and touched his arm. She smiled unsurely. "You are hurt. Come, drink and bathe your body with healing and your soul with peace." She led him to the water's edge. He knelt and cupped his hands to drink. The water shimmered like liquid silver with the taste and clarity of sunlight. And while he drank, the last coldness in his breast disappeared and the weariness began to leave his body. He turned but she was nowhere to be found. Then his eyes roved to a single white swan floating nearby in the water.

He began to laugh. A laugh of joy and renewal. Pleasure erased the deep drawn lines in his face, and he felt hope reappear in his soul. He stripped from his clothes and stepped into the water. The cleansing waves lapped his body and spirit. His wounds ceased to bleed and the staining crimson dissolved into the silver of the lake. He felt revitalized and fresh.

The swan moved closer, leaving ripples in its quay.

"You tease me, my swan heart. But I do know you," he called, and submerged beneath the water and swam to surface beside her. She dived under the glassy water and a few seconds later surfaced, a laughing woman.

He caught her in his arms. His lips touched hers with fierce tenderness while his hands pressed gently on the hollow of her back. Lost in a sea of pure sensation, his lips molded to hers.

Suddenly, from above, he heard a great flapping of wings and more than a dozen swans circled to alight on the lake. "What is this?"

Moira frowned. "I'm afraid word has gone about that a man has passed into Myr. My swan sisters wish to see this man."

He asked, "And what think you?"

"I think it is just as well. Mayhap after seeing you, they will not be so eager to rush out into the world of men as I was."

"Hah! Mayhap they will be more eager." He laughed. "I will swim closer so they have better view of me."

His own amusement was not reflected in her face. In truth her lips firmed. "You need not," she announced, her eyes swirling emerald.

Awareness suddenly tugged his thoughts and he grinned, inwardly thinking she might be green-eyed with jealousy.

"I know what you are thinking," she began. "And I am not jealous." She paused and gave a small laugh. "You may have a peaceful enough heart to enter Myr, but I see you have not lost your conceit."

"Nor have I lost my desire for you." Revitalized by the

healing waters, he caught her close. "Let me love you, Moira, one last time before I return to my own world."

"Must you return?" she asked sadly.

"You know I must" he said solemnly, adding, "Though I will always be a slave to your enchantment."

"Not always."

"What?"

"I must confess to you that the enchantment lasted but one moon month. If you are still a slave to love, it is by your own doing."

"One moon month! Why did you not tell me this before?"

"You did not ask," she said chidingly. She dived under the water and resurfaced a swan.

"I did not ask!" He sputtered, and began to swim after her, but she'd taken safe haven among her sisters. A dulcet-sounding trill circled his ears, and he realized the swans maids were laughing at him. "You might all take the same form and face, but I will find the one among you I love."

Playful splashing and warbling met his vow. One by one they circled him with graceful profiles. He studied them, searching for a clue. He looked into their mystic eyes, over the blackberried bills, and down the sleek necks to feathered bodies. After careful scrutiny, he made his choice. He moved forward, "Come, Moira." Gently he stroked her neck and soft back. The swan let loose a chirring sound of pleasure and dived beneath the water to surface again as woman.

"How did you know?" she gurgled, coming up out of the water.

He caught her in his arms and chuckled. "Woman or swan your beauty is unrivaled. Come." He urged her toward the shore.

Together, hands clasping, they walked slowly beside the lake. Occasionally Wulfsun stooped to pick a flower, and soon he held in his hand a wildflower bouquet. "You spoke true. In Myr I find peace and beauty beyond description." He sighed, "But I fear I stay too long."

She leaned her head against his shoulder. "Do not think it. 'Tis midsummer's eve, and as long as the sun does not sleep, we can go and come freely between the two worlds. Come," she said.

She led him to a shady moss-blanketed spot in a circle of alabaster mushrooms. He stretched his long length down beside hers in the heart of this fairy ring. While he basked in the beauty of this peaceful kingdom, his fingers began weaving a flowery garland for Moira's hair. He placed it on the crown of her ebony head and said softly, "I love you, my swan heart."

Moira's pulse fluttered. Smiling warmly back at Wulfsun, she plucked a brier rose from her garland. She closed her eyes and brushed each lid lightly with the rose, singing, "I see love." Moving the rose to her nose, she smelled its rich scent and sang, "I breathe love." Lowering the rose to her heart she sang, "I feel love." And then pressing it gently against each coral nipple she sang, "I nourish love." Opening her eyes, she took his hands in her own and kissed each palm. "I hold love."

Through their linking hands her flesh felt the force of him, and together their desire coursed as if they were one in blood, one in breath, and one in life. Their eyes held. Her body yearned for his, and her eyes lowered to his manhood and saw the power rose within him as well. She leaned and kissed his brow. In turn he kissed the circle of her neck, and the rash of her bondage disappeared.

Reciprocating, her lips sought to heal his wounds with love's healing balm as well. Kneeling before him, she pressed her lips to the red welts of new wounds and the paled scars of those more ancient. Over his broad-muscled chest, lower torso, and thighs, her lips traced, touched, and healed, until his skin shone smooth and flawless as sculpted marble. She circled behind and brushed the long que of his wheaten hair aside. She kissed his neck, then slowly her lips followed the furrow of his spine. She pressed fervent kisses on each wound in its turn. Gently, across wide shoulders and bare skin stretched tautly over tempered-steel muscle, she molded her lips. Until, down the sleekness of his back below his narrow waist, the gashes from the dragon's three-toed talons vanished as if the battle had never been.

Lastly she moved back to face him. In a tender gesture

he lowered his head and kissed away the arrow's scarlet path on her side. "Now you are a flawless beauty of body, heart, and mind," he said, his voice husky with desire.

He gathered her into his arms, and his lips found hers like a thirsty man discovers water in a sun-scorched land. Their legs, thighs, and hips entwined, instinctively seeking love's unity. She felt the heat of his manhood radiating like fire against her thighs, and she opened to him. Desire exploded between them as the kiss deepened. He pressed forward, blazing a fiery path into the softness of her secret well. Between them the crimson heat began to pulse. She felt the steady rise and fall of his chest against her own, and she matched her breathing to his. She wrapped her legs around his and on a slow wing flew amidst the sweet undulations.

In that rapturous moment her swan mind surfaced, singing her love-lilt in an airy, sweet chant. "Love is before me. Love is behind me. Love is beside me. Love is above me. Love is below me. Love is within me. Love flows from me. Love comes to me. I love." Love's radiance enfolded her, and tears of joy brimmed over lash and slipped down her rose-flushed cheeks.

In answer the soft whisper of Wulfsun's voice caressed her ear. "And you are loved by all that is good which abides in me, my swan heart."

He strained into her and need shuddered through them in unison. "O blessed Goddess!" she cried out, and she felt his power burst into her, filling her with stars and shining. As he held her tightly against him, joy shimmered through her from head to toes. In that exquisite moment his spirit joined with the twin souls of her own.

In the aftermath she was trembling, panting, and glistening with heat, and inwardly she thanked the Goddess for creating her woman. She stroked his head and ran her nails lightly over his sweat-sheened shoulders. He still quivered, breathless and hot.

Moira's eyes wandered to the sun hovering on the horizon and then to the full moon climbing the summer sky.

Her arms tightened around him as if to hold him always. "Do you still wish to leave?"

He lifted his head and met her gaze with the blue intensity of his own. "No! But I must. No matter how sweet, I cannot spend my life chasing butterflies and riding unicorns. Though I am done with war-making, I am a chieftain and many depend on me for livelihood and counsel."

Intuitively she knew he would feel so.

He kissed her gently. "We need not be parted forever," he began. "I will ever return to your arms each midsummer eve to renew our love bond . . . and see our child."

"You return here?" she puzzled.

"Yes, you have my oath on it," he vowed.

She still puzzled. Now he had removed the golden torque from her neck, by her own free choice she would gladly return with him to his world.

Why does he not ask me to return with him? Am I not woman enough for him?

Aye, and more. But swanling, he has not lost all pride. He will not beg, but may wish to give you free choice.

I will tell him I want to return with him.

Nay, don't be hasty. At first let him leave alone and then follow. A few more hours without you will help him better appreciate the magnitude of your sacrifice.

I love him, 'tis no sacrifice.

A man is a man. If he thinks you sacrifice on his behalf, he will better honor you. If he doesn't believe this, he will take you for granted.

Mayhap you speak true. I can see no harm in it.

She drew away from him, saying, "If you are determined to leave, then it must be now."

"You seem in a hurry to send me on my way. Have you another fool waiting in the woods?"

She gave him an impish three-cornered grin. "Now who is jealous?"

He frowned. Saying nothing, he stood up. Even though love's afterglow still clung to his face, she could see him firm his features with Nordic stoicism.

"Then it is good-bye, lady." His voice was thick with heavy emotions, but he bowed stiffly. She was touched by his gallantry, but irritated by his distancing.

"I will miss you," she confessed lightly.

"And I you," he replied with unbearable restraint. He turned heel and strode off as if it were one of many casual meetings.

Watching his back, she let loose a deep sigh, thinking he could be so cold and insensitive. Even so, she knew beneath all his hardness and firmness of purpose lay a softness and sentimentality, a gentleness and tenderness only a very few would ever guess was there. Why else did she love him beyond loving, if not for his strengths as well as his shortcomings? She hugged herself, feeling washed with wondrous love for him.

When Wulfsun stepped out of Myr, it became the longest and loneliest step of his life. Already his heart ached for her. He would miss her delicate, gentle manner, her quick intellect and cleverness, her expressive rainbow eyes ever shifting with the unpredictable. By the gods! He was the fool to leave paradise.

He near turned back, but his eyes rested on Wolf's Claw, thrust point deep into the dark earth. He reached for its hilt and then stopped. The sword became a cold symbol of all the reasons he should not return to Myr this moment. Unlike his will-o'-the wisp swan love, he was rooted in reality and the world of men. Even so, he felt like a man who'd just rediscovered innocence and in a sense rebirth. He would not lose all by taking up his sword again. Turning his back on Wolf's Claw, he left the stonehenge and began a ponderous journey down Ravnjell.

As he approached the valley of the Ravnings, a great bonfire announced that the midsummer's feast was in the offing. Green garlands and sheaves of oats hung on tall poles. He paused by the upper pool and knelt to drink before going down to announce there would be no handfast this midsummer eve, for he had no bride.

Suddenly he heard a winging trill. He looked up. From high above two white swans wheeled to swoop and settle onto the water. Such sweet singing met his ears. He felt like singing as well, and at that moment the grass seemed greener and the sky bluer. His eyes rested on the garland of flowers around one long slim neck. She floated toward him, water rippling in her quay, and as she stepped to shore, she shimmered in the sunlight. Her swan form shed and trailed from her slender fingers in a chimera of down and feathers.

With eyes of a lover he marveled. "I have won you, then!" His voice held the tone of triumphant certainty.

"Yes." She smiled, her eyes flashing quicksilver loveliness. She'd sacrificed much on his account, yet she willingly, like his beautiful black-plumed gyrfalcon, returned to him.

The other swan stepped from the pool as woman, and though she appeared to Wulfsun an aging silver-haired beauty, she was familiar.

She smiled at him and spoke. "To love is to set free. If she does not return, it was never meant to be. If she does, cherish her forever."

Moira laughed. "My grandmother gives you wise advice."

"This time I will take it," he agreed, now recognizing the spakonna. "I have learned my lesson well. To stifle Moira's freedom is not the way to love her."

He took Moira into his arms, holding her close, smelling her smell, a sweet scent like dew on a golden morning. He felt her warmth and softness against his own naked body, and this moment he realized she was really two women . . . one content to nestle happily beside him and the other determined to roam at full moon.

He looked into her eyes calmly with his own quiet ones. "I give you my word, you may ever come and go between our two worlds at your choosing."

"I will hold you to your word," she vowed merrily. "Now let us be go down to the Ravnings. I would not miss the celebration of our handfast."

"You agree to wed me, then?"

"I agree. But do not think to give me a golden necklace as a bridal gift. I would not wear it."

He laughed aloud, knowing this sudden sense of happy amusement would be unending with her beside him. He touched her arm. "Look behind you. A part of Myr follows you as an omen of luck. Look to Odin's bow." A rainbow arched from the peaks of Ravnjell down to the fjord waters.

"'Tis not Odin's alone, but the blessing of the Moon Goddess. Look, she rises within its arc."

"It is true," he relinquished.

Suddenly a festive group of men and women coming up the hillside drew his attention. "Here we three stand as naked as babes. I know you are at ease in flesh or feathers, but those at the Ravnings are not so self-possessed."

"Moira!" came a gleeful squeal as a rosy-cheeked Gyda ran toward them. Moira bent down to embrace her happily. Freya, too, was there, and Ysja. All greeted her with affection.

"Why are you here?" Moira asked Freya.

"When it was discovered you were gone, Wulfsun sent Thorfinn to Olvirsted in search of you. He told us of the handfast. It is not easy to have a handfast without a bride."

Moira looked at Thorfinn. He gave a shrug of his broad shoulders and said, "Life is to my liking. I would not lose it by neglecting to find the chieftain's bride." This evoked much laughter.

"Enough of this," interrupted Brigitta, who bore the burden of the preparations. "I see our honored guests have need of clothing." Her eyes as well as everyone's were drawn to their nakedness. "Here stands my foster brother and his bride naked on their wedding day. I will not ask the tale of how you came to this end. Mayhap you seem more than eager to be wed. Let us prepare you."

The women encircled Moira and separated themselves from the men. The men hoisted Wulfsun to their shoulders and carried him down to the fjord below. Naturally they would try to coax from him the tale, but Moira knew, if a man could keep silent about such an adventure, it would be Wulfsun.

The women washed and anointed her with sweet oils and rubbed dry her hair with pungent herbs from the high meadows.

"Look, Moira, I have your bridal dress." From a basket Ysja lifted the oyster-colored dress to her view.

"Ysja, it takes my breath."

"It is of the finest Frisian silk. I myself have sewn it. It is my gift to you, Moira." She helped Moira slip it over her head, and it fell into a pearl-pale shimmer over her body. Tears sprang to Moira's eyes, and she embraced Ysja tenderly. "I have no better friend than you, Yjsa."

"Quickly, Moira. Your bridegroom waits," hastened Epona, her eyes sparkling with gaiety.

"It will not hurt him to wait," said Freya as she stood back and admired Moira. Lastly she laced ribbons in Moira's garland and let them fall in flashing colors, mingling with her unbound hair. "Another day she will wait when he has gone *a viking.*"

"I think my foster-brother will go *a viking* less and less with such a fair-faced woman beside his hearth fire," suggested Brigitta.

"It is a good thing for the wolf to be kept near his burrow, for then my own man will be longer at my side," rejoined another woman. Moira hoped with them, but she knew as the moon called her, the sea would call him in the spring and send him back to her in winter. His heart was bound to her. That was enough.

The women formed a tight ring around her and began singing a lighthearted ballad as they moved down the hill to the Ravnings. From below the men echoed a rejoinder of song. They advanced toward the women, bowing first before they invited the women to dance. The men, with quickened steps, circled several times to the lilting tunes of harp and flute. Moira's eyes remained steadfastly on Wulfsun in his scarlet cloak, white linen tunic, and leather leggings. He danced gracefully, his arms linked with Thorfinn and Jacob. One by one the women paired opposite their chosen man, leaving Moira alone within the circle and Wulfsun unpartnered. In a moving mosaic everyone smoothly changed positions, forming two circles. Wulfsun and she became the center axis. The unmarried stood in the inner circle and the married couples the outer.

The women again raised their voices in harmonious song, and the men answered in kind. The circle parted slightly. Ragnorvald the Law Speaker stepped inside followed by two thralls who carried a clay vat of frothing mead, which they set in the center. Wulfsun knelt to one side and Moira, following his lead, kneeled opposite.

"You show wisdom in taking such a woman to your side, Chieftain," began Ragnorvald. He gave Wulfsun a golden-gilded drinking horn, which Wulfsun submerged in the mead.

He lifted it out overflowing and raised it to the sun. "We drink our wedding troth, that the gods, Odin, Thor, and"—he paused thoughtfully and looked at Moira—"and the Lady of the Moon, give to us the marriage-luck." He drank deeply and in turn held it to Moira's lips. She took a small sip.

"You must empty it, Moira," he prompted. She took a long breath and drank to the last drop. He took the horn and tipped it upside down to prove its emptiness. Everyone murmured approval. He dropped the horn into the clay vat and outstretched his hands to her. She clasped their reassuring warmth, which stilled the trembling of her own.

"Your hands hold fast, you are bound as sea to earth and wind to sky," pronounced Ragnorvald. Moira's throat swelled with emotion as the unspoken love flowed between them. Wulfsun pulled her to her feet and favored everyone with a lusty, triumphant shout.

The sound of harp rippled the air, and with a burst of song the married couples broke into the inner circle and caught Wulfsun and Moira into their midst. They crowned Wulfsun with a wreath of allheal and summer blossom, and he in turn encircled Moira's waist with a golden chain of keys, the keys of his household.

Their gazes locked tightly, and they joined the skein of dancing, which mimed the abandonment of youth and courtship. The women stepped delicately, skirts swaying, as they sang in sweet, wild voices. All fell under the spell of the midsummer's night.

Eventually Moira found herself seated onto a high seat, which, along with the trestle tables and benches, had been placed in the open yard. Many approached the high seat with bridal gifts.

Haki Gunnarson presented Wulfsun with a finely

crafted battle-axe and to Moira a silver band necklace. Moira and Wulfsun's eyes met, and simultaneously they burst out in laughter. "Haki, your gifts are most pleasing," said Wulfsun, still laughing.

Jacob the Freed's gift was a pair of bone ice skates. Olvir and Freya gave a carved chest. Gyda shyly came forward and set her highly prized painted marble in Moira's hand.

"Oh, thank you, Gyda. Soon our own daughter will play with this." Wulfsun looked at Moira singularly. She gave him a small smile and averted her eyes to another gift giver.

Sverr and Rollo had nothing to give and were to shy to speak their well wishes. "You will honor us by guarding our gifts," decided Wulfsun diplomatically. Everyone thought this appropriate as the grinning boys took stance on either side of the growing pile of tribute.

In turn Ran the Fair stepped forward. She was adorned in a sky-blue kirtle, and her silken hair shown silvery. It couldn't be denied that her beauty was breathtaking, even though she had been sullen most of the festivities, Moira would not fault her for that. Ran never once looked at Moira, but gave her full attention to Wulfsun. She took from her own hand a gold ring and placed it on his smallest finger.

"I would not have this token mark your handfast, but let it be a link between us when I go North to Sigvat's hall, my chieftain." Along the benches heads bent together in hushed whispers.

"My sister, you are generous." Wulfsun embraced her, but it seemed an embrace of brother to sister. A flicker of displeasure crossed Ran's face. Wulfsun had shown openly his attitude toward Ran. This would dispel the wag of gossiping tongues. Inwardly Moira thanked him.

He clapped together his hands in command. "I, myself, have a gift for my bride." He turned to Moira. "Whatever is within my power to give is yours," he vowed.

Another hush rippled through the celebrants. However, the hesitation on Moira's part was only momentary.

She knéw immediately what she wanted. She touched his arm. "There is one thing . . . I would not choose to be a thrall nor shall I choose to be a master. Let it be said at the Ravnings there are no thralls. Free your thralls that I might sit beside you in fairness."

Complete silence suddenly reigned in the open yard.

It was not a small bequest. Wulfsun's face was devoid of expression. He had given much already. Perhaps he had learned the first rule of marital bliss—never give a woman free rein.

He raised his hand on pretense of scratching his upper lip and muttered aside to her, "You intend to hold me to my word?" She nodded slightly.

"Then you stand me on sword's point."

She nodded slightly again.

"So be it, Moira." He gave a half-grin. "I am captured, my good witch. The thralls are free!"

Cheers came forth—mostly from the thrall-born. Ysja fell into Haki Gunnarson's arms, and Moira suspected another handfast would be forthcoming.

After this the feast began to appear, though Wulfsun wondered how, since he had just set all his servants free. The tables were laden with goat and sheep roasted whole, puddings as smooth as satin, sweetmeats, pink salmon, and barrels of mead.

Wulfsun picked up a mutton rib. "You see there is no fowl at our wedding feast. I commanded it thus."

"I thank you . . . and the gander in the open yard thanks you," teased Moira.

"Hah!" he scoffed. "I fear you will soon make grass eaters of us all."

Horns were emptied and filled time after time. Although Moira was enjoying herself, she yearned for Wulfsun's loving again. Her hand wandered to rest on his knee, and slowly she moved her fingers along his hard-muscled leg to lightly caress the heat of his inner thigh.

The canny shift in the depths of his blue eyes told her he welcomed her unspoken message. Every light and shadow of his rough-hewn face, from the golden knot of his brows to the intense line of his determined lips, burned with his desire for her. A tremor warm as sun tumbled through her.

Suddenly he drew her to her feet and led her to the mead vat near the great bonfire. He dropped her hand and hoisted the clay vat into the air and flung it down and it smashed into fragments. With squeals young girls ran and picked up pieces of the clay.

He moved behind her, putting his arms around her, his mouth to her ear. "Needs be, we must hurry the festivities along. The girl who captures the largest piece is destined to marry next, and belief is that she who gets the smallest is fated to remain unwed."

All around them came hand clapping and a rousting by the men. Before she realized what happened, Wulfsun swept her off her feet and flung her over his shoulder. He took off running and leaped the vastness of the bonfire.

She screamed, aghast at his daring. "What if you had missed!"

"I did not," he replied with his maddening confidence. He kept running out the tall gates and up the hillside.

"What are you doing? I see no sense in you carrying me when I can walk."

"Or fly." He laughed. "It is usual for we vikings to steal and bed an unwilling bride."

"But I am willing!"

"I know this." He laughed merrily. "But it is our way."

He found a spot in the dappled shadow of a leafy birch and set her down. He took off his scarlet cloak and spread it out upon the springy turf, and together they lay down. Below, the song of the skald carried to their ears.

"Hear me, O ring bearers, and I shall sing of Wulfsun and his Swan Bride."

Moira lay her head on Wulfsun's chest. "Swan Bride?"

He stroked the softness of her hair as he replied, "This night brings you a new name, Moira. You are the Swan Bride. It is the skald's gift. The saga tribute is held above every other. If our deeds and adventures are sung, such renown will keep my enemies from my door and will bring greater loyalty from my vikings. This night you become a woman feared, a woman respected, and a woman who has power to sway a chieftain."

She pondered this a moment, then said, "All this may be true. Yet I am content to be your lovemate and the mother of your daughters."

"And sons."

"I do not think it," she said cautiously.

"What do you not think?"

"Mayhap I did not tell you," she hedged. He shifted, lifting his golden brow skeptically. She took a small fortifying breath and cleared her throat. "A swan sister only conceives daughters. 'Tis the way of things in Myr. I hope you are not disappointed."

Sun touched his cheek, and his eyes narrowed as he ruminated on this news, then he sighed. "Then I am to sire a gaggle of daughters. Humph! Mayhap I will have to take up my sword again to fight off their moonstruck suitors."

She straightened with apprehension. "Nay, I would not think it."

He chuckled. "Then do not! Give me your lips, woman, I am done with talking."

His kisses let loose desire, and within her breast her heart burned with the consuming fire of the midnight sun. As she lay in her hero's arms, she thanked the Goddess for creating man and blessed the fates, for they had played no cruel trick, laying the fairest of fortunes in her path.

Author's Note

People often ask me why I write romance fiction. And I answer, "I suppose a part of me will always be a flower-child of the sixties, the 'make love not war' generation." *Swan Bride* is a flower-child tale, a tale of healing, reconciliation, and peace. I'd like to credit Llewellyn's Practical Magick Series and author Scott Cunningham for information and inspiration in writing this book. I like to hear from my readers. Write: P.O. Box 118 Centerville, UT 84014-0118

The Best Historical Romance Comes From Pocket Books